THE HUNTER TRILOGY

THREE COMPLETE NOVELS

The books follow artist Paul Hunter from his dodgy youth, *Hunter I*, through his checkered adulthood, *Hunter II*, and into his spectacular aging in *Hunter III*, which began in 2055 when he was 75-years old.

William Serle

Published by the author using kdp.amazon's services.
Contact ~ **billserle@aol.com**
Website ~ billserle.com

ALSO BY WILLIAM SERLE

FICTION

STEALING ALI ~ Written with Daisy Serle

HUNTER I ~ Youthful adventures

HUNTER II ~ A tale of love and crime

HUNTER III ~ 2055

FRED'S GOLD ~ A screenplay

HUNTER TRILOGY ~ Kindle Edition

HUNTER TRILOGY ~ Three novels in one – Hardcover Edition

NONFICTION

BILL'S JOURNEY ~ Memoir*

EDNA'S LOVE LETTERS ~ Biography*

CHIMING OF FORGOTTEN BELLS ~ Selected Essays

SWAYING IN THE WIND ~ Poetry, Essays, and Inspirations

GRANDFATHER UBER ~ Memoir

GAMMY ~ Biography*

LIGHT SONGS WE BREATHE ~ Poetry, Essays, Memoirs, and Ruminations

All available at Amazon.com and Kindle except as noted.
*Visit billserle.com to read.

I dedicate this work to the delightful people of our Southern mountains – The Great Smoky Mountains – where I abided for a quarter of my life.

TABLE OF CONTENTS
Three Complete Novels

HUNTER I ~ Growing Up 1

PART ONE 3

PART TWO 29

PART THREE 55

PART FOUR 85

HUNTER II ~ **A Tale of Love and Crime** 149

CLANCY RIVER MAP 151

PART ONE 153

PART TWO 223

PART THREE 263

PART FOUR 295

POSTSCRIPT 303

HUNTER III ~ **Beyond 2055** **305**

PROLOGUE 307

PART ONE 309

PART TWO 355

PART THREE 411

NOTE FROM THE AUTHOR **447**

v

HUNTER I

BOOK ONE – GROWING UP

First in the series

PART ONE

THURSDAY – August 23, 1990

Paul lounged against the chain link fence and watched Debbie approach. She seemed to be looking right at him. He was puzzled by her eye contact since she had pretty much ignored his existence since the start of Huntsville P.S. 21's fall term. He noticed everything about her. Their too-short lunch break was almost over on this sunny Thursday.

Debbie Malone was tall. Her red hair was pulled back into a ponytail that bounced with every bold step. She seemed to be marching toward him. Her red satin shirt, well-filled blue jeans and matching red sandals gave her costume a finished, thought-out look. Paul considered her the hottest girl in his history class.

He wasn't actually thinking at this moment, though. He was nearing girl-panic but tried to mask it by deliberately keeping his face blank. He stood away from the fence as she came to a halt.

"Hi Debbie." Their noses were just two feet apart, and she had him nailed with her blue eyes.

"Paul. What did you mean when you said that in class?"

"What? Do you mean about the Irish immigrants to New York being luckier than the Poles?"

"Yeah," she almost snarled. "My grandpa was Irish, and he had a terrible time. He got into trouble and ran away to Alabama when he was 21. That's how my family got here, and I think it was very hard. I'm going to be the first high school graduate in my family if I can hold on for four more years."

"Well. I didn't mean anything. I just figured that they had it easier since they already spoke English and could blend in better. Um…"

She interrupted him by saying, archly, "I guess you're Polish. Huh?"

He began to answer but the school bell jangled the end of the lunch period. She spun around and marched away before he could decide how to answer. Debbie didn't say goodbye or even give him a head-bob.

Paul didn't know where his family came from. He guessed they were English and had arrived a long time ago. He decided to ask his brother Mitch, after school or, maybe, his parents at dinner.

"Uh. See ya," he called out lightly. He was glad that the day was half over and gave no further thought to Debbie Malone. His mind was busy with after-school plans.

Paul walked home since it was less than a mile away. Debbie, who lived in the same direction, caught up with him. She seemed a little out of breath. They were approaching her dark red brick apartment building. His house was a few blocks further away from school.

"Hey, Paul."

"Hey, Debbie."

"Say, Paul. I. I-um-…wanted to ask you." She looked a little troubled.

"Paul. Have you ever had a yen?"

"What do you mean?"

"You know." She was looking at him. Her head was lowered, and her shoulders were a little slumped. "Like to do something you shouldn't?"

"Well. I guess. But what do y…" He was interrupted by a sudden shout.

"DEBBIE!" Her mother was shouting from the window of Debbie's apartment. "HURRY UP, DEBBIE! WE'RE WAITING FOR YOU."

"Paul," Debbie straightened up and looked him in the eye. Her lids were half closed, and she hesitated as if she was thinking something over. "Paul. Come to my house tonight at about eight-thirty. Don't ring the bell. Just climb that tree there. There." She pointed to a towering oak growing behind her apartment, "…and wait for me. Be quiet."

She turned and ran around the corner and into the apartment. Her mother was holding the front door open. "Sorry, Deb. Aunt Betty is waiting for us, and we have got to go. Put your books in your room and let's get it on."

Paul continued toward home, deep in thought, anxious to talk to Mitch.

Paul Hunter was not the best student at P.S. 21. He got good grades by listening in class, but he hated homework, except for English literature. He would read anything that came his way, but he preferred novels. His older brother was reading Moby Dick in high school now. Paul was proud that he'd already read it by taking it out of the library.

Well above average height, Paul had erect posture and broad shoulders. On the thin side now, he would gain bulk and become a formidable man in a few years. His hair was dark, and his eyes were a light hazel like his brother's.

For no particular reason the boys never became involved in school athletics. They could have developed team sports skills, but their parents did not push them in that direction.

The Hunter family had moved to Huntsville in Paul's 11th year. Mitch was 14 then and, since school was in recess, they'd formed a tight bond. Strange to say, they never fought other than wrestling and horseplay for fun. They were best friends. Paul, a little shy, was happy to get his older brother's attention.

Mitch tried out for the swim team as a high school freshman, but the coaches were not impressed enough to put him on the team. There were boys who had been honing their competitive skills for years in area swimming clubs.

Paul was anxious to finish the school day because they were going camping and canoeing on the banks of the Tennessee River on Labor Day weekend in two weeks. He and Mitch had a lot to do to get their tent and camping gear together. He hoped they could go to buy paddles on Saturday. He wanted a cool wooden one so that he could say, "No thanks," when the canoe-rental guy told him to choose a plastic one. They had their own tents but not boats.

Money was not a problem. He and Mitch had plenty since they'd been hard at work for several years on several projects. Most of them were legal but a few were not. The more lucrative jobs were often a little evil. So far, they'd never been caught.

As the brothers were not under the benign influence of organized athletic competition. Work, boy adventures, and home life were the center of their first years in Huntsville.

The boys huddled after supper. "Mitch. This girl Debbie wants me to climb the tree outside her window tonight. Do you think I should go?"

"I dunno. What'd she say?" Mitch was very interested in this report from his little brother.

Paul recounted his conversations with Debbie. Mitch was excited. "Paul. You gotta go and I'll go with you, but you have to do something for me later. Okay?"

"What Mitch?"

"Nothing important. Just some fun I want to have at Eddie's house a little later."

"Mom. We're going to see Eddie. Okay? We'll be back in a little while." It was just after eight o'clock and dinner was finished. Pot roast.

"Okay boys. Take care to get back well before bedtime. Tomorrow's a school day."

The door slammed behind them, and Mitch said, "Paul. Wait a minute. There's something I got to get." He disappeared into the driveway that ran next to the house. Paul patiently waited on the dark street.

When he reappeared, Mitch was carrying a little paper sack.

"What's that?" said Paul.

"Well, listen here bro. This is a sack of dog shit that I'm going to leave on Pete Jones' front porch. I'm going to set it on fire and run like hell. You come with me and be a lookout. I don't want anybody to see it."

Paul had been curious about the sudden rank aroma that seemed to emanate from Mitch, "What the Hell, Mitch. What did Eddie do to you? He probably won't answer the door anyways. His mom or dad will have to deal with it."

"Naw. They're going to a meeting tonight. I just want to pay him back for some dog shit he left in my locker at school.

Everybody made fun of me because my books stank, and I didn't know why. He laughed his ass off and I have to get even. Okay?

"Okay. But we do Debbie's tree first. Okay?"

"Okay."

The street by Debbie's apartment was quiet and the boys were hidden in the leaves of the tree opposite the second story window that Debbie had indicated. There was a play of lights inside the apartment as lights turned off and on, people shadows moving inside.

A light went on in a downstairs window and they saw Mr. Malone sit at a window-side table, curtains gently blowing as the evening air stirred. The leaves rustled, too. Mr. Malone placed a briefcase on the table and began rummaging through it as the boys saw a second-floor room light up.

The shade was up, and Debbie walked into the room in a light blue bathrobe. She stood in the center of the room and seemed to be staring through the window at them as she began toying with the sash. They practically fell off their branch when she dropped the robe. She was naked except for white panties that kept her bottom half covered like a bikini bathing suit. She turned away from them, but they had clearly seen her breasts and then her bare aback as she walked out of the room and closed the door.

Mr. Malone was now the only show, and they saw that he was removing cash from his case. He began arranging the bills on the table. He was counting the money and putting the bills into different stacks.

"Holy shit. These are very interesting people," Mitch whispered.

Paul didn't answer but squeezed Mitch's shoulder. A short time later the second-floor door opened, and Debbie walked in again. She still wore her panties, but her breasts were again in full view, and she looked better than a woman in a girly magazine to them. Her pink nipples put them in a trance. They couldn't move.

Debbie's mom appeared in the doorway as Debbie stepped into pajamas and raised her arms to shrug into her pajama top. Her boobs bounced a little. Her mom walked to the shade and lowered it without looking outside.

"Paul," Mitch's whisper was urgent, "Change of plans. I'm going to put the shit on their porch and light it off. When it gets going good, I'm gonna ring the bell and run the other way and make sure that they see my back. Maybe Mr. Malone will chase me. Anyways, don't follow me. Go home the other way. If he gets up to answer the doorbell, grab some of the cash through the window will ya. Be quiet about it and run like hell. I'll see you at home. Okay?"

"Okay, but…"

Mitch was gone in an instant leaving behind a whiff of poop. Paul sat still, wondering if the show was over. He was both scared and excited. Visions of Debbie's breasts and look of her skin sifted through his boy brain. Another upstairs room lit, but the curtains remained closed. Mr. Malone sat at the table busy with his task.

Paul heard the doorbell and smelled smoke at the same time. Mr. Malone got up and left the picture. Paul climbed quietly to the ground and advanced on the window to see that Mr. Malone had been stacking the bills by denomination. There were little piles of hundreds and fifties and larger stacks of twenty-dollar bills and smaller denominations.

Paul caught a loud "God dammit!" from the front of the house as he reached in and took the larger bills off the table. The ones, tens, and fives he scattered off the table toward the windowsill to make it look like a gust of wind might have moved things. As he turned to run, he saw one more thing on the table – a large, black revolver. The sight of the pistol shook him, and he began running for home, stuffing the bills in his pocket.

Mitch looked up and down the street. It was dark except for the occasional porch lamp. He held the bag and a small box of wooden matches in one hand and used the handrail to steady himself. He steeled himself and lit the bag bottom and top in three places. The sack was small but well-packed with droppings. He waited as long as he dared, then rang the bell twice before running.

He paused in the shadow of a large tree trunk directly across the street and was rewarded by seeing Mr. Malone standing over the paper bag. He raised his slippered foot to stomp out the little fire, and the bag exploded into a stinking, smoldering mess that splattered on his legs and over the porch.

"God dammit!" He hopped around, trying to figure out where to put his other foot, and, in a moment, figured out what had happened. He saw Mitch's figure in the deep shadows and began running. Malone thought that he saw two boys and ran toward them. "God damned kids!

Mitch whirled around and took off at a run. Malone was fast and began to close the distance. Mitch heard his pursuer's footfalls, his heavy breathing, and a muttered, "I'll see which of youse bastards can run the fastest." The old guy was incredibly fast. That muttered threat inspired Mitch to shift into high gear, and he got well ahead of the cursing and growling man.

Malone lost a slipper and hobbled to a halt. "I'll getcha, you bastard!" he yelled. But Mitch was around the corner and took a roundabout path home in case the old man spotted him again.

The excitement was over. Home, showered, and dressed for bed, the boys finally had time to put their heads together. Mitch whispered, "$770.00. Holy mackerel, Paul. Hell of a night, eh?"

"Mitch. What are we gonna do with the money? If Mom or Dad finds out about this, there'll be hell to pay. We godda think of something. And, oh, I forgot to tell you, Mr. Malone had a gun on the table. A big one, like in the movie Dirty Harry. You think he might be into something illegal with all that cash? Drugs?"

"I dunno. Sounds like it. I hope Debbie keeps her mouth shut about you. Us. She probably doesn't know about me, but she could figure it out."

After a brief pause, Mitch said, "You know, we already had about a hundred dollars in the jar from the newspaper box break-ins we did. Now it's a lot of money and we have got to find a way of using it; like laundering it so that we can spend it without Mom and Dad getting onto us, and I have an idea."

Paul nodded, "Tell me. Quick. I'm getting sleepy."

"Okay. So, we go over to Cantor's Cash and Carry Restaurant Supply Company and get some gear for selling lemonade at the ball games at the park. We don't have to make a lot of money – we just have got to say that we're making money."

"Sounds good. It sounds like fun. We'll get on it tomorrow afternoon. Okay. I want to get that paddle."

"Okay. Good night."

Mitch left. Closing the door. Paul snuggled under the covers squeezing his erect penis. He wanted to think about the canoe paddle, but Debbie's face was in his reverie. They were nose to nose, and he wanted to kiss her. And touch her…

FRIDAY – August 24, 1990

"Mom. You know I want to buy a canoe paddle at the outfitters store for our camping trip?"

"Yes Paul, and I already told you yes, but you'd have to earn the money yourself and I know that you don't have enough."

"Me and Mitch…"

"Mitch and I," she corrected him archly but with love in her face.

"I mean Mitch and I have an idea. I have enough cash, and Mitch will help me, to buy some stuff at Cantor's. We think we can sell lemonade at the ball games if we have a carrying rack that will hold a buncha cups."

"Yes, but you guys will have to do it on your own. You know how busy Dad is right now and I'm tied up getting ready to take off for our vacation trip."

"Thanks Ma. I knew you'd say yes.

Paul left the house for school on time, keeping his eyes open for Debbie. He was terrified of facing her for two reasons. The least of the two was her father's gun. The other was that he wanted to see her naked again; so bad that it made his throat constrict.

Debbie was not in history class. He looked for her in the schoolyard and on the way home to meet Mitch for their shopping expedition to the Cash and Carry. No sign of her on the street and he was leery of walking by her apartment building.

SATURDAY – August 25, 1990

The boys had an impressive kit gathered for their business venture. They intended to haul the family ice chest, a few gallons of mixed lemonade and a 20-cup caddy with shoulder straps in Dad's big wheelbarrow. They had a carton of plastic cups, straws, and lids. They planned to pick up a supply of ice at a convenient gas station and obtain more water for their jugs with a short garden hose from the tap they'd spotted at the ball field.

There was a carton of instant-lemonade powder packets that made a gallon each. They had pliers to turn the water on since they'd noticed that there was no handle at the park's spigot. They were set to sell hundreds of cups at 50 cents each. They had rolls of quarters and 50 one-dollar bills at the ready to make change. Mitch would hawk their wares and Paul would mix more product or make an ice run if necessary.

"Paul. Remember that there probably are rules against doing this. So, we gotta work fast. I figure if we get busted, they'll just tell us to leave, and we can come back when they aren't looking."

"Okay Mitch."

The big lie would be that they didn't care too much if sales were lousy or if they got chased. "Remember kid," Mitch said with a wink, "we're just laundering money like on TV. We'll tell Mom and Dad that we made $125.00 so's we can get a pair of those swell wooden paddles."

The Park was crowded with junior league baseball fans. It was hot and the work was brutal. The facility had multiple ball fields. The area they worked had four fields with eight bleachers arranged around a bathroom and concession stand. The concession stand sold drinks but no one in an official capacity took notice of them. There was a good crowd – mostly parents and siblings rooting for family members.

The boys sold 220 glasses of lemonade at 50¢ each in three hours when they ran out of ice and the crowds began to thin. They cleared $14.00 after deducting all costs including $50.00 for the strapped carriers. Next time the carriers, cups, lids, straws and mix would be already on hand and not have to be bought. Their net would shoot up.

"And ya know Paul. We could make more if we were more efficient. We'll have to figure out how to get us both in the stands at the same time instead of you just filling cups with ice and juice," Mitch grinned as Paul wheeled the barrow down the street.

"Yeah Mitch. We'll start with more ice too next time. And we'll take the ice pick."

"And tomorrow we'll get our paddles. We can take the bus if we can't get Mom or Dad to take us. Let's say we made $140.00 today. It would take an audit of our stuff to prove otherwise, and no one's going to do that."

SUNDAY – August 26, 1990

The Hunter family sat at the dinner table. With no school and, usually, no work on Sunday, they always tried to gather for the supper meal, conversation and, TV together after cleanup. The sweet aroma of roasted chicken was in the air.

"Well boys, Mom told me you raked in some good money at the ball game. It's a shame you spent it on the paddles, but I guess they'll last for years. Good job! Sorry I was too busy to help."

Michael Hunter was a builder. He held a general contractor license in Alabama but, when he didn't have a project of his own, he worked as a supervisor for others. Sometimes, if he needed to, he could work as a carpenter. He made a good living.

"Thanks Dad," Mitch nodded. "We're going to keep on selling the juice through the football season. We'll do even better now that we've got our gear paid for." Both boys were beaming. It was good to be a Hunter.

Mom worked too. She was a licensed financial advisor. She now worked on a fee basis but had started in insurance sales. She and her husband of 19 years were fairly prosperous now but, at her urging, they always saved for a rainy day. They were comfortable and even thinking of how to get the kids through college. Since the boys were not great scholars, they foresaw community college and, if that worked out, a university education.

"I've been busy too guys," she announced. "But you showed real get up and go there. I'm glad you got your paddles. We'll have a good time camping.

"Say Mike," she turned to her husband. "My friend Patsy who owns the apartment building and I had coffee today. Guess what?"

The three turned toward her expectantly.

"She had the apartment rented to a family named Malone and they left town leaving all their stuff in the apartment. They left her a note saying to go ahead and re-let the place and please feel free to use or dispose of their furniture. They just took their clothing and the TV. The note said they had to leave the area due to an emergency.

The boys eyed each other. In a nano-second they warned each other to be careful. Paul began to feel guilty about the affair. There were consequences he hadn't intended,

"Paul. Didn't you go to school with the daughter? What's her name?"

"Yes Mom. Her name's Debbie. She was in my history class."

"By the way. We had a sort of argument the other day. She said her grandparents were Irish and I didn't know when the Hunters or your family came to America or where they were from.

"So, Mom, what are we anyway? I mean English, Polish or what?"

The camping trip was brilliant. The Hunters felt close in spirit as well as physically. The family tent was big enough for four sleeping rolls and not much else. There was a big awning attached to the front and they faced it right to the water of Lake Surprise.

The rented canoes were pulled up on the beach at their doorstep. There was a fire pit, an iron charcoal barbecue, and a picnic table in their campsite. Shower and toilet facilities, with hot water were nearby. Each campsite was slightly separated from neighbors by trees and brush, but they got to know their neighbors and felt part of a friendly community.

Three days of paddling, hiking, camp cooking, taking all their meals together and enjoying fine fall weather relaxed the Hunters. The boys liked their new paddles. Since no motorboats were permitted, the atmosphere was serene. The lake was large enough for exploration and fishing. They swam from their campsite and a large public beach.

FRIDAY – September 27, 1990

Fall was incredible. The boys were busy with school and their lemonade-vending/money-laundering scheme.

Paul continued to feel guilty about snatching the money from Debbie's father, and even more guilty about her disappearance from the neighborhood and school. He had no way of knowing whether he was responsible, but he suspected that his role had helped no one.

Mitch was more stoic about the matter. "Forget about it Paul, People move all the time, and you can never know if that money had anything to do with it, He may have been getting it together as a part of his moving plan. Lots of people have guns."

For Mitch, the sudden appearance of Molly Kravitz became the focus of his attention. She was a year older than him, but they were in some of the same classes at school. They became friendly when he discovered that she worked in the neighborhood.

Molly worked part time at the corner Bohack's Grocery store until it closed at eight p.m. Mitch was there to meet her almost every night and Paul sometimes tagged along.

The meets with Molly were not dates. They were more like hanging out. Usually there was a walk to Molly's house and a peck goodnight so she could get her dinner and do her homework. Occasionally they'd hang out for a while by Bohacks – Paul would chat with Molly for a moment and then give the couple a little space so that they could smooch in relative privacy in the shadows in the alley.

Paul noticed that there was once a doorway in the brick wall while he was waiting for Mitch and Molly. It was now boarded up and painted brick red; the same shade as the building itself.

He knew the store well and realized that there were shelves of canned vegetables on the other side of the boarded-up door. He pressed his eye up to a knothole. To Paul's surprise he had a clear view of Larry, the owner, emptying the cash register into a little metal box and then putting the box behind the Post cereal boxes behind the counter. He watched for a moment longer and the lights went out.

As Larry locked the store and walked away, Molly and Mitch said goodbye. She walked toward home, and the boys walked together toward their house.

"Guess what Mitch?"

"What."

"I know where Larry leaves the store's cash overnight." Paul said importantly.

"Where? How do you know?"

Paul explained what he saw. "And those boards are just nailed. Nothing fancy. I was thinking when I looked at them that someone could just pry some of those boards out and crawl in, right over the peas and corn, and be back outside of the store in less than a minute.

"And, if it was me, I'd do it right away tonight. Dad's pry bar and hammer are on the basement workbench. If I was to do it tonight, after Mom and Dad went to bed, I'd be back home in less than 15 minutes." Paul was a little wrought up and began breathing hard as he looked at Mitch striding next to him.

"Wow little brother. You're becoming a bad ass. Why do you want to do it?"

"I don't know," Paul said slowly. I know we don't need the money now, but we'll think of something. We're almost done laundering the Malone money. We could keep it going and we're actually making money on the lemonade. We could get rich.

"What do you think? Should I do it?"

"It's tempting. I don't like Larry very much. He's real bossy around Molly and he watches me like a hawk when I'm in the store. As if I'd steal a can of beans.

"If you want to do it, I'll go with you. Stay dressed when you get in bed. We'll need to be quiet getting out and getting back home. We can get the tools off the bench before bed, but we can't put them away until tomorrow morning."

Paul was suddenly a little scared, but he didn't want to look like a chicken. Besides, it was his idea.

SATURDAY – September 28, 1990 – One a.m.

The board gave a loud squeal as Mitch pried it loose.

"Shh." Paul quavered. "Do it slow."

Mitch growled, "Shut up you little shit. I'm doing it as quiet as I can." He began work on the second board and it was quieter. Two boards were enough. Even though the planks were still attached at one end there was enough room for Paul to scoot through. Cans fell to the floor, but he ignored them. He ran around the counter, found the box, and soon handed it through the opening to Mitch.

The boys replaced the board by hand pressing the nails back into their original holes. The nails were not too warped from the prying. Mitch tapped them back into place with the rubber end of the hammer handle. The muffled thumps were not loud.

The streets were empty, and they were back in their beds without incident. Neither boy slept very well. They would count their haul later.

Two weeks later the news in the neighborhood was that Bohacks was closing. Word was that the new Publix had stolen too many customers. Bohacks was a very convenient store for those in the neighborhood, but it could not keep up with modern supermarket innovations and prices.

DECEMBER 31, 1992

Paul was having a happy day. It was his 15th birthday, and his parents were celebrating with a few friends at home and Paul was very much a part of the party. He would get presents, attention and a birthday cake. The only fly in the ointment was that Mitch would not be there.

"Sorry little brother. It's party night and I'm going to a class party with Molly. I'll be thinking about ya though. Happy birthday old buddy."

Mitch was able to buy a 1985 F150 pickup truck when he got his driver's license in the spring. It was a sharp looking rig with a cool fiberglass tonneau cover. Mitch had the $1,000.00 down payment and needed his parents to finance the balance. Having his own set of wheels gave him a lot of independence as well as responsibilities.

The boys' days of crime and laundering money were over. They worked weekends for their dad and his business friends on a variety of construction jobs. They sometimes worked as a team but were more independent now that they were older and had their own set of friends. Paul was now a little too young to run with Mitch's crowd.

Paul went to bed happy. He was fifteen now, getting close to getting his license to drive, feeling prosperous and in control. He woke while it was still dark. His clock told him it was three a.m. He walked into the hallway and saw that his mother and father were dressing."

"Hey. What's up?"

"Paul. You can go back to bed. Mitch has had an accident. He's not hurt, but we have to go to the police station to see him."

"Oh my gosh! I want to go with you." Paul whirled around and was pulling on jeans and a tee shirt before they could stop him. In less than a minute the three were through the front door and on their way.

The police substation was a grim, utilitarian building. The detective was grim too. "No sir. You cannot see him at this point he's under arrest and he'll need an attorney. We are holding him in a cell here until morning when the state's attorney will determine what charges to file. We have quite a laundry list of possibilities including felonies. The investigator was adamant. Mitch was his prisoner now more than he was their child and brother.

"Do you have an attorney?"

"Yes sir. May I use your phone?"

It was noon, the first day of 1993, when they left the police station. They, Mom, Dad and Paul, had to leave without Mitch. Attorney Monroe Gelb had done his best but there were several charges including: vehicular homicide, failure to have a vehicle under control, speeding, possession of marijuana, driving under the influence, resisting arrest, and leaving the scene of an accident.

"They're reaching on most of these charges, but they have a right and the duty to hold him for a preliminary hearing. He'll be okay here at the county lock-up."

The story that emerged from a brief and tearful meeting between Mitch and his parents, from the police officers, and from Monroe, was that Mitch had an accident involving hitting a pedestrian who had died in the collision.

Mitch claimed that he didn't see or believe that he had hit a person on the dark highway but had had lost control of the truck some hundreds of yards further down the highway and had tested positive for alcohol. He thought it was a bump on the road. He was not drunk but, since he was under 18, he should not have had any alcohol.

In the course of the investigation the cops had searched his truck and found a bag of marijuana. Mitch claimed the weed was not his and that several friends had been in the truck over the last few days and supposed that it belonged to someone else.

Molly and another girl had been in the truck with him, and an altercation broke out between the other girl and the arresting officer. Mitch had tried to intervene and that lead to further charges and troubles. The girls had not been charged and their parents had picked them up at the scene.

The truck had a blown a front tire, probably caused by running over a shopping cart. This caused Mitch to lose control and hit a fence. The truck was not seriously damaged, the passengers were okay, but the pedestrian was found dying. He was a vagrant but still had a right, of course, to life. Mitch was deemed responsible.

Life changed for the Hunters. Not in a single day, but over time, the accident seemed like a punctuation mark in the life of each family member.

Mom and Dad were terrified for their children and felt that they had come close to losing Mitch to a darker life. What terrible things would have happened to him in jail? They resolved to keep the boys as close as possible for as long as they could. Family time was given more emphasis. Dinner at regular times; everyone expected, guests welcome. Vac5ations, mainly wilderness-style camping, were scheduled whenever possible.

Mitch paid traffic fines but was not found guilty of the serious charges. His interest in school declined and he settled for a GED and went to work for his father. Molly graduated and moved to Asheville, North Carolina to study ceramics and live with an artsy aunt who welcomed the opportunity to take her in.

Mitch declared that he was moving to Asheville on his 18th birthday and Molly was searching for a job on his behalf. His feelings of guilt and remorse about the accident was sharp and would never be forgotten.

Paul worked with his dad on weekends and, oftentimes, after school. Although he got good grades and was an avid reader, he had no ambition to go to college. His real life was on the job.

Paul began as a laborer. Cleaning up job sites, doing demolition, and, when he got his driving license, running errands. His dad drilled him on the fundamentals of reading blueprints, the math of framing, and the arts of plastering, dry wall, plumbing and painting. His dad insisted that he got regular haircuts and that he shave every day. "You need to fit in with the other workers Paul. They're conservative, handpicked by me to be respectful of our clients and the properties we work on."

Paul's response was all a father could ask for – compliance with a smile and thanks for the job, Dad. Paul loved his father and appreciated all he was learning on the job.

By the time Paul graduated from high school, he was a strong and skilled helper. He earned a good wage and he let his mom salt it away.

With Mitch's hard life lessons, he was not eager to operate a motor vehicle, but he eventually got his own pick-up truck and regarded it as a tool for work. He bought the old Chevy from his dad, so he knew that it was in good mechanical condition, albeit a little dinged up. He had scored a few of the dings himself on job sites where conditions were rough. It wasn't as pretty as Mitch's, but he kept it very clean.

APRIL – 1996

The senior prom was a big dilemma for Paul. He'd had a few crushes and had dated a few girls since his 16th birthday but did not have a prospect for this valedictorian dance. He consulted with his lunchroom crew, and they proposed Sarah Myers.

"Hey. She's totally hot. No way she'll go with me."

"Really Paul, said Betty. "She doesn't have a boyfriend and you have to talk to her now before someone else snaps her up. Go over there you dope and talk to her."

Paul totally liked the idea of Sarah Myers as a date. He'd had classes with her since starting high school. He thought she was smart and popular. She wore jeans and a tee shirt today for Casual Friday. She was on the slender side with dark eyes and shiny brunette hair. His heart was in his mouth when he approached her in the cafeteria.

Sarah was sitting with two other girls and they were surprised when he asked, "Can I sit with you all for a minute?"

"Sure Paul," they murmured while he began a conversation with Sarah.

"Sarah. Say, you know the prom is coming up. I heard that you haven't agreed to go with anyone yet and I was wondering if I could ask you." His pulse was way up but he tried to look calm.

The other girls at the table excused themselves and left. Paul figured that they were sparing his feelings for the turndown.

"Paul. Who said I needed a date?" Sarah gave him an arch look as if she already had more boys wanting to ask her than she knew what to do with.

"Well. I know we haven't seen each other before and I don't have a date. Have mercy. Okay?" He gave her his best smile. "Sarah. Please go with me. I'll get a tux and give you a corsage."

"Well. Why didn't you mention that before?" Her heart was hammering too but she controlled her jitters better than Paul. "Paul, the prom is four weeks away. I need you to do me a big favor if I'm going to go with you. I have needs. I need to go on a few dates with you and you have to pick me up at the house and meet my parents. I know it's a lot to ask, but that's my price."

Paul was ecstatic. This was going way better than he'd imagined.

Paul rang Sarah's front doorbell at five o'clock Saturday night. The plan was dinner at the diner and the movies at the triplex – the movie was Fargo and they found it darkly appealing. Dinner at the diner was deliberately visible so that their high school cronies would be aware that they'd dated in advance of the prom.

"Paul. Thank you for tonight. I had a lot of fun. The prom is definite then?" she sat rather far away from him, yet in the center of the wide front seat. She looked very appealing in her white scoop-front blouse and tan pedal-pusher pants.

Paul had been trying to avoid looking at her chest all night. Her breasts were totally covered but, in his mind, they were about to leap out at him. "Yes please. I had a good time too and I'm glad we could go out tonight.

"Do you think... I mean, are you free tomorrow afternoon? We could go canoeing at the park. I have all the gear we'd need, paddles, cushions and such. I have my own boat. Mitch, you know, Mitch my older brother, and I bought it a few years ago?"

"What time?"

When their arrangements were complete, she leaned slightly toward him and presented him with a glimpse down her blouse pointing to her cheek for a kiss. At the last second, she turned her face to his and gave him a full, lip on lip, kiss.

She laughed as she got out of the car, "See Paul. You never know."

He leaped out of the truck to walk her to the door and was rewarded with another cheek. She did not turn toward him this time, but he gave her a little pat on the back as she slipped through the door.

"See you tomorrow. Two o'clock. Canoeing." And she was gone.

He remembered the feel of her back as if his hand was still touching her. She felt good, smelled good and was fun. Hell of a combination he thought as he ran down her drive to jump in his truck. His heart raced and he was out of breath. He had to drive deliberately to calm himself. He was in a hurry to get home, go to bed, and indulge his fantasies.

Canoeing was a big success. Sarah wore a bikini under her shorts and shirt, and he was in his bathing trunks. So they were able to cool off in the water after paddling along the banks of Wheeler Lake.

It turned out that Sarah loved jokes. "Knock, knock."

She was in the front of the canoe, and he was enjoying a close-up view of her slender back and rounded hips as she plied Mitch's paddle with good energy.

"Who's there?" he sing-songed in response."

"Sam and Janet."

"Sam and Janet who?"

She began singing, to the melody of Some Enchanted Evening, "Sam and Janet evening…" she giggled.

"Why do ducks have flat feet?" he asked.

"I dunno. Why?"

"To stomp our forest fires. Why do elephants have flat feet?"

"I don't know. Why?" She looked back at him inquisitively.

"To stamp out flaming ducks!" he roared, laughing.

Sarah splashed him with her paddle and the canoe was a little tippy for a minute, but they managed to keep it together. The jokes were old but telling them was fun anyway.

At her door he said, "Sarah. I have to work next weekend, but I'll be off Sunday afternoon. Want to do something?" He had his hand on her arm and enjoyed the smooth soft skin.

"Sure. How about a picnic by the river, without the canoe, and then home early so's I can get ready for school?"

"Date."

"Date!" She said emphatically, giving him a peck on the lips and a little chest bump. "See you."

Paul was excited to be dating Sarah and he wondered if they would be able to make love. He was certainly eager. But he understood that girls, women, were not so eager. For good reason he thought with the risks of pregnancy and the social stigma of being a loose woman. A slut, as they said in school.

But still he hoped, indeed he pined, for the end of his virginal state. He read a book that advocated masturbation before every date - just to take the edge off. Men, the theory went, were more interesting to women if they were less eager. And when the big moment came, you'd be less likely to suffer from premature ejaculation. After his first date with Sarah, he began a routine involving masturbating as well as shaving, showering, brushing and flossing. It would have embarrassed him to admit this to anyone, but he felt that it helped.

The weather on picnic day was not so hot. It was showery with occasional downpours. They had their sandwiches and drinks under a rustic shelter but the wind was a problem so they ate up and retreated to the cab of the truck. In a few minutes they were hugging and kissing in a state of passion.

She sat in his lap as the windows misted up with condensation inside the cab. He was exploring her breasts, his hand under her strangely flexible bra. He enjoyed her smooth legs with his other hand.

"Sarah. I would really like to make love. I brought these." He dragged out a package of condoms.

"Oh no Paul." She seemed upset. "I just can't!" Her face was flushed, and she was breathing funny.

He pulled back in alarm, sure that he had offended her. He began to apologize, "Sarah…"

She interrupted him by pulling him closer, giving him a passionate kiss then whispering in his ear, "Paul. Me too. But I have my period and I just can't make love today. Paul I really, really like you. We've had so much fun, and I like kissing you."

"God damn Sarah. You scared me. I thought I'd gotten out of line and that you were going to blow me off." He relaxed his hold on her and they gazed into each other's face in a loving way.

They continued necking. As they lay across the front seat Sarah said, "Paul. Don't bring those rubbers along when we date. You don't need them. I've been on the pill for a year. My mom insisted, but…" she gave him a coy look, "I don't sleep around.

It's just a way for my mom to keep me from getting pregnant if I do make love to someone. She likes to plan ahead"

The shadows grew long, and they grew weary. And Paul had ejaculated in his pants. Sarah seemed not to notice *but*, he thought, *must have surely suspected when he didn't get out of the car to say goodnight at her house.*

Sarah did know of course. She had made sure that he got that little satisfaction. She had felt his body quiver and his muscles writhing as they hugged, and she ground her hips against him. She was happy that he was gentle with her.

Paul spent a fair amount on the tux rental and corsage. He was comforted by the sure knowledge that everyone in his class, including Sarah had probably gone through a similar experience. He came down the stairs to the applause of his parents and had to pose for photos. "Paul, you must ask Sarah's parents to share their photos. We want to see you together."

"Okay Mom. He marched proudly from the front door to his truck. He had cleaned it from bumper to bumper for the occasion. His dark brown hair was neatly trimmed and he had shaved even though his beard was still fine.

Sarah's mom answered the door with a smile. "Good evening, Paul. Don't you look handsome? Come right in. Sara will be ready in a minute."

"Hi Mr. and Mrs. Myers." Sarah's dad appeared next to his wife with and shook Paul's hand with suitable formality.

They sat in the living room until Sarah suddenly appeared in a short, gay, off-the-shoulder formal cocktail dress, and sparkling high heels. Paul was wowed.

"Boy oh boy. Do you look nice! Wow girl."

Sarah paused at the door, smiled and whirled around so that her gown spread out to expose her dancing legs. Paul shyly presented her with her corsage and her mom pinned it to her dress.

Mom took photos with a little camera and promised to get double prints for Paul's family.

The couple left the house in Sarah's family SUV. Paul was a little disappointed when the decision was announced but Sarah's dad said that he thought the SUV safer and comfortable for a formal night. Sarah had said, "Please Paul." It had been easy to agree.

They met three other couples at the steakhouse and had a gala meal to start the evening. Paul was proud to pay their bill, as he was feeling flush with the pay from several summers' work and the remains of the laundered money he'd stolen with Mitch. It was all safely invested with his mother's supervision.

The Marriott Huntsville was the venue. They used valet parking and posed for a professional photo at the entrance to the ballroom.

The dance was in full swing when they arrived. Paul and Sarah had practiced a little and Paul thought that he was not very good. He surprised himself however and they had a lot of fun. He discovered that she could be comical on the dance floor as well as with jokes. Elbows akimbo, stepping high and wiggling her hips, she was hilarious. She got him to match her moves and they became the center of attention when they performed.

The dance went on until midnight, but they slipped away early.

Paul drove the Myers car respectfully. They went to an upper-class neighborhood where his dad was remodeling a lakefront house. He knew the house was vacant and he drove behind it. He backed over a grassy track to the edge of the seawall, next to a sandy beach. Sarah sat close to him and hugged his arm.

The large rolled up quilt and the fact that the seats were down in back to create a carpeted area had not escaped Paul's attention. Sarah had prepared the car and herself with care.

Paul inhaled her perfume as her dress, pantyhose and bra came away. He quickly removed his clothing, and they locked in a passionate embrace on top of the soft comforter.

Paul tried to speak to express his feelings, but Sarah gently shushed him. Whispering into his ear. "Paul, just do me. Do me now!" She helped him align his engorged penis with her ready vagina.

They made love twice before they had a chance to really appreciate their surroundings. The air was cool, the bright moon shone on the water and there was a beautiful grassy aroma drifting through the night. The leaves rustled softly as the couple lay intertwined, breathing into each other's ears. He was able to see the curves of her thighs, hips, and belly. Her dark nipples, standing erect in the moonlight, drew his fingers and his lips. She shuddered with pleasure as he explored her body.

"Paul. You are so beautiful. Thank you for being you."

"I don't know how to say this differently but Sarah, I'll always love you and always remember this night and this moment. You are too beautiful for words."

"Me too. Me too you."

Then it got complicated. Sarah was late for her 1:30 a.m. curfew. "Paul. I have got to go."

"I know. Just let me hold you one more time." And she did.

A little later they found use for the towels she had thoughtfully rolled into the center of the comforter roll-up.

Redressing was a little awkward. But they looked presentable, perhaps even elegant, when Paul walked her to the front door, and she turned her cheek up for a kiss.

He leaned in and she twisted her head quickly to present her lips – but not quick enough. Paul turned his head to press his slightly scratchy cheek into her lips. They laughed loudly just as the porch light turned on and the door opened a crack.

He said, "Goodnight Mrs., Myers," to her mom's eye and gave Sarah a peck on the lips before trotting to his truck. It was two a.m. but he felt totally awake and ready for anything. He dropped off to sleep thinking about Sarah's lovely body.

Graduation was held the next Saturday morning in a gala tent on the school grounds. Paul spotted Sarah and waived sadly. Their affair was coming to an end. Sarah was leaving right away to be a summer camp counselor and then would report to The University of Alabama in Tuscaloosa.

They had dinner the night before and Sarah was reserved. She declined the opportunity to "park" with Paul. "Paul. My folks are a little mad at me. Not you. I was late on Saturday, and I have to – just have to be home early tonight. I'm sorry," she said with a smile and a tear.

"Paul. Thank you for promming me. You saved my life and I love you, but I don't think I'll be back home until Thanksgiving and that seems so far away."

"Yeah, I guess you're right. Are you saying that you don't want to see me again until you get back?"

"Yes." Sarah's eyes teared up and she held his arm. "I hate to say it, but I think that's best until we figure out a little more about life."

Paul had already confessed to her that he did not want to go to college. He planned to visit Mitch and Molly after graduation and then decide his next moves. He could earn a good living in construction, but he wanted to explore other avenues. He was correct when he thought that Sarah was concerned about his lack of direction.

Paul's path was not clear to Sarah. She wanted to be a nurse or other health-care professional. She did not understand Paul's lack of ambition. It scared her that she liked him so well.

PART TWO

JUNE 1996

It was beautiful in Asheville. The mountainsides were carpeted with fully greened trees. Flowers bloomed everywhere. It was cool in the mountains unlike Alabama, where summer had already taken charge.

Mitch and Molly rented a one-bedroom apartment near the UNCA campus. They were very proud of their independence. Molly was in an arts program with an emphasis on ceramics. The area was famous for ceramics art and her ambition was to "throw" pots and such for a living. Paul thought that her finished pieces looked good enough to sell anywhere. She beamed when he gave her that opinion.

Paul was crashing on their couch. They made him feel so welcome that he had no hesitation in agreeing to stay for a while. Mitch held his arm for emphasis as he said, "As long as you like little brother."

Molly was busier than Mitch. Her schedule of classes and work schedule were brutal. She worked at the university bookstore. The wage was not high but there were serious benefits. She got discounts on textbooks and merchandise, Since she was considered to be full time, health insurance and tuition. Her demeanor gave no clue to the frantic schedule she kept. She was always smiling and her neat blond hair and placid blue eyes radiated happiness.

Mitch had two jobs involving antiques and collectibles.

He worked at a huge antiques mall named the Cotton Mill. It rented space to dealers who would tag their own merchandise but, in return for a modest rent, they did not have to man their stalls. The mall collected the money from merchandise sales and cut the dealer a weekly check after deducting the rent. Mitch worked for minimum wages plus they let him have several well-located stalls at no cost. He bought inexpensive 'must goes' at negotiated prices and sold them for as much as he could get. He also sold Molly's ceramic work and she was a willing supplier. Her pottery classmates were eager to sell their stuff too and this was a very good sideline for all concerned.

His second job was to haunt flea markets, yard, and estate sales in his off time to acquire the 'must goes.' The owner of the Cotton Mill took a shine to him and fed him tips and advice on an ongoing basis. Mitch loved old man Milt Friedman and in an incredibly short time he was making regular profits in addition to his salary.

On this cool Saturday evening, the sun still hanging over the mountains, the brothers were enjoying a beer while they waited for Molly to get back from Ingles Supermarket with their dinner. They had comfortable plastic chairs and a little table on their diminutive patio.

"What now little brother? I mean what do you want to do for work now that you're finished with high school? And what about college?"

Paul was not certain. His internal life consisted mostly of trying to forget about Sarah while taking a summer vacation. He enjoyed working for his dad and felt like it was a good learning experience. He had no ambition to study for his own contractor's license.

"I really don't know Mitch. I want to take a few weeks off and then I'll probably go back to Huntsville and work with Dad. I don't feel any money pressure, after all, I'm mooching on you and Molly for a while."

"I've got all my camping gear locked in the truck. Any chance that you and Molly could get away to hang out with me for a bit?"

"I don't think so. I can get away for some day trips, but Molly is scheduled at school or work almost every day and needs to rest on her time off. We can ask her though."

Paul gave Mitch a serious look. "Mitch. Do you ever think about the things we did in school? I mean the thefts from Debbie's dad and Bohacks. Like the lies we told about the money and all?"

"Sure. I guess we did some crummy things, but they were more like adventures than crimes. I'm glad we didn't get caught."

"Yeah. Me too. But I feel guilty about Debbie's family disappearing and Bohacks too. I wonder if we were responsible."

"Well. Me too. But we were pretty young. I wouldn't want to do it again. Would you?"

"Hell no! I believe I'm cured."

"Hi lovers!" Molly called out as she walked up to the patio with paper bags in her short arms. She was a tiny red-haired woman with an enormous supply of appealing freckles. They each took a bag and she rewarded them with a hug and a kiss and said, "Dinner in three minutes. Then I'm going to crash."

They ate roast chicken, coleslaw, and apple pie still warm from the store's oven.

"Why don't you take Paul whitewater canoeing while he's here Mitch? You love it and he will too. If you go tomorrow, I'm only working half a day and I can go check on the stalls at the Mill." She really wanted to know how her stuff was doing.

"What do you say Paul? We can go to Clancy, Georgia and rent a whitewater canoe. Do you have our paddles?"

"Yep. I mean yes to the paddles. Canoeing sounds great but I've never done white water. Is it like that old movie *Deliverance* with Burt Reynolds?"

"It's way more fun and there are no mean hillbillies," Mitch laughed. "We won't need a reservation since it's a weekday. You're gonna love it."

Molly and Mitch were right. Paul loved the whitewater experience. Mitch rented a two-man canoe with big airbags in the bow and stern for floatation and special saddles to keep their weight low in the boat. There were foot braces and thigh straps to keep them in the boat when it bucked in the rapids. The straps were adjusted for easy exiting in case they spilled.

It was a two-and-one-half hour drive from Asheville to the little town of Clancy. There were continuous mountain vistas as they rolled along through deep country with few towns and villages. The roads were great, and traffic was sparse. Paul felt at peace in the mountain terrain. He told Mitch that he was missing his girlfriend and how they had parted. Sarah's somewhat hasty departure from his life became a little less painful as he shared the story with his brother.

Mitch listened until Paul was talked out. "Bro. You'll get over it. Today, on the river, there won't be any room in your head for negativity. Only joy and terror."

That seemed a little strong to Paul, but he knew that Mitch was joking about the fear - he hoped. He already felt good about the day.

There were two options for paddling the Clancy River from the town of Clancy: upstream or downstream. They chose up because they wanted to end up near their truck which was parked at the outfitter's take-out beach.

The outfitter that rented them the canoe provided transportation upstream to a public put-in area on the Clancy River.

They carried the boat to a practice pond near the drop-off place. They got in the boat and Mitch drilled Paul on what he'd have to do on the river. Paul learned to paddle on the left side of the boat with his right hand firmly on top of the paddle. He practiced paddling on both sides of the boat without shifting his hand position so that he could shift sides as fast as possible with a minimum of commotion. He learned the high and low braces and sweeps to help turn the boat in either direction. He had good natural balance, no fear of the water and the strength and flexibility of his hardworking, youthful body.

"Mitch. How did you learn to paddle like this?"

"In Asheville. The first job, that Molly got me, was a seasonal gig with a canoe rental outfit on the French Broad River. I was mostly a cashier and 'Yard Monkey' because they were a little leery of my driving record. The folks there took me in hand on my days off and taught me the basics.

I could be a guide and trip leader there but it's seasonal and I needed a steady job. I'm saving to open my own business when Molly graduates from college. I think it'll be next year. Mr. Friedman, my boss will give me a steer when I'm ready."

"Wow Mitch. You're going to get rich. Molly too. Are you two planning to get married?"

"Yes and no. Yes, but we don't want to set a date until she gets out of school and learns what her options are. I really love her, but we're getting along great just now, and I don't want to push her. She's the boss you know."

They were soon on the river. There the light, fresh smell of the water, the lush forest odors and shifting shadows transformed Paul into a whitewater devotee in minutes. He liked the feel of the boat as they powered along with their old wood paddles. He was aware of the cold splash of the water, the moving wind and brilliant sunshine when they were out of the shadow of overhanging trees.

An idea formed in Paul's mind. He began to see a path for the next few months. *I'll find a way to camp near the river, buy a boat and get a job – on my own for the first time.*

He knew that it was a juvenile plan, but he shrugged his mental shoulders and mused, *what the hell Paul. I'm young and life is long.*

He outlined it for Mitch.

Mitch agreed that it wasn't much of a plan and somewhat lacking in goals. "But Paul, it's okay. Where do you think you can camp for free?"

"That's the 64-cent question wise one. I don't know. I'm not broke. Just ugly. If I only score two out of three of my wishes, I'll be happy for a while."

Paul got a resounding three for three on his wish list.

He returned to Clancy a few days later and began shopping for a boat. He asked about work at every enterprise on both banks of the river as he moved upstream from the village of Clancy.

No one needed help but he found a boat for sale. A handsome Mohawk canoe, rigged for white water and not bruised up. It sat on sawhorses, bottom-up, next door to a little eatery called The Barbecue Shack with a 'For Sale' placard taped to its red side.

The Shack could be seen and approached from the river as well as the road. There were no immediate neighbors on the road or on the other side of the river. Just trees. People ordered food through a window with a generous stainless-steel shelf and could use the benches and picnic tables scattered about.

He rapped on the closed service window and heard someone approach from inside.

A cheerful woman in a spotted apron and chef's white jacket stepped through the door. She looked a little stocky in her cooking outfit and her red hair was trying to escape the confines of its hairnet. Up close she smelled like cooking smoke. She smiled and said, "We open at 11:30."

"Ma'am. I just want to ask you about the boat. How much is it?"

"Oh. Good," now she was really grinning. She came out and they walked to the boat together.

"I just put it out here today. I decided that I'm never going back out on that danged river again." She hitched up her shorts a little to show him a very big bruise that went up her leg, out of sight. I thought I'd get beat to death before I could drown properly. Never again!" She laughed. "Help me roll it over so you can see inside.

"I paid 600 bucks for it when I bought this place a year ago. I thought I'd found paradise.

"It's fully rigged as you can see. Air bags, bow and stern. Saddle and leg straps. It's had very little wear."

The boat looked indestructible. Large floatation air bags were laced into the bow and stern. The center of the cockpit was dominated by a kind of saddle for the paddler to sit on. It allowed the operator to sit lower than the built-in thwart seats that were made of a varnished wood.

"Yeah. This is a very nice boat. I've seen the Mohawk brand before." He walked around the boat petting it as he went.

"Say. My name's Paul Hunter. I'd like to make an offer."

"Megan Smith. But I won't take a cent less."

"Megan. I'm looking for a place to camp and this is really nice by the river here. I don't know how long I want to stay but could I give you your asking price and you throw in permission to park over there at the edge of your parking lot and pitch my tent by the river, out of sight, for a while."

"I don't know, er…Paul."

"I could give you a $100.00 cash deposit and a check for the balance."

Megan was not convinced. Paul looked like a nice guy, but she didn't know if it was even legal to camp there.

"I don't know. Where would you go to the bathroom?"

Paul thought he'd just use the abundant woods, but Megan had a point.

"Megan. Let me sweeten the offer. I'll use your facility," he pointed to the single door that was marked 'His'n n' Her's.' If you'll let me use the bathroom, I'll take responsibility for cleaning it up every day. Keep it clean. I'm sure that's a chore you'd rather not do."

Megan was 34 years old and escaping from a bad marriage. Her planning and execution of the change from city office worker to rural free spirit was not without complications. The barbecue business was working financially, but the work and the hours were long and hard. Paul struck a note when he offered more than just money for her little boat. She sensed the possibility of an even better outcome.

Megan was ready to accept the deal – Paul pitching his tent and using her bathroom, but she was moved to say, "Paul. I like your offer but there's one more thing you could do that would make it work for me."

"Uh oh. What is it?"

"First I need to ask you some questions. I need to know who you are and where you are from and what you have been doing."

Paul explained that he had just graduated from high school and that he had a worked for his dad in construction. She asked him to write his parents' and Mitch's names, addresses and telephone numbers on a lined pad. She asked him for references and all he could think of were his bank, his high school Lit teacher and the pastor of the church they attended on holidays. He wrote the contact information on the yellow pad.

She seemed satisfied.

"Paul. This business is a little too much for me. Do you think you could work one day a week for me? Minimum wage plus tip jar. And I want you to pick up the parking lot trash every day? For that you can camp here, use the restroom and, on your one day of hourly work, you can eat your lunch and dinner on the house."

Paul grinned and offered his hand. "Great Megan. I promise to do all that. When do you want me to start?"

"Today. You can pitch your tent. Give me a check for the boat now, and I'll let you know what day I want you to work. I need to think it over. I'm assuming you don't care too much. I mean about which day."

Paul went to a payphone at the Caverns Outdoor Center. The center was a big whitewater raft rental, restaurant, and motel complex a few miles downriver. He soon learned to call it COC. He called his parents and Mitch to let them know where he was and what he was doing.

"Mom. I'll be home when it gets cold here. Give Dad my love. And," he laughed, "yes, I'll send you ten percent of my paycheck. Don't expect much."

'COC' was the largest enterprise around. He had lunch in a restaurant there; one of the three restaurants on the property. The café was named 'The Takeout' because it was close to a sandy beach where rafters pulled their boats out of the water after running the last big rapid of the run. There were plenty of customers, mostly family groups just off the river and hungry for something warm. Paul liked its homey feel.

He snooped around and found that the public restroom there had showers and he supposed that he could use them if he liked. There were no posted signs to the contrary.

There was a mailbox on the wall near the office for the little hotel attached to the center. He asked the woman at the motel desk in the office if they sold stationary. He was given a piece of copy paper and an envelope. She sold him a stamp. He wrote:

Hi Sarah

I think about you every day. Wish you were here.

Hope you are having a beautiful summer at Camp Karamac.

I just bought a canoe and found a part time job at a barbecue joint that will let me spend time learning to be a whitewater paddler. I'll be camping by the Clancy River - it's nice here. See you in the fall.

XXX OOO

Love Paul

Paul erected his tent on a flat spot well above the river. It was not visible from the road or from the barbecue shack parking lot. One would have to get very close to catch a glimpse of it.

He rigged a line over the limb of a tree to haul food supplies off the ground. He didn't want to attract a bear or the skunks and raccoons that were famous for their thievery. He did not want a fire pit. His one-burner propane camp stove and a propane lantern were enough. He'd be content with the simplest of diets, but hot coffee was a blessing in the morning.

It rained that first night and he woke wet in the morning. He had failed to dig a trench on the up slope, above his tent, to divert ground water. The price of this oversight was wet bedding that had to be spread out to dry. He was philosophical about it. He reckoned that he'd make a few more mistakes before he learned to live without a house. He moved the tent to let it dry in the sunshine.

After he used and cleaned the restroom, he patrolled the parking area for litter, and tamped down the trash already in the large containers. Megan watched him approvingly through the service window with the built-in stainless-steel counter.

"Hi Paul. Thank you for a job well begun. Paul. Would you mind working on Wednesdays? I want to go to Asheville and spend time with some friends. If you will spend tomorrow with me, I'll show you everything you need to know. I'll spend the night in town and be back on Thursday morning. That'll be our regular schedule. Okay?

"Oh. And I'll pay you for the training time. But Wednesday will be your regular day from morning light until dark. I'm just going to pay you cash. Is that okay?"

Paul nodded an enthusiastic yes. "That'll be great. Say Megan, today's Monday. Right?"

Paul was an apt student. They began in the screened room she called the chophouse. Megan started each day by loading pork butts in a stainless-steel smoker above a wood fire lit with a built-in gas ignition system. She then made coleslaw and heated large cans of beans on a two-burner stove.

"Follow this list, Paul." She handed him a handwritten list of daily chores arranged in the correct sequence. "I've learned how much prep to do each day and it usually works out. If I run out, I just apologize, and folks are generally okay with that. I mean I just can't stop and make coleslaw or smoke a new batch of pork butts when I'm by myself with a line at the window.

"The menu is simple: pulled pork sandwiches; pulled pork platter with baked beans; bread and slaw; hot dogs and hamburgers. They can order anything to drink as long as it begins with a 'lemon' and ends with an '*aid*.'" They laughed at her little joke.

She showed him how to handle the lemonade powder, how to apply the dry spice rub to the pork before slow cooking in the smoker. She taught him to preposition trays of little paper cups of barbecue sauce. Her barbecue sauce, baked beans enhancement, and coleslaw recipes were taped to the refrigerator door for him. Other condiments were in plastic pouches including sauerkraut and diced onions.

She showed him how to clean and sanitize the chophouse, the hot dog steamer, the hot table and all the associated gear. Thin burgers were cooked to order on a small grill.

"I usually clean the chophouse before opening but, if I get busy with something else, it may have to wait until closing.''

The last thing she did each day was to he haul all the garbage to the county garbage station a few miles up the road. She had a heavy workload and Paul admired the cheerful face she put on everything – especially with customers. He decided to haul the trash for her even on his days off.

Paul's Wednesday was relatively easy. He bagged the cash register tapes and cash before locking up and hauling the trash. The vinyl bank envelope was hidden behind the big number-ten cans of beans. He guessed that Megan did her banking on Wednesdays.

There was still some daylight left when his work was finished. He dragged his canoe into the water. He braced himself and turned the boat downstream in the lee of a rock so that he could accelerate into the faster moving water. This was his fourth outing in the boat and he was getting good at self-rescue because he flipped the boat at some point during every trip. It was a hard learning process.

Two large air bags filled the entire bow and stern spaces of the sturdy boat. Nylon laces served to prevent water from filling the canoe when it flipped. There were a number of stainless-steel eyes screwed into the gunwale and thwarts to help tie down loose gear such as watertight bags filled with lunches, cameras, wallets, keys, and such.

He leaned the wrong way. Again! And found himself immersed in the cold water, gathering up his bow rope and paddle in his left hand and stroking for shore with his right hand. The water was not moving fast here so he had to watch for rocks as he floated with the current and keep his feet downstream to push off any of the boulders that came close. He knew not to try and stand up in waist-deep water, but it was soon shallow enough to let him plant his feet on the bottom and haul his water filled canoe to shore. He was bruised from bumping into underwater boulders. The water was freezing. He thought he'd buy a wet suit when Megan paid him.

He was not upset. He knew that counter to his intuition, he had to lean and paddle on the downstream side when leaving calm water on the shore and turning into the current. I can do this he muttered while rolling his boat upside down to empty the water. He was back in business in a few minutes and managed the rest of the short run with pleasure.

He expected to learn a lot by the end of the season. He wanted to hook up with paddlers who would suggest other, more challenging rivers. He would be glad to provide transportation as an inducement for others to make the journeys with him. But the

Clancy was his favorite, his only, river for now. He eddied out behind rocks, surfed standing waves, and rode the bigger rapids down to COC. There he left his boat on the shore, bought a soda and hitched a ride back upstream to so --return in his truck to retrieve the canoe.

He was in bed soon after sundown. He closed his eyes to dream of Sarah. He drifted off remembering her feel, her smell, and the sound of her voice as she said "Do me now…"

Some days Paul would go upstream to the most distant put-in and paddle all the way to Clancy. After a few weeks he became familiar with some of the regular paddlers. They were mostly kayakers who thought of canoes as less than hip. Nevertheless, he did make friends, and was delighted to learn better boat handling techniques and river lore. He decided that he'd sell his canoe at the end of the season at COC's Guest Appreciation Festival at the end of October and start the next spring off with a kayak. There was no shortage of advice on this subject.

His new friend Marvin Redman told him, "COC sells most of their boats at the festival. They start fresh in the spring with new rafts. The rafts are used heavily and soon display patches and scars. They're tough boats, those used ones, and will last an individual owner for many years. But the patches are not good for the company's image."

Marvin worked for COC in the kitchen of The Takeout Café. He was very short, almost a midget it seemed to Paul. But he was dark and powerfully built and very manly with a full beard and copious body and arm hair visible. His beautiful, natural kindness drew him to accept Paul, the outsider, as a friend and Paul liked and appreciated him very much.

The two men sat in their boats in the quiet water behind a large flat rock. The sky and river filled Paul's senses. They were face to face for easy conversation while they waited for the rest of their party to catch them. Each man had a hand on the others gunwale and the boats bumped together with a little hollow sound. Marvin's kayak was scarred up from hard use. Paul's red canoe was clean and new looking.

Marvin was explaining, "...but for rafting companies to put two seasons' use on boats is not their best course. The employees buy their boats through the COC retail operation and get enough of a break on the price that they can sell them at the end of the year and just about break even. The reason I don't do the 'sale' thing every year is that I think it's better for the planet to use our possessions until they're worn out."

Paul laughed. "I was wondering why so many paddlers had raggedy shorts and sandals held together with tape."

"Yep. That's it. Sort of a cult. I think that's the COC ideal – like taking a vow of poverty when a priest joins up.

Through Marvin and his friends, who were now Paul's paddling buddies, Paul learned that Caverns Outdoor Center was a good place to work. The company mission statement declared that it was a community of athletes and philosophers. Good caretakers of the environment and a sort of disdain for money. Marvin laughed, "That means that the pay is lousy – don't ask for a raise."

COC was a seasonal operation from April through October. The mountain air was too cold for safe paddling in the off-season although, being in the South, there were many nice days in the winter. Snow fell often as moist air masses moved north from the Gulf of Mexico. But it didn't usually linger too long. Starting on the first of November the area would be quiet and almost deserted. Along the river only The Takeout Restaurant operated on a limited schedule. The Barbecue Shack would close too. Marvin would work at The Takeout Restaurant on a limited schedule.

"Paul. If you want to work for COC put your application in before the end of the season. You can use Megan and me as references. You'll be glad you did it. You know the work will be hard, but you'll have a lot more paddling friends and you can bunk in staff housing. That will be more comfortable than that raggedy ass tent of yours."

"Thanks Marvin. I have a slightly different vision. I spoke with Megan, and she'll let me camp at her place whenever I want. I'm going to take the raft guide course at COC in March. I'll use the lodging offered by the school during the course week and sign up as a reserve raft guide on the Clancy River. She'll work with me on scheduling so's I can work for her one or two days a week then work whenever I can get guide work at the center. I don't need a more regular job because my expenses are close to zero and winter construction work with my dad pays well.

"Maybe I can get a regular job at COC the year after. I gotta keep moving up because I'm near the bottom now. And I'm loving it."

Marvin thought it was a good plan. As a senior COC employee, he didn't earn much but with staff housing, a working wife, and low expenses he felt rich. "I love cooking and I love paddling. My wife and I aren't getting along so well though. She wants me to get a real job. Go figure. More money but no time to enjoy it."

The summer slipped away, and autumn colors and the smell of chimney smoke tickled the senses. Paul had not shaved since the prom. His beard was dark but he kept it trimmed with scissors that had become a part of his kit. He was used to living rough and his was getting stronger and building muscle mass from paddling and work. He had plenty of free time so he was able to take frequent hikes on the nearby Appalachian Trail.

Paul was very happy to see October coming to an end. It was getting too cold to live in the tent and his last day with Megan was scheduled for October 30th. He planned to sell the canoe at the COC Guest Appreciation Festival. Molly and Mitch invited him to visit in Asheville and his dad was more than ready for him to get back to a real job. Life, Paul thought, was good.

He was canoeing alone one brilliant autumn day. The hardwood trees were dressed in gay hues of red and yellow. He made frequent turns into minor eddies trying to be totally technical with his strokes and balance. He was practicing whitewater skills. Just behind a half-boat sized rock, he nosed into the bank only to find a screen of bushes that masked a side stream entering the Clancy. He pushed his way in with a couple of light strokes.

It was a flat area, and the shallow water was crystal clear. It was just inches deep. His boat floated above river stones and pebbles strewn on the bottom. Grasses and bushes screened the wilderness garden from sight in every direction.

He stepped out of the boat to look around and wound up sitting on the mossy bank, basking in the sun. There was a carpet of green moss in the dappled sunlight and the rustle of leaves.

He liked the peaceful spot so well that he always, thereafter, paddled there when he was by himself. It was his chilling spot, his private paradise. Sometimes he fell asleep. Sometimes he just daydreamed about his life and where he was going.

NOVEMBER – 1996

Thanksgiving was a bust. Sarah disappointed him. They spoke on the phone the Friday morning after Thanksgiving. She seemed older and remote, and her words shocked Paul, "Paul. It's over with us. I want to be in school without any entanglements and you are a definite entanglement.

"You know that I love you and what we had in High school, but I can't see any future for us. I'm going to be a nurse and marry a doctor. I know that sounds shallow, but I want you to have it straight. That is my dream."

Paul had suspected that it was over with Sarah, but he held out hope until the end of the call. She declined his invitation to meet for lunch. He felt that high school was a very long time ago.

Paul was so sad that evening that he broke down and told his mother, "Mom, I thought about her all summer and wanted to go back to the way we were, but she wouldn't even talk about it. She's husband-shopping at the medical school." His eyes welled up and was glad to bury his head in his mother's shoulder.

She gave him every comfort a mother could. "Paul. You'll soon be over this. There are many women in our wonderful world, and you will find the one meant for you. You'll know when you're ready"

"Thanks Mom. I think you're right. I'm not ready for a relationship. I was wrong. Sarah and I were not thinking in the same track at all. I'll wise up after a while."

Paul went to work for his father with the understanding that he would have the boating season off to take his River Guide Course and spend the summer in Clancy. He telephoned Megan to confirm their previous deal and she seemed fine with the prospect having her Wednesdays off again next season.

The winter sped by. Paul fell in love with a slightly used kayak he bought at the local outfitter store. On warmer weekend days, he donned wetsuit and neoprene boots to practice in Huntsville's rivers for summer on the Clancy River.

SPRING – 1997

The third week of March was relatively balmy in the mountains of North Georgia. There was lots of sun and only a few snow flurries. His weeklong training class as a river guide exceeded his expectations. There was a mix of instruction including short, indoor classroom theory and long days outside, in all weather, learning everything one could know about running whitewater rivers in rafts. He learned how to maintain them on the river. Guest satisfaction and safety were a big part of the program.

There were 18 male students and six females. Some were trained professionals including an ER physician, a CPA, a police lieutenant, and a high school teacher with an MBA. This lot all professed to want more adventure and less money. They were willing to live in poverty (staff housing) as a part of a package that enabled them to spend days on the regions' rivers in good company.

The ER doctor, Lucy Lu, told Paul, "I can work full time here and odd 24-hour shifts in my hospital in Atlanta. Maybe even one day a week, to keep my position. Off-season I can work normal shifts there."

The CPA planned to work his profession only during tax season. Each of the professionals was making a financial sacrifice. Each had a different story.

COC provided all the gear the students needed including wet suits, first aid kits and rescue bags. The bags included a variety of ropes to help haul people and boats out of the water. The students learned to manage heavy rafts full of inept guests with paddles but without skills, perform rescues and avoid dangerous situations before they developed. He was told that most whitewater injuries were caused by novice boaters hitting one other with their paddles. The course was much more intense than his high school studies.

Paul spent a happy week with Mitch and Molly in Asheville. Mitch was more prosperous and talking about a shop of his own.

He returned to working for Megan one day a week. His first day was a Wednesday on the second of April. The river gorge area was not busy in the spring, but she liked having a day off. Since the days were short and the nights cold, he spent as little time in his tent as possible. Oftentimes he spent hours drinking coffee at The Takeout Restaurant or doing errands in town. The laundry was one of his favorite places because of the warmth of the driers and occasional company from COC employees on a similar mission. He saw every movie within a 50-mile radius.

Paul took a two-day class at the YMCA's swimming pool in Atlanta to learn the Eskimo roll. This one maneuver made kayaking much easier and safer than canoeing. The roll enabled him to stay in the boat and turn himself upright whenever he capsized.

When he made a mistake, he could recover without having to deal with a boat full of water or total immersion. His life vest and helmet offered him a good deal of protection from rocks. The deadliest whitewater threat was foot entrapment in rocks and crevices hidden by moving water. In a kayak, his Eskimo-roll techniques meant that his feet were likely to spend less time on the river bottom. Marvin began giving Paul kayak tips on their days off.

Paul hung out at the COC rafting area on weekends hoping to get work as a guide. He made sure that they knew he was there and that they had him on the list of accredited guides. He got his inauguration trip in the first week of May. COC paid him a flat $20.00, and he collected $40.00 in tips from six happy passengers. Regular guides would get three or even four trips on lucky days.

As they pushed off, he told his guests that it was his first trip down the river as a paid guide. His passengers felt a frisson of unease when they heard those words.

His confident manner of instructing them and guiding the boat down the first few rapids allayed their worries and they were soon engulfed in the whitewater experience. He was a hit and he loved the job. He would get a trip every few days, but it required time and effort. He looked just like all the other guides with well-worn river shoes and khaki shorts. He bought a Tilly floating hat and sunglasses. His guests always wanted to have their pictures taken with him after the raft trips. Especially the girls and children.

SUNDAY – May 18, 1997

A huge rain event occurred in mid-May. Megan arrived at his tent at nine in the morning to find him re-digging the moat that led water away from the tent. His breath was visible in the cold morning air. He was muddy and a little out of sorts. The tent was fighting the wind.

Megan pulled up in her little truck and jumped out shouting. "Paul! Come quick. The ceiling of my trailer is collapsing, and I can't get the tarp in place by myself! I've got leaks and there's a branch lying on top." Megan was breathing hard and on the verge of tears. She wore a yellow raincoat and matching hat. She was mud splattered.

His mood changed in an instant. "Let's take my truck," he said. "I've got tools and stuff in the back." They made their way to her simple home place a mile upriver from the Barbecue Shack.

Her site was a beautiful cut into a mountainside. It was on a side road a few hundred feet away from the main route. Its principal feature was a long view of the Clancy River. The river was brown with silt this day and the muddy approach to her driveway was not easy.

The house was a 32-foot, 1-bedroom, house trailer. He had been there before to help her with chores. He and Marvin had built a deck and steps for her on their day off last fall. The deck was 12 feet on each side and not far off the ground so there was no rail. It comfortably held a table, four redwood dining chairs and a park bench.

The first problem was that there was a rather large tree limb on the roof. It was still attached to a tree that leaned over the dwelling. "It scared the hell out of me when it hit just before dawn. Bam! I fell out of bed."

A large blue tarp was partly unfolded and just sitting in the water and mud at the bottom of her steps. There was a clothesline tied to the grommet in one corner.

"I just couldn't handle it," she croaked. "Do you think we can do it together?"

He peeked around to the back of the trailer and confirmed his suspicion that the ground was too slick and steep to just climb up to cut the branch away.

"Sure," Paul reassured her, "But it'll take a little doing. I've either got to get on the roof or climb the bank with my saw. I want to try the bank first and I'll need your help."

He dove into the space behind his front seat. He emerged with a braided polypropylene rope he kept for river emergencies. It was rigged inside a weighted throw bag. He took his carpenter's saw from the back and led the way.

"Come on Megan. Follow me." He scrambled to get to the narrow space between the bank and the trailer, reaching his hand back to help her along. He paused directly below the offending tree's trunk. The base of the tree was out of reach ten feet above their heads.

She held the saw while he gently tossed the weighted rope to get it around the base of the tree and fall back to his feet. The rope enabled him to scramble to the base of the tree. He reached back for the saw. He couldn't reach the crotch where the branch had snapped so he put the saw down, pulled the rope until he had enough to work with. He tied the saw, through the handle with a hitch that let him carry it on his back while he climbed the tree and cut the offending limb free.

The cold rain continued to fall while she anxiously watched his progress. They were soaked despite their rain gear and hats.

"It won't be pretty Megan," he said, "but we'll get it done." He cut the offending limb close to the trunk.

He dropped the saw to the ground and again used his rescue rope to snag the now-severed tree limb.

"Let's carry this rope to the end of the trailer and start pulling. See if we can get the branch off."

As hard as they pulled and worked the rope the branch didn't move. Paul wound up tossing it over the trailer and wrapping the end around his trailer hitch. They used the truck's horsepower to get the branch to the ground.

"Okay," he grinned at her. "Let's cover the roof." Their faces were streaming with rain.

The tarp took a good deal of effort and time. There was a blustery wind accompanying the rain. And it caused the large tarp to balloon and flap furiously, the corners flying threateningly about their heads. By noon they had managed to spread it over the trailer's roof and had it tied down with clothesline through the grommets.

Although she hadn't been up to doing the morning's jobs by herself, she had proven herself agile and fit. Now, at the end of the rescue projects, she was emerging as the leader again.

They were wet, chilled and dirty. To Paul, she seemed younger, small, and in need of care.

"Paul. You can't go back to your tent in this mess. Come in and clean up while I fix us something to eat. I'll make coffee too."

Things looked normal inside the trailer. Megan pointed to a puddle on the kitchen floor. "The water must have come in near the ceiling," she said. "I think the crack is behind the ceiling paneling and cabinets."

Paul noticed a slight distortion in the ceiling and said, "I'll have a look under the ceiling panel after I get cleaned up. Might be something simple."

His clothes were in an impossible state of grime. "Here Paul," she grinned impishly. "Take my bathrobe and hand me out your muddy stuff. I'll put it in the washer." She bustled around while he stepped into her shower and bathed.

The only problem was that after his wash, her robe was too small and a tad too pink. *What the heck*, he thought, *at least I'm dry and warm*. Megan had waited for him to emerge from the bathroom before starting the washer. She had changed her clothing and combed her hair.

"Have some coffee and a roll," she said as she stepped into the bathroom. She was smiling over at his somewhat comical predicament of being stuck without his clothing. "You'll have to hang out here with me for a while. And by the way, there's no way I can even try to do business today."

After couple of cups of hot coffee and a pair of big sandwiches they sat on the couch with their feet up.

"Paul. Would you watch a movie with me? I've got *Quest For Fire* in the machine. Okay." She did not get any reception from broadcast stations and cable had not reached her branch yet.

The rain continued and Paul noticed that the puddle on the floor was not smaller. "Let me look at the ceiling first. See if there's anything I can do." He dragged a chair to the middle of the floor and stepped up, too late realizing that he would suffer a complete loss of modesty when he reached over his head and the robe rode up. He paused, embarrassed. Megan stood next to the chair, interested in what he'd find.

Megan saw his problem. "Here Paul, let me help you with that." She pulled the robe's hem down as he reached up. Trouble was she did this one handed and placed her other hand on the back of his thigh and slid it higher as he began to raise his arms.

Paul felt a little unbalanced at this development and placed a hand on her head for balance. He looked down and saw only beauty. There was a pause in home repairs. They moved to the sofa for the unveiling of their bodies and to the bedroom for the ravishment. Her shorts and tee landed on top of the robe on the floor.

Paul was amazed and Megan was delighted.

In her case she had been without a man for two years and had been happy enough with that. Her life was challenging and this development with Paul had not been her intention. It was an impish impulse that took her by surprise. At 33 years she was in the best condition of her life and ready for love before the robe had hit the floor.

Paul was too surprised for words. He had thought of Megan an adult woman, well above his status as an 18-year-old recent high school grad. But he had become aroused the minute her hand had moved to his thigh and doubly inspired as he looked down at his hand on her head. Her clear face, shiny hair and eloquent eyes galvanized his nerve endings. She was a desirable woman and he acted like a man.

Sated after their third round of intercourse, they lay naked in her bed as the wind buffeted the walls and the rain pinged on the roof. He toyed with her nipples, and she burrowed her face into his neck.

"Paul," she declared, "That was something. You are a bull my young friend."

"Thanks Megan. You too…" She giggled.

"No. Not that. I mean you are a wonderful lover. You know I've never made love in a bed before. S'funny, I didn't know how nice it could be. I don't want to leave."

"I don't want you to go either, but there is a problem."

"What's that?"

"You know. I'm old enough to be your mother. Today was priceless. I wouldn't change a thing, but I'm at least 15 years older than you are and this is just a fling for you. A thing that is good. But not a thing that will last beyond a day, or a week, or maybe this summer. We can have lots of fun, but our life needs are different. You need a girl to fall in love with you and have babies."

"Yeah. But I'm confused about something."

"What?"

"Can't you have babies?" he said with a leer.

She leaned back slapped his shoulder - hard. "Damn right buddy. But not with you – you're a baby yourself."

"Am not!" he shouted and rolled her over and began to spank her buttocks. She scrambled to get away. He got in a few good licks and her cheeks turned pink before she could sit on them to make him stop.

They laughed at the horseplay, but a note of sadness gripped them too. Paul knew that she was right. "Well Megan, that may be true," he said ruefully. "But I'd give anything to spend the night with you. They hugged. They slept. They ate more sandwiches. They made love again and then they watched *Quest for Fire*.

It was a rowdy movie about cavemen and survival. Rae Dawn Chong was costumed only in blue dye. She played the role of a homo-sapiens girl interacting with a bunch of Cro-Magnon people. They loved the movie.

Paul decided that he was having the best night of his life. He was reluctant to sleep. Lying with soft, sweet-smelling Megan was so much better than his usual hard, rock lined, sleeping arrangements, that he could not wipe the smile off his face.

MONDAY – May 19, 1997

They woke late, gazing at each other in the morning glow filtering through her bedroom's skylight. The day was clear, and the sun was just coming over the mountain. She declined his advances, whispering, "Wait Paul. I'm a little sore down there."

He nodded understanding.

"Let me make you feel good." Her face descended and her hands and lips began stroking his chest and then his belly. She engulfed his morning erection with tender lips and gentle hands. "Paul," she murmured, "just lie on your back and let me do the work."

Her hair was soft on his skin and he floated in ecstasy until, at length, he exploded in her mouth grasping her hair with both hands to prolong and deepen the penetration. "Oh my God Megan. Oh my God…"

She released him when he began to squirm, and wiped her face along his body as she sought his lips and strong embrace. "That was a gift my friend she breathed. Thank you for being you."

Paul just kissed and hugged her in a loving way. The taste and stickiness of his ejaculation made the kissing and embrace even more intimate. This was officially the best morning of his life.

Megan's washer and drier did their magic. Paul showered and dressed in his clean jeans and tee shirt. She now wore the pink robe.

He got back up on the kitchen chair and loosened a ceiling panel to reveal a sharp branch tip poking through the insulation and outer skin of the trailer. He pushed it out, observing that the hole was minor. He pounded the jagged edge of the break with the rubber handle of his hammer and replaced the insulation and tile. They had not noticed the puncture when they were putting the tarp in place.

"I'll have to get up there with some repair goop.

"Say Megan. Was there a repair kit when you got this thing?"

She gave him the key to the exterior storage spaces, and he found a can of black glue and a metal panel intended to fix the kind of damage the unit had suffered. He remembered a 2x8 plank stashed behind the trailer, where they had walked the day before. He leaned it against the roof and used it as a monkey-walk ramp. On the roof, under the tarp, he saw a small depression where the tree had punctured the roof. He was able to pop the ding out with a little ingenuity and a piece of wire. He applied the patch neatly despite the stickiness of the black goop he was using to plug the hole and bond things together.

The tarp was dry now from sitting in the sun. Together they folded it and stowed in an outside, built-in storage compartment.

They had coffee and cereal and a kiss goodbye. "Paul. Take me to my truck. You'll be working Wednesday and then I'll see you on Thursday."

TUESDAY – May 20, 1997

He whiled away the day working on his tent and trying to get his feet back on the ground. Holy Moly! he mused. Why had he not noticed before that Megan was so hot? And how can we get together like that again?

Paul's tent and gear were a wet mess. He spent the day taking care of his stuff, cleaning the restaurant bathroom and policing its parking lot. He was able to smile and wave to Megan who appeared in the service window from time to time. They would have to talk, he mused. Where could this go for them?

Megan closed shop and walked over to Paul where he sat on a log outside his tent. "Paul honey. I'll be in Asheville tomorrow and I need the night off. I'm bushed."

"Me too," he grinned at her as she sat next to him.

"I'll be home late, and we need to talk. So. How about dinner at my place Thursday night? You provide it. Okay. Just a pizza would be fine. Anything but barbecue or coleslaw."

She gave him a peck and a pat and they parted. He went to have supper at The Takeout Restaurant and, afterwards, went right to bed. He had sweet dreams about making love to Megan. In his dream it was raining hard, and they were trying to make a baby.

WEDNESDAY – May 21, 1997

The day was normal. Not too busy and plenty of time to think. He planned the Thursday dinner. Definitely not pizza. Maybe a couple of candles and a bunch of flowers to tell Megan how much he cared for her.

Paul planned to go paddling Thursday morning – all the way town. He envisioned a nice solo to Clancy to do grocery shopping. He wanted to buy some shaving cream and aftershave lotion, thinking he'd be sexier without facial hair.

Despite being alone much of the time, he was in contact with his paddling buddies most days and interacted with customers every Wednesday. He had learned to treasure solitude when he could manage it.

THURSDAY – May 22, 1997

His run down the river town was totally enjoyable. He pushed off early and stopped to surf on standing waves and major eddies along his way.

He got a haircut, and the barber threw in a professional shave for an additional five bucks. This was a first for Paul. Later, his face was glowing, as he cruised the supermarket aisles.

He toted his grocery bags to the kayak and left them in the cockpit while he hitched a ride to his vehicle. He was always gratified by how easy it was to travel by thumb in this area.

He was surprised when Megan's truck was not in place when he arrived at his tent. She must have been delayed in Asheville, he thought as he drove the few miles to The Takeout Restaurant for a late lunch. It was not busy, and he enjoyed the privilege of eating outside, behind the restaurant, with Marvin.

They sat on the retaining wall overlooking the river. The waitress would let Marvin know when he was needed to fill an order.

"Paul. You look great. What did you do to yourself?"

Paul debated with himself as to whether to fess up his affair with Megan. He decided to say nothing about it. He felt protective of Megan's reputation; at least sensitive to her possible preference to not being outed with an eighteen-year-old.

"Just trying to clean up," he replied. He told Marvin about his fine river run to Clancy and they agreed to meet on the river on Marvin's next day off.

It was late afternoon when he got back to his campsite. He was surprised that Megan's truck was still not there and the closed sign was on the door. He loaded the fixings for their late supper, and he decided to check on Megan by driving up to her trailer. There was no sign of her or the truck. Paul went home and bedded down wondering if her absence had anything to do with their wild day and night of lovemaking. He still felt her on his private parts. He was partly sore and partly buzzed by their multiple contacts. He assumed his sleep position with a sigh and drifted off thinking about sleeping in a real bed. With Megan.

PART THREE

FRIDAY/SATURDAY – May 23 and 24, 1997

Megan did not appear on Friday morning and that left Paul restless and out of sorts. He made his morning toilet and cleaned the rest room in his usual way.

When nine a.m. passed, he decided to open the kitchen and prep for her eventual arrival. It was intended as a favor. The Friday, semi-weekly, food delivery was a slight problem. Megan was a c.o.d. customer. The only funds available were the $50.00 change in the cash register. So he paid cash out of his own pocket and got a receipt. They'd need the stuff for the weekend rush.

Paul guessed he should call the police to see if there had been an accident. Surely, he thought, Megan would find a way to him a message if it were only a simple delay.

He closed early and drove to the COC motel pay phone. He dialed 911 and announced to the flat male voice answering, "What is your emergency?"

"Sir. This is Paul Hunter. I work for Megan Smith who owns the Barbecue Shack Restaurant. She's been away for three days and I'm worried that she may have had an accident."

"Hold one," the voice commanded. After a short silence the voice said, "Mr. Hunter. We can check that for you, but can you come down to the station and give us some ID and details in a report?"

"Yes sir. I'll come now. I'm calling from the pay phone at the Caverns Outdoor Center."

"Could I please have your address and telephone number?'

Paul answered, "I'm camping near the Barbecue Shack. But I don't have a phone number."

The police sergeant wore a nametag announcing that his name was Clancy. Paul introduced himself and was told "We have a report of a bad single-vehicle accident Wednesday night in Asheville, involving a Megan Smith of Clancy, Georgia. 33-years old. She was driving a Ford pickup truck and was admitted to Mission Hospital in Asheville. Sorry. That's all I can tell you. We have no information about her injuries. Is she a good friend?"

"She's been my boss for two years and yes, we are friends."

"Officer Clancy. My brother lives in Asheville. Would you have a phone here so that I can call him? Collect?"

Paul was given a phone and told not to worry about the charges. He called Mitch and gave him a quick rundown. "Mitch. Could you meet me there in two hours? Say about nine. At the front Desk."

"Paul. Molly and I will be there. Drive carefully."

The hospital's main lobby was a cheerful and well illuminated. Mitch and Molly were waiting for him. Looking worried.

The receptionist looked up Megan on her computer and turned to a second receptionist with a question, "Excuse me honey. What does this mean?"

The second receptionist wheeled over on her chair, looked at the screen for a moment and said to Paul, "Megan Smith has been transferred to another location. She went, this morning, to the Willis Rehabilitation Campus. It's not far but you should drive." She gave Paul a map.

"Cripes Mitch. I'm worried."

Molly looked at him with tears in her eyes. "Paul. Were you close to this woman?"

"Yes. Very. She's my boss and I've been trying to take care of the Barbecue Shack for her. Let's go now? Can we drive together?"

The rehab hospital was sited on a hill nearby and they had a little difficulty navigating to the driveway. The receptionist gave them a room number and an encouraging smile. "Talk to her nurse if you have any questions."

Thirty minutes later they sat on a bench in shock. "Oh my God guys. I'm sick."

They were all somber faced and near tears.

Megan had been horribly broken in a high-speed accident on I-40 Wednesday night. She had head and spinal injuries. She was unconscious but her eyes were half open and uncomprehending. Her face was twisted in a grimace.

The nurse was kind but offered little hope or information. "I can only give information to immediate family members. You'll have to talk to the doctor."

They fared little better with the information specialist at the front of the hospital. "You are her first visitors. We have no information on her other than her address and the police investigating the accident are looking for relatives.

"Do you know her next of kin or any relative we can inform of her condition?" Paul could not help but he promised to get in touch with the Asheville police in the morning. It was after midnight - too late to consider driving home, so he bunked with Mitch and Molly. It was the worst night of his life.

The awful night was followed by a terrible morning. He started by tracking down Megan's doctor – the physician on duty that is. Dr. Singh. Megan was not a private patient.

"Paul. I understand that you are the only visitor she's had and admin is trying to find her next of kin to consult with them on her treatment plan.

"I can only tell you that her condition is grave, and she might not survive."

Paul eyes teared up.

"I'm not saying that she can't recover. We will do everything we can, but we must be honest with each other. Yes?"

Paul nodded. "Thank you doctor. Can you put my name down to call if there is any change?"

Doctor Singh agreed, and Paul gave him Mitch's telephone number. Paul slept on Mitch and Molly's couch that night having nightmares involving a terrible automobile accident in slow motion. He was at the wheel but could not steer. It was wintertime and he was on black ice.

SUNDAY – May 24, 1997

Sunday morning, he made his way back to the hospital to find no change in Megan. He assured the nurse that he would be looking for a family member and drove to the Barbecue Shack pondering what to do?

He saw several options including shutting the business until others, he did not know who, decided how to proceed. He could keep the place picked up. He would put a Temporary Closed sign in the window. Or maybe he could continue to camp by the river and paddle the summer away, trying to get trips as a standby guide. That meant showing up at the COC rafting office in the mornings and waiting around.

The standby crew did not get paid unless they caught a trip so they worked a bit around the rafting area stacking, deflating and cleaning rafts and gear. This was a kind of suck-up procedure where they hoped to get favorable notice from the regular rafting guides and supervisors. It could be very dull and unrewarding for a rookie this time of year.

Paul thought long and hard on the drive back to Clancy. He thought that just pocketing the money and letting things slide might put him in jeopardy of being declared a thief of the business. He wanted to erase his history of stealing and become a better man than he was a kid. He didn't like the idea of standing by while the food went bad, and vandals discovered opportunities to spoil her property.

He finally decided to keep the place open for Megan and make sure that it suffered no damage from neglect. But for how long? And to what ultimate end? He would have to go through her stuff to find leads to her friends and family information.

One thing he did not feel was a suitable option was just folding his tent and stealing back to Huntsville with this terrible calamity hanging over Megan.

MEMORIAL DAY – May 26, 1997

Paul rose early and opened the restaurant at the usual time. The third of the Memorial Day weekend was busy but uneventful.

After closing the Shack, he went to Megan's trailer and unlocked it using the spare key he found hanging from a nail she'd driven into the side of the deck. Somehow, he knew it would be hanging there on the deck he had built for her a year earlier. He walked the path to her pole-mounted mailbox and found a week's accumulation. He reckoned that the mailman must think she was away.

The floor was dry, but the air smelled a little musty with a slight overlay of sex. The bed was made and there were no dishes in the sink. Megan was neat. Like me, he thought. He opened all the windows. There was a screen door in front, and he left this open as well. The late spring day freshness soon aired the place out.

He looked at the mail hoping for clues. "Megan. Who are you? Where is your family?" he muttered.

The electric bill, the phone bill and a variety of advertisements did not tell him what he needed to know. There were no long distance calls on the bill.

He made a cup of coffee and found nothing good to eat in the refrigerator. There were a number of leftover bits and pieces and a brownish hunk of lettuce. He tossed it all.

Business was slow and Marvin sat with him as he devoured a steak and fries. Marvin looked natural in his cook's hat and white tee. He sat at ease with his arm resting on the back of the booth and a twinkle in his eye.

"We on for tomorrow bud?"

"Naw Marvin. I can't make it. Something's come up."

Marvin's jaw dropped as Paul related Megan's sad story.

"So, I'm going to be working at the shack every day until she's out of the woods."

"I'll stop by and look in on you. If you need help, I'll ask Susan to find someone to give you a day off when you need it." Susan, Marvin's wife, was something of a hippie as were many in the COC orbit. She was a food service pro but now somewhat limited by the need to care for their three-year-old son.

"We have lots of friends who could use work."

"Thanks Marvin." Paul's eyes suddenly leaked tears. "Oh God. She's so hurt."

Paul called his parents for advice. "I want to help her but I'm worried that someone might claim that I'm stealing her business,

"Mom? What should I do?"

"Paul honey. I can see that this is very upsetting for you. I've had a lot of business experience over the years, but this is a first for me. How about I call my cousin Fred, the lawyer, and ask his opinion? Get back to me tomorrow and we can talk again."

When he called her again his mother said, "Be careful. Keep records. Stash the money in a bank account and make deposits for each day's receipts. You're doing all right, but you'll have to try harder to find her relatives. Fred said so too. Find her family. Talk to a local lawyer.

MONDAY – June 2, 1997

The days slid by. Paul's doubts and fears about his own position began to intrude on his concern for Megan. She lay in a coma, unattended by family. Paul was weary of working six days a week. He went to Asheville once each week to check on Megan. Her facial bruises healed but she lay slack jawed and unresponsive. Dr. Singh still expressed hope, but Paul was discouraged

Bills began to pile up on the trailer's kitchen counter. There was a mortgage notice in the mail, an electric bill and many others that demanded attention. His least favorite bill was the demand for a sales tax report. The notice required a weekly payment and Paul felt that he had to act fast.

He had not found her checkbook or purse. He assumed that they were in her vehicle. He'd have to find how to claim her stuff.

Paul had searched her trailer and the nooks and crannies of the restaurant. There were no clues about her family of friends. Maybe, he thought, he'd get more information from her bank statement when it came.

Paul was now sleeping in Megan's bed. His tent and gear were neatly packed in the back of his truck.

One of his many concerns was the pile of cash that he was accumulating. He wrote each day's cash register total on a lined pad and noted all expenses that he paid. As the season approached business grew stronger. He was taking in over $2,500.00 a week and paying the food truck driver about 20 percent. There were few other cash expenses but the bills piling up in the trailer were getting serious. He had over $7,000.00 in a bag under the front seat of his truck.

"Marvin. I've gotta have a regular day off. Can you find someone who'd be trustworthy to handle the Shack for me on Wednesdays? I need someone who knows about foodservice. I can pay $8.00 an hour plus the tip jar."

"Sure. Easy. How about me?" Marvin grinned at him. "Susan wants me to work longer hours at COC, but I can do this for you for a while. We'll be looking - Susan and me that is - for someone who can spell you as much as you need. The whole season if necessary."

"I'll need to show you what to do first. Could you make it Tuesday and Wednesday this week?"

WEDNESDAY – June 11, 1997

Paul lay in Megan's bed, sleeping in when he got the idea. He picked up the telephone and looked at the caller ID list. There had been several incoming calls from the same number in the 828 area code. He hit the redial button.

Somewhere a phone rang, and a pleasant woman's voice exclaimed, "Megan! Where the hell have you been girl?"

"Er… Hi. It's not Megan. My name is Paul Hunter and I work for Megan. I just hit the redial on her phone and you answered.

"Are you a friend of Megan's?"

"This is Martha Nelson. Yes. I have been calling her for days, but the phone doesn't answer. Is she there?"

There was a silence on the line as Paul began telling her about Megan's accident.

"So, I need to find a family member to take charge at the hospital and take over her business.

"I'm going to be in Asheville late tomorrow afternoon. Would you be able to meet me at the rehab center? We could vis her and then compare notes about how to contact her family."

"Yes. But I might not be able to help much. What time?" Martha thanked him for calling.

Paul opened a bank account in his own name the next day with a single deposit of $6.000.00. He got a temporary checkbook using Megan's mailing address. He visited the offices of the power and gas companies to make payments with his new checks. No one seemed to notice or care about the situation.

The agent at the tax office wasn't so easy. Paul had found the sales tax reporting forms and filled in the appropriate information. He knew that there was a tax office in Clancy.

The man asked about Megan and Paul gave him a complete answer.

"You'll have to fill out an application for yourself for the weeks you are paying. We'll need to get some more information about Miss. Smith's situation because there are two weeks missing."

The tax application troubled him, but he sat and completed it in the office. He had to use his social security number and register as a new business. There was a section where he could narrate details pertaining to the previous owner of the business.

He wrote – *I am just the present operator of the Barbecue Shack. The owner, Megan Smith, has been in a coma in the Asheville Rehab center since May 15, 1997. I intend to keep the business going until she returns and will be responsible for collection and reporting of sales and taxes.*

He later told Marvin and his wife Susan, "That was gnarly. I was scared that they'd bust me for something. In the end the guy said that he was glad that I'd come in before a situation developed. I guess Georgia really needs its sales taxes."

He intended to pay the mortgage and some other necessary bills by mail as soon as he got back to the trailer.

Martha Nelson was a tiny woman. A thirtyish, slim and black-haired bundle of energy. She bustled into the waiting room and immediately spotted Paul.

"Thank you so much for calling me. Megan is a dear friend. We met at an art class at UNCA a couple of years ago. Usually we meet for drinks, dinner and a movie. I'm single. I work as a nurse at Memorial Hospital. Tell me more about you."

Paul recited his history with Megan and concluded, "I've known her since last year. We've become great friends and I don't want to see all her hard work destroyed by neglect. So, I've kept the Barbecue Shack open. I've been paying the bills and taxes and my salary out of the store's income. Keeping the records and so forth."

Martha frowned but relaxed as Paul added, "It's all legal. I'm using the advice of a lawyer and a county judge approved me as a temporary guardian of Magen insofar as the Shack and her bills are concerned."

He hesitated, a little embarrassed..."I'm living in Megan's trailer. Going through her things to find a relative. I only know that there is an ex-husband and a brother she doesn't talk to… I mean get along with."

"Well Paul. I'm in the same boat. I know the ex's name was Robert Turner and he lived in Los Angeles. Her brother's first name is Marty and he's in Chicago. I guess the name is really Martin Smith.

"I don't envy your position. We have a little circle of friends for our girls-night-out. I'll talk it up with them.

"Let's go see her."

Megan was the same. She seemed a little smaller than last week. It seemed that she might be losing weight despite her feeding and therapy programs. They stayed and spoke to her and stroked her arms. They were both crying when it was time to go.

"Paul. I tried to call her so many times. Why don't you get a good answering machine to monitor the telephone? Maybe someone will call."

They hugged, sharing their sorrow.

"Molly," Paul said at dinner. I've bought an answering machine for Megan's phone. I don't want to chance missing any more calls. Would you record the answering message for me? I don't want a male voice.

After a bit of practice, they recorded a minimalist message in Molly's sweetest voice; "Megan's phone. Leave a message.

WEDNESDAY – June 18, 1997

Paul's hair was long enough for a ponytail. The long hair and beard were not formulated in his mind as a policy or deliberate statement. It was the easy way to get through the days.

The saga continued without change until the county health inspector arrived. She was Miss. C. White, according to her nametag. Fortunately, she came on a day that Paul was there.

He followed her around like a puppy while she looked into every nook and cranny with a flashlight in one gloved hand and a clipboard in the other. She made notes and checked squares on her form.

"Where is the thermometer in this reefer?" she said, indicating the under-the-counter refrigerator where coleslaw, uncooked hot dogs and miscellaneous groceries were kept.

"Uh. Sorry. I don't know." He got on his knees and stuck his head in the cooler. He saw the thermometer hanging from a wire shelf and proudly brought it out.

She smiled. "Very good. And I need your grease pump-out record."

He shrugged his shoulders and gave her a rueful look. "Sorry. I don't know where it is."

Miss White gave him a hint. "Megan usually has it under the cash register."

Sure enough. There was a pick-up record indicating that a company that specialized in recycling the nasty stuff had emptied the grease trap on the 16th of May. He saw that there was another envelope under the register. He left it there while she finished her inspection.

"Very good inspection," she said. "But there is one more thing. I need to see your health education certificate or schedule you for a class at the County health Department." He signed up for the class scheduled for the next Monday morning at eight a.m.

Miss White left him a certificate indicating an "A" rating of 92. He had lost points for not having his certificate of training.

He looked at the envelope under the register as she left. It contained sales tax reports for the two missing weeks with a single check attached for the total amount. He saw that she banked with First National, and he resolved to hand deliver the reports as soon as possible. He checked one small worry off his plate.

That same day, the mailman left the bank statement along with a few bills and ads.

He popped the statement open and studied the checks she'd written. There were no surprises. Her balance was a $1,050.00 and he guessed that the check for the sales tax would the only one outstanding.

Paul had a stack of unpaid bills including:

The mortgage for both the trailer and the restaurant property
Automobile insurance due to Geico
Business liability Insurance
Car payment
Sears Department Store
JC Penny. (This had a small credit balance)
The county annual business license renewal
The Power and Light Company
Gas company for both the trailer and restaurant tanks
Magazine subscriptions
Chamber of commerce dues

He wrote checks for utility bills and others that seemed essential for both the residence and business. He wrote checks from his new account and prepared the envelopes for mailing as he had seen his mother do every month.

Finding the tax forms under the cash register inspired him to search the trailer again, even though he had worked hard at it before. He checked under the mattress, in the freezer, in the cups and bowls in the kitchen and in the pans under the sink. He looked under the rugs behind pictures.

It was almost midnight when he found Megan's address book in the couch. It was way down under the cushions. He thought it might have fallen there when they made love.

There were about 20 names. Some had area codes, and some had addresses. Some were cryptic - just initials or numbers without a name.

MONDAY – June 30, 1997

This was Paul's sixth week of despair. Megan seemed to be failing and Dr. Singh gave him little hope. He had exhausted Megan's address book and had no leads to her ex-husband or brother. The working numbers were all businesses and the people answering could or would not give him much information about their business with Megan. There were a few disconnected numbers.

He was banking the receipts from the Shack. They increased a little every week and the last weekend in June was very busy. Every day would busy in the upcoming month of July and the weekends were already brutal. Kids were out of school and families prowled the area looking for mountain recreation and roadside barbecue.

Paul kept the restaurant going for six weeks before he threw in the towel. He was tired of working seven days a week and the constant worry about his uncertain position. And he opened a notice from Geico including a check for $15,000.00 payable to Megan and The First National Bank. It was to pay off the loan and compensate Megan for the total loss of her truck. He closed at noon and headed for town with a bagful of Megan's bills, cash register receipts and all the miscellaneous paperwork he had collected.

Throwing in the towel meant consulting with the town's biggest law office, Johns and Johns. The firm occupied a Victorian mansion on Main Street. The dated building was perfectly maintained and looked as good as new. His appointment was for one o'clock.

Paul wore a clean outfit consisting of jeans and a shirt with a collar. This was the best he could do for this occasion. He was conscious of wrinkles in his shirt and scuffs on his boots.

The elderly receptionist asked him to have a seat in the waiting room. It was nicely furnished, and Paul felt slightly intimidated. She offered him coffee or water, but he politely declined.

After a time, an elderly man entered the room and said "Hello."

He was nattily dressed wearing bright red suspenders with a matching tie over a very white shirt. No suit jacket.

He introduced himself. "Johnny Johns," he said offering a firm handshake. "Step this way young man so we can talk in my office." He led the way into the back of the office suite. It was a somber place with antique furniture and expensive looking pictures on the walls.

The lawyer sat in a leather chair on the client side of the desk and motioned Paul to sit in a matching chair. "How can I help you today?" he asked kindly.

Paul was surprised to be sitting on the same side as the desk with Attorney Johns. It was a down to earth way to conduct business.

"Well sir. I've gotten myself into a situation. I need advice, but before I ask my questions, I should tell you I'm willing to pay for your time. Excuse me for asking but I need to know how much you'll charge. I'm embarrassed to ask so bluntly, but I feel a need to know." Paul sat on the edge of his chair.

"Good question Mr. Hunter. May I call you Paul?"

"Yes sir," said Paul venturing a smile.

"Paul. Call me Johnny. Everyone does. If you say *Johns* people won't know whom you're talking about.

"Let me tell you that I've been in business here in Clancy for over 30 years with my late brother George. I never charge for an initial consultation.

"If I agree to help you, I'll probably charge $75.00 per hour billed in 15-minute increments. If it is a criminal matter, I'll need to be paid in advance. So, you see I'm not cheap, but my advice is usually pretty good." He winked at Paul in an avuncular manner and sat attentively in his chair, looking directly at Paul in a friendly manner.

"That will be fine sir." He began to tell Johnny the story of Megan. He told him everything except that they were having a relationship. "I've been staying in her trailer to better look after things but I'm very uneasy that I'm getting into trouble.

"My uncle who's a lawyer in Alabama told my mom that I should just pack up and leave. She told me to leave the keys with the police in Clancy and make sure they have the whole story.

"But here's what I'm worried about. If I just leave someone might break into her house and trash it. Probably the business too and she'll have nothing when she gets better. I mean if she gets better." Paul was very emotional and close to crying as he concluded his recital.

Johnny was quiet for a moment. He leaned toward Paul and said, "Paul. I'm sorry to learn of these circumstances. Do you want to take over the business?"

"No sir... I mean Johnny. Megan's my friend and I just want to have her come back to work and tell me what to do."

"How old are you, Paul?"

"Nineteen sir... er, Johnny."

"Paul, were you intimate with Megan?"

Paul hesitated trying, to find the right words. "She was my employer and landlord since last summer. We were very good friends, but we made love the night before she had her crash. She was older than me, but we had just started. We were supposed to have dinner when she returned."

Johnny did not seem to pass judgment. His face remained alert and interested,

"What is your education and work experience?"

Paul told him about his recent graduation from high school and working construction for his dad. "Oh yeah. I forgot. I got a health department certificate for taking a sanitation lecture and test and I'm an accredited raft guide for Caverns Outdoor Center. I took the seven-day course."

Johnny nodded. "Paul, based on what you have shared with me, you haven't done anything wrong. Yet.

"You could step over the line if you continue after Megan passes, if indeed she does." Johnny paused, rose, and crossed the room. He handed Paul a tissue.

Paul wiped his eyes and blew his nose. "Thanks Johnny. This is scary stuff for me."

"Paul. I will be willing to help you in this matter for my usual fees that can be paid as we go along. It's really not too complicated but it will take some time. At $100.00 per hour I'm guessing that you may be looking at a bill for one or two thousand dollars plus modest court filing fees.

"I see you as a guardian of Megan's assets until she gets back or dies. From what you tell me her condition is deteriorating. You have done her heirs, should there be any, your community and the state of Georgia no harm. Indeed, you are the good guy."

Paul smiled to hear this. "Johnny. How do you mean her guardian?"

"I believe that we could apply to the Clancy County Superior Court to appoint you as a guardian of her real property, and that would include the business. Paul. I like the way you have conducted yourself. Since you are young and inexperienced, I would be willing to join you in the effort.

"Paul. I'm on the verge of retirement. I have no need of fees. I'll be closing this office at the end of the month – this would be one of my projects in retirement. I'll go easy on the fees but we will need to use an investigator. That may be our main expense.

"As a part of conserving her property and business affairs she would need to become a ward of the court and, should she pass, we would need to take steps to not only locate her family but liquidate her business and sell the real estate.

"Should you be willing to continue to work for Megan and her heirs, when and if we find them, I'd expect you to remain in place for a period of time.

"Today is the last day of June. If you will agree to stay on, I'll need a few days to file the petition. My fee for that will be $200.00 but I'll need a check from you for $1,000.00.

"I also need to investigate you. I want to be sure that you are who you told me you are. I'll need personal references.

"We'll have to get a statement from this Dr. Singh in Asheville. I'll do the legwork on all of these matters, but we need to act swiftly at this time to be sure that we can get the blessings of the court on your actions.

"Do you want to continue Paul?"

Johnny seemed to shift into another mode as he laid out a plan of action for Paul. His demeanor was very friendly and supportive. But he seemed to become younger and more animated as he spoke.

"Johnny. I need to talk to my mom to get her advice. Is there a phone that I could use?"

"Paul. You have just revealed yourself as an intelligent as well as a kind man. Use the phone in the conference room if you like and I'll make a few phone calls on this. No fee yet. But I want to get a few things lined up." He showed Paul into an adjacent room with a library table surrounded by comfortable chairs on wheels. There was a large picture window and lots of light.

There was a stack of yellow pads and pens on the table and a telephone with several lines indicated by buttons. He pushed a button and punched in his mother's number.

Paul's mother heard him out and concurred that he needed Johnny John's help. He made a note of his second cousin's address and phone number in Birmingham to use him as a reference.

"Good luck honey. I know that you are doing the right thing."

Paul walked back to Johnny's office and waited at the door for Johnny to put the phone down. Johnny's last words into the receiver were, "Thank you sweetie. I'll wait here for your phone call."

He looked up at Paul, smiled, and gestured for him to be seated. Johnny stayed on the working side of the desk this time.

"What did your mom say Paul?"

"She told me to stay as long as I needed and to say thank you for helping me Johnny.

"And I need to show you this check and ask you what should I do with it?"

Johnny looked at the $15,000.00 check and glanced at the form letter from GEICO. "We'll just attach this to the file for now. We may need to negotiate with the insurance company after looking at the vehicle, the loan papers and the black book. We'll talk about this later. The main thing is to get you settled.

"Well then. Let's you and I get moving. We have a lot to do. My investigator's name is Carmen Cabrera. She is a retired Florida State Highway Patrol officer. She is right now heading for the

Barbecue Shack to make sure that it is as you say it is. I hope she likes the food," he chuckled.

"I'm sure she will if she likes to eat. The slaw is made fresh, and the pork is smoked on a daily basis. The only thing we freeze is the bread so that it stays as fresh as the day it's baked. Please let me know what she has to say. My friend Susan Reed is running the show today. She and her husband Marvin take turns helping me so that I can get days off to go to Asheville every week."

"I see. Are they legal employees?"

"Yes and no. But I get the point. I'll get their Social Security numbers right away and withhold taxes. Is that what you mean?"

"Yes Paul. We are about to enter the real world. We need to dot our 'I's and cross our 'T's.

"Paul. We have a great deal to do if we are to succeed in our efforts right away. By Wednesday I expect to have the court appoint you and me as guardians of Megan's property. Friday is the Fourth of July weekend, and the court will begin its vacation recess for four weeks. I want you to go to the office of Smith and Company. They are accountants. Just down the street. I have already spoken to them, and they will help you apply for an Employers Identification Number, by phone. They'll give you the forms you need to legalize Marvin, Susan, and yourself as employees.

"Paul. Please write your name, Social Security Number, your address and telephone numbers and the names and contact numbers for as many references as you can. Please give me your brother's and parent's contact information too.

"I'll need you to return to my office at ten o'clock Wednesday morning and be prepared to go to court with me. My secretary has already made an appointment with the judge and the county attorney for a hearing on the matter at noon.

Johnny questioned Paul closely about the income from the Shack and the expenses of both the business and Megan personally. He got all the details about how Paul handled the cash register tapes, expenses and deposits.

Paul took the time to write all that Johnny requested on a lined pad. He gave his second Cousin Fred McDowell, the lawyer, Marvin Redman, his friend, and his high school Lit teacher as references. He gave the list to Johnny with a personal check for $1,000.00. He felt that he was doing it for Megan and, for the first time in weeks, enjoyed confidence in his actions. He felt like he'd been in a state of uncertainty since he said goodbye to a healthy Megan.

"I want you to get a good start in the right direction. Please shave, get a haircut, and wear a jacket and tie. You'll clean up fine my boy!"

Smith and Company's offices were not as elegant as Johns and Johns. Accountant Regan Smith was alone and on the phone as Paul entered with his paper beg of records.

Smith had a ruddy face. He was a white haired, handsome guy in his fifties, and he spoke with a musical, high-pitched voice. "Yes. Yes. No." He smiled and motioned for Paul to be seated on the other side of his cluttered desk. "Hold on a moment please."

"Paul. Hi I'm Regan. I'm on the phone getting your Employers Identification Number from the IRS.

What is your Social Security number and address?" He paused for a moment, and then said, "Paul Hunter? Do you have a middle initial?"

Paul answered his questions and presently Regan said goodbye and put the phone down.

"Johnny briefed me on your situation. I'm sorry about Ms. Smith. I don't know her by the way. We're probably not related.

"Paul. I told Johnny that I would not charge you for today's work. He briefed me on your situation. I've gotten you an EIN and have here a file of information of your responsibilities as an employer relating to Workman's Compensation Insurance and Georgia State Income tax.

Go through this stuff and come back to me after your court date on Wednesday and I'll answer any questions you have. Just read it all over. A lot of it is self-explanatory." He handed Paul a manila file folder containing a neat stack of pages.

"Thank you. How do you charge for your services?"

"Good question. It depends on how much work I must do. In the case of your business, I would guess $50.00 per month plus

$200.00 next spring if you want me to do your taxes. Sound Good?"

"Yeah. I'm mean yes sir." They both laughed.

Since it was too late to go the distance to Asheville, and because he had not made advance arrangements with Mitch and Molly, he decided to shop for clothes and get a haircut. There was a Walmart in Clayton, Georgia but the drive put him off.

Solomon's Menswear on Main Street was his best and only choice. There was a 'Summer Madness' sale. He left the store, under the kindly eye of Sol Solomon, with a complete 'Go-To-Court' outfit; chino pants, blue short-sleeve shirt, black knit tie and blue blazer. He bought a pair of black loafers and several pairs of socks at the neighboring Shoe Heaven. These were all cash transactions.

Then to the barbershop. The barber remembered his name from his first visit. "Say Paul. I'm going to have to use the electric shaver on you before I can give you a regular shave."

"No problem. Thanks for taking me on." Afterwards the air felt cooler on his face.

"Marvin. I need a big favor from you and Susan."

"Sure bud. What is it?" Marvin was just finishing his daily clean-up work. He didn't comment on the change in Paul's look. He was a patient man, and he was sure Paul would explain.

"Actually, two things. I want to keep our business; I mean Megan's business, confidential. I don't want folks around here or at COC to know what I'm up to."

"Why Paul. You're doing good things. I'd be proud if I were you."

"Yeah. I don't disagree but I'm going to court Wednesday to ask to become Megan's Legal Guardian along with lawyer Johnny Johns. I figure that this won't last long. I don't think Megan is going to make it. By the way, Johnny made me shave and get a haircut."

Paul was frankly crying, and, to his surprise, he saw that Marvin was crying too. Marvin put down his dishtowel and gave Paul a hug. "I know it's tough bud. We'll do what we can to help."

"The thing is that I'm 18-years old and I feel way in over my head. I don't want people to think I'm some smart guy. I want to fit in and just be a working stiff. Maybe at COC next year. However long this lasts I want it to end clean and not follow me around as a part of my rep. Ya know?"

"I see what you mean. I'll talk to Susan, and we'll not gossip about you. I promise. We haven't said much so far because I don't want my boss to know that we're working for the competition, although she probably already knows. Cornelia Johnson is a smart lady and there's not much that gets by her.

"Thanks Marvin. And there's something else. I need to back track on our deal here. I want to give you and Susan a 10% raise in pay but, in return, you have to go on the books, and I need to start paying you by check and deducting Social Security from your checks. I'm not exactly sure how that works but I'll find out Wednesday. Okay?"

"Yes, sure. We'll be glad to cooperate. Just figure it out and let us know."

That night he settled down to read through employer and employee manuals, state and federal income tax forms, workman compensation rules and a handful of forms. He understood them well. Even at the low rates of pay for Marvin, Susan, and himself, he would have to deduct taxes, account for them and pay them to the appropriate authorities. He wondered how Megan had avoided all this bother. He guessed she was a rogue, bootleg business operating outside the system. He imagined the worry this must have cost her over the three years she'd told him she'd been in business.

He arrived at Johnny's office at ten o'clock on Wednesday morning. The secretary invited him to sit in the conference room. She gave him a cup of coffee and some heavy reading material. "Johnny will be here in a few minutes."

The main document was a petition to the Superior Court of Clancy County to appoint him and Johnny as Guardians. It was a beautifully typed and bound document. It proved to be an interesting read for him. He was impressed by the amount of research and initiative it revealed about Johnny and his team. There was no way the old man could have done this on his own.

PETITION FOR THE APPOINTMENT OF A GUARDIAN FOR AN ALLEGED INCAPACITATED ADULT
Clancy County, Georgia

TO THE HONORABLE JUDGE OF THE SUPERIOR COURT: Roland E. Sequoyah

IN RE: Megan Smith, ALLEGED INCAPACITATED ADULT, And PROPOSED WARD:
1. **Paul Hunter**, friend and employee, whose residence address and telephone are 1901 Georgia Route 72, Clancy, Georgia 31955, and **J.P. Johns**, Attorney at law representing Paul Hunter as counsel and advisor for fee, and who is a proposed friend, in absence of family, of the proposed ward, is a resident of Clancy County with offices at 12 Main Street, Clancy Georgia, 31955.
ATTACHED HERETO as page 6 and made a part of this petition is the completed **affidavit** of Mohamed Singh, M.D., a physician licensed to practice medicine in both the states of Georgia and North Carolina. (Megan Smith lies in a coma in the Asheville, North Carolina Rehabilitation center) Dr. Singh has examined the proposed ward within 10 days prior to the filing of this petition.
2. Megan Smith, proposed ward, age 33, (May 1, 1964), social security no. XXX XX 2198, is a resident of Clancy County, Georgia has a residence address of 1 Robbins Cove Road, Clancy, Georgia 31955 and is presently located at the Asheville Rehabilitation Center in Asheville, North Carolina, where she lies gravely ill and in a coma since May 22, 1997. (The full S.S. number is in possession of Petitioner J. P Johns)
3. The proposed ward lacks sufficient understanding or capacity to make responsible decisions concerning her person and is incapable of managing her estate, and the

property of the proposed ward will be wasted or dissipated unless proper management is provided.

As per the attached notarized statement of Dr. Singh and the North Carolina State Police Report 0522196744, Megan Smith lies in a deep coma resulting from a single car accident in North Carolina in the early morning hours of May 22, 1997; cause unknown. **(Alcohol, drugs, and foul play have been ruled out pending final disposition of the case)**

The duration of the incapacity is unknown.

4. There are no known relatives or spouse at this time other than a brother, Martin Smith. His whereabouts is under investigation so that he can be notified of Megan Smith's circumstances.

In accordance with the stature, notice is being given to 2 adult friends of Megan Smith. Copies of their signed response will be provided within 7 days:

Martha Nelson (Friend of Megan Smith)
21 Bowery Street
Asheville North Carolina
(828) 555 2121

2. Alice Gordan (Friend of Megan Smith)
1211 Meyers Court
Asheville North Carolina
(828) 555-7676

5. There are no previously appointed representatives from prior proceedings pursuant to Official Code of Georgia Annotated Chapters 37-7, 37-3 or 37-4.

6. All known income and assets of the proposed ward are hereto attached.

7. The nominated guardians have consented to serve have consented to serve as shown by the consent on page 5 attached hereto.

WHEREFORE, the petitioners pray: that service be perfected as required by law; that pending receipt of any evaluation reports, required by the court, the court order an immediate hearing to determine the need for a guardian for the alleged incapacitated person; and that a guardian of the property be appointed for the alleged incapacitated adult.

PAUL L. HUNTER (SIGNATURE)
J.P. JOHNS (SIGNATURE)

J. P. JOHNS
12 MAIN STREET
CLANCY, GEORGIA 31955

VERIFICATION
GEORGIA, CLANCY COUNTY
Personally appeared before me the undersigned petitioner who, on oath, states that the facts set forth in the foregoing petition are true.
MARSHA GRANT, NOTARY PUBLIC

Sworn to and subscribed before this 2nd day of July 1997

RE: Petition for the appointment of guardian for Megan Smith, an alleged incapacitated adult.

I, PAUL HUNTER, having been nominated as guardian of the property of the above-named alleged incapacitated adult, do hereby consent to serve as such.
Paul Hunter (signature)

I, J.P. JOHNS, having been nominated as guardian of the property of the above-named alleged incapacitated adult, do hereby consent to serve as
such.
J.P. JOHNS (signature)

**AFFIDAVIT OF PHYSICIAN OR PSYCHOLOGIST
STATE OF GEORGIA, COUNTY OF CLANCY
SUPERIOR COURT OF CLANCY COUNTY**

**RE: Petition for appointment of a guardian for MEGAN SMITH,
an alleged incapacitated adult**.

I, being first duly sworn, depose and say that I am a physician licensed to practice under Chapter 34 of Title 43 of the Official Code of Georgia Annotated. My office address is Asheville Rehabilitation Center, 1000 Mars Avenue, Asheville, North Carolina, that I have examined the above-named alleged incapacitated adult on the 1st day of July 1997, **and I have found her to be incapacitated by reason of an automobile accident**, to the extent that said alleged incapacitated adult lacks sufficient understanding or capacity to make significant responsible decisions concerning her person and property and is incapable of communicating such decisions.

WITNESS MY HAND AND SEAL this 1st day of July 1997.

Mohamed Singh, M.D. (Signed and Notarized in North Carolina)

INCOME AND ASSETS

Below are listed all of the known income and assets of the proposed ward:

REAL PROPERTY

Parcel- 1 - A Manufactured Home at one Grant Cove Road, Clancy, Georgia sitting upon an acre of land. Value undetermined, mortgaged to GMAC with a balance of $95,000.00

Parcel-2 - A one-acre lot at 1901 Georgia Highway 72 occupied by a business known as the Barbecue Shack. Value undetermined and also subject to the mortgage cited above.

It is estimated that he Barbecue Shack produces a net income in excess of $25,000.00 per year. No other income is known at this time.

YEARLY TOTAL OF ALL INCOME is estimated to be in excess $25,000.00.

PERSONAL PROPERTY

Checking account – First Citizens, # 45454555 - Balance - $1,050.00
Savings Account - Unknown
CERTIFICATE OF DEPOSIT - Unknown
BONDS - unknown
STOCKS – unknown

AUTOMOBILE 1995 Ford 150 pickup truck - wrecked. This vehicle has been totaled. GEICO Company has tendered a check of $15,000.00 intended to pay the loan off and compensate Megan Smith for the total value of the vehicle. This amount will be negotiated should the court appoint the petitioners as guardians of Megan Smith's estate and property.

OTHER ITEMS
Furniture and incidental personal property including jewelry, business inventory of the Barbecue Shack and other personalty.

TOTAL PERSONAL PROPERTY - Estimated to be in excess of $25,000.00

TOTAL YEARLY INCOME + TOTAL PERSONAL PROPERTY VALUE Estimated to be in excess of $50,000.00

GEORGIA SUPERIOR COURT OF CLANCY COUNTY

Roland E. Sequoyah Judge of the SUPERIOR Court

APPOINTMENT OF ATTORNEY

This Court has not been notified of the retention of counsel by the proposed ward within the prescribed period, **J. P. Johns** is hereby temporarily appointed as attorney for the proposed ward in this matter. This 2nd day of July 1997

Roland E. Sequoyah Judge of the SUPERIOR Court

The main document had yellow arrow stickers placed where he was to sign. There were several other documents including orders for the judge to sign creating the guardianship. He noted Dr. Sing's notarized affidavit and realized someone had traveled to Asheville to get his signature. He was paying for this work, but he found that he liked the way Johnny had taken charge and was getting things done.

Judge Sequoyah was a sturdy man of about 45 years. He had black hair and dark features that revealed a Native American heritage. He, Johnny, Paul and a man named Sam Silvers sat at a conference table in the judge's chambers. Silvers turned out to be the State's Attorney. He was there to represent Megan's interests. "So. What's the real story Johnny," the judge said looking directly at Paul.

Paul was dressed in his new clothes but felt out of place among these dignitaries. The judge was in his shirtsleeves with the cuffs rolled up. He was clearly in charge of this proceeding. The others wore jackets and seemed to know each other well.

"Judge. Young Mr. Hunter here is a hero in my estimation. He fell into a bad situation and conducted himself well." He told the story in as few words as possible and concluded. "So, like a true friend he kept the business going and has folded his tent, so to speak, and moved into the trailer to keep it clean and repaired. He has paid Ms. Smith's bills.

In addition to going to the police he consulted me and then with Smith and Company, accountants, to help him find the correct path to follow. He is current with the sales taxes and has paid utilities and mortgage payments."

The judge looked at Paul and said, "Mr. Hunter. I was very sorry to hear about your friend's accident and dire medical condition. I am going to permit you to continue as you have been, but I will require a weekly report to be filed with Sam Silvers and the court detailing both Ms. Smith's condition and the financial situation of both from the business and her personal finances. I don't want to see Mr. Hunter enrich himself but I see the need to pay him appropriately for maintaining this seven days a week business. I propose to pay him not more than $700.00 a week if that is possible given the nature of the business. I want also to see a proposal for closing it down if it can't support itself when the tourist season is over.

"Do you concur gentlemen?"

The attorneys and Paul all nodded and chorused, "Yes Sir."

"Johnny. Get the paperwork ready right away. Okay?"

"Yes sir. It will be here by close of business, and I'll make sure that it's all signed off by Mr. Silver first."

It was a one-block walk to Johnny's office from the courthouse. Sam Silver's office was in the courthouse. Silver and Johnny had paused to confer out of Paul's earshot. But he saw that were looking at their watches and setting a time to review the orders that Johnny would generate for the court.

"Paul. How do you feel? Did we do good for Megan?"

"Yes sir Johnny. Thanks to you. I think so. I don't know about the $700.00 per week. It may be a little too much after the season is over. Everything will slow down in the shoulder season."

"Let's not worry about that right now." Johnny said kindly. "Just come to the office and I'll figure out what you need to sign. Most of the forms we use are on the computer now and it doesn't take too long to fill in the blanks and print them."

Paul sat in the waiting room thinking. There were magazines and a newspaper, but he wanted time to absorb all that had transpired in the judge's office. Johnny came out after a while and said, "Paul. Take a walk for a few minutes. We'll not need you until three o'clock. And then it will just take a few minutes."

Paul, feeling liberated, made his way to Smith's Accounting and found Regan finishing up with a client who nodded politely to Paul as he entered. He sat and waited until the man left.

"Paul. What happened in court today?"

Paul told him that he was going to continue to run the business, try to achieve his paycheck and that he would stop by before the end of each month with cash register tapes, an account of receipts and expenses and checks for taxes.

"Paul. Speaking of checks I would appreciate you paying me now. $100.00 will be enough to get me started. I'll work with you for a while, but it is my goal to have you do most the work by yourself and I'll just be your coach. Johnny will tell me what he needs, and I'll just bill you as we go along."

They agreed on meeting times and dates; weekly at first. Paul returned to the law office with a determination to be a good client for Smith. He liked him very much and wanted his approval.

Johnny sat Paul at the conference table and presented him with a series of legal papers, some requiring signature and other just a nod of understanding. These were the orders that gave him the legal authority to continue doing what he had already undertaken as an act of friendship for Megan. He just wanted her well and back in charge.

Paul was given a folder containing copies of all the documents relating to the case. It was fat enough to make a thump when he put in on a table.

"Paul. In addition to the things, we have just discussed there is that matter of settling with the insurance company. Megan probably had personal items in the car, and I want you to take a copy of Judge *Sequoyah's* order with you and go to the police in Asheville next time you go there and see what you can do. I'm thinking about her purse and wallet mostly but there may be other stuff of help in tracking down a family member."

A week later Paul brought a sealed cardboard box to Johnny's office. He wanted them to open it together. Megan's purse and wallet especially were examined in detail and, sadly, there were no further clues, telephone numbers or addresses.

Business grew stronger each day until the weekdays were indistinguishable from weekends. He really needed the days off that Marvin and Susan gave him. Wednesdays and Thursdays were his days to travel to Asheville and see Megan's sad situation and gain comfort from Mitch and Molly's company. He usually spent a night on their couch and returned to the trailer Thursday afternoon to do housework and bookkeeping.

The money worked out just as it had before except that he deposited the excess to Megan's bank account each week. No one had thought about charging him rent for the trailer or some fine points that developed as he worked the days away

The tip jar, for example, yielded a dividend each day. He saw that the more he interacted with customers the bigger the take. It was a funny thing. It supplied him with a regular side income every day he worked. He always put a few dollar bills and a few quarters first thing in the morning to give customers the idea. He thought of it as 'salting' the jar. Most put in loose change and some folding money. He didn't really care because he felt happiest when he smiled and said a friendly hello to everyone. He kept that money to himself.

Paul took all his meals at work except for his days off. His little scams also involved getting the weekly food delivery to include some extras like cereal, milk, coffee, and his favorite brand of baked beans. The food was an efficiency move for him rather that a ploy to save a few dollars a day. He was able to open earlier and stay a little later.

He mailed his mother a check for $500.00 on a weekly basis and accumulated a balance in his personal checking account. His opportunities to get out on the river were limited.

Paul made a few office visits to Johnny and Regan who worked together, from the information Regan extracted from his checkbook and cash register tapes. He prepared his own Sales Tax Reports and Regan made a copy. Regan taught him to make Withholding Tax and Social Security payments to the IRS. The reports were easy enough.

Susan and Marvin didn't care that a little was withheld each week. The tip jar probably made up for their small contributions to the government. He put posters and official notices on the back walls of the Shack advising the employees of their rights and responsibilities.

He saw many new faces each day and a few regulars and friends too. It was not a hard job, but it did require good organization and proper prepositioning of all the supplies he needed every day and always thorough cleaning.

Paul enjoyed working with the food. Turning cabbage into delicious coleslaw and raw pork into savory barbecue was fun.

The bank balances grew even though Regan had him make checks to Megan on a weekly basis. He no longer had to pay the mortgage because Johnny found out that there was a disability clause, and no payments were due while she was unable to work. In fact, the mortgage company refunded one month's payment and that went straight into Megan's bank. Her account had also grown by an additional $1,500.00 from the automobile insurance policy.

Johnny had negotiated a better payout.

PART FOUR

SEPTEMBER 5, 1997

Dr. Singh called and said, "Paul. I have sad news for you. Megan did not survive the night. As you know we have no relatives to call. There was an investigator here a few weeks ago and she gave me the hint that you are being appointed as Megan's guardian. Is this true?"

"Yes sir. Thank you for calling… I've been bracing myself for this."

"What is the situation now? I mean about her body."

"Paul, as you probably know from her driver's license Megan chose to be an organ donor. Unless someone comes forward to object, her body will go immediately to the state coroner and there it will be decided what to do with her remains. The state of North Carolina will incur expenses that will probably be dismissed due to the complexity of collecting. There will be a large hospital bill that may be filed against her estate in Georgia. You'll need legal counsel if you have an interest in these matters.

"I wish I could tell you more, but matters are now out of the hospital's hands, and I can only say that I'm sorry that we couldn't save her."

Paul sniffled a goodbye and thank you. He felt defeated. He felt he had failed Megan utterly.

Mitch and Molly took over. They sat down with Paul in their living room. "Paul. This is an intervention. We'd like to ask the hospital chaplain if they could help us conduct a service for Megan. We never knew her, but we feel like friends and family. We want to say goodbye to her in a proper way.

Phone calls were made that resulted in a solemn service conducted in the chapel on the Tuesday following her death. Paul was surprised that over two-dozen people attended. She had several friends in Asheville and there were members of the hospital staff.

Paul rode to the occasion in a COC van with nine people from COC and Clancy including the judge, Johnny, Regan and their wives. Marvin and Susan brought their child. He had arranged for and driven the vehicle. Carmen, Johnny's investigator was there, and he recognized a number of Megan's nurses. He was touched by their attendance.

A party of 14 went to a downtown tavern that had been frequented by Megan and her friends and had a meal. Mitch and Molly had been right – the activity and memorial service made Paul feel better about things – Megan had a good sendoff.

"Paul. We must carry on as the court dictates and as the laws of North Carolina and Georgia dictate. I believe that it will be in the best interest of Megan's estate if you will continue for a short while until we get instructions from the court. I believe that it will order Megan's property liquidated. As to the business, I think it can be sold quickly. There are brokers who deal in the buying and selling of businesses. Thanks to you; Megan has a valuable business that might well be continued under a new owner.

"Do you have any interest in acquiring the business?"

"No Johnny. It's not that I don't like it but if I could buy it, the Shack would own me. Remember I'm only nineteen and I haven't figured my life course out yet." Paul was embarrassed to admit this, but he did not have a real plan beyond getting a job with COC for a season to be able to continue playing on the river.

Many of his river friends were a good bit older but they seemed content to enjoy nature's bounty and each other's company without much concern about the future. He admired that about them but thought that something important would catch his interest one day.

FRIDAY – September 12, 1997

Judge Sequoyah, Johnny, Paul and State Attorney Sam Silvers sat in the judge's conference room again. They were a somber group gathered to decide the fate of Megan Smith's property and business.

"Gentlemen," the judge said in a gravelly voice, "The law dictates what we do now." It seemed to Paul that he was getting a lecture, the same lecture Johnny had given him. "We must act with deliberate speed to liquidate the deceased's assets and that means selling her business and her real estate. Are we agreed?"

All nodded. "Therefore, Johnny you will produce documentation, and you Sam will approve or amend it as necessary until complete agreement is reached."

The judge turned to Paul. "Mr. Hunter. It is my understanding that you will occupy the real estate and run the business as a conservation manner, as you have been, until a buyer is found."

"Yes judge." Paul was very nervous. "I'll do the best I can."

"I understand that you are young sir, but I have trust in the fact that Mr. Smith is partnering you and that you will work under his supervision.

"Mr. Silverman. I expect you and Mr. Smith will be able to work this all out together." Silverman nodded. They all rose as the judge stood and everyone shook hands.

Judge Sequoyah held Paul's hand a moment longer than he did the lawyers and said quietly, "Megan would thank you too sir. I thank you for being a stand-up guy."

FRIDAY – September 19, 1997

Johnny was a man of action. Paul was at the Shack window serving lunch on this quiet day when Johnny and a couple showed up just before noon.

Paul had quit shaving again and would grow a beard and long hair by his birthday in December. Today he looked a little windblown and had a heavy five o'clock shadow on his chin and cheeks.

Johnny introduced them as Paula Pruitt from Atlanta, the New Horizons Business Brokers owner, and her client Jerry Marks who was very interested in buying an income property in a rural mountain area.

Paul thought he recognized Jerry as a recent face in the service window. Perhaps he had previewed the place on his own.

"Paul." Johnny addressed him. "Could you please show Paula and Jerry around and then hang a closed sign for the afternoon. We could either eat here, at that restaurant at COC, or bring some food to the trailer. What do you say?"

"Sure Johnny. It's a 'break-even' kind of day and I didn't do much prep. I'll show them around and then pack us a lunch to eat at home… I mean at Megan's."

"How do you do Jerry? Are you from Atlanta?"

Jerry gave Paul a very hard handshake and a rather unfriendly glare, as if they were unfriendly opponents. "No. Miami. How about you?"

"Huntsville." Paul did not embellish. "Come on I'll give you a tour."

"Mind if I tag along?" Paula asked.

"Sure. No worries. There's not much to show." The three explored the property while Johnny sat comfortably at a picnic table. Since it was such a basic enterprise, few questions were asked. Jerry seemed very interested in the exposure to the river and remarked that there wasn't much signage.

"Jerry. There are virtually no signs on this river. That little tin BBQ nailed to a tree stands out like a neon sign for boaters. This is the only place available.

As if on cue, two rafts with a dozen people on board rounded the bend and edged up to the bank. The boaters beat it up the path to the shack, lining up at the bathroom door on their way. Paul hustled to his place in the window. While he was taking care of this group, two pick-up trucks appeared, and four more people joined the line.

Paul had them all served in minutes. Their money was registered, and the tip jar was anointed. Paul gave every one of his customers a smile and a benediction, "Thanks. Enjoy your Meal."

Paula and Jerry seemed impressed. Paul told them, "Saturday and Sunday will be busy."

Paul quickly prepared take-out barbecue for four people, hung a paper sign that said closed until two p.m. He figured that he wouldn't be missing too much and that he could clean up later. We might even stay open until dark to make up for the missed hours. He treated the business as if it was his own.

Paul set the lunch out on real plates, with Megan's stainless-steel flatware and glasses. He thought it looked nice as they sat to eat together. The river view was pretty, and the picnic table and benches gave them ample space.

Presently Paula sat back and said, "That's very, very good. What do you think Jerry? Would you be happy to serve food like this?"

"Sure. I like it fine. Good job Paul. Thanks for feeding us.

Paul gave them all a tour of the trailer and a little lecture about its features. "I find it very comfortable. This is how people hereabouts live. Manufactured housing is the best cost per square foot living space available." He felt like an expert since he had read through Megan's files containing the original mobile home brochures.

As the company was getting into their car Johnny held back a little and said, "I think it's a sale. He's been here before, and I had Regan fax all the numbers to Paula last week. I didn't tell you because I wanted to give you peaceful possession as long as practical. Okay?"

"Sure Johnny. If I'd known you were coming, I would have spent days cleaning everything up. Thanks."

"Paul. Everything's fine. You're a good housekeeper."

They sat in the judge's conference table again with two new players: Paula the broker and Jerry Marks the buyer. Johnny's secretary was there to notarize the documentation. There were several purposes for the meeting:
- Convey Megan's property and business to Jerry
- Discharge Paul from any further involvement
- Appoint Johnny as executor off Megan's estate
- Receive appropriate cashier's checks from Jerry to pay the broker's commission, to pay off the bank and to pay Megan's estate the balance.

Paul had to write final checks to Johnny and Regan for final fees. Now that Paul was out of the business, Megan's estate would need to pay them.

There was a veritable raft of paperwork. Paul had to give Johnny final sales tax reports and withholding tax submission forms with checks attached. There were dozens of documents.

When the meeting and the signing were over, Jerry had the keys to the business and the trailer.

Jerry received one day's training from Paul. It had not gone well in Paul's opinion. Jerry never worked in foodservice before, but he exuded an attitude that he could do it all better. The customers were hicks and jerks, and Paul was a dumb kid. He did not like Jerry and Jerry seemed to like no one. And the food was "…for shit."

Paul's worldly possessions were packed in his truck. He was homeless and jobless bus somehow satisfied that he had brought a sad situation to a satisfactory conclusion. For once in his life had done the right thing.

WEDNESDAY – October 1, 1997

Paul and Marvin were sitting on a bench in the early October sunlight waiting for Susan and their son Mars.

COC customers, mostly rafters, and employees milled about in the near distance. The day was a gift from heaven. Blue skies and mild temperatures ruled. The slight breeze was pleasant.

"Marvin. It's a little early for me to go back to Huntsville. Now that the Shack is gone, I'd like to stay here a while to go back to playing on the river."

So, what do you need, a place to stay or a job?"

"Yeah. Both Marv. Who do I talk to?"

"See that woman. Right there." He pointed, "That's Betsy, our personnel director. Wait here a minute."

Marvin jumped up and approached a woman hanging out with a small group of paddlers. Paul could see that she was young, in her early twenties, and dressed outlandishly in figure-hugging wetsuit and a pink trimmed, tutu-like, spray skirt. She had a pink helmet on her head and matching pink water boots.

Paul saw Marvin gesturing, grinning, and pointing at him. After a moment the two left the group and came to Paul. He stood to greet her with a handshake. "Hi. I'm Hunter. Paul Hunter." He was aping the James bond character in the movies. She got it and they smiled at each other.

"Bowman. Betsy Bowman. Pleased to meet you.

"Marv tells me you need a job, a place to stay, and that you'll do anything and work for peanuts. Could this be true?" she asked with an incredulous smile and a shrug of her shoulders.

Paul started to reply but she interrupted him… "He also says that you're his hero and that you are the best man he knows and that is a really good reference."

"Well. Marvin and I are friends. Susan too. I sure will work for peanuts. Do you have anything at this late date?"

"The only thing we really need is a dishwasher at Corney's Cavern Restaurant. Do you know the place?"

"Sure. But I'll need a little training. I haven't worked at a real restaurant. Oh yeah. I forgot. I do have a current Clancy County Health Department Certificate."

"You're hired. The pay is minimum wage and the possibility of tip sharing with wait staff. Marvin will train you if you can start Saturday morning. Most employees pay for the meal Plan. It gives you three square a day and we deduct the cost from your paycheck.

"What do you say?"

"Yes!" Paul said eagerly and shook her hand. "Thanks. That's great! Is there any paperwork?"

"We'll do the paperwork later – I've got to get on the river now or turn into a zombie. You can stay at the main staff house down the road. It's just a bunkhouse and shared bathroom. Marvin will show you."

Paul liked bunking with other people for a change. Sharing space and the toilet facilities were not problems. He was, in fact, far more comfortable than in his tent. He felt more secure too. He'd never had a problem, but it was just a thin piece of fabric between him and nature.

The COC bunkhouse was not a properly winterized dwelling, but it was a step up from canvas. Living in Megan's trailer had been a mixed blessing because of his emotional state.

Friday night – Paul was never much of a drinker. A little beer. Mostly just a bottle or two. So, the staff party should have been a mild night for him. But he had a few more than usual because he was excited about having a real job and his mates were urging him on. He was feeling liberated. He got drunk.

It was a major effort to make it to Corney's Cavern Restaurant at five a.m. The alarm rang for a long time before he could rouse himself. He felt horrible. He was nauseated, his head was splitting, and he was muttering under his breath.

The dishwashing station was a royal mess of greasy pots, pans, and stacks of dirty dishes left from the previous night. The Thursday night fill-in dishwasher had not done a proper job. The stainless-steel machine was littered with nasty looking food and grease. It smelled bad and looked disgusting to Paul.

Marvin was waiting. "What's up Bud? You don't look so good.

"S'okay Marvin. I think I have a hangover. I didn't get to bed until after three."

Marvin said sympathetically, "We have an aspirin bottle here. Maybe you could take some with a little OJ."

Paul looked at Marvin with gratitude in his bleary eyes. He could not speak. He turned away from Marvin and vomited on the on a stack of dirty dishes in machine's main sink.

"Oops. Sorry about that." He rinsed his hands and face in the employee hand sink.

Marvin suppressed a laugh.

"Marv. Thanks, but I don't think I could hold anything down right now," he croaked. "Maybe in a little while."

"I'll be okay. Just show me how this thing works." He was not smiling.

Marvin showed him how to turn the works on and told him that he had to wait for the rinse-water temperature to reach 180° before running the first load. Aside from its messy state, it was an impressive setup. The dishwashing machine was a Hobart. "This is the Cadillac of dishwashers Paul. Learn this and you'll always have a job at any restaurant in the country. Guaranteed!" he laughed trying to cheer Paul up.

Marvin explained the machine and procedures. It was a U-shaped table, with a 12-foot-long base. There was a six-foot dirty side where bussers and wait staff could unload dirty dishes on the left. On the right was six-foot clean side where washed dishes emerged for drying. The washing compartment was centered. The clean dishes came out hot, so they dried quickly.

The large racks held 20 dirty plates on their edges, separated from each other, so that the operator could use a conveniently dangling hose to rinse debris into a large sink, before the machine wash began.

The main sink drain was protected from clogging by a square stainless basket with perforations to let the rinse water flow into the drain, but not the solids.

The basket of rinsed dishes would slide into the washing compartment. The doors, front and rear, opened and closed with a single lever. A rack of clean dishes would roll out to the clean side when the dirty dishes were pushed in. Detergent and rinse agent were fed from easy to replenish bottles. Glasses and silverware had special racks. The powerful wash, rinse cycle took less than a minute.

Paul was impressed despite his queasiness and pain. Marvin showed him the special racks for glasses, cups and flatware. Flatware went through twice – first lying in a jumble on a rack and, second time, vertical in special containers, handles down, to prevent water spots from forming on the business end.

Once a rack of dishes was clean it could be placed on a wheeled dolly. Dollies would support as many racks as one cared to place on them. Usually, four racks would be high enough. Clean dishes were rolled to the line-cooks or staff cafeteria line. Glasses and silverware would go to the servers' work area.

It was a strong washing system, but large pots and pans would need scraping, scrubbing, and hand washing before going through the machine.

Despite his pain Paul saw that he had to sanitize the 'clean' side before he could start. He replenished an almost empty rinse agent bottle and then used a wall-mounted hot water hose to wash down the clean side and its tile walls and floor. He used a hand squeegee to get the water off the walls and the stainless-steel elements of the unit itself. He thought that it looked nice when he finished.

He noticed that he was soaking wet from the waist down but, in his concentration on the task, he forgot how bad he felt and, to his relief, he felt a little better. Marvin and the other breakfast cooks cheered him on. Peter the shift manager appeared and kindly suggested that Paul don a rubber apron and handed him a pair of rubber gloves.

The servers started at six a.m., and he saw that despite the banter throughout the establishment, everyone worked hard. They were expecting to serve about 200 morning meals including 40 staff in the staff dining room, 120 clinic students taking weeklong whitewater courses, and an unknown number of regular customers. The 120 clinic students would eat box lunches away from COC. There was a special table set up for preparing these lunches

Paul dumped the strainer into a heavy-duty garbage can fitted with a plastic bag. The can was very heavy and mounted on a wheeled dolly. So, he rolled it through the kitchen to the dumpster container located by the back door. He was afraid that if the bag got any heavier, he wouldn't be able to boost it into the container. The outside air was crisp and soothing.

He began to clean and organize the 'dirty' side. He racked and rinsed plates, glasses, and cups first.

When the big gauge on the dishwasher reached the required temperature, he ran four racks through the washer and began scrubbing pots.

He soon worked up a sweat and, began to feel in control. He liked the work. The results of his efforts were immediately apparent. Every steaming, squeaky-clean rack was a little success and he soon felt normal. He loved this work!

Breakfast was over at 10:30 a.m. Time passed quickly. Paul was told that no lunch would be served at this time of year. People, including employees could eat at The Takeout Restaurant. The dinner crew would not start until after noon. Marvin and one other cook continued to work cleaning the kitchen. One server, a paddling friend that Paul knew from the river, vacuumed the dining room. Everyone remained busy even though the restaurant was closed. Paul was learning that everyone involved worked hard before and after the public came in and after they left.

Peter sauntered over at about noon and said, "Paul. Let me help you wrap this up. I'd like to take you on a tour of COC and then treat you to lunch at the Takeout."

"Great. I'm getting hungry."

Corney's Cavern was the largest building at COC. The first floor was divided into several areas. He knew the kitchen and the general layout, but he enjoyed the tour. "The building is only two years old. COC staff did most of the construction labor over the 1997, 1998 winter. It was built the old-fashioned way using post and beam construction." Peter was proudly pointing out hand-hewn timbers and the beautiful craftsmanship of the building. "I'm not a carpenter but I learned a lot. My ambition is to build my own home one day using the skills I picked up that winter."

There was a long dining porch looking out over gardens that supplied the restaurant. It looked over the cave entrance that gave the center its name. "They say that it was dug by hand to mine clay by Indians. Really old."

Paul appreciated the attention that he was being given. They went through the staff dining room and up a with hand hewn stair treads. They walked into the largest room in the building; a room carpeted and high ceilinged that could be used in a variety of ways. For banquets it would sit over a hundred guests. During the season it might be used for overflow dining. There were generous windows looking out over the mountains.

They went through a couple of doorways checking out a storage area, a small laundry room used for napkins and tablecloths, and into the two-desk restaurant office where he was introduced to Cornelia Johnson.

"Call me Corney," she said by way of an introduction. Glad you could help us out today'" she said as she shook Paul's hand. "Our staff is very seasonal and lots of folks have left for school and winter jobs already. Are you planning to apply for a job here next season?"

"Yes ma'am. I live in Huntsville but, if I work out, I'd like to come back in the spring." He gave her his best smile. "Thanks for having me now."

Peter contributed, "Corney. He's doing great. He may look funny, but he be strong and smart." They all laughed at this jibe.

They walked away and Peter continued his narration, "Corney is a founder of COC. She and her husband Rolf Johnson started small about 25 years ago and built it into this. We are an employee-owned company now. You are a full-time employee now. If you sign up for the 401 plan, you'll acquire shares in the company."

The tour continued through the garden, past the cavern entrance, just a big hole in the hillside, and to a farmhouse that was now the administrative office. There he met the company president and filled out a couple of forms for the payroll clerk. He was now legal for the meal plan and staff housing. His employee code was Hunpa. Peter Jackman was Jacpe and Corney was Johco.

The staff lunch was a hamburger and fries. He could have opted for a veggie burger. Paul was able to eat. His hangover was replaced by fatigue and his hands were sore from handling hot dishes and pots. After saying goodbye to Peter, he took a nap in his pickup truck. He was free until five a.m. Sunday morning.

He made it back to the employee dining room by closing. He sat with several other employees at a picnic style table. He enjoyed becoming part of a group. He went into the kitchen, which was open to the staff room, and was surprised to see Vila Thompson, the president of the company, washing dishes, wearing his apron. He approached and reminded her that they'd met just before lunch and that he was the morning dishwasher. She was a very short woman with a very big smile. She kept on working, in the job groove, but gave him a greeting and an invitation to chat. She nodded, "How was your first day Paul?'

"Really good. I hope that I left the station in good shape for you."

"No complaints at all. I can't really talk now but I'm glad you said hello. If I stop the mess will overwhelm me." She added, "I like to try my hand at all the jobs at the center so I can better understand the challenges the staff faces every day. This is a hard job," she grinned up at him as she rubbed perspiration off her brow with her sleeve. As he turned to leave, she bent to her task, and he noticed that she was standing on an overturned plate rack.

He left feeling good about his first day. Getting this job had been an adult decision - he was planning for next year. He felt that he would have played this entire year away had it not been for Megan's accident. That would not have been a bad thing, but he was feeling mortal and in need of shaping his life. So far COC had treated him very well indeed. The pay wasn't much but the deal included housing, food, and good companions. He was careful not to mention his role at the Barbecue Shack and had asked Marvin and Susan to do the same. By spring, he thought, his face would no longer be associated with anything but the river and the dishwashing station.

The weather was benign in the last weeks of the 1997 season. Clear skies, mild sunny days, chill nights, and the smell of wood smoke in the evening air, became his permanent personal signals of fall in the Georgia Mountains. He worked a four-day schedule - some mornings and some nights. Off days were for paddling or hiking amidst the fall colors. The responsibilities that the Shack had imposed were left in his wake. At night he dreamed about Megan. Mostly work scenarios where he had to do things for her. The making slaw ream was his favorite. They had food fights that he let her win.

Paul stopped at the Barbecue Shack on the last Wednesday in October. Jerry sold him a drink and a barbecue pork sandwich. He was not very talkative, but he did say, "I'm closing for the season Monday. I'm tearing this crap building down and I'm working on a design to replace it that will be much easier to work. It's gonna be better than paying for the new roof and termite repair bills I'm facing."

"Good luck with that," Paul replied. "I'm heading home myself and Sunday will be my last day at work."

"Oh yeah. Where are you working?"

"COC." Paul wished that he hadn't told Jerry anything. He didn't know why but he felt that Jerry was a troubled man and he didn't want anything to do with him. He swallowed his last bite and carried his drink to the car. "See ya." He said but Jerry had already turned his back and didn't seem to care.

Paul was heading for the put-in to meet Marvin for their last paddle of the season. COC's Guest Appreciation Festival was going on all weekend, and he planned to sell his boat and gear at the annual whitewater yard sale.

His money situation was strong. There was more than enough cash in his waterproof wallet to last the year. His COC paychecks and most of the balance in his checking would go to his mother for investing. He didn't know why he was saving money, but he had little urge to spend.

Paul had appointments with both Johnny and Regan for Monday and a plan to stay with Mitch and Molly for a few days in Asheville before heading home to work for his dad and spend the holidays at home.

Paul and Johnny were now close enough to share a bro-hug rather than just a handshake. They met at Johnny's home and sat on the front porch overlooking a broad lawn and stately trees. His house was right on Route 72 just a mile or so shy of the city line. Few cars passed. They were out of the wind and the sun kept them warm. Paul commented on the 'For Sale' sign on the lawn. Madelyn, Johnny's wife came to sit with them bringing a coffee pot and cookies. The screen door made a little double bang behind her as she settled down to sit with them.

"Paul. I'm afraid I won't be around much longer, and this place is too big for Maddy."

Paul said, "Johnny, are you sick? I'm so sorry."

"I've been sick with a kind of blood cancer for a long time. It's a form of leukemia. I don't want to burden you with the details, but the docs give me less than a year so we're going to move to Jacksonville, Florida to be closer to our children and grandchildren and leave dear Clancy behind forever.

"But Paul. Remember, I've been around for a long time now. I'm ready for the next world. Try to look on this as a good and natural event. Don't be troubled."

Madelyn said, "Paul. We're both okay with this. I've been wanting to move to Florida for a long time, but Johnny's work wouldn't let us. You are his last client." She smiled as she spoke, and Johnny seemed so serene that Paul tried to join them in their attitude toward their life cycle.

"They, the docs, have plans for me. I've been to the Mayo in Jacksonville. They suggest that we move quickly, before they start the radiation and stronger meds. Then I might be a candidate for a bone marrow transplant.

"At my age I probably won't be cured but they may get me a few more years. And we don't know how well I'll tolerate the treatment. It could be worse than the disease. I've been feeling a little sick for a long time now." He smiled warmly as he spoke to Paul. He seemed at peace.

They moved the conversation to Paul's plans. "I got a job with COC for next year, I hoped that you'd be around so we could visit once in a while."

"Good for you. What will you be doing?"

"It may not sound like much for educated people like you, but I'm going to be a dishwasher at Corney's Cavern Restaurant. You know, the new one on the hill. And I'll be on the reserve Raft Guide Squad on days' off. It's my first real job where I won't be working for my dad. The kindly slave-master." He laughed. "So far I'm really enjoying the work. I like cleaning things up and serving people. Maybe there's a career up there for me. It's an employee-owned company with health benefits and a 401K plan."

"Paul. We're not all cut out to be college graduates. The world is made up of two kinds of people: those who are happy with what they do, and those who wouldn't be happy no matter what. They'd complain if you fried them in real butter."

They all laughed at the joke.

"I agree with Johnny, Paul," Madelyn ventured. "Follow your heart and you will find happiness, wealth, and satisfaction with the world. Look at me. I graduated from Hofstra University, summa cum laud, with a degree in math science. I worked for years before I met Johnny and I wasn't happy for a day. Now I've been a housewife and mother for over 40 years and I'm as happy as I can be. I love doing the dishes too."

"On another subject Paul. We are closing the book on Megan. We have tried very hard but there are just no clues. We've looked at her papers, her phone and bank accounts, her loan applications, her tax returns, and we're at a dead end. There's quite a bit of cash in her estate now that everything's been sold. There was mortgage insurance too. But there is a big hospital bill to be settled by her new representative. I trust him to do the right job. The money will escheat to the State of Georgia eventually. But I have turned everything over to lawyer Bunny Johns. You have a special interest and status as Megan's late guardian. You can go to her if ever you want to find out more."

When the visit was over, Paul said "Johnny. You have my number in Alabama. Call me if you need help with anything. I'll come right away." Paul, emotions easily roused, had tears forming as he waved goodbye to his friends.

After stopping by to see Regan at his accounting office. Paul drove off through the mountains at a measured pace to visit Mitch and Molly in Asheville.

NOVEMBER – 1997

The weather in Huntsville was milder than at COC. Paul took one day off and went to work with his dad on a major home remodeling project. He worked as a laborer to start. He was part of a crew that had been with his dad for years. They were used to bossing Paul around and he did not mind. They sometimes called him 'Twinkle Toes,' remembering an incident when he was in high school. He had kicked over a pan of paint. There hadn't been any real damage, but he still wore the work boots he'd had on that day. The right one had a lick of red paint on the right toe.

He was a neat and careful worker. He had experience as a rough carpenter, painter, sheet rock hanger and all-around construction skills.

The main job Paul worked on was a remodel involving gutting the kitchen, dining, and living areas and tearing down walls to create a sizable great room. His dad was there for a few minutes every morning to check progress, manage supplies and confer with the owners who were living in the basement where they could escape some of the dust and noise. Demolition was almost done when Paul arrived and by his second week, he was into laying floors, nailing floor and ceiling molding and sheet rock.

The hard physical work felt good to Paul. All in all the work was not harder than the restaurant dishwashing he had been doing. His mom and dad were very happy to have him at home and they pumped him for all the details regarding his adventures at the Shack, at COC and on the rivers.

"Did you mind camping out so long," Mom asked at dinner.

"Yes and no. At first it was like vacationing. Like last year. But the weather wasn't always nice and when it turned cold or wet, I longed for my bed at home. When I took over for Megan and lived in her trailer, it felt insanely comfortable. And when they gave me a place in COC staff housing, I liked that a lot better than camping too.

"Next year I want to go back to COC."

His parents watched him with wary eyes. They had been talking, with and without Paul, about the possibility of him staying in Huntsville and studying to become a licensed contractor. "What else would you like to do Paul?" they asked.

"I'm embarrassed to say that long-term, I don't really know. I have an ambition to become a better kayak paddler and maybe a full-time river guide at COC. That thing with Megan turned the year bad for me. I worked and worried myself to death.

"But when they hired me as a dishwasher - I know it doesn't sound like much - I really liked it.

"Dad. This is the first real job I've gotten by myself, and I can't wait to get back to it. I love working for you too. Don't get me wrong. I'm not in rebellion. It's just that I feel like working there in the mountains is good for me."

"Right now," his dad pointed out, we would be able to support you if you want to go to school. So now is good, eh?

"Five or ten years from now we may need you and Mitch to support us." Times are good now, but it may not always be so easy for us.

Paul had a healthy bank account. He had worked as Megan's replacement for four months. Carefully following the rules established by the court, he had taken out over $10,000.00. He had given most of it to his mother to add to his investment. He accumulated the tip money in his shirt pocket and had more than

$1,000.00 tucked there now. He was proud of his financial results, but he would rather be poor and still have Megan alive and well.

"So, Dad. If you'll have me, I'd like to work until the first of March. I'm scheduled to report to work on April fourth and I want to take a three-day whitewater rescue course they offer before I start."

"I only wish you could stay longer. Of course, I'll have you."

"Me too," said Mom. Please stay as long as you can and come back home as soon as you can."

MARCH – 1998

Paul learned more about the construction business than he anticipated. His dad suffered a health reversal on the second day of March. Paul was unable to return to COC as planned.

It may have started with the fall or, perhaps, with the heart attack. Either way, the result was a broken arm, a broken leg, and a heart attack. He was climbing a ladder with a heavy tool belt on a construction site when it happened. The arm and the leg injuries were obvious; the heart attack was more insidious. The result was a week in the hospital and then confinement to the house until his leg healed enough to get around on crutches. The Hunter's health insurance was limited and did not completely cover the large bills that came flooding in.

There wasn't much damage to his heart. He was placed on a drug regimen to lower his cholesterol and control his blood pressure. He was told that he could look forward to regular medical checkups for life.

Mom and Dad were strong people and could have no doubt been able to survive the problems incurred when it became impossible for him to immediately go back to work. Paul had to step up and do the things his parents needed.

"Honey. I know you want to go back to Georgia, but it would be a blessing if you could stay until Dad gets back on his feet. We have insurance and savings but frankly we're in trouble.

"As you know a lot of the profit in the jobs Dad does comes in at the end of the job and not the beginning. He's got four jobs underway and there's a 'holdback' in each one of them that doesn't get paid until the final walk-through and punch-list are completed.

"There's about $50,000 in profit to be made from the jobs underway but, if they're not finished properly, there may be no profit at all," his mom was frankly crying. "Paul. I know that this was not a part of your plan. We're asking you first because Mitch and Molly are so involved in Asheville and, frankly, you are more flexible and closer to hand too."

He sat next to her and hugged her, as she had comforted him so many times over the years.

"Mom. I'll do whatever I can. You know that I have no plans for my investment account, and I also have $2,000.00 in the bank besides that. It's all yours. What else do you need?"

"Honey. Thank you, thank you, thank you… It's not so much the money right now. We must organize things while your dad is laid up and you may be the only one who can do it.

"Between you and me we can keep things going but you must be out on the job for him every day. Be his eyes and ears and keep in close touch with his customers and employees.

There were several jobs underway at the moment. A $20,000-basement apartment, the $25,000-kitchen remodeling, a $150,000-home addition, and a $50,000-sunroom, garage combination. The basement apartment was almost finished and the others nowhere near completion. The promise dates were clear, and Paul could see that he would not be a dishwasher-paddler-raft guide and free spirit this year.

Paul reviewed the paperwork with his mother and father. Contracts, material receipts, bills, time sheets, and such, in manila folders. There was one jacket for each project. There was a ledger sheet stapled to each folder help them allocate expenses. Some jobs were more profitable than others. The larger the contract the greater the risk of miscalculation and misfortunes. There was a hand-wrought calendar on the front of each folder to help schedule the many jobs required to produce a finished project.

His dad was a good record keeper but the primary force behind each job was not in the record keeping. It was in the relationships with customers, workers, suppliers, subcontractors, inspectors, permit authorities, unions, competitors, utility companies and the banks.

There were seven employees including Paul – each one he thought more experienced than himself. He was not full of confidence, and he was afraid that he would make mistakes. When he confessed his doubts to his father, he expected comforting words.

"Paulie. Don't worry about how you feel. Just make sure the other guy sees that you are interested in him, his point of view and his welfare. If you act confident and happy, that's how people will see you. It's an act for all of us.

"If you don't have the answer to a question or a problem, have the balls to admit it. Remember these words. 'That's a good question. Let me get right back to you on that.'

"Nobody much cares about how you feel or what you like, other than your family and friends. They care about their own stuff, but they will like you, help you and trust you if you care about their stuff too.

"What do you think about that?" His dad was sitting in his armchair with his legs elevated.

"Good question. Let me get right back to you on that." They both laughed.

Paul crafted a plan with his dad. He started by carefully prioritizing his time. He had a talk with each owner assuring them that their work would be done properly and on time. He told the employees that their jobs and paychecks were secure.

He told each employee and supplier, "You know, this may be a good thing. There is a great crew of workers and fine subs to do the work. Now Dad can concentrate on selling and estimating new jobs. He's the brains. I'm just his feet and eyes."

Paul did a lot of chores around the house too. He mowed the lawn, kept the gardens neat and took care of garbage can and other mundane tasks usually done by his dad. He shaved every morning and visited the barber every second Saturday.

He was quite over Sarah. She had not given him the slightest encouragement on the few school breaks when he had called her at home. Her words reverberated in his head, "I do like you Paul but

I'm hell bent on getting my degree, my doctor and a rich life in the suburbs. I think you should get over it and not call again. I mean this as a kindness honey. I don't want to string you on or to get derailed myself."

They both cried as they rang off. Paul was fully convinced and ready to move on to other women.

JUNE 1998

Friday was payday and the crew usually met at Duffy's Tavern for the beer and chicken wing specials after work. These men he worked with were mostly married and he usually found himself alone before the clock rang seven. His folks had approved the idea of his picking up the tab as a company expense. Paul had to limit himself to coke since he was not yet twenty-one.

The Tavern hired extra help on Saint Patrick's Day. He met a temporary server named Irene Linnick there on that special Tuesday holiday and she had caught his eye with her unusual grace and strength as she managed heavy trays, pitchers of beer and baskets of wings. She had red hair and an animated face with frequent outbursts of humor and jokes. She kidded Paul as his tablemates left him alone at the regular hour. "You forgot your deodorant honey?" she joked as she cleared the table."

"Nah. I just can't find the right kind of friend," he replied. "I need someone who has more endurance. Are you available?"

"Not tonight honey. I'm heading for the barn as soon as they let me off. I have to get up at seven o'clock."

"Me too," said Paul. "I'm in construction. What are you taking? He had her pegged as a student.

"I'm studying for my AA in Outdoor Recreation at UAH. I'm thinking resort management. I teach dancing. Ballet and jazz in the evenings. Gotta go." She bounced off but, before she left, when he paid the tab for himself and his crew, he got her phone number and gave her his business card.

Paul Hunter
Hunter and Company
Construction Management

Paul was proud of his card. He was not yet 20-years old but felt like an old hand now with heavy coaching from his parents and OJT.

Irene sounded very reserved when he called her the next evening. Reserved and tired.

"Irene. Would you like to go out with me this weekend? Say a movie and dinner?"

"I'm a little overscheduled right now Paul. I don't really date but I eat every day. Would you like to have dinner with me?"

"I'm busy too. I don't really date either, but I sleep every night. Would you like to sleep with me one evening soon?" There was a shocked silence on the line. Then Irene burst out laughing… At first a titter, then a guffaw… "Paul. You are a darling. Let's have dinner first."

They both laughed and finally settled down. "Irene. You know I'm just kidding. I'm not really this bold. You are literally the first girl I've ever called for a date. I don't date either.

"I'm not overbooked, and I can make it any night but Sunday. I always have family dinner with my mom and dad on Sundays. Sometimes my brother drives all the way from Asheville to be there with his girlfriend. I can make it any night you choose. What's best for you? Your call entirely. Time, place and day. You could even meet my folks."

"I'm sure I'll love your folks but let's get to know each other first. Okay?"

"Sure."

"Friday night I don't have classes. I usually crash and burn, but I could rise to the occasion if Friday is good for you."

"Perfect. I can pick you up any time or if you'd like to come to Duffy's we can go from there. Or I could pick you up anywhere. I usually hang out there for a little while on Fridays. I get there at around five with the guys from work."

"Good there's fine. I'll meet you at Duffy's at six. Can we go to Argos on the river? Dutch."

"No. No. I'll pay. This is my…"

"Dutch. Double Dutch," she said. "That way I can order anything I want. Or I could pay for you, but you'll have a limit of…"

"No limits. No limits. We can go Dutch this time, but I really want to treat you next time. When we get to know each other a little."

"But look. There's something else. I'm coming directly from work. Please can I just wear my jeans and I'll put on a sports coat for dinner. Very California ya know. Would that be okay?"

"Sure. Me too. I'll dress California."

The spring weather was sublime, and work was good. He was feeling very relaxed and in a playful mood when he met Irene at the bar. He'd had his usual coke but offered Irene a drink before going to dinner.

She declined saying, "Paul. I don't drink and I don't date." She looked at him with a friendly smile when she said this. Her California consisted of designer jeans, a fuzzy red sweater and red shoes with two-inch heels.

She seemed to glow. Paul guessed it was the reflected color from the sweater, but she looked hot in his eyes. "You go ahead and have another. I don't mind."

Paul wore a white turtleneck shirt with jeans and a tweedy jacket. Irene thought he looked fine. He seemed to have plenty of energy, and she liked the way he moved. He had real muscle under his clothing.

"I have to admit that I don't drink either. I had a few too many one night last fall to celebrate getting a job at the Caverns Outdoor Center in Georgia. It made me sick on my first day at work. I vowed to quit."

"COC. You gotta be kidding! I go to school with people who work there in the summer. She gave him several names but he didn't know them."

"There are a lot of people there. I came in just four weeks before the end of the season."

"I'm supposed to be working there now." He went on to explain his dad's injuries and illness.

They left Duffy's tavern in Paul's pickup truck. He was on his best behavior. He held the restaurant door for her and opened the truck door too. He made sure she was well seated before he closed the door. Irene smiled her appreciation for the formalities. The truck was more battered than ever but the inside and the glass were spotless. He wanted to make a good impression on Irene.

They were seated in a booth at Argos. They ordered steaks and cokes. Their sides were identical, and they both said "medium" when the waiter asked them how to cook the meat.

They grinned at each other across the table. Paul offered her a high five and a grin. She reciprocated saying, "Fine choices!"

They enjoyed the intimacy of sharing a meal in a nice restaurant. Candlelight, white tablecloths, and expert service moved things along and they lost track of time.

"Too bad about your dad," she commiserated. "How is it going?"

"Dad's doing well. His heart attack was minor. A warning the doctor said to take better care of his health." He launched into telling her about the jobs they had working and the relief he had felt when he finished the punch list on the basement apartment and the joy at getting the check for the balance. "That check represented the entire profit for the job. The prepayments and progress payments had gone entirely towards materials and labor. So, my folks are solvent at the moment.

"Dad thinks he has sold another job to begin in July. He'll be on crutches, but he ought to be able to get out and about on a limited basis. Now it's just back and forth to the doctors' offices. I'm taking care of supervising the jobs, under his supervision. Plus, I do carpentry, sheet rock and painting. Not so much electrical or plumbing."

"Wow Paul. You must know a lot about the construction business. Do you want to continue that line of work when your dad's better?"

"No," he said slowly. "I think I want to go back to working at COC and being a river rat. Just messing about in kayaks." He told her about working at the Barbecue Shack and camping out but did not tell her about the real events and Molly's demise. He felt that those details about his life were still too raw for casual conversation.

"I wish I had a career goal, but it just hasn't hit me yet. What do you want to do Irene? Like, I mean besides your school?"

"Well. I'm not too driven either. I worked some in restaurants in the summers and after school. It's kind of addicting. I can see why you liked it at COC.

"My mom took me to dance classes when I was little. I studied ballet and jazz. When I got to my teen years, I was so into it that I began to work, without pay, as a teacher's assistant with the little beginners. I just sort of grew into a paid employee. When I began college, it was paying me enough to get an apartment with schoolmates. My folks still pay my school expenses. I'm 21 so that won't last much longer. Dad's an architect and Mom is a domestic goddess."

"Oops. You're an older woman," Paul grinned. I'll be 20 this year."

"Sigh," she breathed. "You're too green kid. I guess I'll have to put you back for a while."

"Oh please. Just let me sit in the sun for a little bit and I'll be all right."

They passed on dessert. When the check came, they left a 20% tip and thanked the waiter profusely. He had just let them sit without feeling neglected. He was glad that he didn't have to ID them.

Paul held doors and when they got back to her car at Duffy's, He politely escorted her. "Irene," he asked her through her car window, "Would you like to do this again?"

"Sure. Could we wait for Friday though? This is really my best night."

"Sure. Oh, and can I follow you home to see you safe."

"Nope. I'm fine. It's been a long day for both of us. Call me. Okay?"

"Good. Will do. Drive safe."

He stepped back as she started the car and they smiled goodnight. He admired her posture and felt that he had missed an opportunity to shake hands or give her a kiss on the cheek. No matter, he thought. I had a great time.

JULY – 1998

The weeks slipped by, and Mike Hunter recovered his abilities. The casts came off and he walked – at first with a cane, then with a limp. The limp would go away by the end of the month as exercise and activity restored his muscle function to previous levels. He had lost a few pounds but was ready to work as a construction supervisor, perform as a salesman of home-remodeling projects and recover his place as man of the house.

Mike's work was easier with Paul as his alter ego. Paul had saved the Hunter fortunes and both he and Sam, as he was wont to call his wife, made sure that Paul knew their gratitude. "Paul," his dad said at Saturday dinner, "You've done a great job. Everyone I've talked to has nothing but praise for 'Young Hunter.' Thanks for being you."

With his dad getting back in the saddle, Paul's work was easier too. They had two new projects and Paul participated in the planning and preliminaries. He saw that his dad approached authorities in the building department permit sections with a humble and respectful attitude. He learned, from him, to establish better relationships with competitors and suppliers.

He and Irene had continued Friday dinners. She was becoming Paul's unattainable dream girl. He wanted to progress to a deeper, sexual relationship, but she was not having any.

"Paul. I have to confess something," she said anxiously.

"Don't worry Irene. What is it?" They were at their regular table at the Argo Restaurant. Dinner was done and they were speaking very quietly.

After a long pause, Irene ventured, "Paul. I know that you want to have sex with me. And I like you too that way. But I'm damaged goods. What I haven't told you is that I got knocked up in high school, got married to my boyfriend and lost the child to sphingolipids. I gave birth but the docs couldn't save her.

"I went into a funk and our marriage was busted." Irene was crying and her head was down as she spoke.

Paul got up to sit next to her and put his arm around her. "I'm so sorry Irene. I see you lost two people you loved at the same time. How long ago was this?"

"Going on four years now. I made such a mess. I felt retarded." He hugged her and she turned her head toward him for a salty kiss on the wet cheek."

"I have something to confess too," he told her.

"Wait Paul. You don't have to. I really appreciate your comfort. Thank you. But there is something else I have to tell you. Something you won't like.

"I made a vow when Robby took off. I decided that I wouldn't have sex again until *after* marriage. I love sex and the intimacy it brings, but I just think I owe it to the world, my parents and myself to abstain. I'm now officially saving myself for marriage. Got to put the horse before the buggy this time." She was crying and embarrassed again. He hugged her hard and returned to his seat.

"Gosh I'm sorry about what happened. I can see that it was rough and that you are on a path. You know, I can learn from you.

"I had a bad experience last year that I haven't told anyone but my family in Huntsville." He told her the outline of his affair with Megan and her death.

"You've got me thinking. Men can take a vow of chastity too and it might be the best thing for me too. I feel so guilty about what happened that being, what d'ya call it, celibate, might be a good way for me too.

"Irene. Maybe we could be non-fucking buddies. What do you say?" he meant what he said even though he wanted to jump her right there in the restaurant. He said it as a kind of joke, trying to get her back to an even keel.

She looked at him levelly and said, "Paul. You are a lovely man. That might be too hard for us. Maybe we should switch off the regular Friday thing and let our emotions settle down now that we know the truth about each other."

"Only if you insist." I'm not doing anything on Friday."

He turned off the lights and engine when he parked in front of her apartment. He turned to her and dragged her into a hug. She willingly came in for a kiss too and did not pull back when he stroked her back through the thin fabric of her blouse. He wanted to hold her harder and was drawn to grope her breasts. She sensed his need and moved his hand from her waist to her chest. He felt both the lean hardness of the dancer and the softness of a woman.

"Paul. I want you too but it's so hard right now."

He interrupted her with a chuckle. "Ooh I know what ya mean."

"Please Paul. I don't want to be a tease. If we don't stop now, I'm going to wet my panties."

"Me too," he confessed. They both laughed and the spell was weakened. He jumped out and rushed to get her door before she could get out.

They kissed goodnight at the side of the truck. Her lips were soft and moist. Their thighs met and he felt her against his chest. "Good night, Irene, good night, Irene," he crooned. "I'll see you in my dreams."

She gave him a big smile and walked away lightly; her dancer's body strong against the earth's pull. Paul leaned against the truck and sadly watched her disappear into the apartment building's shadow.

He remembered a joke that Mitch had told him once when they were younger teenagers. They were walking home after school. "Hey Paul. Do you want to meet my girlfriend?"

"Sure," Paul glanced at his brother who grinned and stuck his hand out as if to shake hands. He had a big grin on his face as Paul innocently reached out to shake.

Mitch held the shake a tad longer than expected and burst out laughing. Paul had just shaken hands with Mitch's 'Girlfriend.'

He smiled as he drove home for a date with his own girlfriend. Irene's beautiful image danced in his head.

Irene moved to Miami when she graduated in December. They had eased away from their Friday dinners because their sex urge was making them both uncomfortable. But they spoke on the phone every week and, before she left, Irene invited him to attend a dance recital held by her school at the Huntsville Civic Auditorium. "This is a big deal for us Paul. The kids, the teachers and the parents look forward to it each year. It is not a professional grade show, but you'll be surprised at how good the kids are. Especially mine – I mean the little ones. We'll fill the theater for two shows."

Paul asked his parents to come but his dad had a conflict. He and his mom arrived at the theater at six p.m. There was a good crowd, but they had prime reserved seats and Paul did enjoy the show. His mom was thrilled that he had asked her. "Will I get to meet the mysterious Irena?"

"Irene." He corrected her. "Sure Mom. Maybe we could take her to dinner."

Samantha was excited to finally meet one of Paul's few girlfriends. She had never met Megan, of course, but she had shaken hands with Sarah at graduation.

The dance teachers had all received bouquets from their students on stage after the performance. So Samantha easily recognized Irene as she approached them on the theater steps afterwards, carrying her flowers. She was struck by her beauty and grace.

They did not have dinner as Irene was heading for her parents' home for a farewell Saturday supper. She and Paul hugged hard. This was their goodbye.

Paul had a tear in his eye as he drove his mom's car home. "I'm sad to see her go. She got a great job with the Marriott Hotel in Miami. We had a good friendship and I wish it could have gone further Mom. But I'm drawn to return to COC and the Clancy River next spring. I don't want to work in construction right now. I don't know why but I feel compelled to go."

"Honey. Dad and I understand. You have many, many years ahead. You will find the perfect path and we'll always be proud of you." She smiled and put a comforting hand on his leg. "And Dad will always have a job for you.

"Paul. Try to stay in touch with your friends even when they are far away."

MARCH 1999

Paul was back at COC on the fourth Saturday of the month. He was scheduled to start work as a dishwasher on Sunday. He was happy with his assignment to a three-bedroom cottage with five other restaurant employees. He spent the day organizing his bunk area, cleaning his truck, and shaking hands with everyone he met. There were no old faces.

Paul drove past the Barbecue Shack and had a kind of mental pause and confusion he had never experienced. What the hell...he thought...wasn't that where...

He pulled over, backed off the road and slowly returned to the shack's parking lot. It wasn't there! The parking area was overgrown with foliage and fallen leaves. There was no trace of the actual building or concrete foundation. Even the utility pole was gone. He got out of his truck and poked around, unable to figure out what catastrophe had occurred here. The path to the river was overgrown and his former campsite looked just like the rest of the forest floor.

He made his way down to the river and sat on a boulder for a few minutes remembering Megan, his peaceful time in a tent by the river, and his sorrowful summer of waiting for his friend to die. He stroked his beard and wiped away a tear. He was set on a course – to fit in at COC. His hair was shaggy but not yet long enough for a ponytail.

He drove the few miles to COC and stopped in at the front desk. He did not recognize the young woman at the desk. She greeted him with a smile, thinking he was an off-season guest.

"Hi. I'm Paul Hunter. I work here but I skipped last season. Do you know what happened to the Barbecue Shack that used to be a couple of miles up-river? I used to work there"

"No. I never saw it last year, but I may have heard that the owner was going to demolish it and couldn't get a permit to rebuild.

"Look for one of the old-timers at the store. They'll probably know."

He thanked her and reported for work up the hill.

At dinner, in the small staff cafeteria, he was happy to see shift manager Peter Jackman sitting at an indoor picnic table with several other employees. Peter asked Paul to join the table.

He met the general manager of the restaurant, Peter, and a couple of instructors. They all gossiped about winter activities that included world travel as COC whitewater trip leaders to Nepal and South America. Others at the table had worked at ski resorts and one had a Christmas tree business. Paul was very impressed and began to see some benefits of the seasonality of the COC business.

Paul found out that Marvin and Susan had moved to Florida to be with aging parents. They were his only close friends from 1997 - *Megan's Year,* as he liked to call it. He asked Peter if it would be possible to get an address for Marvin and Peter said he'd try.

No one remaining at the center knew of Megan's tragic love affair and her sad ending. Only Paul remembered. It was a sadness that he carried with him. He threw himself into his dishwashing duties and spent days off on the river in his new kayak or waiting for work as a raft guide.

Paul ventured to Clancy a few weeks after his return and looked for Sam Silver, the State's Attorney that he and Johnny had worked with. Sam was cordial and seemed to have plenty of time for them to catch up on each other's lives. They had a friendly visit

"Paul. You know that Johnny passed away?"

"He told me he had very little time just before he moved to Florida. I didn't know that he died. I really liked him."

Sam knew exactly what had happened to the Barbecue Shack.

"Damn shame. There was a huge conflict with that guy Jerry Marks. About two years ago. Just after you left. He all of a sudden tore the place down, hauled away the debris and then applied for a permit to build a little better, more modern facility. Not very big.

"But they couldn't give him a permit. Clancy County had an agreement with the state and the USDA to not permit any new construction on the river for ten years, to give authorities time to work out a plan to designate the Clancy as a Wild and Scenic River. It's a valuable program with the Bureau of Land Management National Park Service US Fish and Wildlife Service US Forest

Service and the state of Georgia. No one here really knows if it can happen, but the County was obligated to deny the building permit.

"Jerry could have updated or improved on the existing footprint if he had applied before a complete demo, but he was impatient and he paid a heavy price.

"He's gone now. There was no lawsuit, but I think it was close."

A few weeks later, Paul spent some quiet time at his special, 'secret garden' on the river. He thought again about Megan and her fear of the water. He mused about Jerry's abrupt and rather bad attitude. And about his own failings.

He decided that he was happy with a simple life. Sometimes he took pleasure from being on his own. His problems seemed few.

Paul liked to watch the cooks perform their duties and, without thinking much about it, learned a lot of their routines and duties. There was a particular cook that he enjoyed watching and talking to as she worked. She was Eddie Mitchell, half of a husband-and-wife team there for the summer. Her husband, Slim, was the baker, producing bread, rolls, pizza, pastries and other items for the clinic and public tables. Eddie was the prep cook responsible for doing prep work for the entire kitchen operation including the restaurant, the staff cafeteria, and the clinic dining service.

She was a graduate of the Culinary Institute of America, known as the CIA, had a professional set of cooking skills and was happy to show them off whenever Paul had time to watch or had questions.

Eddie was good with her knives. She did not share her tools with the other cooks who all used house knives and tools. She brought them to work in a special briefcase and sharpened selected knives before clocking in.

She would process whole bags and crates of vegetables at the start of each shift. Cleaning, peeling, slicing, dicing and otherwise getting everything ready to be cooked for the evening meal. After the prep she would cook the evening meal for the clinics and that item would also serve as the staff meal and the daily special in the restaurant. Her movements were economical, her tools sharp and her techniques interesting – different from anything he had seen while growing up in and about his mother's kitchen.

Eddie was not a happy go lucky person. She would mutter things about her fellow cooks, the wait staff, the kitchen layout and her husband Slim. Like "Piss-poor preparation produces piss-poor performance," or "mise en place, mise in place," over, and over again.

She would take a few minutes before each shift to make sure that she had the recipes and specs together for each item on her job list along with the actual foodstuff, storage pans, pots, and platters. This was the mise en place procedure. Her work volume would seem like an overwhelming task to the uninitiated, like Paul, but she flew through each project, never leaving her station until it was time to deliver something or time to assemble a dish for cooking.

Head down, muttering, hands flying, a bag of carrots would suddenly become plastic containers full of sliced carrots. Potatoes would lose their skins, have a bath, and be evenly diced or sliced for further cooking operations.

Eddie told Paul that she had been a cook in the army and that her service benefits had paid for her degree in culinary arts. She and Slim had been in the army together. She said he was a Blue Cord infantry soldier.

Paul had never heard of the CIA and was very impressed by all she said. The buzz in the kitchen was that she was here for only one season and that Corney and Peter expected that everyone would learn from her.

Corney's Cavern Restaurant was widely known for its food quality due to several important factors. The breads they made were freshly crafted every day. The biggest sellers were tender beef shish kebab marinated in honey, oil and teriyaki sauce, and local farm-raised trout. Cornelia Johnson's food had a lot of style and was appreciated by all who sampled it.

The salads served with every dinner were presented with Corney's secret-formula ramp dressing and decorated with an edible flower. The blossoms came from the garden and the ramps from the forest.

Corney would spend days wandering the forest every spring to gather ramps in burlap sacks. The ramps would be cleaned and frozen in quantities sufficient for the entire season. Pungent, finely chopped ramps would be mixed with sour cream, buttermilk and other seasonings every week. No one loved this forest bounty more than Corney. The salads were one of her signatures.

Eddie seemed an odd bird with her checkered pants, black military dress shoes, short stature, and attitude. Everyone was in awe of her including her husband, Slim. She recognized a desire to learn in Paul's eyes and she would give him mini lessons in cooking each time he visited her station.

"Paul. You see that I am the only cook in this kitchen who has his own tool kit." She opened the briefcase she carried into the kitchen each day and pointed out some knives and their cost.

He was flabbergasted. "$100.00 for a single knife. Wow. I hope they're paying you big bucks here."

"Naw. We're here for the fun of it. Slim's just learning to bake and I'm his coach. When we go back to real life after the summer, we'll worry about getting bigger salaries. These knives are heirloom quality and they'll be around for my children's children." She laughed at the thought of her knives' afterlife.

"This toolkit was a part of the CIA training. I had to buy the stuff at the school bookstore or at a local restaurant supply company. If you want to be a cook, I suggest that you visit a restaurant supply company and assemble a kit of knives and a carrier. Could be just a simple canvas roll-up. You'll need a sharpening kit, a sharpening steel, and a few knives.

"Buy commercial and they'll be heavy duty but not so expensive. You'll just have to sharpen them more often. To tell you the truth the government paid for these tools along with tuition and books. Slim chose to go to community college, and he has an AA in outdoor recreation leadership. That's what pointed us here toward COC. Who knows? Maybe we'll come back every summer from now on."

Paul learned a lot from Eddie, and he took his day off with them to go to a large restaurant equipment store in Atlanta's outskirts. They planned dinner and a movie afterwards. Paul made a deal with the couple, "I'll drive and buy lunch and you advise me on how tool up to be a self-trained chef.

"I want to read some books, hang out at your station and practice on COC time. Maybe I can snag a promotion sometime." He had already confessed to her that he had a little cash burning a hole in his pocket and that he'd like some decent tools.

He wound up buying three knives, a sharpening steel, a sharpening stone and several little books about sauces, meat cooking methods and restaurant operations. He also bought a canvas roll-up with tie strings to carry the knives to and from work. The cost for the whole lot was just over a hundred dollars.

"Don't worry," Eddie said. "If you start cooking in a big restaurant one day, you can always upgrade to more expensive gear. Chances are that you will never wear these knives out."

The ten-inch-blade chef's knife was the most expensive buy. It was made very strongly. It was very sharp and heavy. He liked the feel of it.

"I'll teach you how to use these guys if you want to come in a little early tomorrow." said Eddie. You too Slim. Sit in on the lesson please."

Slim who had been following them around, admiring the endless parade of stainless-steel tables and gadgets, agreed. They set a date for a ten-a.m. meeting as they drove to see *Primary Colors*.

Eddie's demonstrations attracted several other cooks besides Paul. She began by sharpening her knives and laying them out near a large poly cutting board along with a peeler and a folding slicing machine, she called a mandolin. She taped her copies of the day's menu and prep list that had been supplied by the shift supervisor.

She needed to prep a box of romaine lettuce, a box of iceberg lettuce, a bag of potatoes, a bag of onions, a bag of carrots and several other items as well. The items were neatly stacked near her workstation as well as the clean containers and tools that would be needed. She had to cook 125 portions of beef stew to be served to clinic guests, staff, and the public as the daily special. She needed to produce a large pot of mashed potatoes, 125 portions, and a vegetarian entrée for 25 as an entrée for the staff vegetarians. She already had a dozen frozen cherry pies in the oven – part of the daily special. "Everything I will use is *mise en place*. On hand and ready to use. She had the spices and other ingredients all at hand.

Eddie began to lecture about knife skills. How to be safe above all else as a cut would slow a cook down or even put him out of action. And it was nasty and painful too.

Peeling carrots first, her peeler flew, working in both directions. The peels landed on the stainless table and in the lined garbage bag she kept at her side. The carrots landed in her prep sink for a wash before further processing into shredded and sliced carrots. She kept her head down and began to hum.

Suddenly, without warning, as the little crowd watched her techniques, she flung her head back and yelled, "Shit! Oh, fucking Christ!" She banged the tool onto her board, whirled around and ran to the oven where her pies were giving off smoke. Her nose had tipped her off before the others noticed. She had forgotten to set a timer.

"Damn! I forgot. My fault. Fuck me hard!" Her red face was screwed into a frown as she removed the three large sheet pans holding a dozen smoking pies. The outer edges of the crusts were black.

They expected her to dump them, but she fooled everyone by announcing, "Peter. Take the pie off the menu. We're having cobbler instead.

"Paul. Bring me 12 dozen monkey dishes." While Paul ran to get the little plates, she began knocking the black edges into her garbage can and placed the pies on a clean area of her table. She got a large ice cream scooper and neatly scooped the unburned parts of the cherry pies into the little monkey dishes. She had over a hundred cobblers in a flash.

"Peter," she commanded, "$3.95 each," as she placed the dishes onto clean baking sheets and then onto a rolling rack. "No waste. The burned portions go to the gardener with the mulch.

"Slim. Clean these aluminum pie tins up and do something with them." Her speed was impressive, and she finished peeling the carrots before the smoke had been sucked out the kitchen exhaust fans.

Eddie began cutting the carrot ends off into her garbage pans and then slicing them on her 'mandolin.' She had the slices into a pot of water on her stove before she began shredding some for a salad garnish.

Her next job was the romaine lettuce. The carrot mess and the pie goof were behind her. The audience dispersed except for Peter and Paul who were not needed for prep. She dipped the lettuce, four heads at a time into a sink full of cold water to knock the dirt off them with the heads down to let the sand and other debris flow into the sink.

She refilled the sink with clean water and dunked the heads several times until her standards for clean lettuce were satisfied. She set the lettuce aside, leafy part down, to enable the water to drain off for a while before further cleaning and processing.

Eddie stopped to hone her knives with the steel sharpener several times during the demo.

The audience left and Eddie really picked up speed. She needed a coffee break and a smoke as soon as possible. Almost all of the cooks used cigarettes and had a regular smoking area well away from the kitchen's back door.

Over the next few weeks, she continued to start an hour earlier than scheduled for training and demonstrations. Eddie was rapidly attaining high status as a skilled kitchen worker and other cooks began to emulate her ways when doing prep.

Paul came in early to hang out with Eddie and Slim. He began to know more about cooking and restaurant work as she shared her professional training. She had attended cooking schools while in the army and then had gone to culinary school, full-time, for two years and She was a pro with practical ways to handle every kitchen situation from over-seasoned dishes to substitutions for missing ingredients.

She used her sharp knives to create flowers and little animal statutes from a wide variety of ordinary vegetables. "Paul," she confessed, "I didn't make this stuff up. I got it out of books and magazine articles."

Paul was the star dishwasher in the 1998 season. He became an expert paddler, gained experience as a raft guide and learned to cook. He was cooking on the line or prep-cooking several days a week.

Socially he was not so successful. He had work and paddling friends but no matter how hard he tried he could not find a girl to hold. He had his memories and hope for the future. At the Friday night staff party he was always a shy loner and he always abstained from a second bottle of beer.

The college students had to go back to school toward the end of the season and COC was, as usual, short of help. That's how Paul learned to wait on tables.

Peter approached him one busy Saturday night at eight o'clock. and said," Paul. We need help in front. Could you please put on a clean server's apron and help us out?" A raft guide was washing the dishes and Eddie was working the line with Paul. She was so fast that Paul was not really needed.

"Sure. I don't know much about it, but I can learn fast."

His first table was a four-top. First-timer-tourist types. He was asked a series of questions.

"Do you serve alcohol?

"What's the special of the day?"

"How is the shish kebab made?"

He gave them a big smile and said politely, "Sorry. No booze but you can bring your own if you have it. The beef stroganoff special ran out at 5:30." He knew because he had cooked it.

"I recommend the kebabs or the trout. The kabob meat is marinated top sirloin with onions, peppers and cherry tomatoes. Cooked to order, served on rice pilaf – it's to die for.

"Where ya'all from? What can I bring you to drink?"

His answers to their questions and his own little barrage of questions and obvious good will obviated his need to explain to them that he had never waited on a table before.

They were from New York City and wanted water and four wine glasses. They all ordered kebabs, medium, and one of them left for their car to get a bottle of wine while Paul disappeared to fetch water and wine glasses.

"Peter. I need a corkscrew and a bucket of ice. Can you help me?"

"Sure Paul. When you're ready, take table nine. Six-top. They'll be seated before you get back."

Paul hustled to get four glasses of water and four empty wine glasses. He had to compete with other servers in the service area for room for his tray, for the glasses, for the ice and even for the water. He was a little surprised that it was so hard to arrange.

Peter had set up the ice bucket and Paul arrived as the same time as the wine. He offered to open it, but the guests said no need. "We're starved. Can we be served soon?"

He left the glasses and said, "Absolutely. Right on it!"

He greeted his second table before returning to the kitchen. Big smile. "Sorry the special is out. Have you tried the shish kebab or trout? Can I bring you something to drink while you're deciding?"

They wanted cokes and iced tea.

Paul thought to himself, *this ain't too hard but I'd better write something down soon.* He paused in the kitchen and wrote his first order and turned it in to the line cooks. He was familiar with the tickets and the timing involved because he worked the line from time to time.

He got a large tray and loaded it with ten salads, three loaves of herb and onion bread, six glasses of ice and pitchers of coke and iced tea. The salads each had a little ceramic container of ramp dressing. Each loaf of bread sported a little ramekin of butter and a knife. The load was heavy, but he was strong and was accustomed to handling the large trays with non-slip, rubberized surfaces from bussing tables and from toting things in the kitchen. He centered his hand, palm up, bent his legs to lift the weight and steadied an edge of the heavy tray on his shoulder. He picked up a folding tray in his other hand as he passed into the dining room. It seemed natural to him, and he tried to move deliberately and efficiently rather than hustling like some servers did.

He delivered four salads and two loaves of bread to his first table and said, "Here's your starter. Your order is in. Can I get anything else now?" They seemed happy so he turned his attention to the other table. His folding tray stand was in place, and he gave them the glasses of ice and pitchers of soda.

They ordered two trouts and four shish kebabs and were pleased when he immediately began placing the bread and salads in front of him.

Peter intercepted him on his way to the kitchen and said, "Well done. Can you take one more table now?"

"Sure."

"Table 12. A four-top." I'll seat them now."

When Paul placed his second order Eddie told him, "Paul. Tone down the shish kebab a little. We're going to run out if we don't get more balanced orders."

"Okay. Sorry." He grinned and shrugged in apology.

He appeared at his third table with four salads, a loaf of bread and four glasses of ice. "Hi folks. No special tonight. Everything else is delish."

He faintly heard his name and "Order up!" from the kitchen as he took an order for iced tea.

"I'll be back in a flash for your order," he told the new table and marched to the kitchen to load up his first dinner order. The kebabs looked and smelled wonderful to him. He placed a steak knife on each platter, added a pitcher of tea to the tray hoisted the load.

The dining room was humming, every table full and a short line waited at the host station. He delivered the tea and kebabs, removing the empty salad plates as he placed the platters in front of each guest. "Paul. Order up," He heard again, faintly, thru the din.

"What else can I get you?" he asked as he went from diner to diner removing the skewers using a napkin and fork. They seemed happy.

Table three was eating their salads as he took their order for trout, kebabs, and roast chicken. Their salads and bread were under attack. He took their tea pitcher for a refill.

Peter waylaid him as he walked to pick up his next order. "Paul. Can you take a two-top?"

"I think so."

"Table 11. I'll seat them in a minute."

Paul hurried to the kitchen to pick up his third table's entrees and a pot of tea for refills along with two new salads, a loaf of bread and two glasses of ice. He delivered the food, took the order from table four and saw that table one was ready for dessert. They declined dessert and said, "just bring us a check when you can. No hurry. Good job tonight, Paul. Your manager told us we were your first table."

"Yep. It was a pleasure. Thanks for being patient. Any suggestions?"

"Yes. Don't change a thing. You're a natural. You made us feel at home."

Table One had a check of $67.00 and they left a $20.00 tip. Table two, the six-top left him $12.00. The evening ran by quickly in a blur of greeting, feeding, checking, and pocketing tips. Paul was exhausted by the time the last guest left and cleaning up began in earnest. The servers, mostly local women, were very cordial to him. He knew them from their forays into his areas of the kitchen, the dishwashing station and, more recently, the cooking areas.

Cleaning the restaurant was a grind. Bathrooms to be swabbed, carpets vacuumed, decks swept, and tile mopped. Every seat and every table had to be sanitized and then the grand finale. The servers moved about filling salt and pepper, sweetener caddies and condiment holders. They cleaned the coffee urns and drinks stations, then set up the supplies of clean glasses and cups for the next shift.

While the servers were cleaning, the designated person was washing and drying napkins in the laundry room. Spot remover was used, and each cleaned napkin was inspected and laid flat to prevent wrinkling.

When all the other chores had been finished, they gathered around a single table and sat to fold napkins into the signature COC fold. It was like a little party, without hors d'oeuvres. They gossiped and joked as their fingers flew.

"Paul. Did you learn rule number one?"

"What's that?"

"Never go anywhere in the dining room with empty hands. If your tables are clean pick up someone else's dirty dishes. Thank you very much." There were several hundred napkins to fold, and the kitchen crew had left and the kitchen was dark when they folded and put away their last napkins, clocked out, and locked the back door.

As they clocked out, they had to declare their tips. "Paul. Make up a number. I'm putting down $65.00. Put anything you want but keep it low."

"Okay." Paul agreed. He wrote $45.00 and would consider what to do next time when he was less tired.

Paul had a new respect for the servers. He had really worked as hard as he could to keep up with a few tables. His efficiency had risen a little with each experience and he hoped to be asked again. He had not counted his tips during the evening but, when he was alone in his bunk, he found that he had $130.00 in cash. He was stunned – this was much better than washing dishes or cooking. He determined to ask Peter to use him again – anytime!

With his head and heart full of the summer's memories – and as fall morphed into winter, Paul packed his stuff and left for Alabama. He had sold his canoe and other gear at the Guest Appreciation Festival and was comforted by the bulge of cash buttoned into his shirt pocket.

His earnings had exceeded his expectations and he was in love with the restaurant and food service business. He mulled his future and decided that he'd like to do it again. Peter and the GM had given him good reviews and he was assured of a job there again in the spring,

MIAMI – November 1999

What the hell is it all about? mused Paul. His 22nd birthday was coming, and he was moping around the house in Huntsville. There were a few chores to keep him busy, but no construction work with his dad. Business was slow and Dad was looking for projects. His big project was painting the upstairs bedrooms. The COC season was over too quick he thought. His life was yet not mapped, and he envied those who knew where they were going.

He had been working the phones trying to get in touch with Irene and his paddling buddy Marvin. Both in Florida. He reached Marvin first.

"Paul! Damn it's good to hear your voice. How ya doin?" Are you at COC? Tell me everything."

"Me too buddy. I'm in Huntsville with my mom and dad and wishing I was on the river. I'll be going back in the spring as a cook at Corney's Cavern Restaurant. Tell me about yourself."

Marvin was back in Miami where he and Susan had met and married. They were both working in the Marriott Hotel kitchen as cooks then and had migrated to COC after experiencing whitewater sports there while on vacation in 1995. Now Susan's mother was ill, and they had returned to help her. Marvin was cooking at the Marriott again and Susan stayed at home to tend to the kids and her mother.

"We won't be able to go back to COC for a while. Maybe never old pal,

"The Marriott!" That's where my friend Irene Linnick works. On Brickell Avenue. She's at the front desk. Do you know her?"

"Sure. I see her every day. I'll say hello to her for you." Before they hung up, they hatched a plan for Paul to visit them in Miami. Marvin's mother-in-law had a house with plenty of room for a guest and Paul couldn't wait to hang up, pack and hit the road.

He called the hotel to see if he could talk to Irene and was not disappointed.

"Paul! How are you? Hold a minute while I switch phones."

She picked up an extension in the office and kicked back, anxious to hear about Paul's summer at COC.

He explained about Marvin's offer, and she was suitably excited,

"Paul. It'll be so good to see you. How long will you stay?"

"It depends. I could be talked into a long-term visit. It depends on you Irene and on the situation at Marv's house. I don't want to be a pain, but wouldn't it be wonderful to reacquaint?"

"Yeah. Sure. Thing is though Paul, I have a boyfriend. To tell you the truth I'm living with someone." There was a long silence on the line as Paul digested the news.

"I broke my abstinence vow and I think I'm in love. Pablo is Cuban and a very nice guy. I think you two will hit it off, but I still want to see you if you're game."

"Well sure Irene," he said. You are a friend and not just a woman. I'll try to be good. I want to see you too."

The drive to Miami was not difficult. He used the interstates. Birmingham, Atlanta, Jacksonville, Miami. Paul didn't need a map until he got to Miami. He had lots of time to think about what he was doing now and where his life was heading. It made him a little sad and embarrassed to be on his own so much. He felt best at COC where work and play were engaging. He was proud, even though he knew it was silly, of his abilities with the Hobart. He'd never be unemployed. It was a start.

He recognized his mixed feelings about women. He wanted sex, of course, but he felt that he'd had bad luck with each of his girlfriends. He had not been totally serious when he told Irene that he would be celibate too but, in fact, he just had not found the right woman at the right time. His attitude toward Irene's announcement was sadness. Not surprise – she was just too lively to be good.

He used his sleeping bag in a rest area under the camper top amid a litter of paddling gear and other possessions. He arrived in Miami late on a Sunday morning. His good jacket and dress wear were on a hanger, but he was basically a tee shirt and jeans guy. The weather was warm – just right. No cold and no tropical heat. He had thought it would be hotter.

Paul's long hair was tied in a tight ponytail, and he used an electric razor to keep his beard short. Easy maintenance he thought.

He was, in fact, a man to be reckoned with, but his cheerful countenance, good manners and ready smile made him instantly welcome everywhere. He did not see himself this way, however. He felt somewhat unsure of himself – always ready to learn, but a little shy.

Marvin and Susan were living in Little Havana a few blocks south of *Calle Ocho*. The house was a 50's era CBS with a tile roof. It was on a large corner lot with tall tropical trees. An enormous hedge and vine covered walls and fences made it seem like an oasis in the modest, mixed neighborhood. The towers of downtown Miami loomed over the neighborhood trees. One could easily walk to stores on 8th and 9th Streets. There were apartment buildings on many streets.

After greetings and introductions at the door, Marvin opened the gate to let Paul park on the concrete apron of the separate garage. The kids, Mars, seven, and Sally, two-and-a-half, were excited to have company. Paul had seen them at COC, but they had not had any real contact. Over the next few days, he learned that he liked kids and that they were fun to play with and teach. Sally was in preschool, Mars in second grade.

He later learned Susan's father had remodeled the garage into an apartment for Susan before she moved away from home. He lined his truck up neatly between a sharp old Chevrolet Impala and Marvin's old VW bus that he remembered from COC days.

"This neighborhood is safe, but the folks here carry a cultural desire to bar windows and lock gates. It's from childhood memories in old Cuba, The bars work, of course, but they're mostly for decorative purposes."

"Ah. I see. What kinds of trees are these Marv?"

"We have tangerine, mango, avocado and limes. The Cubans say *limon* when they want a lime. Oranges are *naranjas*. Those big leaves growing in the corner are banana trees.

"We have to chop the bananas down every time, after we get a crop. A big new plant will come up in a few months. We have fruit coming out of our ears just now. It's wonderful," Marvin grinned, rubbing his belly.

He learned that Susan's mother, Carmen Alonso, a widow, was Cuban and that the local language was half Spanish and half English. They called it Spanglish.

"Call me Carmita. Por favor. Welcome to my house. *Mi casa es su casa.*" Susan's mom was a slender woman about his mom's age, late forties, or early fifties. She kissed him on both cheeks and drew him instantly into the family circle.

They sat in the living room watching the two children play and Susan, fixing dinner, moved in and out of the room. She declined Paul's offer of assistance and said, "Later Paul. You can help clean up. You have guest status for the next 45 minutes. Then you're part of the family. You'd better make friends with my children and my mom."

"Just relax and enjoy it bud," advised Marvin. "There's plenty to do and you can help.

"Carmita is in chemotherapy and can't work much. The grass grows every day, and we need to put rice on the table.

"By the way. Irene said, 'Hi. Come and see me.'

"What is the plan, Paul?"

"Thanks. We were good friends, and I can't wait to see her again."

"She told me to tell you come on over to the Marriott for lunch tomorrow if you can. You can either eat in the restaurant there or in the staff dining room. I'd recommend the restaurant. Or I could I'll pack you a lunch if you like and make you brown bag it. You can call her there now if you want.

Paul did want. He got her on the phone, and he spent the next few minutes letting Irene know that he'd buy her lunch the next day.

"Paul. I want you to meet Pablo. He is the kitchen manager here at the Marriott and I've told him all about your big adventures."

"Not so big maybe," said Paul shyly. "I want to meet him."

Paul was glad he'd worn his go-to-court outfit, jacket and slacks, shirt, and shoes. Irene was more beautiful than ever – she made her Marriott-prescribed business suit look like high couture. Only her nametag identified her as an employee, they embraced in the lobby then sat in lounge chairs, waiting for Pablo to join them at one o'clock. The Brickell Avenue hotel lobby lounge area was richly paneled and formal in a very comfortable way. The air was cool, and it seemed an oasis from the energetic bustle of Miami. Paul told her about his shifting work pattern at COC. "I thought I wanted to be a cook. It was hard work and a little more interesting than washing dishes, but now I love being a server. I doubled my income and, after a few more months as a waiter I think I could fit in at any restaurant.

"It just started as a job to be near the whitewater paddling, but I now feel like I have another skill set that would work just about anywhere.

"Construction too. I think I would hate college. I learn so much every day in the working world."

"Me too Paul. I studied for my degree, and it got me in the door here. But honestly, I think I could have done without it. I spend my days learning about Marriott systems and culture. They're very good about developing staff... Oh here comes Pablo."

Pablo was taller than Paul. He looked well-tanned and appeared heavy in the arms and chest, with an athlete's build and grace. He was wearing an open collared white shirt under a nice, Marriott style suit. The damp, dirty, white apron didn't quite match. He moved towards them quickly, gave Irene a peck on the lips and drew Paul's handshake into a bro-hug. He felt very strong to Paul, but his manner was brilliantly sunny and friendly. "Good to meet you, Paul. Irene talked about you so much I feel as though I know you."

Paul gave him his best smile and said, "*Mucho Gusto Pablo.*"

"Oh*! Hablas Espanol*! *No me digas. ¿Eres otro Cubano*?"

"No. No. Just kidding. I have a Cuban friend I'm visiting who taught me to say, '¿Cómo está usted?'"

They all laughed at Paul's humor.

"Pablo," Irene's voice rose an octave as she said his name, "Do you know that you're wearing an apron?"

Pablo looked down and removed the garment in question. "Oh, I forgot. I was helping out in the kitchen, and I had to run to meet you." He removed the apron and walked it over to a desk clerk and asked him to send it to the laundry.

They walked to the dining room. It was cool and quiet with a pretty view of the palm fringed pool and gardens. Biscayne Bay glimmered in the background.

They talked about working in the hotel and about Paul's experiences at Caverns Outdoor Center.

Pablo was 28 years old and had just recently been promoted to Kitchen Manager. The hotel had three restaurants and banquet facilities that served hotel guests and meetings. Room service was still another dimension. "I've been here for three years. I started as a cook and worked in every position. I managed the poolside bar and grill, then the coffee shop and later, as situations unfolded, I became the banquet manager and, after that, the main restaurant manager. Each of these facilities has its own manager but the main kitchen serves them all. Now as Kitchen Manager I have a much different set of challenges. Today I'm very challenged; two line cooks are out ill, and the dishwasher didn't show.

"I'm going to have to eat fast, but you two take as much time as you like." He glanced at his watch.

"And. By the way, this meal is on the house. My job requires that I eat in every day, and I am encouraged to have guests. My treat."

They thanked him and enjoyed the food. Irene got a fancy salad and Paul the best hamburger he'd ever eaten. Pablo had a shrimp bisque soup and a toasted cheese sandwich.

"Paul. What are your plans? Are you moving to Miami?"

"No big plan. I can stay as long as I like but I'm committed to returning to the Caverns Outdoor Center in the spring. I want to wait on tables next season. I've had a lot of kitchen experience."

"Really." Pablo looked keenly at Paul. "I don't suppose that you could consider working here for a while.

"We're so in the weeds. If you could even start today, I'd be thrilled to have you."

"Well. I'd have to call home first then get my knives from my truck."

Pablo gave him a big grin. "Irene. This is karma. You have brought Paul here at a time when he could do us the most enormous favor."

"Glad to help. I've got to get back to the desk now. You boys talk and do what you need to do.

"Paul. I hope you will stay forever." She gave him a hug and a kiss on his face. Very near his lips. He felt a drop of her moisture on the corner of her mouth and was very affected by this show of friendship. He was jealous of Pablo and at the same time very glad that two such beautiful people could find their happiness together.

"Me too. See ya later."

"Pablo. I'd be happy to help. Could you help me make a phone call to the house?"

"Of course. Let's go to my office."

They went through a staff-only door and instantly entered a different world. The wall finishes were utilitarian, the floors linoleum tile, and the doors painted metal with aluminum kick plates. The long, wide hallway led them past offices with signs marked with their functions. Accounting. Finance. Executive Suite. Event Planning. Foodservice. Human Resources.

"Paul. I assume you are human?" Pablo joked. "Let's stop in here a moment and get you registered.

Paul was introduced to a young woman working in Human Resources, Patricia Cross. "Patty. This is Paul Hunter. He's clocking in today. Just as soon as you can get him signed in at $12.50 an hour. Use Irene Linnick, and Marvin Smith and me as references. He'll need a chef's pants, jacket and toque. Issue him work shoes as well. Okay?"

It was okay so Pablo left them, asking Pat to bring him to the kitchen as soon as she could. "Quick Patty. We're dying in there and Paul may save us." It did not escape Paul's notice that Patty was about his age and that she had very blond hair and was pleasingly well rounded. A very pretty woman. Her hair was very shiny and pulled back into a neat bun. Her skin was fair, and freckles were visible under transparent makeup of some kind. She was very kind to Paul, and he admired her efficiency and professionalism as she explained various elements of the hiring process. She gave him Marriott new-employee literature in a manila envelope.

It had taken Patty over an hour to get him into the system, uniform him, and give him a lightning tour of the back of the house. He had been introduced to a number of people including the General Manager. The GM was cordial and told him that he had started with Marriott as a bellman in Salt Lake City, Utah.

Paul made a quick trip to his truck to get his kitchen toolkit and change in the men's locker room. They had given him three complete uniforms so that he could have them cleaned in the house laundry as necessary.

The kitchen was vast, much larger than COC. It was the biggest kitchen he'd ever seen. Pat led him to a door marked MANAGER. Paul saw Pablo and Marvin in earnest conversation. Pat left him at the door.

Marvin glanced up and was astonished. "Boy. That was fast. Fine looking outfit." They were now dressed in identical checkered pants, leather shoes, white chef's jackets and sported tall toques on their heads.

He was given a training schedule that involved a lunch meeting with different managers every Wednesday. He would be one of ten new employees learning about the company. Paul was impressed.

"Marvin will be your mentor, Paul. He'll give you an overall tour of the kitchen from the receiving dock to the grease pits. We have many different stations, and we'll get you through them all before we finish. I hope you like it." Pablo was tying on a fresh apron. "I myself will be doing dishes until six o'clock. Ciao."

Marvin handed him a list of the workstations he'd be assigned to for the next 30 days for OJT: Fried Chicken, Cold Prep, Prime Rib, Desserts, Cook Station Number One - Vegetables, Cook Station Number Two - Deep Fryer, Line Cook, Sanitation, and Expediting. He would also work Receiving at the loading dock, in Cooler Organization, in the Employee Lunchroom, and on the Room Service Table.

"Marvin. I didn't expect to even look for a job here in Miami. I'm on vacation. Pablo begged me to help, and I couldn't say no."

"Paul. You're such a slut."

Marvin started Paul at the fried chicken station explaining the system and the environment. "We have fried chicken on every menu: main dining room, coffee shop, pool snacks, and room service. It's all cooked right here. There is a special part of a big refrigerator reserved for covered, white, 55-gallon plastic barrels on wheels. Chicken parts are marinated in them for at least 12 hours. The barrels are rolled to the fryer station and the chicken, 40 pieces at a time, are dipped out and allowed to drain, dusted with a coating and pressure fried." Marvin showed Paul how to handle the big chicken dipper used to get the birds out of the barrel. He showed Paul three pressure fryers joined together. They were table height and their kettles each held about 40 pieces of chicken. The adjoining breading station had a steel mesh pan for draining, dusting and staging chicken parts close to the fryers.

"We use three or four barrels of chicken a day. More if there is a banquet. Your job at this station is to open boxes of chicken parts, breasts, leg quarters, thigh pieces and such. Wash and inspect them, trim off bits you would not want to eat. Maintain good sanitation at all times. There should be at least four full barrels when your shift is over.

"Dump a packet of marinade powder in a clean barrel, half fill it with water, and then put in as many cases of chicken as will fit. When the marinade water rises to the full mark, stop putting the chicken in. Stick a time label the barrel and roll it into the reefer.

"When a barrel is empty, wheel it to the floor drains and use the built-in bottom spigot to drain the liquid. Wash and sanitize the barrel to get it ready for another batch." There was a carton opening station with double sinks to wash the birds. A box of rubber gloves stood at the ready to keep hands out of the chicken mess.

"Meanwhile, like a chicken with its head cut off, you will be dipping the marinated chicken parts out onto a drain rack, breading it, frying it, and moving the finished product to the holding ovens."

He showed Paul the pressure fryers full of hot oil. "Drop your 40 pieces, gently, four at a time. Close the pressure lid and set the timer for 12 minutes. Got it?"

"Sure. It looks like fun. Lots of fun."

They investigated the holding ovens and found only one hotel pan heaped with delicious looking fried chicken. There was a wire rack on the bottom of the pan to keep the product from sitting in a puddle of oil. The pieces had a good brown and were crisp and fresh looking.

"Paul. We gotta hurry buddy. Let's get to frying us some chicken and loading this holding unit up. Serious dinner hour starts in two hours have to get going. He showed Paul how to coat 40 pieces of chicken into a basket and drop them into the hot fat and close the pressure lid and set the timer.

"I'll come back and check on you after a while. I'm gonna cut some vegetables." He saw Paul frown and recognized a set of concerns. "Don't fret bud. You'll get the hang of this in one day and we'll move you to another station tomorrow or the next day. There are about 20 workstations to master. When you get 'em all you'll have a better appreciation of how we feed thousands of people a day, 24 hours a day, seven days a week. We are scheduled to work until ten p.m. We'll keep you busy.

"I'll show you how to filter the oil and clean up later."

Paul managed to get the holding oven filled to his spec sheet and found the work hard and not so interesting. It was so one-note.

He reflected on his wage of $12.50 an hour. It seemed fairly high, but he had no standards to go by. He got $6.00 an hour at COC plus tips. This Marriott work paid enough to start.

Paul received visits from Pablo and Irene during the shift as well as regular contact with Marvin. He had dinner with the three of them in the staff dining room. He enjoyed a taste of his own fried chicken. The price was modest for staff. He could even charge it against his paycheck. *Pretty damn good chicken*, he thought.

He learned a lot on his first day. In the days following he also learned how Marriott cold-prepped vegetables of all varieties, cooked massive quantities of mashed potatoes, steam vegetables, roast prime ribs and even how to work on the line where he thought, *the action was best*. He liked his job and thought that he was building a skill set for life at COC and afterwards.

Marvin approached him with a deal before the first week was up. Paul had expressed a desire to get an apartment in the neighborhood because he didn't want to wear out his welcome.

"Paul. Stay in the garage apartment and take your meals with us. We can work the same shift and either drive or walk to work together – it's only a mile away. We'll give you a terrific deal on rent. Say $155.00 per week including utilities and board. *Todas las comidas* you care to eat." Paul was learning a little Spanglish every day. "What do you say? *¿Que dice?*"

Paul didn't answer for a moment because he was so happy to be wanted.

Marvin jumped in again, "We all like having you around and it will help Carmita. She gets social security from my father-in-law's death benefits but Medicare won't kick in for a few years. She gets Medicaid benefits, from Uncle Sam thank you, but she needs more to keep this house going. That's why we're here.

"That, and the fact that she loves having us around. Especially the kids. She says they bring life into the house."

"Ah Marvin. That would be great, but you have to promise me something."

"What?"

"We have got to have a three-way conversation with me and Susan to promise me to let me know if any of that changes. I don't need the job really, the money is not a big issue, but I like the idea of learning more about the hospitality business. I want to be a pro like you and Pablo. I believe that I'm going back to COC in the spring.

"And I'm having a great time. Here in Florida, it's so different. I feel like I'm visiting another country."

"*No problema hermano.* Let's have that talk now."

Paul's new digs were very pleasing to him. The garage space was now a 450 square foot efficiency apartment with a bathroom and walk in closet. The garage doors had been left on but were just a sham and not functional – Carmita and her husband did not want to get a building permit. Taking down the doors would have tipped off any inspector in the area.

Inside, the garage doors were concealed by a properly built and insulated sheetrock wall with decorative wainscoting. The curtains were not too girly and there were landscapes and family pictures on the walls. HVAC included a ceiling fan and a through-the-wall, reverse cycle, air conditioning, not much needed this time of year. A love seat, a recliner chair, a double bed, 1 bathroom and a walk-in closet provided most of the comforts Paul needed. He needed six inches of hanger space. There was bedding and towels but no television.

Paul thought it was just right. *Way, way better thana tent in the woods.*

Windows provided cross ventilation and nice views of the tropical back yard. "Marvin. Would you all mind if I got a TV and cable set-up?"

"Not at all. Let's call our cable company and see if we can just add you on. Shouldn't cost much."

Paul made a beeline to the nearest Sears store and returned with a mammoth box containing a 32" screen television set. The first piece of home furnishing he ever bought.

The weather was beautiful in Miami, and they walked to work most days. Virtually every shop and advertisement they saw was in Spanish. Conversations on the street were in Spanish or, sometimes, Spanglish. People seemed lively, happy, and busy.

"The Cubans are hustlers Paul. They work hard and play hard and try to live the good life.

"I grew up in the Southwest section of Miami in an American neighborhood that gradually became all Cuban. The natives all moved to the suburbs. My father was in his early twenties in 1960 when Castro came into power and the middle-class Cubans fled to the U.S. – mostly Miami. He said that the area we call little Havana now, was going downhill fast. The shops along the main streets were all empty. People preferred driving to the malls and local merchants all went broke. It was a disaster.

"Most of the Cubans who came here were poor. They had to leave a lifetime of material accumulations behind. They had no money, no houses or furniture, no jewelry, and no jobs. Coming here was a leap into the unknown for them.

"The government helped them a lot but more than that, they helped themselves. They began to open little shops selling the goods and services they were used to at home. And restaurants. They revitalized the whole area. Miami is way up on other cities with respect to having people living close to the city center.

"Now, four decades later their kids are voting republican and are more educated and professional than most of the rest of America."

They stopped for a Cuban coffee and pastry most days. "*Un cafe' y uno pastelito por favor*." Paul loved ordering and the people behind the counters enjoyed hearing his American accent. They appreciated his attempts. They ate their *pastelitos* and drank their coffee standing at the counter. If other customers appeared they'd move a few feet and lean against the building.

Paul reluctantly called his mother to declare that he would be away for Christmas. She said she understood but he could tell that she was disappointed. "Mom. I'm learning so much here. And I'll be sending you money every week.

"Do you or Dad need money?"

"No honey. Thanks for asking. Dad and I are doing all right. We just need a Paul-fix once in a while. Call me every week. Okay."

"Okay. Love to Dad. I love you too."

Paul learned everything he wanted and needed to know about frying large quantities of chicken in two days and went on to the hot vegetable station.

He learned how to create tons of sweetly delicious, skin-on, mashed potatoes in the big Hobart mixer using cream, butter, grated Parmesan cheese, salt, and pepper. He steamed fresh green vegetables that others had prepped and, following his script, kept the holding cabinets filled to a prescribed level, gradually cutting back as the dinner hour slowed and then ended. Room service, coffee shop and poolside needs were lighter than the main dining room.

His paycheck was directly deposited to a new bank account and, to his surprise; the bank offered him a Master Card. He accepted it, activated it and left it in his wallet. He thought that he might use it sometime, but he was so used to paying cash and having no monthly bills that he was leery of credit.

Paul had no social life outside of his new family and a few acquaintances at work. He was eager to make friends and took every opportunity to chat it up at work. Because there was an older guy in the kitchen also named Paul. They began calling Paul 'Hunter' at work.

The slightly grizzled Paul-1 chatted with Paul as they worked side-by-side prepping vegetables. Hunter felt like a pro using his own knives.

"Hunter. I'm lucky to be here. I just got an early release from prison. I got caught doing something stupid. I broke into a grocery store and stole cash from the registers. About $400.00, I think.

"The reason I don't know is that I didn't have time to count it. They busted me as I went out the back door. I got two years but only had to serve nine months."

"Oh my God Paul. I'm sorry for your problems. I guess I've done worse than that myself. Stupidly. But I didn't get caught."

"You were lucky Hunter. Prison was for shit. The only thing is that it got me clean of cocaine. That was my main problem and I rehabbed in jail. I guess I did good. And it wasn't my first crime – only the one I got caught for."

This conversation played over again in Paul's mind many times. He thought back to the thievery and mischief that he and Mitch had gotten away with and wondered why they were so blessed. He'd seen pain and trouble in Paul I's eyes. He was glad his wayward childhood was behind him.

Paul attempted something very scary ten days before Christmas. He called Patricia Cross while on his break and said, "Hi Pat. This is Paul Hunter. Do you remember me?"

"Yes, of course Mr. Hunter. What can I do for you?"

"Well Pat. Call me Paul please or I'll think you're Cross."

She laughed at his little joke.

"Say Pat. I, uh. I mean," He stammered a little, "Do you think you might like to see a movie and have dinner with me sometime?"

"Let me think..." She paused for a fraction of a second. "Yes!" she said. "Do you mean now?"

"Well yes. But I have to work tonight. Until ten. What nights are you off?"

"Weekends only I'm afraid."

"I'm free Sundays and Mondays. So, Sunday then? What would you like to see? I haven't been to a movie in like forever so you pick, and I can say I haven't seen it. I was thinking we could see *American Beauty* or *Toy Story II*. Pick One."

"American Beauty," she said immediately. "Where and when do you want to meet? By the way, call me Patty."

"Can I pick you up at your house Patty? I'm afraid I drive an old pick-up, but I promise it's clean. Almost clean anyway."

She gave him a Coral Gables address along with some complicated directions involving circles and streets with names instead of numbers. They agreed to a five o'clock time, dinner at the Versailles Restaurant, then eight o'clock show time near the restaurant.

Paul was excited and he thought that Patty sounded pleased. When Sunday came, he spent a great deal of time grooming for his date. He followed his high school rules. Shower, shave, masturbate, brush and floss. He wore his only jacket, slacks, and clean loafers.

Her apartment was on the second floor of a tired old building. It was in a middle-class neighborhood at the edge of an opulent district of beautiful homes and estates. He climbed dark, narrow stairs to knock on the door of 201. He heard her footsteps and the door unlatching.

When he saw what Patty wore, Paul thought he should have jerked off twice. She was very fetching in a scoop neck, white peasant blouse and form fitting jeans. She wore fuck-me red shoes. The outfit was topped off with a red, Spanish style shawl. Her hair was different.

"Hey Paul. Come in for a minute. We have plenty of time"

The corner apartment was neat and plainly furnished. There was a Formica table with two kitchen chairs, a sofa and two easy chairs. Her bed, behind the couch and the kitchen were all in the room. It was a 1950's efficiency with a combination bathroom and closet. She had it fixed up with bright curtains and pillows on the chairs and couch.

The walls were somewhat crowded with travel posters from France, Italy, and Spain. Filmy curtains fluttered at the windows. The through-the-wall air conditioning unit was off in the mild evening.

"My God Patty. This place is so much like mine. I'm living in Marvin's family's garage apartment. I like your posters better than my pictures. Where'd you get them?"

"Thank you, sir. I got them here and there. All over actually – if you like I'll take you shopping one day soon.

"Gimme a few seconds." She stepped into the bathroom without closing the door and leaned toward a mirror to expertly apply and blot lipstick and give her hair a fluff. She turned out the bathroom light and they left the apartment for their date.

They were apparently in the landing and takeoff zone of the Miami International Airport. Several jets roared overhead while they were there. "Sorry Paul. I'm used to the noise now but, because of the jet noise, the rent is very low here.

He led the way down the stairs offering his arm to give her support as she negotiated the stairs in high heels.

Paul was so proud of his date. He held the door while she settled in the truck and made her wear her seat belt. He drove gently through the beautiful Coral Gables streets as she directed him back to *Calle Ocho* and S.W. 36th Avenue.

This was the first real Cuban dinner restaurant Paul had been in. He knew he liked the *comidas* that Susan and Carmita provided and the *café* and *pastilitos* that he and Marvin had been eating. But this restaurant was amazing. It was plain and fancy at the same time. It had a neighborhood vibe and fancy mirrors on every wall with world class Cuban food. The place was very busy, but they were seated quickly in a mirrored back room. The background babble was entirely in Spanish as far as Paul could tell.

The waitress bid them *buenas noches* and offered them a choice of Spanish or English menus. They chose one of each. Pat ordered the house special salad. "I've got to watch my figure, or you won't," she flirted. Paul had *masas de puerco fritas.* They shared Galician White Bean Soup as an appetizer.

Paul wondered why he kept thinking, *best ever. The soup was super. Best ever,* he thought again. His pork chunks fried sweet plantains and black beans were wonderful. Pat's salad was beautifully made. He realized then that Cuban food and Mexican food were not the same. Mex, as he knew and loved it, had the heat of peppers and the richness of coriander lurking in every bite. Cuban food was well seasoned with lots of garlic but no sharp edges or bite. It was heavenly.

They took their time with dinner since they had three hours to go and just a few miles to the theater. They talked about childhood memories from Huntsville - him, and Long Island, New York – her. Patty was 23, on her own for over a year, and thrilled to be working at the great hotel chain. "My goal is to become competent in Spanish. I need it to apply for a post in Spain. The company will give me a Spanish test when I think I'm ready. Soon. I've had courses in hotel management, and I have had experience in a few smaller American chains."

Paul gave her his work history and she was suitably amazed when he got to the Barbecue Shack episode.

"Holy Mackerel! You must have been scared."

"A little bit. It wasn't half as scary as calling you however." They laughed.

After their Cuban coffees and flan dessert she said, "Paul. I'm so full. What would you think about taking a walk before the movie?"

"I'd love it. Can you really walk in those heels?"

"Girl Scouts are always prepared," she smiled at him as she reached into her ample purse and removed a pair of flat shoes. "The red shoes are for show. Attitude, you know. These booties are made for walking."

They strolled a block down *Calle Ocho,* AKA S.W. 8th Street, then went south on Douglas Road, AKA S.W. 37th Avenue to Miracle Mile, AKA Coral Way. Downtown Coral Gables' fancy shops were decorated for Christmas. Patty held Paul's arm as they moved along window-shopping for things they didn't need or want. "God. I love looking at this stuff," said Patty. Maybe I'll buy some of it when I grow up."

They discussed Christmas plans and discovered that they were both working second shift, she at the front desk, he, and Marvin, in the kitchen as usual.

The company had asked for volunteers to allow employees with families to get the magic Christmas off. Marvin said his kids wouldn't miss him after they opened their presents. He and Paul would start work by one o'clock on Christmas day.

On impulse Paul invited Patty to spend Christmas morning with his new family at *la casa*. He knew them well enough to know that they would rejoice at having her with them.

When the time came to hike back to his car for the movie she said, "Paul. I've had such a good time. I like being with you. Would you mind skipping the movie? I'd like to walk back to my place and have a night cap."

Paul felt a little woozy thinking about what she might mean. Her words had been a little slow and sort of breathy. "Of course. Lead on." He took her hand. It felt natural, and they walked a mile or so back to her place.

It turned out that the nightcap was a glass of water since she had no booze.

Afterwards he held her in his arms, and she began crying. "Oh Paul. I'm sorry I did this to you. I feel like such a slut. I'm so lonely and it just felt so good to be with you." They were sated with sex and with passionate kissing. Wrapped together in her sheet they sat on the couch and cuddled, drinking from the same glass.

She knew that he would be leaving in March. She ventured, "Paul. I'm about ready for my Spanish test and I think I'll leave in the spring. If I can't get to Spain, I'll try for New York."

"Like I said, I'm kinda lonely here. I have a few girlfriends but no men friends. Would you consider being my Sunday boyfriend for a few months?"

"Hm. Let me think. Yes." He got his arm under her and turned her so that he could plant a good kiss on her soft mouth. She opened her lips, and they were soon back in her bed.

When they were resting, he said, "Patty. I'm going to get you a little Christmas present tomorrow." He looked at his watch. "I mean later today so that you'll have something to open next Sunday. I'm doing my Christmas shopping tomorrow, I mean today." It was after midnight. I need something for my folks, for my brother Mitch and for Marvin and Susan's family.

"Say, Patty, it's getting late. Can I spend the night with you?'

She answered by setting her clock for 6:30 and turning off the bed lamp. "Paul. If you try to leave I'll hurt you."

He laughed and they snuggled until they slept. Both were tired from the emotional coupling and togetherness they felt.

Paul had a wonderful Monday morning. He attacked Patty when the alarm went off and they made love before the sun peeked in the window.

He washed her in the shower enjoying her luscious body. Each breast, pointy and pneumatic, got kissed, suckled, washed and hand rinsed. He did not miss anything, including the ticklish bottoms of the feet. "Paul. I've never had such a bath."

"Me neither," he said as she began to work on his body.

When he became aroused, somewhere between his toe scrub and shampoo, she said, "Not again Paul. My heart is ready, but my other organs are done for the day."

"Me too, but the next time I see this beautiful body I want to count the freckles."

After their incredible shower she was rushed to be on time for work. "Paul. Do you need a ride to your car?"

"No. Thanks Patty. I want to walk my mind back to earth. Have a great day. See ya at work Tuesday."

They walked down the stairs, she to roar off downtown and he to hike through the beautiful neighborhoods to *Calle Ocho* and get his vehicle. He drove to Dadeland Mall and bought Christmas gifts.

Paul found the UPS shop and sent his store-wrapped gifts to his parents and Mitch and Molly – they all went to Huntsville where they would celebrate the holidays without him for the first time. The season was not without sadness on that account.

Christmas morning was a party. Patty came just before eight. with wrapped toys for the kids, a tea set for Carmen, matching hats, watch-cap style, for Marvin and Susan.

Paul's gift was a Hermes scarf.

"Oh Paul. This is too much! You shouldn't have spent so much." She handed him a long thin package that turned out to be a walking stick that unscrewed into two pieces for storage and travel. It had a built-in compass on top and a knife in the hollow handle.

The walking stick brought the wonderful hikes he'd enjoyed in the mountains. He felt a pang of longing for those winding trails and cool breezes and giving up the city sidewalks.

Susan and Carmita had not met Patty before this day. They gave every sign of approval for Paul's guest. Patty was delighted to feel a part of the family.

While Marvin and the other women set out the lunch, and the kids played with their new treasures, Patty sat close to Paul on the couch taking it all in. "Thank you for having me here," she whispered. This was wonderful. By the way," she sat even closer and hugged his bicep, "you can unwrap your big present at my place after work tonight."

"With pleasure Patty. It'll be late. But tomorrow's Sunday and we can stay in bed all day." Paul leaned in close and whispered into her ear, "By the way, next Friday is my birthday…" She growled at him and the kids looked up expectantly, thinking that they might be about to fight.

Susan stepped into the room singing, "Come and get it lovebirds. Y'all can clean up after we eat. You've lazed around long enough."

JANUARY 2000

Patty passed her Spanish test and was offered a 1-year employment contract by Marriott in Malaga, Spain at the A. C. Palacio Hotel. She would start in reception and perhaps be rotated into other areas of the operation.

Paul was very happy for Patty, but he saw that the end of their idyllic relationship was near at hand. He hosted a farewell dinner for her involving Irene, Pablo, Marvin and Susan. They ate in a small private dining room at the Versailles Restaurant and presented her with a little electronic translating device. It handled all the several major European languages.

Patty started her adventure with a visit with her parents in New York on the 15th of February. Her car was already sold and Paul gave her a lift to the airport. "I boxed my stuff and UPS'ed it to New York. I won't be taking much to Spain. Mostly clothing and a few pictures. The company will give me a mentor to get a rental apartment and whatever I need for making the big change.

"I wish I could take you Paul."

"Yeah. Me too Patty. But we have to part for now. Send me postcards. Okay?"

MARCH 2000

Paul was happy to be back on his river - the Clancy River - in the budding Georgia spring. He was in his secret garden on the riverbank out of sight. Quiet. Peaceful. Alone.

He sat erect in his kayak in the quiet water. His double-bladed paddle rested athwart ship on the gunwale. Paul was protected by his wet suit, basking in the noon sun with his eyes closed. Dreaming about his life. Experiencing wisps of memories, fears, sorrows and happiness.

He deliberately let his mind drift to the people who were important to him. Mom and Dad were always in place and formed a base for footing for his emotional security.

Brother Mitch, his idol, had first gone to Asheville to be with Molly. He seemed to be heading in a direction Paul envied – toward stated and rational goals. Gone to make a life with his girlfriend – more than a girlfriend – Molly. They were living in Charlotte, North Carolina where they had bought a consignment, antique shop.

Sarah, his first love, had gone her way without him. The other women in his life, Irene and Patty were gone. His friends Megan, boss, landlord and lover, and Johnny, his lawyer, were gone forever. The Barbecue Shack was gone.

Paul had spent a lot of time living alone in tents. Even now, living in staff housing, he felt slightly alienated from the COC culture. The hardcore, permanent employees were the athletes and experts in whitewater matters. The most prominent were past Olympic participants and the hopeful youths actively competing at a high level.

The hardcore people worked in Administration and Retail as well as serving as instructors and guides. Some of them were involved in the International Adventure Travel Department, making trips to far-away places like Nepal and Costa Rica. These elite folks tended to look down on foodservice workers.

The cooks, servers and other restaurant workers were mostly locals and summer-employed students. They were socially inferior to Olympic heroes and hopefuls.

Paul sensed patterns in his affairs. He wanted some do-overs.

###

HUNTER II

BOOK TWO – LOVE AND CRIME

Second in the series

Henry David Thoreau – As you simplify your life, the laws of the universe will be simpler.

A man is rich in proportion to the number of things he can afford to let alone.

Go confidently in the direction of your dreams!

Live the life you've imagined.

Jesus – Do not be anxious about your life, what you shall eat, or what you shall drink, nor about your body, what you shall put on.

Life is more than food and the body more than clothing.

Look at the birds of the air: they neither sow nor reap nor gather into barns, and yet your heavenly Father feeds them.

Are you not of more value than they?

Which of you by being anxious can add one cubit to his span of life?

And why are you anxious about clothing?

Consider the lilies of the field. They neither toil nor spin; even Solomon in all his glory was not arrayed like one of these.

But if God so clothes the grass of the field, which today is alive and tomorrow is thrown into the oven, will he not much more clothe you, O men of little faith?

Seek first his kingdom and his righteousness, and all these things shall be yours as well.

Do not be anxious about tomorrow, for tomorrow will be anxious for itself.

Let the day's own trouble be sufficient for the day.

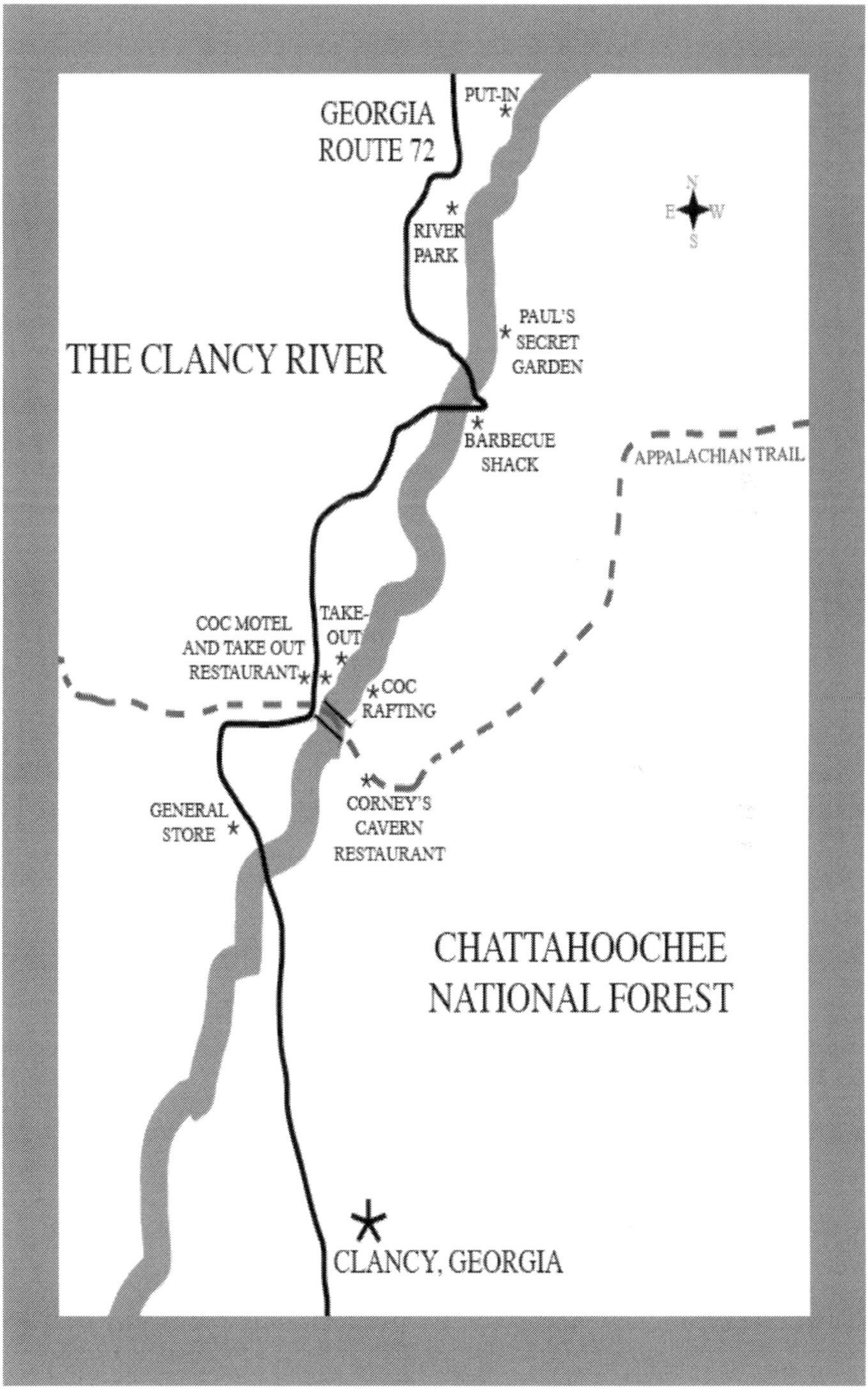
GEORGIA
ROUTE 72
PUT-IN
N
E
W
S
RIVER
PARK
PAUL'S
SECRET
GARDEN
THE CLANCY RIVER
BARBECUE
SHACK
APPALACHIAN TRAIL
COC MOTEL
AND TAKE OUT
RESTAURANT
TAKE-
OUT
COC
RAFTING
GENERAL
STORE
CORNEY'S
CAVERN
RESTAURANT
CHATTAHOOCHEE
NATIONAL FOREST
CLANCY, GEORGIA

PART ONE

Once upon a time ago, in a peaceable land of rivers and mountains, a drama unfolded. The telling may entertain you for a day or two. And it's all true, I swear by Mom's tattoo…

CAVERNS OUTDOOR CENTER (COC) – April 2000

Dahlia Schmitt was a delight. Her pretty figure and boyish haircut caught Paul's eye on her second day at Caravans Outdoor Center. She seemed taller than her actual 5'- 4" because of her confident posture and long neck. She was in the United States on a work/study visa, and she planned to be in the states for the summer.

COC seemed like a paradise to Dahlia when she'd first planned her visit from her home in Germany. She hadn't yet made friends with the women working at the center and felt shy about the men. Her English was good and getting better every day. As she bantered with the staff while bussing tables and taking her turn at the dishwashing station her accent and vocabulary improved. She missed her family in Berlin.

Archie Phillips, the manager, liked her, but she spurned his advances, partly because he seemed too old for her, and partly because he thought he had a right to touch her when they spoke. He would put his hand on her arm or shoulder, and it creeped her out. She was scared by the lust she saw in his eyes.

Paul was cooking when he first met Dahlia. When he became a waiter, he sometimes helped her with overflowing bus tubs, or crinkled his eyes as he held doors open for her. His beard was full, and he had a ponytail. His hazel eyes were beautiful. He stood six feet tall and looked strong and solid. She jumped at the chance to get away from staff housing when he asked her to go rafting on her day off.

Paul was thrilled when she said, "Oh yah. Dat vould be nice." He loved her accent.

Paul did not like the way some people treated her as he often felt something of an outcast himself. He hoped to make a friend.

Archie, standing nearby, out of sight, overheard the invitation with displeasure. He marched off angry at Paul's success.

Paul reserved a boat for the next Monday. He ordered a two-person "Duckie," as they called the slender rafts propelled by double-bladed kayak paddles. He felt it would be more fun for a novice like Dahlia. He had taken the guide course the previous year and knew the Clancy River well. Sometimes he got work as a raft guide on his days off.

Monday, in the staff-housing washroom, he did his morning routines with great care. He scissored and razored his beard to a fashionable buzz. His ponytail was pulled tight, and his teeth were brushed and flossed. Clean shorts and a new tee shirt made him feel fashionable in the woodsy way. He donned his visor at a jaunty angle. He wore his neoprene river shoes.

There was no charge for employees if equipment was available. Guided rafting trips on the Clancy River cost clients forty dollars per person. They received their gear and attended a five-minute safety lesson before riding to the put-in by bus along with other guests and employees. Dahlia wore a pink baseball cap, shorts, tee shirt and sturdy Teva sandals. Paul thought she looked smashing.

The two boarded the bus for the put-in after donning wet suits. They carried their paddles and Paul's waterproof wet sack containing their clothing. The rubber suits were needed because summer heat had not yet set in. Paul had packed cool cokes, crackers, and apples for sustenance. Their deflated boat was on top of the bus along with the larger rafts and other duckies.

The Clancy River was great fun for the thousands of people who ran it in rafts, kayaks and canoes each year. A hydroelectric dam Water levels controlled the river to provide appropriate flow for recreation and electric power at different times of day.

"Don't worry Dalia," Paul said.

"It vill be my first time on a river," she said quietly. "You vill have to show me how to do it."

"No *problema*. You'll love it. It is the most peaceful place on earth. We'll be close to nature, but your wet suit and your PFD will keep you safe and warm. I know the river and I'm sure you will want to go again. I'll be happy to take you anytime."

She smiled up at him and felt her trust building. Her grayish blue eyes were clear and direct. He seemed so strong and sure of himself. "Vat's a PDF again?"

"A personal flotation device. PFD. Your life jacket."

"Oh, yah. I forgot the initials."

She liked the confident way Paul conducted himself. He did not swagger. His attitude was deferential, and he greeted everyone he encountered with a polite smile and strong eye contact.

Paul explained that the rapids they would traverse were Class I, II and III, in the parlance of the white-water river sports authorities. Class I and II are mild and easy enough for even inexperienced boaters. Perhaps boring for hard-core paddlers. Class III requires a degree of skill and effort that may be within the limits of inexperienced but fit people. Class IV and V are increasingly challenging. Class VI is over the line - too dangerous for recreation.

There were about forty people for the last trip of the day. Paul sat on the aisle next to Dahlia. Their shoulders pressed together as the bus made its turns on the forest road in the leaf-filtered sunlight. Paul felt a great peace in Dahlia's presence, but she showed some apprehension about their upcoming adventure.

The drive was a bit over five miles on Route 72. They saw the Clancy River from time to time as it romped alongside their route. The pace was slow, and the driver deliberate as they maneuvered along the winding road. The trip leader stood near the driver and regaled the passengers with funny stories, jokes, and river safety reminders. There was a lot of laughter and kibitzing.

The bus turned off into the raft staging area by the river called the put in. The deflated boats were quickly unstrapped, lowered to the ground, and inflated by the put-in staff. Paul helped handle the boats as guests and guides formed into groups and departed on the water. Dahlia stood to one side holding their paddles. The number of people watching dwindled as rafts departed.

Dahlia and Paul were the last boat of the day. Paul planned a leisurely pace to make sure that Dahlia would not get too tired and to ensure that they would be alone in the river world.

The shouts of the other boaters from their bus faded and the magic environment asserted itself. The sunlight was intermittent with great rocks and green forest on the banks. The air was still and cool and the mineral smell of clear water bubbling over river rocks added to a sense of change from land animals to river creatures.

The initial Class I and II rapids were interesting rather than frightening for the novice. She paddled as Paul directed, sometimes pulling forward with her twin blades, sometimes resting, and sometimes using a reverse stroke on one side of the other to help him steer around rocks.

Dahlia's seat in the bow of the boat was supremely comfortable. The inflatable boat's bottom was just a big, long flat air cushion to make the boat self-bailing. The thwart was a firm backrest and the stiffly inflated sides rose to a comfortable height. The rubberized fabric of the craft was strong enough to resist the daily assault of shallow water and sharp rocks.

Her wet suit, PFD, and neoprene shoes made her feel like she was wearing a comfortable suit of armor. The dollops of water that splashed aboard as they progressed down the river did not discomfort her. The whole process was exciting.

Paul, in the stern, was alert to the flow of the river over its bottom rocks, and banks. There were many large rocks all around them and he picked their way through waves and rocks with respect for his passenger's enjoyment.

"There's Eddie's 'Bathtub,'" Paul said.

She saw his paddle reach along the side of the boat to point at a huge rock ahead on their left side. The water noises grew loud as they approached, and she could see the water curling around the giant boulder with great force. "What do you mean?" her voice quavered slightly with fright.

"That's where Eddie Minton's kayak got broken on the big rocks just where the water moves the fastest. He had to bail out and swim in the whirlpool with a dislocated shoulder.

"Don't worry," he called out. "I know just where to enter the big eddy behind the rock. Let me paddle and you give me a big reverse stroke on the left side when I tell you. It's like a carnival ride. Raise your left hand. Yeah. That's the side you need to reverse when I tell you to do it."

They drew ever closer to the 'Bathtub,' and the roar of the water got louder. This was far bigger than the other rapids they'd experienced.

They moved faster and faster toward the maelstrom. She could feel Paul paddling hard. Then they went over a giant drop of rushing water as Paul yelled, "Now Dahlia. Hard left reverse!"

She dug her paddle in and the boat spun into a tight left turn into the calm water behind the rock. The boat bobbed quietly now, and the river was certainly rushing by faster, and was higher than their boat. They were nestled in the eddy that was like sort of quiet hole in the water.

They both vocalized. "Wow!"

"Yay!"

"Good job Dahlia. Was that fun?"

"Oh my God. It vas vonderful. Thank you for showing me. I feel that you saved my life. How is Eddie now? Did he recover from his injury?"

"Yeah. He's fine. Eddie is COC's head of accounting, and he runs the river almost every day."

They ran several rapids and Dahlia grew more confident. Paul pulled to the shore at deserted Riverside Park. She wrestled her wet suit off to pee in the lady's room. It was a smelly wilderness toilet, like a big outhouse, but her empty bladder made her more comfortable, and she looked forward to their next rapid as she buckled her PFD and helped paddle away from the shore.

Paul surprised her by steering for shore into a thicket of flowering bushes. "Bring your paddle up into the boat," he directed.

As the bow pushed into the bushes, she realized that they were entering a hidden branch of the river. The trees were thinner here, so the sky was brighter. Transparent water revealed pebbles and green algae flowering just under the surface.

"Let's rest here a while," Paul said as he stood and stepped out of the boat into the shallows. He offered his hand to steady Dahlia as she stepped out next to him. She gave him a shy smile.

"This is the most beautiful spot I have ever seen."

The nearby river murmured. Bird songs trilled and the slight breeze was welcome. She spotted some blue and gold flowers at the edge of the water and stooped to get a better look.

Paul kneeled in the stream next to her and then sat back on his heels. "I like to come here. This is my favorite chilling spot. I don't think anyone else knows about it. This is the reason I love COC so much."

He splashed to the boat, dragged it to shore, and flipped it over. He sat on the boat and leaned back. He looked so comfortable that Dahlia had to join him. They lay on their backs quietly and took in the smells, sounds and sights around them. They did not talk at first and spent a quiet half hour. Their silence was warm, and they both slipped into a light sleep with late afternoon sunlight brightening their eyelids.

After a time, Paul said, "My parents live in Alabama. I have a brother living in Charlotte. His name is Mitch, and he is doing very well. He owns and operates a secondhand furniture and consignment store.

"I'm sorta the black sheep of my family. I save my salary and try to live simply. The money I get this season will last me all year. This is my second season at COC. I cooked all last year. Mostly on the line but sometimes I baked and did general cooking for clinics, staff, and the daily specials. I liked working in the kitchen"

"Yes. I know about Charlotte. That's in North Carolina, yah? How long does it take to get to Alabama from here? How far is Alabama?" The cadence of her voice was slow as she formed the words into English from her native German.

"Huntsville is a six- or seven-hour drive from here. It's even further from Charlotte to Huntsville. Do you have sisters and brothers?"

No but I have a lot of cousins. Mostly on my father's side of the family. I am an only child. When I get home, I hope to work for an airline. My English is good. Yes?"

"Very, very good," he replied. "Where did you go to school?"

"After high school I attended a hospitality school where we learned about hotel, restaurant, and amusement company management. How about you?"

"I graduated from Huntsville High school four years ago. I did a lot of construction work as a laborer and carpenter in high school – mostly for my dad. I've done a lot of other jobs but guiding rafts is my favorite. I do it here at COC on my day off sometimes. Waiting on tables pays about the same but it's steady. Sometimes guides wait all day and don't get a trip. They make their money from tips too."

They were both twenty-two years old.

She nodded and they spoke intermittently, getting to know each other. She would have to leave the country in October to go back to her real life in Berlin.

She said that her mother was a "*haus frau* with lots of friends and community activities. Mine dad is an architect."

"Cool," said, Paul. My mom and dad both work. Mom sells insurance. She's a certified financial planner and gives investment advice. She is why I have money in the bank. Dad is in construction. Sometimes he's employed and sometimes he free lances. He let me help him every summer when I was in school, so I know a bit about carpentry, and I can do plumbing and electric work too."

They returned to the river after a time and enjoyed the miles on the water, as the solitude, and peaceful mountain scenery that unfolded around them. Paul never tired of it and Dahlia was beginning to love it.

Two weeks later, on their third trip down the river, they took two one-person duckies. Paul led and Dahlia followed him through the rapids. She felt empowered as she successfully managed her duckie. This was her first time in a boat alone. They pushed though the bushes to their secret spot, flipped their boats, removed their

PFDs and flopped down to rest. They were hot and the sun was strong this day.

Dahlia was sweating and pulled down the big center zipper to expose some skin to the slight breeze and reclined. Paul, right next to her, unzipped his wet suit to the waist slipped his arms and torso free of the garment. He too lay back, facing her.

Her baseball cap was off, and he could see a slight sheen of sweat on her forehead. Her short hair looked a little spiky and damp in the warm air. He thought it gave her a pixie look.

Without thinking Paul reached out and touched her zipper. She looked hot. His finger lingered on the zipper, and she looked at him with wide eyes. She licked her lips, and he touched the zipper again with two fingers and ventured to lower it an inch more.

To their mutual surprise, she sat up and pulled the big zipper all the way down and slipped the garment half-off just as Paul had. Her beautiful breasts, freckled shoulders, and back were covered with goose bumps. To Paul she was the most amazing sight he'd ever seen.

Paul was not a virgin. He had girlfriends in high school and had first done the deed in the back of his prom date's Ford Explorer. The tailgate window was up, and the back seats folded. They had spent a happy night rolled up in a comforter in the back of the truck. They'd broken up the next afternoon when he'd suggested a ride in the Explorer. Paul was not sure why she had blown him off but, gentlemen that he was, he took it like a man and never saw her again.

Dahlia lay back making no attempt to cover herself. She filled his eyes and then his hands as he began to stroke her smooth skin.

Her armpits were unshaved in the European fashion that many female COC employees followed. He saw that her body hair was sparse. She had never used a razor. Her leg fuzz was very soft and blond. They kissed gently at first then with rising passion as the intensity of their situation took hold of them.

She had been naked under the wet suit, and they were soon rid of the heavy garments. She tugged at the damp waistband of his boxers and now they were together like Adam and Eve in a wilderness Garden of Eve. She noticed that Paul was a beautiful man in the nude. His body hair was dark, and it accentuated the muscles of his chest and abdomen. Paul's skin and hair were soft to her touch.

They made love twice. Rough and quick the first time. After a rest, they entwined again and made love on top of her duckie with delicious care and deliberation.

Their kisses were passionate and their words breathless. "Oh Paul. This is vonderful. Ve are like a natural man and voman."

Paul murmured an assent and, in a few minutes, came up with a question. "Dahlia. What about, uh – protection. I mean you're not ready to get pregnant. Are you?" His voice rose slightly as he managed the question.

"Don't vorry Paul." Her accent was showing itself. "My mum gave me a supply of der *Morning After* pill in case... You know, in case I made love mit somebody."

She smiled at him. "I never thought I vould need them. I'm not a virgin but I don't make love very often. Not for two years maybe." Paul fell in love.

Their stay in the secret garden was almost too long. The power company dam at the head of the river shut down at eight o'clock most nights and they got back to the take-out just as the river water receded to its dammed flow rate. They dragged their gear to the designated drop-off area, changed out of their wet suits and sat on the riverbank, dangling their feet in the clear cold water for a few minutes while they snacked on Paul's crackers and split the last coke. The staff dining room had closed at seven. They could have bought snacks at the store, but he didn't want to face his fellow employees with the taste of Dahlia fresh on his lips.

They hitched a ride to staff housing by hanging out near the bridge. It was fully dark when they were dropped off. Paul kissed her lightly on the lips and they went off to their separate buildings to sleep and dream about paradise.

The Caverns Outdoor Center, COC, had grown from humble beginnings over its quarter-century existence. The heart of the business was located on an eighty-acre parcel of land in the

Chattahoochee National Forest where Georgia Route 72, the Appalachian Trail and the Clancy River cross paths.

Despite its distance from any city, rafting, restaurants, and boat rentals served thousands of people every day during the season from April through November. Many customers came from Atlanta. The Motel, the Restaurants, the Outfitter Store, the Instruction Department, and Guided Travel departments each generated substantial revenue, but the guided raft trips down five nearby rivers were the biggest moneymaker

The mountain elevation here kept the nights cool and the days mild. The woodlands were beautiful now; they had recovered from destructive clear-cutting that previous generations had wrought. Rivers and streams abounded. None were more beautiful than the Clancy River.

Paul Hunter was now a pain is the ass so far as Cornelia K. Johnson was concerned. She ran the restaurant operation. She managed it, and had created it from scrub pine, sweat, and wisps of her dreams. So, Paul had to go. God damn it! She liked him, but she heard that the staff, including cooks and shift managers, were complaining about him.

"He stinks like a dog," Archie told her. "Paul even looks dirty, and he refuses to follow the rules," the breakfast manager had whispered.

"Which rules?" Cornelia asked. She was surprised because Paul was always polite.

"He won't give customers water when they're first seated. He insists on asking them if they'd like something to drink... they only get ice if they ask for it. Paul says it's better for the planet to conserve water.

"Then there's that crap about aluminum pans poisoning us. It's something about light metals causing Alzheimer's and memory loss. He won't recite the specials if they're cooked in aluminum pots."

"But all our pots are aluminum!" said Corney.

"Exactly," said the manager. And I can't budge him. He talks about this stuff at shift meetings. I either look weak or the servers begin to grumble. They may be joking to tease either me or Paul. The situation gets worse every day."

Corney thought back to other conversations over the last months. Complaints from the kitchen might have been motivated by jealousy over Paul transferring from line-cook to server. Some cooks tended to look down on people whose *only job* was to deliver the beautiful food they created in the hot and confused kitchen. Paul was a traitor. The head chef had warned her that Paul was too generous with salads and bread and that he seldom served a dessert.

"Corney, you got to shape him up. He's costing us money."

She nodded. Paul Hunter had to go.

Serving food was something Corney knew well. It was a sales job and took a special mindset to do it well. The best waiters brought a measure of happiness to their guests along with food and drink. They made them feel welcome and anticipated their needs. She herself, a retired English teacher, had waited on thousands of tables over the years.

Cornelia was a formidable woman. She was not tall but her gray eyes, mobile eyebrows and sun-darkened complexion were striking. Her confident bearing and direct gaze made her stand out in a crowd. On her days off, particularly in the shoulder seasons, she sometimes guided rafts full of vacationers down the wild rapids.

When she and her husband, Rolf, started their ever-burgeoning white water rafting business 24 years ago, they'd bought a failed 16 room motel and general store near the river. She became the foodservice person. She had started it as a hot dog stand on her summer vacations from teaching. They called it the Take-Out Restaurant because it was located right next to the rafting Take-Out Beach. At first it was literally a hole in the wall with a counter and a sliding window.

Rolf had been a philosophy professor at the University in Athens, Georgia. He had vision and a love for white water river activities. Cornelia was a willing and able partner. Their first seasons at COC were short as they coincided with school terms for themselves as well as their three children. Financial success led them to leave conventional education and devote all their energies to the company and a full-time life in rural Clancy County. They often spoke of the business as being a kind of Experiential Education. They had two other partners in the first years, but they bought them out and continued the business as a couple when it became their only occupation.

People were hungry when they finished the six-mile downstream paddle from the upriver put-in. Very busy from the start; the foodservice operation had grown into three successful restaurants. The simple motel and raft rental business had become a monster, attracting visitors from all over the planet.

Their enterprise had grown mightily. Food was provided in huge quantities now. The company still offered lodging and now sold high-end outdoor sporting goods. COC was a magnet for Olympic-quality kayak paddlers and canoeists. Many of these expert paddlers worked as raft guides, store clerks, waiters and in the many clerical positions created by success. Many of the athletes were supervisors and managers and also taught White-water leadership and paddling skills. Classes, styled as clinics, ranged from a weekend to two weeks in length. Students lived in dorms and obtained their meals at the restaurants. Lunches were usually packed out to the rivers where the actual teaching occurred. Other popular activities such as rock climbing, mountain biking, fly-fishing, and hiking were taught too.

The newest restaurant was named Corney's Cavern Restaurant. The original take-out restaurant was now a 120-seater with wonderful views of the river. The hot dog stand moved across the river and was reached by a sturdy steel bridge. Its sign proclaimed it to be THE Hamburger Stand. The bridge was only two years old, and it had made Corney's Cavern, a fine dining, multipurpose, establishment, possible by opening parking and service areas that could be reached by food suppliers' trucks.

The restaurant had a large porch overlooking the gardens, the cavern mouth, and scenic Swan Pond. The covered screened porch was the most popular spot when it came to seating the large numbers of diners that arrived daily during the seven-month season. The Swan Pond sparkled, flowers danced in the garden breeze, and the mountains did scenic duty in the background. Spring twilight brought out fireflies. At night the cavern entrance was lit, and the river's murmur could be heard in the background.

The full moon on the mountain horizon was a glorious sight from the porch.

In early spring and late fall it was often too cold for people to sit outdoors, so inside tables filled early. Clinic students had their own dining room. The staff ate in their own cafeteria. The kitchen serviced all three dining rooms.

Cornelia Johnson was not thrilled by her nickname, but she realized that it was good for business and came to think of herself as Corney.

She regarded herself as tough. Tough enough to deal with the riffraff that sometimes gravitated into the foodservice business. She was fit and liked to explore the forest by herself, at her own pace. She wasn't afraid of anything in the forest. She could bluff a bear, chase a bobcat, or kill a snake with her walking stick.

She always carried a short-barreled .38 caliber revolver on her person. Usually, she had it in a holster under her arm, hidden by a shirt or vest. She had a permit and knew her limitations. If she was in a swimsuit or dressed in a manner that made concealment impossible, the pistol would be in her backpack or purse. This weapon was not for snakes or four-legged animals. It was for use against deranged humans she might encounter in the forest or elsewhere.

Her dad had been an army officer and had taken pains to teach her about weapons and shooting. Carrying a weapon was a habit of twenty years – since her friend Carmen had been assaulted and left for dead on the AT. Carmen had survived but the event had altered her life and she no longer enjoyed the wild country and hiking.

Corney and Rolf never locked their doors at home. No one in the area did - even when away on vacation. But since Carmen's attack they had bought two shotguns and kept them loaded in childproof, quick-release wall clips behind their front and bedroom doors.

Corney mulled over the Paul problem.

The trouble, she thought, is that Paul isn't liked. I might be able to get him work as a raft guide or maintenance worker, but he'll be a source of grief for us as long as he is around. She decided to bite the bullet and fire him when he came in the next day. She sighed and rubbed her weathered face.

COC – Saturday, May 6

It was one o'clock in the afternoon when Paul got word to go to Corney's office. She greeted him with a serious face and gestured for him to sit in the wooden chair next to her desk.

"I'm very sorry but we have to let you go Paul," Corney told him.

He was floored. "Why…" His face was clouded, and tears began to flow.

"Paul," she patted his hand. "You know that I like you, but your coworkers have been complaining about your work attitude and your hygiene. Corney's face was rigid, and her skin was mottled red. Her face seemed to glow.

"I'm telling you straight out that this is a final decision. Rolf and I have thought about putting you in another position but in the end, we agreed that you must go.

"You have until the end of the day to get your things out of staff housing. We'll make an announcement this evening at the restaurant that you have left for personal reasons so this will not be any kind of negative thing on your work history." She sat straight and looked at him with what she hoped was a stern but understanding look.

Paul tried to speak in his defense but just stammered. He saw from her look that there would be no reprieve. This was no warning. He was just shit-canned, like the jerk he was, he thought – blind-sided and without a clue.

"Paul. I know that you don't have transportation so I will have my son, Joe, give you a ride to staff housing to get your stuff and he'll take you anywhere, within reason, you'd like to go." She handed him an envelope, which he pocketed without looking at it.

"S'okay Corney," he choked out. I'll be okay. He was mad as well as sad. It was just good manners speaking – not his heart.

Paul didn't have many things. His possessions suited the life he'd chosen. His vehicle, a 1979 Volkswagen bus, had a pop-up top and was outfitted as a camper. Trouble was that it had died on him and the mechanic in town wanted a thousand dollars to rehab the engine and transmission. So, the vehicle sat at the mechanic's in Clancy. He used it as a storage shed on wheels to hold his tent, spare paddles, and such. His needs at COC were simple. His clothing needs were mostly tee shirts and shorts.

Corney watched him depart. Funny she mused. He didn't smell as far as she could tell. His grooming seemed good. She had the sinking feeling that she'd made a big mistake. She should have warned him. Archie the restaurant manager had reported counseling sessions, but she didn't have a lot of faith in him.

She sighed and trudged up the hill to the restaurant. She smelled a foul odor when she paused at the back door. She looked down and realized that she had doggie doo on her left foot. She spent five minutes scraping, rinsing, and drying her shoe.

Corney's face was red and her brow damp as she squared her shoulders to face the rest of her day – happy that she wouldn't be stinking the place up.

Paul didn't need much time to put his stuff into boxes. He took his boat from the staff racks and loaded it into the back of Joe's pick up. Joe sat patiently while Paul left a note for Dahlia.

> Dahlia,
>
> They fired me today. I'm not sure why.
>
> I'll get settled in a few days and then come and see you by the bridge, on Monday Morning at ten o'clock.
>
> Love Paul

Joe dropped him off in Clancy at his mechanic's shop. He had his final check for $650.00 from Corney and almost a thousand in cash, buttoned in his shirt pocket. His mom in Huntsville was keeping ten thousand dollars for him - his life's savings. She worked as his financial planner but, of course, didn't charge him the usual fees. He didn't feel broke - just at loose ends.

The mechanic promised to fix the Volkswagen by Tuesday and accepted a $500.00 deposit. Paul could have had the repairs made at any time he wanted but he had been taking pleasure in the perceived economy of not having a vehicle. Now he looked forward to getting it running right again.

Paul took his tent and camping gear from the vehicle and fit his kayak into the space. His boat would remain inside the bus for now with most of his clothing. He wasn't much of a reader, but he had two favorite books: Euell Gibbons' Beachcomber's Handbook and Thoreau's Walden Pond. He took them figuring they would keep him occupied while he thought things over.

He walked two blocks to the downtown diner and ordered a meal of all-you-can-eat pancakes and coffee.

His tip was generous. The waitress let him use the phone as it was three o'clock and the restaurant was quiet.

"Mitch." he had said to his brother's answering machine, "I've lost my job with COC. They let me go and I'm not sure why. Maybe I didn't fit in well enough. Anyway. I'm okay. I'll be camping out for a while." I'll call ya in a coupl'a days and let you know my mailing address. Anything comes up leave a message at the Crossroads General Store. Look up the number. See ya."

He walked to the Clancy taxi company's office and asked for a pickup in front of the Piggly Wiggly Grocery store at four o'clock. The grocery was in sight, and he walked over and shopped carefully for camp supplies. He had enough to last him for about a week.

The taxi arrived as he walked out of the store with a cart.

He loaded his supplies in the trunk and asked the driver to go to the auto repair. Once there he added his tent and camping gear to the groceries in the trunk of the cab and gave directions to his chosen campsite on Route 72.

He had no big plan really. He thought he could just camp in the National Forest near COC and his lover. He knew that he needed a plan, but he was tired and emotionally drained when he unloaded everything on the side of the road. He'd plan tomorrow.

It took him another hour to climb the hill three times with tent, camping gear and groceries. He left five gallons of water in bottles hidden near the road to retrieve in the morning.

He had a ground cloth, a six by eight-foot tent, and a log to sit on. The awning-flap on the front of the tent protected his cooking stuff from rain.

He coiled a fifty-foot length of nylon cord and tossed it over a branch 20 feet off the ground to hoist his food in the air where coons and other animals could not get to it.

He had a can of cold beans for supper and crawled into his tent to rest. It was getting dark on this troubling day.

He dreamed of Dahlia. She was lying in his arms on a big mattress under an open sky. She was weeping and he comforted her.

COC – Thursday, May 7

Paul woke at first light and systematically stretched, to loosen his body, before he rose to pee in the rear of, what he now thought of, as his camp. He was on top of a 200-foot high, rocky, and totally undeveloped hill nestled in a curve of Georgia's Route 72, a curve so sharp that vehicles had to slow to ten miles per hour.

The wooded top was not more than one hundred feet in diameter. This was a very private site with interesting views. Paul had been here before and knew that a few feet from his tent he could clearly see Corney's Cavern Restaurant, the cave entrance itself, The Swan Pond, Corney's house, the bridge over the Clancy River, the rafting reception building and, in fact if he circled the edge, he could see the entire COC compound.

He used his lightweight propane stove to heat water for oatmeal and instant coffee. He sat on a rock and passed the morning hours watching the comings and goings at the Outdoor Center.

The cooks and wait staff showed up at six a.m. They smoked at the back door of the kitchen for a few minutes. Clinic guests and staff came next, coming for breakfast before spending time on one of the area's rivers or lakes.

Rolf was observed as he walked from his house to the rafting center. Paul judged that he would be leading rafting trips today – an activity he loved. He told staff every chance that he got that rafting was the center of the operation and that everything else was in support of that core business.

Paul saw Corney go to the cave and sit in its shady entrance for a few minutes before striding off to the admin building. As the day progressed, Paul saw the pageant of people pursuing work and pleasure. Saturday would be a busy day for everyone but himself.

Since Paul could see things from his campsite, people could see him if they knew where to look. He was not spotted for a time but then the word passed quickly, and everyone knew where to look by noon Sunday.

Corney resented his presence. "He should go away," she declared to herself and anyone else who would listen. She fretted but Rolf refused to take any action. "Leave him alone," Rolf advised, "He'll be gone when the cold season arrives, if not sooner." It was hard to stir Rolf up.

Paul missed his job. He wasn't exactly bored, and he very much looked forward to hooking up with Dahlia on Monday. He sat and brooded about the unfairness of life. He thought that he'd been doing a very good job and was totally blind-sided by Corney's bombshell. He decided that he had to be very polite when talking to or about her. But his resentment was high and he thought about revenge.

He walked to the general store, on Route 72 to use their pay phone. He spoke to his mom and dad in Huntsville. He told them that he was on vacation and camping near the Appalachian Trail. He promised to keep in touch and see them in November when the season turned cold. He left a message for Mitch. "Mitch. Come and see me. I need your help with something. I'm camping on that hill over COC that I showed you last time you were here. Come soon. I'll be here every night until I see you."

Paul was always observant and early in his first season he'd noted a stream of messengers at the close of business each day as zippered, vinyl bank envelopes filled with cash, checks, and credit card receipts were carried to the Corney's Cavern Restaurant back door. Each department would place the day's receipts in the bags. These vinyl bags would be taken to the safe in the manager's office upstairs. He knew that the Accounting Department would pick the envelopes every weekday morning but on weekends and holidays the pouches would accumulate.

There was no armored car service so far out in the woods and area banks would be closed on holidays. So, there was no point in taking the envelopes out of the safe. On long weekends, they would sit for the duration. Paul pondered the situation and looked at his wallet calendar to ponder October. He found himself thinking about how much cash would accumulate over a busy weekend when the banks were closed.

The Center would close for the season on Wednesday, October 31. The five days beginning October 28th would be the annual Paddlers and Peddlers Festival. Devoted COC fans would plan entire years around this weekend event. It would be insanely busy and in past years November first and second would be declared an official COC employee holiday.

In the winter the outfitter store, its huge mail order department, and The Take-out Restaurant would stay open with limited hours of business to match the area's annual tourist hibernation. Staff housing would be closed. The last weekend of the season was always the biggest of the year.

Paul was awakened from a nap by approaching footsteps. He had been dreaming about Dahlia. Their mattress was covered with a leafy fringe of green currency, fluttering in the breeze just like leaves. They were sitting up, naked and eating bowls of ice cream.

As he rolled over, he heard Dahlia's voice.

"Paul," she called. "Paul. Is it you?" Her shadow fell on the tent fabric."

"Hi Dahlia!" He jumped up to zip open the flap and she fell through it into his arms weeping.

"Don't cry honey. It's okay. You're okay." He stroked her; very much aware that he was wearing his boxer shorts and had an erection. He had to pee so bad he could taste it.

"Wait here a minute," he whispered.

"Okay." she whimpered

He stumbled out and put on his sandals. In a moment he was at his pissing-tree and wished that it was further from his tent. He resolved to change his ways. He wiped his face with the damp cloth hanging by the jug of washing water and brushed his teeth.

He was back in the tent in about a minute to see Dahlia slipping out of her shorts and work shirt to present him with parts of his dream.

They kissed, cuddled, stroked, and joined so hard he thought she'd split in two. But she was up for it. After the first round they lay in each other's arms. He told her, "I don't know why I was fired. I guess somebody didn't like me. I had no warning. Corney just fired me, but I don't want to leave because I don't want to lose you."

"Oh Paul. I'm so glad you're here." She kissed him passionately and they made love again. Eventually they got a little sore from the prolonged contact and just lay still, linked in sex but not willing to break the contact.

"Paul. Do you need money? I can help if you do."

"No Dahlia. I'm okay. I'm getting my bus fixed and will still have enough cash to last for the year. Maybe next year too," he said smiling at her pretty face so near to his. I have money at home too, so I'm okay. I love you for caring about it though."

"Sveetheart. I think it's Archie the restaurant manager. He's been saying dat you stink like dog shit and dat you are not a good waiter or cook. He's glad you are gone."

"Dang! That's rough."

"Paul. You don't smell bad. I promise. I love da way you smell. And you are such a gentleman. I tink that peoples like you very much. It's just that bastard Archie. He's da one who stinks."

Paul slapped his forehead. "I know what he's talking about. It's a joke. I stepped in dog poop a few weeks ago and didn't realize it. I think it was Corney's old dog. He hangs out by the dumpster looking for scraps and he must have taken a crap there!"

Oh Paul. He's so awful."

"Naw. Don't worry about it Dahlia. I have a plan and you are in on it."

She looked at him wide-eyed and naked. Her short haircut had a couple of twigs in it. She said, "Tell me. Tell me now!"

Paul wasn't dressed either. He had a twig or two in his beard and his feet were dirty. He held her tenderly. "Well. I haven't worked out all the details yet, but I want to stay right here for the summer and teach you to kayak on your days off.

"In the fall you must go home, and I want to see my mom and dad in Huntsville. Then, my dream is to send for you. But I want to assure you that my intentions are honorable, and I want to make sure that I can provide a home for you..." Paul blushed, "and our family..."

"Yeah Paul. Dat sounds wery gut to me." Dahlia was crying and could not speak further. Her German accent was very pronounced when she got excited

"Dahlia. I want to marry you but let's not rush. I want us to know each other better first. I'm an odd duck, but I do what I say I'll do, and I want to do everything in my power to make you a happy woman."

Paul quit talking while he was ahead, but he was thinking, *Let's make love on the river, play in the woods, and sleep in on your day off.*

Dahlia was quiet now. "Paul. I have to go now. To work. Tonight, I get off late and I'll be too tired. Ve meet tomorrow, yeah. By der bridge at ten o'clock?"

"Yes, my love. Call extension 191 when you get to work and order kayaks for the noon bus. We'll gear up when we meet but I have to be your guest since I don't work there anymore. Let me take care of you now." He brought a bar of soap, a jug of water that he had left to warm in the sun, a washcloth, and towel. He dried her off when she had finished her abbreviated bath and helped her dress. He picked the twigs out of her hair and gave her his comb.

"Soon Dahlia, I will buy you the biggest and best bathtub you can imagine." She gave him a dazzling smile, a hug, and a kiss goodbye. Then she was gone.

If Saturday was a bad day in his life, Sunday was the one of the best. He glowed all day as he went about his camp chores, napped, and watched from above.

The evening lights came on at COC as the sun went down behind the mountains. Paul saw the soft lights on the restaurant's dining porch. He could hear the murmur of diners and the faint clink of silver. He saw a low light come on at the Johnson house as either Rolf or Corney went about evening chores.

There was a streetlight illuminating the bridge and it sparkled on the water rushing underneath. The path through the garden outside the restaurant had foot lamps from the entry to the parking lot. Corney's Cave was lit with low wattage spots giving it a real presence in the landscape. Paul appreciated the beauty of the place and felt sad to have lost his job.

The exterior lights, all on a timer, all went dark 30 minutes after midnight.

COC – Monday, May 8

It was dark and deathly quiet at two a.m. Paul silently picked his way through the edge of the woods toward Corney's Cavern Restaurant's back door. He was on the Appalachian Trail that wound its way through COC. He stepped off the trail and went to the back door of the Restaurant, just 100 feet away at that point. He tried the handle and found it locked. He methodically tried every door in the building and found them all latched against easy entry. *No problema*, he thought.

He quietly and quickly gained access to the nearby roof at the second-floor level. He was able to use a board to make a narrow footbridge, lifted from a little pile of debris that was left over from a recent landscaping project on the side of the hill. The steep terrain made it so easy that he was able to walk rather than crawl. The board was only slightly slanted. The first window he tried was unlocked. He noted that the AT was just a few feet away.

Moving like a cat, stopping to listen every few minutes, he determined that the building was empty. Staff members were known to sleep on the carpeted upstairs lounge if they had to start early. The wooden building seemed to breathe and sigh as compressors started and stopped at odd intervals.

He went to the kitchen and took a steak knife and a pair of rubber gloves. Then he made his way back upstairs to the office.

Gloves on, the cheap lock yielded easily to his knife, and he was in.

After carefully listening again, he used the knife to disable the side window lock. He did this in a way that was not obvious, and he thought that it might never be noticed.

Shielding his tiny pocket flashlight, he began to examine the shelving edges, doorframes, and the bottoms of the chairs and the desks. He found the safe combination taped in three different locations and memorized it. 13-69-13-78. L-R-L-R. He didn't need to write it down. Unlucky cocksucker, unlucky old-timer he thought... Got it!

He listened for a long time before making his next move. He sat on the floor and leaned on the safe. He dialed the numbers and the safe opened silently. Inside was a jumble of zippered blue and red vinyl, bank envelopes. He opened a thick one and saw neat bundles of credit card slips, checks, and cash. He noticed that instructions for changing the safe's combination were conveniently stowed in a pocket inside the door. He memorized the simple procedure.

Paul pocketed ten dollars and put the bag back before locking the safe and spinning the dial back to the number 78 where he had found it. "Let's see if these ten bucks will feed me for a week he whispered." He returned the rubber gloves and steak knife.

After slipping out the disabled office window he returned to his plank and crossed back to the side of the hill. He stowed the plank behind some bushes and slipped back into the woods.

Corney was also out and about that night. She sat in the shadows near the cave entrance. Some people thought that settlers looking for white kaolin had dug it, but she believed that it was an Indian artifact. She felt a spiritual connection.

She often patrolled the woods around the center by night. She heard owls fly. She was aware of certain staff trysts, of families of raccoons, shy foxes, and other nocturnal animals. In fact, she considered herself nocturnal. She heard soft rustlings in the woods as Paul drew neigh, but she did not move a muscle. She wanted to see what it was.

Paul stopped every few steps to listen and watch. He saw a shadow on the far side of the cave entrance and stopped completely. It was only fifty feet away.

It looked like a rock shadow where there should be no rock. A half hour passed, and the shadow rose up. He identified it as Corney standing still by her cavern's mouth. His blood curdled and he lowered his face slightly to present as little reflected light as possible.

Corney was tired. She looked all around, saw nothing in the dark woods and decided to call it a night. She was there just for the pleasure of being out in the night and hoping to spot wildlife. She would creep into bed and, if she got lucky, Rolf would not wake up. If she were unlucky, she'd have a good bed workout before sleep. She was an early riser, but her calendar was blank in the morning and a sleep-in would be welcome.

Paul restarted his day at seven a.m. with a huge bowl of oatmeal. He made PB and J sandwiches and packed them in his small dry bag along with a couple of apples. He arrived at the COC Outfitters Store and shopped for Dahlia's beginner kayaking needs. He would rent gear for himself, as he would not be recovering his stuff from his bus the next day.

The bill for Dahlia's stuff was $150.00 and he spent another 50 bucks for a large, black waterproof backpack. He packed her spray-skirt, a helmet, and nose plugs in the backpack and went to the bridge to wait for her. He didn't get boat shoes for her because she'd already bought them on her own. Paul had shopped carefully and was excited at the prospect of gifting her.

Dahlia was on time and curious about the backpack. They sat on a bench under a large tree, and he went through the bag with her. She squealed, "Paul. It's too much. I should pay for my own stuff."

"Dahlia. It was so much fun for me. Please don't say anything but thanks."

"Thanks Paul." She gave him a peck on the lips and a little hug. They were a little shy in public. He didn't think anyone paid much attention to them and he was surprised when Corney strolled by and nodded a reserved hello.

He made Dahlia try the helmet, the neoprene vest, and wet skirt on. It all fit well, and he explained, "When you sit in the kayak the neoprene skirt fastens to the boat to keep water out; even if you should roll over upside down."

She saw that the hem of the skirt had a sturdy cord that would fasten into a flange around the cockpit opening.

"The vest will keep you warm from splashing. The days are getting warm now and we won't be needing wet suits."

She nodded her understanding. Men and women and families were walking around the center preparing to get on the busses. Many wore the spray skirts and they didn't look so ridiculous to her now that she had her own.

"Paul. People here seem to all know you. Some think you are crazy to be camping up there, but most admire you for being, how do you say, 'in their faces.' Archie's mumbling about you. I don't like him.

"They all know that we are seeing each other. The girls talk to me now and ask questions about you. They are much friendlier"

"What do you tell them?"

"Everything," she joked with a giggle.

"Naw. Do you tell 'em that you love me yet?"

"I think they know. They seem to like me better. I'm like a person instead of der German chick. There is a policy now of sharing tips when there are bussers and dishwashers working. I'm making more money and I'm saving to buy you a present."

He gave her a smile. He couldn't remember when he'd gotten a present from anyone other than his family.

"Dahlia. About today. You already know a lot about kayaking and paddling from being on the river with me. You know to never stand up in moving water and, if you fall out of the boat, you keep your feet downstream to fend off rocks. You know to hold on to your boat and paddle with one hand and to use the other for swimming.

"Kayaking is way more fun than duckies, but we have to go to the practice pond for a while before we go on the river, and I'll show you the rest."

"Paul. Should I be nervous?"

"No Dahlia. Not even a little. We'll start in the practice pond, and you won't go on the river until you think you're ready."

"Gut," she said.

They stood in lines to register for the trip, get paddles and gear for Paul and board the bus. Their rented kayaks were strapped to the roof with an assortment of rafts, duckies, and canoes. There was no charge for the gear as Dahlia was an employee.

The bus to the put-in was full, as usual, but soon enough they were walking, carrying their boats the hundred yards through the woods to the practice pond. There were other students and teachers there and they watched for a while before starting.

Ken Kaster, an experienced kayaker was teaching a twelve-year-old girl the ropes and they sat close for Dahlia to get the lesson too. "Hiya Ken. Do you mind if we watch for a while?"

"Hi Dahlia and Paul. We're doing Eskimo rolls. This is Lottie. Lottie can my friends watch?'

Lottie grinned at them. "Sure. Watch this!" With that she leaned over and capsized her boat on purpose, bringing the paddle parallel to the hull. A quiet moment passed with Ken standing close, smiling at Dahlia, who clearly saw the girl move her paddle to the crosswise position and pop back out of the water. "Hey Ken. How was that? I used my hips and head and hardly used my hands or arms."

"Perfect Eskimo roll Lottie. Tell Dahlia how to do a wet exit."

"Well. If I go underwater and want to get out of the boat, that's called a wet exit, I hold the paddle and this exit strap on the front of my skirt. I pull the strap hard, hang onto the paddle with the same hand, and straighten my legs. I hold my breath until I'm clear of the boat. I never stand up in moving water. I hang on to my bow rope with the hand holding the paddle while I swim to shore. Legs downstream to fend off rocks."

"Great recitation Lottie." Her instructor beamed.

"Ready to try it, Dahlia?" asked Paul.

"Sure. Thank you, Ken and Lottie."

"Thanks buddy," Paul addressed Ken. "Say hi to your wife and don't believe everything you hear."

An air hi-five and he took Dahlia a little distance away to show her the ropes: how to get in and out of the boat, how to fasten her spray skirt and how to paddle about. "It's so tipsy Paul," she noted, struggling to stay upright and still.

"Here's the thing Dahlia. If the boat were more stable it would also be hard to do Eskimo rolls and to brace in the rapids. It's a tradeoff but it makes the boat fun too. You'll see."

Soon Dahlia was paddling with authority, tipping and righting the boat with ease and feeling at home. "Paul. Let's get to the river. I can't wait." Never was there a more willing student.

"Let's do it," he said, and they retraced their steps to the put-in area for the Clancy River. It was deserted. Paul asked her to sit and have some food before they set off. They each wolfed down two of the PJB sandwiches and a bottle of water.

"Follow me Dahlia. Go where I go, and I'll pick out the best routes for your maiden voyage. We'll stop at River Park for a restroom break and, if you wish, take a break at our special spot too.

So it was that Dahlia learned to be a paddler. She made not one mistake. She paddled hard when Paul did, rested when he did and watched him doing low and high braces where the river demanded.

They made a pit stop at the river park and then headed for their secret garden. Paul," she said. "I haf my period and I don't vant to make love now. Could you just kiss me and hold me for a while?"

He held her tenderly. They rested in each other's arms for a long while kissing and hugging. In the peaceful garden the world receded.

"Dahlia. Will you spend the night with me? I know you'll need work clothes for tomorrow, but we can get what you need at the store if you like."

"Yeah sure. Dat vill be nice. But all I need is a shirt and I already have one in my locker at the restaurant"

She was clearly getting emotional. "Paul. I am in love with you, and I don't care about anything else. But I vant to stay mit you ven you are ready to leave here."

"Okay Dahlia. Me too."

She hugged him tightly and they rested in preparation for the rest of her first kayak run.

At the end of their run, they returned the borrowed gear and dined at the crowded Hamburger Stand. No sex that night. They were bushed.

They bathed each other in the morning while sitting on a log. Dahlia said, "Paul. I vant to love you like this." She kneeled in front of him as he sat on the log and took his instantly erect penis into her mouth and slowly worked with her fingers and tongue until he came in a rush.

"Oh my God Dahlia. I didn't know it could be so good."

She placed her hand on the back of his head as they wiped each other down and peered into his eyes.

"Paul. I am a happy woman. In a few days I come back, and I'll teach you more. Thank you for the best days of my whole life!"

They agreed that she would come to him in a few days - probably Thursday morning and they'd hang out for a while.

CLANCY – Tuesday, May 9

This was a very interesting day for Paul. Later in life he would recognize it as a grand turning point. In the moment, he just felt like he had a lot to do.

He set out with a couple of sandwiches in his backpack and hitched a ride to Clancy. As usual, the first car that came along picked him up. He didn't know the driver well. Jim Bob Bryson, the man at the wheel, knew him and that he was living in a tent over COC. "Wow dude! Why are you staying there?"

"Well Jim Bob. I have a lot of time and I love to paddle. This is the greatest place in the world. I'm going to town to get my bus out of the repair shop, so I'll be able to carry my boat strapped on the roof rack.

Jim Bob dropped him off at the garage and his bus was ready. He paid cash and had working wheels and his gear again.

He had heard that he needed a bank account to apply for unemployment benefits and that was his first stop. But he hit a hitch. He needed an address to give the bank and couldn't use his employee box at COC. So, he went to the post office across from the bank and rented a box – number 1378. That was the same as the last four digits of the safe's combination. He would have thought that the number was a sign if he was superstitious.

Now that he had an official address, he was able to open a bank account with the $650.00 check that Corney had given him.

He left his bus in the bank's parking lot and walked to the Unemployment Office because he felt a need to walk. He felt good that his ride was properly licensed and insured. The inspection sticker was brand new. The owner of the garage had done the state inspection free.

At the state unemployment office, he learned that he would qualify for two hundred and forty dollars per week for thirteen weeks as long as he was looking for work. After that time elapsed, he could reapply. He didn't show any emotion but was ecstatic at the generosity of the State of Georgia. The money would appear in his bank account as a deposit every week he filed a form describing his job search.

Then as he was leaving, he read a notice on the bulletin board showing classes at the community college. He saw that, although it was between semesters, there was one class that was available – private watercolor lessons by a local gallery just down the street.

He ambled over to the gallery and met Elizabeth Aubeson, the owner, a woman somewhat north of her fiftieth birthday. Her work was on display. He liked her nature studies and landscapes so, on a whim, he signed up for a class on Tuesdays which would be the same days he needed to visit the employment office.

Elizabeth accepted a $50.00 deposit, gave him class outline, a little book about painting, and a color wheel. Paul was to make some sketches of things he'd like to paint and bring them to class. The fifty would be used when she went to Atlanta on Thursday. She promised to buy him watercolor paper, brushes, a few colors, and supplies. Elizabeth said that the supplies would probably be a bit more, but she would collect the balance on Tuesday.

Paul looked for a job on the way home. He shopped at Piggly Wiggly and got an application for stockman but got no encouragement. The gas station where he filled up did not need help and the general store near his camp also did not need help. He would have to do an ongoing job search, but he was not well motivated. For the rest of the summer, he asked for work whenever possible, but it was just window dressing for his benefits qualification. There was no work available. Good, he thought. He had a lot on his plate - good stuff.

His very last stop was at the town jewelry store where he bought a diamond ring with a gold band. It cost two hundred fifty dollars and it gave him a warm feeling- almost a glow as he thought about presenting it to Dahlia.

Paul had about five hundred dollars cash left in his pocket, six hundred and fifty in the bank, and unemployment compensation would add to that every week. He was relaxed and comfortable. He was ready for the next step.

Paul pulled into the parking lot near Corney's office. He had to talk to her. As usual she was not in her office, and he was reluctant to walk all over COC looking for her. So, he resolved to wait. He opened all the windows in his bus and sat in his folding chair between the built-in bunks, reading his new art book. He examined the color wheel and began to think about what kind of drawings and paintings he might be able to do. This was happy work for him, and two hours slid away.

Corney was letting herself into the office as Paul stepped out of his old red and tan bus. Her first thought was that he was here to beg for a job, but he surprised her.

"Hi Corney. Thank you for the check. It was a nice severance. Could I talk to you for just a minute?"

"Sure Paul. Would you like to sit here on the bench outside?"

"Yes please." He felt that she must feel safer outside where people could see them. She was clearly on edge, and he didn't blame her.

"Look Corney. I forgive you for what happened. I'm sure it was my fault, and I don't want my old job back." He gave her a big grin and she couldn't help herself – she smiled back at him, and they both felt some tension receding. "On the other hand, if you need a trained guide on the reserve river guide staff, I'm available."

"No Paul. Thanks. But, as you know, we always have more people than we need. I don't think that will happen. But you never know. I'll pass the word to Rolf."

"I want to tell you that I just got my bus back. The reason I'm camping here is because I had no other place to wait for it to be repaired and I needed to be close to Dahlia. I don't know if you know it, but we've become great friends and I want to stay close to her until she goes back to Germany."

Corney nodded. She had heard that they'd been going about together, and she'd seen them a couple of days ago, under a tree, with their heads close together. She could read signs.

"Corney. I need a big favor. Could I please park my bus somewhere at the center until the end of the season? Anywhere would be fine. I need it to store my boat and I'll probably need to use it a few times every week or so. I'm taking art classes from Elizabeth Auberson."

She said, "Paul. You made me nervous hanging out so near, but I understand it better now. So, the answer is yes, subject to Rolf's veto. Where are you thinking?"

"Out back by the boat repair and warehouse building."

"Okay." I'll let you know if things change. You will leave; when…?"

"I guess I'll leave after the Guest Appreciation Festival. I'll want to sell my boat and a lot of junk I've accumulated."

She understood. Staff members could buy boats at a discount, and they got a good price when they sold them at the end of the season.

"Is this your bus?" She ran her eyes over it and thought it looked good. There was a clean-looking red kayak mounted on a homemade roof rack. "Nice rig. Is there anything else?"

"No Corney. I think you may change your mind about the things you said to me someday, but meanwhile, I'm okay and I thank you very much for tolerating me up there."

They shook hands in a rather formal manner, but they resisted the urge to hug. She did not spot any flaw in his grooming. He looked just like the other hundreds of paddlers they'd employed over the years. He was slightly shaggy but wholesome.

Paul was fuming after left Corney. He had hidden his feelings while talking to her, but he was hurt and angry. He stomped his way back to the tent in an unusually bad mood. He was worried about his ability to spend the summer without having a real job to keep him busy. He was angry.

COC – Thursday May 11, 2000

Paul was at loose ends, so he decided to take a day hike on the Appalachian Trail. He was interested in exercise, but he was even more focused in the route and terrain.

During the hours he spent around camp he had begun to dream about stealing a great deal more than the ten dollars he'd taken on his test run at two a.m. the previous morning. A lot had happened to him but his desire for revenge and the fun of planning kept him teasing the idea along.

The main elements he thought about were striking fast, leaving no physical evidence behind, getting rid of the loot and facing the world afterwards. He knew that the police would come and that he would be a suspect.

He worried about Corney more than anything. She was so smart, and he knew for sure now that she could be in the woods at night. If he waited until the Guest Appreciation Festival on the last weekend in October, there would be a huge amount of cash in the safe and he could probably delay discovery until a week after Dahlia left for Germany. Her ticket was reserved for October 25th. She had promised to be home for her father's sixtieth birthday party. He would take her to the airport on the 24th and they would have a night in Atlanta.

Paul set out with water, apples, PBJ sandwiches, and a flashlight in his daypack. The AT wrapped around the foot of his hill, very close to his camp. He turned north so that he climbed the trail as it converged with the back of the restaurant at the second-floor roofline. He saw that the plank he'd used was still in place behind grass and bushes. He walked slowly and did not stare too much but rather concentrated on the contours of the path. If someone saw him, it would obviously be the kind of day hike that many staffers took. On his big night he'd turn south toward Route 72, but he wanted to know the way in both directions.

He made good distance considering that the way was steeply uphill. He ate at two p.m. and husbanded his water. He turned back and walked quickly downhill in the waning afternoon so that it was quite dark as he walked the final hundred yards toward his campsite. Rather than going to his tent however he continued south through COC property and hiked the scant mile on Route 72 to the General Store. He bought a sandwich and bottles of water and went back to his tent.

He arrived at his camp home in total darkness and was able to feel his way along without using his light. He meant to do this sixty times between this first night and zero hour when he planned to strike. He would know more about that portion of the Appalachian Trail than anyone in the world.

COC – Thursday, July 6, 2000

Paul rose from his sleeping bag at two a.m. He dressed in black including his one pair of black socks. He slipped out of the tent with his new black backpack and crept down to the Appalachian Trail stopping to look and listen every few minutes. It took him an hour, but he was finally satisfied that there was no one out this night. He paid great attention as he circled the cave entrance looking for Corney.

She must be sleeping he thought. When he got to Corney's Cavern Restaurant he found the back door unlocked. Someone goofed and forgot to lock it he thought. He checked the entire building and once he was satisfied that he was alone, he took a pair of rubber gloves from the kitchen and made his way outside. Always alert, he got back on the AT and climbed to his plank's hiding place. He used it to get onto the roof and enter the office.

He opened the safe and stole ten dollars from the fattest envelope. Reversing course, he was back on the AT in three minutes with the plank restored to its usual place.

He stealthily made his way back to his tent. He estimated that he'd been gone an hour and a half and that he was in the restaurant a total of fifteen minutes. His actual time in the office was only two minutes. The plank took too long, and he mused about finding a quicker way to get to the roof. If he could jump to and from the roof, he could do the safe and everything else in an even shorter time. The problem was checking the building for sleeping staff. He'd need to enter quietly.

Paul repeated his Breaking and Entering routine many times over the summer and early fall. He got better and quicker and soon figured out how to do it without the plank. There was a sturdy electrical meter and other utility boxes on the back wall near the office window. He learned to use them and their piping to scale up and go in quickly and quietly.

To leave the office, he jumped to get to the road and became adept at hitting the ground in a tucked position and rolling. If there was someone in the building, he felt, he'd be out and gone before they could investigate the little noise he made.

On the occasions when he found sleepers in the building, he continued his activities with extra care. The crime he was planning was well rehearsed.

Paul developed a routine that filled the hours when he was not obsessing about his planned crime. He and Dahlia went paddling on Mondays. She would spend the night camping with him and go to work from the tent on Tuesday mornings. If the weather was foul, they would have an early dinner in town and drive to the triplex movie house in on the highway near Clancy.

He thought that his art lessons were fabulous. He loved Elizabeth's carefree approach to her craft. "Wet and sloppy," she called it: full of happy accidents.

Paul was more careful but soon developed a painting theme and a style. He painted his vision over and over again with many variations.

He portrayed a male face in the shadowy branches of a tree in the upper left corner looking down on the angelic figure of a woman or girl kneeling in the near right of the picture. The man was faint, almost a part of the tree. Dark and light. Man and woman. Rough and smooth. He would often include a riverbank or pond.

His paintings were impressionistic except for the eyes. He masked the white paper where the eyes would be and later dry brushed or inked clear lines and colors, with the whites of the eyes so sharply defined so that the beings seemed to float off the page. Although the woman was clearly kneeling, her figure was just suggested by little curved lines with a lot of white paper left bare. His women seemed to glow.

He sketched leaves and plants between lessons so that he had a collection of elements to bring to the finished paintings. To his surprise he loved painting and it occupied much of his thought process. By the fourth week, in mid-August, Elizabeth had taught him *plein aire* techniques so that he could do complete paintings for her evaluations on Tuesdays.

He shared his painting endeavors with Dahlia but not his dreams of grand theft. He didn't want to risk involving her and feared that his dark intentions might affect their relationship.

Brother Mitch arrived at the tent unexpectedly on a Sunday morning. He caught them making love, but they were all fine with that.

Mitch was taller than Paul, had darker hair, and was very fond of women. He and Dahlia hit it off right away. Mitch told them that he had to return that night to open his shop for business on Monday morning. That was fine with the lovers. It meant lying in each other's arms Sunday night and Monday on the river.

They had begun to read to each other from Thoreau's *Walden Pond*. For Dahlia this was a way to perfect her already good English. Paul sometimes helped her with pronunciation.

Paul thought it was a validation of his lifestyle and it was a lesson in living to both. He knew Elizabeth better by this time and told Dahlia, "Dahlia. This book about living simply reminds me of my art teacher and her husband.

"They do exactly what they please every day. He writes books about nature and submits articles for the Atlanta paper. They don't pay him much, but he loves it. She paints all day. Her earnings cover her shop expenses, but the thing is that they have no personal bills. They live in a tiny trailer parked in the woods. They have no rent, no mortgage, light bills, taxes or anything. They are almost like Thoreau."

CAMP – SUNDAY, July 16, 2000

Dahlia left the brothers to report work just before noon. They sat on the ground in the shade, leaning back on the logs Paul had dragged to the campsite with a herculean effort involving rope and levers.

"So. What's up little brother? What do you need? The answer is "yes." Paul gave Mitch a serious look. "I'm so mad at Corney and COC that I could spit!" He told Mitch the story of his season. He detailed his unjust firing and of his successes in other areas. That he was okay financially, but he wanted revenge.

"Mitch. They are leaving thousands of company dollars virtually unprotected every night and I intend to pick them up on October 30th and I need you to transport and launder the money for me."

"Huh. You've got to be kidding." Mitch's mouth dropped in surprise. "You're talking about jail time bro. big, long jail time and we could both go to the slammer.

"And it's a nasty crime too. Not something you'll ever be proud of. Besides how much money is involved?"

"Mitch. C'mon. The insurance company will pay. COC will be inconvenienced but they'll get their dough back."

Paul added this kicker, "I think there will be over fifty thousand in cash. But, however much it is, I'll guarantee you that your help will take less than six hours and will net you $10,000.00 in cash. If I get as much as I think I can, your 50 percent cut could be way, way bigger. What will that do for you?"

Mitch fell silent for a time. Then he answered, "My business is all right. Word of mouth and a little advertising have only gotten me so far. With ten thousand dollars I can put up a properly lit electric sign that will more than double my business. Trouble is that I don't have the money and my credit as a single man who doesn't own a house is not that strong. With that much money I can take myself to the next level.

"Give me details Paul."

Paul told Mitch about his nightly rehearsals, his instant access to and egress from the safe, and his thoughts of Mitch just driving by COC on route 72 at three in the morning on October thirtieth, Sunday night-Monday morning. "Mitch the crime can't be discovered until that Monday afternoon, and it might not be discovered for days.

"I'll toss a black bag into the bed of your truck, and you'll be away in a flash. Home by dawn. You will have at least a full day to dispose of the evidence, the zipper bags and credit card receipts.

"We can't throw the cash around, but you can work it into your business receipts over a few months. I'll take my half and launder it myself. I'll need you to hold it for a while. I'm in no hurry. I have plenty of cash to take care of myself for a year or two, and my paintings - I can sell plenty of them. I never knew I could make money so easy.

"So, Mitch you'll hold on to my half until I'm ready for it." Paul spoke as if Mitch was already in the plot – as if he'd said, "yes I'll do it."

Mitch nodded. "I'll do it. three a.m. – Monday. I'll gas up at home and there'll be no trace of me in Georgia.

"Only thing is, if one of us gets caught, we each have to promise to take the fall. I won't rat you out no matter what happens."

"I'll never tell bro. I'll take the fall if I have to."

They hugged and patted each other on the back to seal the deal.

They talked about the heist in detail, but the plan was so simple that they both understood it perfectly.

Main thing was that Mitch would get his truck to the bridge over Route 72 before three a.m. and wait as long as necessary.

The bridge in question was less than a mile downstream from Paul's camp. He would bring the contents of the safe it into the truck's bed by three a.m.

He envisioned himself napping afterwards and then spending a few last days on the river after the caper. He wanted to hang out there as long as he could so that the crime would be discovered before he left. He was sure that he would be questioned and didn't want to leave until then. Otherwise, they might think of him as a fleeing felon.

"Mitch. Y'know that at least twenty people have the combination to that safe. I don't have any reason to know it but I'm going to peel the combination off the shelves and chair bottoms and put them in the backpack. Perhaps they won't realize that anyone with half a brain could learn the hidden combinations and open the safe.

"Good idea Paul. Let's make a point of not telephoning from here on out, unless there's a change in plans. I'll gas up the truck a few days before the thirtieth and make sure that it's up for the trip. It's pretty new, and I don't expect any problems."

"Got to go now. See you in ah - he paused to think... about three months."

They hugged in parting.

Paul crept into his tent to sleep. And dream. And scheme while he waited for Dahlia's shift to end.

Dahlia walked into the camp a few minutes before midnight. "Big news," she breathed, after a warm kiss hello.

"What's up?"

"Wait. I have to pee first. Get ready for bed and I'll tell you all about it." She left for her special place while Paul stripped to his shorts and laid down atop the sleeping bags they had zipped together."

"You'll never guess what happened!" She announced as she scooted into their nest naked.

"They fired Archie. They caught him dipping into the restaurant cash register. Apparently, it has been going on since the beginning of the season and there's a lot of money involved. But I don't know how much."

Paul was very, very interested. "How do you know all this?"

"They had a meeting of the whole crew at the restaurant and told us he was gone and why. Later there was an all-departments manager's meeting and they all seemed upset. Archie was not popular but now they hate him. He caught the first shuttle to housing and took off in his car quick. No one knows where. Corney said they'd have to change the safe combination and re-key the doors."

Paul absorbed all this but, with the first burst of news out of the way, Dahlia wanted to get on to the main course of their evening together. They had a huge portion of loving including the ardent oral sex which she had initiated for them soon after they became lovers.

As they finally drifted off to sleep Paul thought about Dahlia's bombshell. He had three months to try and recover from a combination change. He'd have to think about taking the higher road and not do the theft. Ah well, maybe it's for the best.

Paul missed seeing Corney and Rolf's visitors on Monday morning. He and Dahlia were on the bus, heading for the river when two men in slacks and long-sleeved shirts climbed out of their tan sedan. The men were insurance agents in for the annual review. The most interesting questions discussed were the theft coverage and the possibility of rate decreases if certain security procedures could be adapted.

Alarms, a heavier, more modern safe, armored car services, employee screening, safe combination changing practices, a reduction in the number of people with access to the safe and other measures were reviewed. They asked about ex-employees who might pose security issues. Several names were mentioned including Archie whose malfeasance had been recent.

Later, as they reviewed the meeting, they agreed that many of the items were possible and good, but not for this season. They decided to work on the issues of improved security in the spring before opening day 2001.

Corney showed Rolf a catalogue of security equipment for banks and stores. They opted to order an exploding dye pack now to plant in the safe for unwary robbers. It came in a zippered, red vinyl bank bag. Unfortunately, they had to share its secret with everyone who had the combination. They had already changed the safe's combination and shared the new numbers as necessary. The system included a telephone alarm feature that would activate automatically if the dye pack went off on COC property within reach of a telephone device which would be located near the office area.

CLANCY – Tuesday, July 18, 2000

Elizabeth and Paul were becoming painting buddies as well as student and teacher. They enjoyed sitting and painting together. She had just framed his very first painting, labeled it Man Watching Girl and had it tagged for fifty dollars. He was very proud of joining her on the gallery wall. This was Paul's sixth lesson. They had discussed his project of the day. He meant it to be a woodland stream with rapids and rocks. No people were planned for this painting.

They chatted as he began a light backwash for the picture. "There are several places I love to paint she said. Not only the mountains. I love the seacoast and rivers of every kind. My husband George and I try to make trips for my painting and his writing four times a year. Winter, spring, summer, and fall."

"Paul. Have you ever been to Swan Harbor, North Carolina?"

"I have heard the name before. Where is it?"

"George and I went there last fall. We camped at the River campground and I loved it. The town of Swan Harbor is so tiny and quaint. I think I would consider retiring there if my grandchildren wouldn't be so far away."

Paul had been wondering where to go when November rolled around. He rejected Huntsville, Alabama for no good reason. He'd graduated from high school there and had not had a very prosperous or happy life. He drifted until he discovered white water paddling sports in the mountains of Georgia and North Carolina. He wanted to live on the water.

"Is there water Elizabeth? In Swan Harbor."

"Yes. That's one reason why we liked it so much. There are wetlands, rivers, bays, and the ocean. Camping there was wonderful in the fall – it's probably hot in the summer.

"It is almost like a little island surrounded by the River, the Intercostal Waterway, and the Bogue Sound. There are a multitude of little islands creating Hawkins Bay that is like the town's front yard. The town has water views everywhere and the streets go uphill and downhill and you give glimpses of the water

"And don't forget cozy and quaint. It's a real town with some tourism in the summer. I want to go back again."

She showed him some photos, clippings, and junk that she had in her gallery, collected during her trip. He was transported by the pictures the old buildings, homes, and shops. She showed him a marsh painting she had hung. There wasn't much paint on the board; just some light strokes of pastel colors and dry brushed curves representing water and grasses. He thought it was elegant

Paul stopped at the library and poured over some maps and camp directories. There wasn't much material available on Swan Harbor, but he liked what he saw and began to dream of life after COC."

Corney noticed everything. She had seen Paul leave on Tuesday mornings and disappear for most of the day. She wandered toward the restaurant but veered onto the AT and disappeared from the view of COC staff that might have been watching.

When she arrived at his camp she called his name a few times to be sure he was gone. Then she began to go through his things methodically. She was puzzled by the rubber gloves tucked into the pocket of a pair of black jeans. She found no documents of any kind. She presumed, correctly, that he kept them in the bus. She did find his portfolio of sketches and watercolor studies as well as a few more finished works. She liked what she saw.

She noticed a strong smell like a bear's den when she first got to camp. It puzzled her for a moment and then realized she must have been close to his latrine area. She did not look for it but concentrated on the tent area and his cooking supplies. She saw that he was spending very little money on food and admired his parsimony.

Corney was a rich woman, but she did not lightly spend money. She and Rolf had done well in life, her family had left her a fortune but the best thing they had ever done was to engineer an employee buyout at COC. They were rapidly becoming minority owners while employee's 401K plans bought them out. The buyout would be complete at the end of 2005, and they would withdraw completely soon thereafter. The interest on her CD's exceeded their salaries.

But meanwhile she enjoyed her snoop. She didn't learn much: just that Paul was artistic and probably kept his papers in his bus. She'd have to check that out. She already knew his Tennessee tag and vehicle identification numbers. A glance at her watch told her it was time to go to work. She liked to arrive at the restaurant after noon to be able to visit both the night and day shift managers whose work hours overlapped between noon and two p.m.

Since Archie had been fired, she worked his job as Corney's Cavern Restaurant manager as well as Foodservice director for all restaurants. She could set her own hours but she took her duties seriously. Everyone knew she was the boss of bosses and employees reckoned that she even bossed Rolf who was Chairman of the Board of the corporation and CEO.

Paul returned to his camp and knew that someone had been in the tent. His portfolio was lined up precisely with the tent wall and he clearly remembered tossing it casually when he'd left in the morning. Also, there were two small, dried leaves inside near the entrance. He recalled pausing as he left that morning to pick up a few leaves so that the place would be neat for his return. Dahlia? Corney? Who???

He would depart carefully from now on. He wanted to know who had been there.

COC – Wednesday, July 19 – Two a.m.

Paul left his tent after a six-hour nap. He was wearing black, as usual, carrying his black backpack. He wondered if he should get a black bandana to wear under his broad brimmed hat to further reduce the shine of his face in the faint light of the night. He believed that his night vision was improving as his time in the woods increased.

He patrolled COC looking for Corney or, in fact, anyone out and about. By three a.m., seeing nothing out of the usual, he was in the second-floor office. As he had expected the old safe combination didn't work. The dial was left on the number 78.

He could see that Corney had taken over the office. Her stuff seemed neater than Archies.' He checked the usual places for a taped combination but found only the old numbers in place. He felt that there was time, but it irked him a little that he did not have his old super ability to just open it at will.

As an exercise in focus Paul spent a lot of time listening as he returned to his tent. He wondered if he could do the trip blindfolded using the sound of the river and feel of the trail as guides.

The rest of July and August passed pleasantly for Dahlia and Paul. He was painting a lot and happy to share his work with her. She was always there for their Monday paddling dates. She spent Sunday nights and Tuesday mornings with him as well. A regular pattern developed that accommodated her work schedule and his town day for painting with Elisabeth and errands.

Dahlia turned out to have a talent for making wreaths from twigs, evergreen bits and things found in the forest. She would sit weaving them for hours while Paul sketched her from every angle. Sometimes he would clothe her paper images in flowing robes, sometimes she would appear partially clothed and often just as she really was, in shorts, sandals and a tee shirt.

Paul usually just ate from cans, reluctant to build a fire in the national forest. He thought that there might be a rule against fires or permits required to camp as he was doing. No one ever challenged him. Dahlia usually brought treats that varied his diet and gave her more than beans as well.

Besides Elizabeth on class days, and Dahlia, when they could arrange it, his main social outlet was on the river. His former work mates from COC accepted his dedication to kayaking. The fact that he no longer worked at the company was not a problem. No one ever asked him about unemployment. COC knew about his drawing unemployment since they got monthly reports on all COC former employees who applied. Officially they were against former employees applying but since there were so few it didn't affect their costs.

Once or twice a week he'd go out on the Clancy. It was almost like a club or play group. The kayakers would gather to play in the best rapids. They applauded each other's stunts and achievements.

He was invited to go to other rivers with his pals, but he didn't feel comfortable in leaving COC, his mission, and his stuff. He returned the kayak to his bus after each outing, always keeping the vehicle locked. But when he went out in his boat, he hid his keys inside the curve of his bumper.

Corney caught on to his ignition key hiding spot so, on the second Wednesday in August, she boldly let herself into his vehicle in front of God and anyone else who cared to look; not that it mattered since no one noticed her.

She was surprised to find that his August bank statement from the Citizens Bank showed a balance of $2,950.50. There were regular weekly deposits, but no checks had been written. She saw that the deposits were his unemployment system checks. She learned that he was a saver and not a spender. "Good for him," she muttered. She found receipts from Elizabeth Auberson, a tiny book with some phone numbers and not much else. Paul seemed to have a thin paper trail. She already had Dahlia's address and phone numbers in Germany from her employment records. She saw an address and telephone number Mitch Hunter. She thought he might be a brother or other relative and, not knowing why, she made a note of the name and number.

Her most interesting find was a brochure and some photocopied information for a town in North Carolina called Swan Harbor. She made a hurried note of the names and addresses and put everything back where she found it. The whole process took ten minutes. She returned to her office in the restaurant to think about what it all meant.

Boy Corney, she thought to herself, *you are something. You're a nosey old woman who does things she should not be doing!* She was angry with her bad behavior. She stuffed the note into her desk and went to tour the kitchen, going about her legitimate work again.

COC – Tuesday, August 1, 2000

Dahlia and Paul woke to the singing of birds and the rustle of the warm summer morning. They made their morning toilet and settled down to read and snack the morning away.

Paul said, "Dahlia. I have something to ask you." He reached under his laundry and took out a little black box. He kneeled beside her and opened it up so that she could see the sparkle of the diamond. "Dahlia..."

Dahlia sat up in surprise, tears streaming down her face. "Oh Paul. I didn't..."

Paul was terrified but he struggled on, "D-Dahlia. I want you to wear this. I want to marry you but, if it's too soon, just tell me. I'll wait forever."

She sobbed. "Paul. I was afraid I'd have to ask you." She giggled and he too began to laugh.

"Paul..."

"Dahlia..."

Words failed and they just hugged and snuggled on top of the covers. She held her hand up to try and see the ring and it made her so happy that she wanted to share her joy.

"Dahlia. Let me tell you about my big plan. But first let me ask you, can we live here? In the U.S. I mean, or do we have to go to Germany."

"Paul. Your people will be my people. Ve must live here. Not at COC, but here in the U.S."

"Good. I'll go anywhere you want but there is a town in North Carolina that is attracting me, and I want to go there in the fall after the season is over. I know you need to see your father and mother in October."

She nodded. "Ya but I vant to marry here. Maybe they will be able to come for the wedding."

"Great. But Dahlia, I want to pay for your ticket here when you come back to marry me, and we'll find a way to make a good living and be happy either in Swan Harbor or anywhere you want to go. Okay?"

"Okay," she sighed. "It sounds vonderful."

They napped, made sweet love, and she left for work. Paul went to his vehicle carrying his empty one-gallon plastic water bottles strung together. He looked like a peddler. He drove to Clancy to claim his unemployment compensation, check his mailbox, take his art lesson, and shop for groceries.

Elizabeth had a nice surprise for him. "Paul. I sold your painting. Your work is attracting a lot of attention." She handed him $30.00. His percentage.

She had previously framed several of his best pictures and suddenly they were selling as fast as he could make them. At first, she priced them at fifty dollars but because the demand was good the prices swiftly rose to one hundred dollars and then one hundred and fifty. That seemed to be the top price for the people who came into her gallery. Her primary source of income came from selling prints of her own works. They shared the revenue from Paul's paintings. Paul got 60%

It would turn out that by the end of October, Elizabeth had sold thirty Hunter paintings and held an inventory of twenty more. Paul had received over fifteen hundred dollars from her. His bank account was prospering, and his lifestyle was virtually free.

He smiled at the money and his smile got even broader when she said, "...and I want to sell some more. I have a place in the window for your biggest painting and I'll frame a few more for inside the gallery if you like."

"Yes Elizabeth. I like very, very much."

She thought that he looked wonderfully excited, and she imagined it was the appreciation she was showing for his newly minted talent.

"Boy am I motivated. Let's go to work." He began working on a new variation of his theme. The girl was wearing a halo made from twigs that looked just like one of Dalia's wreathes.

"That's nice Paul," Elizabeth said. "Why not stop right there. It is understated but anyone looking at it will fill in the blanks with their own image. Automatically. They won't think it needs more paint. As you know too much paint can make the work look muddy."

Paul was a little doubtful but stopped and washed his brushes. As soon as the paint was dry, less than fifteen minutes later, Elizabeth had the work mounted on a foam board. She had a clear plastic corner frame kit that just snapped on over the foam board. The piece looked finished and polished as it hung in the window with a tag for $100.00.

"Elizabeth. Guess what? I'm getting married. The girl in the painting is my fiancée, Dahlia. She said, "Yes" this morning and you are the first person I've told."

"Congratulations Paul. Can you bring her by so that we can meet?

"Well, she works six days but I'm sure we could come on Monday."

"Okay. Come to the trailer and we'll have dinner. George will be happy to have company there." She gave him a warm hug. She was a tall and trim woman and felt very youthful to him as his hand rested on her waist.

She smiled at him, and he felt very happy.

Paul stopped at the county's freshwater station spring outside of Clancy. The water flowed from a pipe fixed into a cliff on the side of the road. The spring's overflow was carried away by concrete channel made for the purpose. He rinsed his bottles and filled them one at a time. He had been doing this since he'd gotten his bus back and it represented a real savings over buying drinking water at the general store. The burden of carrying the containers to his tent was less than from the general store because he unloaded the bottles from the bus and left them behind a roadside bush near his camp. Thus, he didn't have to carry them so far.

Dahlia came to the tent after midnight but was too tired to talk. They slept close, breathing the same air and soothed by the gentle breeze and katydids singing in the woods. He felt the engagement ring as he stroked her hand.

Teeth brushed, breakfasted on cereal and fruit with milk, too early to even think about going to work. She was a full-time server now, making more money than a busser and, truth be known, working harder too. He told her about the sale of his painting.

"Dahlia. I told Elizabeth that we are going to get married. She was very happy for us and can't wait to meet you. She's invited us to come to dinner on Monday at their home. The trailer in the woods."

"Yeah. Dot sounds nice. We've never been to anyone's house together before." What time do we leave? Vat should I wear?" Clearly Dahlia was ready to socialize and so was Paul. It would be refreshing to be with other people.

"We need to leave here at six o'clock on Monday to get there before sunset and we must carry a flashlight to walk back to our car. It's not very far to walk but Elizabeth said it can be very dark."

"Everyone at work likes my ring, Paul. They say congratulations and we should go the end-of-the-month staff party on the twenty-fifth of August - the last Friday of the month"

"Okay," he said. He had heard the party noises on certain nights and sometimes felt left out. He wanted to go to please his Dahlia.

CLANCY, Monday, August 7, 2000

This was another of the special days in Paul's life. They got to see Elizabeth and George's home after a busy day on the river. Dahlia was now an accomplished kayaker.

They heard the story of the Auberson marriage first hand over a simple meal which was mostly rice and vegetables, flavored with wild herbs gathered by their hosts. A kerosene lamp provided light. The trailer was warm from the heat of the wood cooking stove.

Elizabeth and George took turns talking about their life and philosophy. They were out of a page in *Walden Pond*. They took turns telling stories about the way they raised two kids without the benefits of television, indoor plumbing, running water or even electricity. The kids had done well in high school and college but, when the time came, they couldn't wait to leave home.

Elizabeth and George did more than make a living from their efforts. They had just bought the forty acres of beautiful woodland and meadows they had been renting for twenty-five years. They had traveled widely and told the stories they loved through her painting and his writing. Their children seemed on the right tracks. The Aubersons seemed content.

Later, on the way home, after they had followed a footpath and crossed an unsteady log bridge on foot, Dahlia said, "Wow Paul. Elizabeth and George are really special people. I want to live simply too and still be able to do the things I enjoy. But I want electricity and an indoor bathroom when we leave here at the end of the season."

"Are you troubled by this?"

"Dahlia. I love what we are doing but it's just a lark. When you return to marry me we'll have electricity and protection from the elements. Our kids will never want to leave home."

Camping was fun but modern living was better.

Pillow talk. "Dahlia, I haven't told you everything about my finances."

"By the end of the season in October I should have some money saved. My mom has the account papers for my $10,000.00 savings account, and I should have at least $5,000.00 more from this year. It's funny but when I stopped spending money my bank balance went up every week.

"That's not enough to live on forever but it should give us a start. I'm not afraid to work."

"Sweetheart. Thank you for telling me. I bring some money to our marriage too. Let me think. In dollars it should be fifteen thousand and I think my family will give us gifts of money too."

They hugged in the dark and tried to imagine what it would be like. They had previously agreed to marry in the states but that did not fully answer the questions of where and when. They agreed that it would not be here, in the area of COC.

Maybe, they speculated, they'd get hitched in Swan Harbor. If they did the deed within the year, they felt that their parents would all be available to make the trip. Spring felt good to them and they tentatively decided on March 31, 2001.

They both sighed a relief at their new understanding. They kissed and found sleep in an instant.

COC – Thursday, September 28, 2000

Paul was living a double life. Every night he was alone he'd be asleep by dark. There were no telephone or television presence to interrupt and no car or other human noise to disturb him. He would sally forth in the wee hours with a dual purpose.

First, he had to be sure that Corney or other people were not prowling about. This was the more difficult mission. Maybe twice a week he'd spot Corney and would take care to move away from her and then watch until she headed home. The easy job was to gain entry to the office. He'd move from the bank to the footholds on the side of the building, and through the window, quietly and quickly. He wore the rubber gloves he now kept in his backpack. He had never touched anything in the office with naked fingers.

Paul's routine was to check the desk drawers and two drawer file cabinets for information. He was a little rough when he opened the wide middle drawer of the desk. When he lit it with his shielded flashlight, he noticed a slip of paper that had slid out from under other papers, receipts, and such. He saw the word 'arbor.' He slipped the note out and was stunned. His mother's and Mitch's address and telephone number were written down and the word "Swan Harbor." Nothing else.

He closed the drawer and sat, heart pounding, head spinning, confused.

Damn! What could it mean? Why and where could this information have come from? Maybe Dahlia had talked about their plans. Why the information on his mom and Mitch? Why anything?

He pocketed the note and decided to think about it later when he was safe in camp. He deliberately slowed his breathing and listened intently for human sounds.

Hearing nothing untoward, he did his usual search for the combination and found it in taped in two places: underneath the desk drawer and on the back of a framed business license from the State of Georgia. He reasoned that as some of the managers who used the safe were back in school their replacements needed a reminder. 55-12-31-77. It was his birthday with the number fifty-five tacked on the front. He successfully opened the safe and took one hundred dollars from the fattest envelope. He felt behind on collecting his weekly grocery money and that this would be his last theft until the big one.

His mood was mixed when he fell into his bed an hour later. He was jubilant over regaining the combination number but troubled by the meaning of the note.

As he reviewed the possibilities, he came across a scenario where Corney was watching him and had invaded his car. It made sense only if she suspected his evil intent.

What could he do about it? After mulling it over he decided that taking the note was a good thing. He had given his mother as an emergency contact on his employee application, but they wouldn't have Mitch's number. It might be a casual thing with Corney, and she'd never miss the scrap of paper. By the time the suspects were being evaluated for the theft he'd be just one of many. He ripped the little paper into shreds and swallowed them with the help of an apple and a cup of water. Much ado about nothing he thought and went to sleep.

The last thought on his mind was the Friday night party scheduled for the next day. He'd see Dahlia there and they might have another night together. The August party had been loud but he'd been well received. He and Dahlia had done some comical dancing together. She was very good, and they'd gotten a round of applause before slipping away into the night.

ATLANTA – October 25, 2000

Dahlia and Paul were feeling blue. They were on the shuttle to the airport after having spent a comfortable night at the Day's Inn. It was their first night together in a real bed with a real bathroom and electricity. That part was wonderful.

They were feeling subdued because Dahlia was leaving and they would be separated by an ocean. Their agreement and understanding were now that Dahlia would spend as much as six months in Germany and return when Paul sent for her but not later than the end of March. Paul promised to write every day even though her letters might be a little delayed depending on when he could change his address at the post office. "Dahlia. I have my passport that I got when I made a paddling trip to Mexico. If it's better for you I will come to Germany."

"Don't vorry Paul. I am yours forever. Just let me know when to come."

They had a light breakfast, and he was able to accompany her to the gate. She had a carry-on backpack, and nothing checked. She had left a few things for him to store in his bus. There was a cashier's check for $5,000.00 in her pocket representing her summer's savings.

The plane began to board at ten thirty and they parted with a kiss and a hug. They both wept openly.

Paul drove to Huntsville, Alabama to see his mom and dad before his planned caper and move to Swan Harbor, North Carolina.

COC – October 27, 2000

It was getting dark when Paul pulled into his parking spot at COC. His ride through the fall colors had been marred only by Dahlia's absence. It was cool. In the thirties he thought. There had been frosts but he liked the cold. The summer's heat was just a memory.

He had stopped for a hamburger and was feeling full but ready for bed. He had a two-a.m. mental appointment to scout the territory and check on things at the office. At this hour all of the restaurant parking spaces were full, and it was obvious that the October Guest Appreciation Festival was in full swing. His plans included moving his kayak and some other paddling gear to the side of the road early in the morning with his For-Sale sign. He had bought it all wholesale in the early spring and would recover most of his eight-hundred-dollar investment.

When he woke, in a sweat, it was a little later than he intended.

He crept about and caught Corney's shadow passing in front of the cavern entrance. He thought that she was heading for home. He followed her and got close enough to hear her steps on the porch and the squeak of the screen door. Satisfied that she would be home for the night he walked to the AT and then to the restaurant on silent feet with frequent listening stops.

As he looked at the contents of the safe, he noticed one bank bag in particular. It was on the bottom and looked thick with loot. The problem was that he had seen the same bag in the bottom position for several days, perhaps a week. He didn't touch it but he thought about it.

Thick red bag. Always in the same position. Maybe it was a dye pack like he had seen on the crime shows that his mother liked to watch on television? He resolved to never touch that particular bag.

COC – October 28, 2000

At a half hour after sunrise, he had set up shop at the side of the road. He had hardly finished wiping his kayak with a rag when he sold it to a guy in a leather jacket driving a big SUV for $750.00. It was a package deal complete with a PFD and paddles. The guy took everything.

Paul was hungry and felt like celebrating with a big breakfast. The Takeout restaurant was packed, and he had to first wait for, and then share a table. To his surprise Corney waited on him. "We're a little shorthanded, "she explained.

He grinned at her, "I'm available."

"No thanks Paul. You know I might be tempted if I didn't have two extra servers due to show up any minute. Thanks for offering."

"You're welcome. Corney. Could I have the two-egg special with grits please.'

"Paul. You know they're cooked in an aluminum pot."

"Of course," he said. "So what?"

She cocked her head and said, "I was told that you didn't want to eat anything cooked in an aluminum pot."

"Not me," he replied. "That nutty idea was Mark Zee's. We used to tease him about it at pre-shift meetings. He said it caused Alzheimer's,'' he laughed.

Corney laughed too. "No kidding. Let me put your order in." She marched off upset about having fired Paul. I was just so wrong she thought. It was that rat-fink manager Archie out to get Paul that had ruined Paul's career at COC. She had no time to think what, if anything, she could do now to fix matters.

Paul telephoned Mitch from the pay phone in front of the store to confirm their predawn Monday morning meeting. There was no debate. "I'll be there for you little brother."

From there Paul drove to town to visit with Elizabeth. He gave her a folio containing most of the finished paintings he'd been accumulating.

"Some of these aren't so good," he told her. "You can edit them if you like or just toss anything you don't believe will sell."

Elizabeth smiled at him. He knew that she hated to throw anything away. He knew too that she would sell most of his work and 'Edit' the rest.

The editing would consist of cutting the bad parts of his work out and pasting the better parts, that wouldn't stand alone, into collages. She then would take the remaining scraps, that others would trash, and paste them together paint side down. On this hodgepodge of paper she would in make a work of art with bold strokes and vibrant color.

If she liked the result she might sell it. In the end, she sold almost everything she could make and threw very little away. She could always add the last forlorn scraps to her slurry when she created handmade paper.

Elizabeth handed Paul a wad of cash. "Four hundred and eighty dollars. It was your best week," she said.

"Thank you. For everything," he said. "You have been a good friend. Say goodbye to George for me."

"You too Paul. " You are the best student I've ever had." She knew that he would not be back next year and wiped away a tear.

He deposited most of his cash in the bank and made his way back to his tent. He felt sad at his impending departure and excited at his upcoming adventures; first to strip the contents of the safe in the wee hours; then to a new life in North Carolina. He missed Dahlia.

October 30, 2000

The hour had come. Paul eased from sleep to wakefulness at Two a.m. It was quieter than usual. As he stepped out into the cold he understood the silence. There was a great low cloud settled in on the mountain. He'd never seen such a dark condition at COC. He couldn't see his hand in front of his face.

The moon was in its first quarter and wouldn't give much light even on a clear night. Dark and quiet, he thought as he made his preparations. Just the way I want it. He donned black clothing and a ski hat that would roll down and cover his face should he feel the need. He made a little mud and rubbed it around his eyes, neck, and ears. He'd look like a coon if anyone could see him.

His challenge became apparent to him immediately as he set out. There was no light whatsoever. He would have to feel his way to the goal.

He got a little guidance from the fog-muffled ripple noises of the Clancy. On a clear night he would be able to hear better. He felt his way off his hill, along the AT and to the rear of the restaurant. It took him much longer than usual.

When he finally got his head through the office window, he heard the rumbly hum of the nearby clothes dryer. Someone was in the building! Maybe it was an employee who couldn't find the way home in the fog.

Paul eased in and wedged the rubber doorstop under the office door just in case that the person using the drier had an office key. There was a barely visible glow of light coming under the door so he took off his jacket and blocked the light in case his own light showed under the door.

The safe opened quietly. He couldn't believe how many zippered bags were stuffed in there. Many more than on the July fourth holiday. His backpack was filled to its limit, and he had to sit on it to get the zipper up. He left the fat, red, zippered, envelope alone on the floor of the safe.

After another spell of listening, he used his pocket light to help him change the combination of the safe to its old setting. 13-69-13-78, reading the instructions conveniently taped inside the door. Now, he thought, I am the only person able to open it until a manufacturer's representative locksmith made a call in a day or two. Longer he hoped.

Light out, jacket on, he eased himself and the stuffed bag through the window. He closed it quietly and prepared to leap from the roof to the AT pathway.

He heard it just before he could make the leap. A scraping noise. He paused, wondering if was an animal. As he crouched, coiled, on the edge of the roof a loud buzz went off behind him. His body responded with an involuntary, explosive jump off the roof. He flew through the darkness.

Crashing into another human being in the dark was one of the worst surprises of Paul's life. He landed, legs bent, ready to absorb the impact and roll. The maneuver turned out to be a big thump into a man who "oofed" and groaned. Arms still wrapped around the lumpy black bag, Paul belatedly recognized that it was the drier's end-of cycle-signal, just as a loud yelp and a grunted, "God Damn It," emanated from the man lying underneath him.

He recognized the voice. It was Archie!

What the hell was he doing here! Thought Paul. He realized that Archie must have fallen in the ditch, perhaps trying to get on the roof.

"You okay," he croaked, rolling off onto the ground.

"Who the hell are you!" Archie snarled. "Jim Bob. Where are you," he hissed out in a loud whisper.

Then he said the awful words, "Is that you Paul Hunter?"

Paul became very fearful. His plan had gone bad. He rolled a few feet away, across the trail and resolved to not say one more word. He snapped the gloves off and pocketed them so that he could feel the ground better. The time he thought was after three a.m. He found a patch of grass and knew where he was. He crept away silently.

When he realized that his tackler was gone, Archie muttered, "Never mind. C'mon Jim Bob. Let's get this done." Paul heard the words, softened by the mists.

The last thing Paul heard from the scene was the bump and scrape of a ladder on the roof.

Dawn was still hours away, but the going was slow. And he worried that Mitch might not have made it in the pea soup fog conditions.

The Clancy was on his right side as he felt his way along the riverbank path. A gentle rain began, and he felt rather that saw that the fog was thinning.

At last, he came to the square concrete base of the bridge. He crept to the side of the road and gave a credible owl "Whoo."

There were two metallic thumps in reply, and he knew it was Mitch tapping the palm of his hand on his door. Paul felt his way toward the sound and found the side of the vehicle. He tossed the heavy black bag into the truck's bed. His rubber gloves were inside.

He clutched his brother's arm. "Mitch. Something crazy happened." I bumped into somebody as I jumped off the roof. He thinks he knows who I am. Said my name. But I think we're good. Leave as soon as you can. It'll be a couple of days before they get the safe open because I changed the combination."

"Okay," Mitch whispered.

"Open your shop at the usual time this morning. Get rid of everything but the cash. Take your half and launder mine for me if you can." Paul was reciting the plan. "Love ya."

"Okay. Me too. See ya."

Some visibility was coming back even as they spoke, but it was still very dark. The pickup lumbered slowly onto the road and away. Silence.

Paul was tired when he got back to his camp. He stripped off his black clothing and scrubbed the black dirt from his face and hands. It was cold and he put on gray sweatpants and a fleece sweater before crawling into his sleeping bag. He fell asleep before he could think about or analyze the events of the night. But he thought, *Attaboy Paul. You did it.*

COC – Monday, October 30, 2000

At nine a.m. he woke to the sound of his name. "Paul! Paul Hunter. Come out of the tent with your hands up. THIS IS THE POLICE!"

"Oh shit! Already! Here we go." He muttered to himself.

"I'm coming. Wait a sec." He crawled to the zippered door, opened it all the way, and emerged into the misty morning head and shoulders first.

"Keep your hands in sight."

He complied and stood to see four police officers pointing their guns at him. They had leaves and mud sticking to their uniformed legs. The whole area was still wet from the fog. Corney stood behind them glaring at him.

He was shaken. He thought, *I could be dead in a few seconds.* His hands and legs trembled. "What's up guys? Was it something I said?" He offered as a joke.

No one laughed or even cracked a smile. The guy with the most stripes informed him, "You, Paul Hunter, are under arrest on suspicion of breaking and entering, trespass, and grand larceny."

"Sir. I have permission to be here. Ask Corney, I mean Mrs. Johnson. And I didn't take anything. Go ahead and search the place. It's all my stuff."

"Mr. Hunter, we have a warrant to search your person, your vehicle, and your premises. Do you want to read it?"

"No sir." What am I being accused of?"

"You'll be told more details when you go down to the station."

"Corney!" he called out. "What's happened? Are you doing this? I thought I was okay here."

"Paul," she called out. "You shouldn't have done it."

"Done what?"

"Shut up!" said the man with the stripes. "You'll get to talk later. You too ma'am." He glared at Corney.

"Where is the money, Hunter?"

"What money? Corney. What is he talking about?"

"You know Paul. Just don't struggle and make them hurt you." She too was trembling and, obviously upset. "Archie turned you in. He told us everything"

Two officers took Paul to the side where he could not talk to Corney. "Don't run. We are going to put your hands in front." The older officer moved Paul's hands to the front and cuffed them together. "Now sir, empty your pockets. Do you have any weapons on you?"

"I don't have any pockets in these sweats. No weapons, Sir."

The cops glanced at each other as if to consult on an unexpected turn of events.

"Lean on this tree while I pat you down."

Paul complied and the officer's hard hands confirmed that he was unarmed.

"We are going to search your camp and your vehicle for evidence. Do you have any weapons in the camp or in your vehicle?"

"No sir."

With Corney watching, they looked over the contents of the tent and examined the entire camp. They turned over logs and looked in his small aluminum saucepan.

"What's this?" The cop held out an Uncle Henry folding knife for Paul to see.

"My camp knife. I bought it at the store here two years ago."

The officer dropped the knife in a plastic bag wearing a sneer of satisfaction. It was clearly a weapon and the perp had lied about it.

The officer held out a sheaf of currency. "Why do you have over a thousand dollars in your shirt pocket?"

"I haven't had a chance to deposit it yet."

"I meant. Where did you get it?"

Corney had edged closer now so that she could hear.

"I sold my boat yesterday."

Corney volunteered something to help Paul. "Most of our employees sell their boats and paddling gear during the festival."

"Yeah." said Paul. "Even the company sells its inventory of boats so they can start fresh in the spring."

"Officer," said Corney, "I suggest you move the tent and see what's underneath it."

The police thought that was a good idea. They pulled the stakes and let the poles fall where they stood. They pulled the entire setup to the side and raked through the ground under the tent. They found a baked beans can label under one corner. "Littering," one of the younger men laughed. They had found evidence of a misdemeanor.

They allowed Paul to don shoes and socks, jeans, tee shirt and jacket before marching him down his hill, through COC, along the AT, through parking lots, and over the bridge. His hair was shaggy, and his beard tangled. He needed to brush his teeth.

There were not many people around to see them, but those who saw the procession stopped and stared. Paul was embarrassed.

When they got to his bus it stood alone since few employees remained in the area. The sergeant demanded the keys. "They're in the bumper in front," Paul informed them.

The entire bus was emptied, and the interior studied. "Nice job on the bunks and shelves," the sergeant remarked to Paul as the work progressed. "Did you do it yourself?"

Paul nodded, feeling disturbed, as he watched them paw through his stuff.

Soon a new plastic evidence bag was produced. Paul's wallet was emptied. More cash, forty-eight dollars, a three-year-old passport, 1999 Alabama Driver's License, an expired health insurance card, his social security card, and a Clancy County Library Card were inventoried. Still another bag was marked to hold his passport an address book, bank statements, unemployment papers and all the receipts and other paper records they could find. Nothing sinister was revealed and Paul was informed that they were taking him away for questioning.

"Hey. Officer Brown. Please lock my bus." The sergeant complied and dropped the keys into the final evidence bag.

"Corney," he pleaded. "Help me with this. What's going on? Please set my tent up so there won't be any rain damage. Tell me what's going on?"

They were sitting him in the back seat of a police cruiser.

She stood, face twisted as if she were in pain and shook her head. "Archie told on you," she said coldly as the door was closed.

"Huh? What have I got to do with Archie?" he said to her as the door slammed shut to prevent further communication between them.

They encountered patches of heavy fog on the way to town. It took two hours to get Paul to an interview room.

As they walked down a long hallway with green floors and tan walls Paul was stunned to see Archie and Jim Bob, handcuffed together in a room, sitting on a wooden bench, as they passed an open doorway. Archie was red. His face, hands and clothing were covered with red paint. Jim Bob's head was down, and Archie was looking away. The sighting took a split second and Paul was past and being led into a small room with three chairs and a metal table – all bolted to the floor.

Sergeant Brown and a man introduced as Captain Myers sat with him and stared him down. Paul lowered his gaze and did not even try to test them until the captain said, "Mr. Hunter. I am going to read you your rights…" When he got to the magic words, "You are entitled to an attorney…"

Paul interrupted him, "I need to make a phone call. I want my attorney here."

Sergeant Brown sneered, "So. Who's your attorney?"

"I don't know yet, but I want to make a phone call. Maybe two."

After a brief discussion they brought a black cordless phone set into the room and said, "Local calls only. You will have to reverse charges on long distance. You have five minutes. They locked him in. He presumed that they would be watching them through the mirrored wall.

Paul dialed the restaurant office expecting Corney to be there, trying to investigate the damage the theft had caused and working with insurance companies and credit card information. He was correct.

"Hello."

"Corney. It's Paul. How're you doing?"

"Fine. What do you want?" She sounded upset.

"Corney. They think I did some kind of robbery. It's not true. I saw Archie here and that Jim Bob Bryson. Archie was covered in some kind of red paint."

"Archie said you were in the robbery with them and that you got away with the loot. The cash."

"No. Just no. Archie has been telling lies about me since the beginning.

"Anyway. I need your help. I know that your cousin Bunny is a lawyer in town. She's probably just two-hundred feet away hoping the phone will ring. I want you to give me her number and call her to ask if she would stand by me just during the next day or so for an hourly fee. I have money to pay her, but I can't spend my life's savings to protect me from something I have nothing to do with."

Silence.

"Corney. Are you there?"

Paul was sweating her answer. If she said no, he'd be at the mercy of a total stranger.

"Her number is 208-7222. She is there. I'm not sure why, but I'll just call her for you.

"I expect she'll come right over, and you can make your deal with her."

Corney made the call to Bunny, then sat at her desk and thought about things for a long time. How in hell had they gotten the safe open? Were any other managers or staff involved? She thought about the accounting department, the various managers and their assistants who would all know the safe combination. The list of possibilities was long.

The safe had been open when she got to the office. She locked it, for no good reason, and then, for no good reason, twirled the dial to reopen it. No dice. Must have miss-dialed, she thought. But after five attempts she did not get it open and gave up. She wondered about the scenario. What had happened here?

There was red paint spray all over the room. She sighed, thinking about new paint and carpeting.

Corney began her own search of the room.

She went corner to corner, checking out the ceiling, walls, drawers, and underside of the furniture. She discovered what the police had failed to notice - the combination of the safe was taped to the underside of the chair and to the underside of the desk.

The police had found the inoperable window lock and faint signs around the office door of a forced entry. She herself had once forced the lock rather than return home for the key. Their security had seemed so simple and safe.

They found lots of fingerprints and would try to match them with the suspects as quickly as possible, which meant within weeks. Finally, stumped, she locked up and took a hike in the woods to clear her mind. She would go back to work tomorrow to get the information the insurance company needed to file the company's loss claim. The bookkeepers were working on the same problem, and she needed to rest her mind.

Paul hung up and a few moments later Brown and Roberts came in without knocking.

"My lawyer is Bunny Johnson. She should be here in a few minutes.

"Can you guys tell my why I'm here?"

Captain Myers wore a white shirt with a pair of sunglasses peeking out of his shirt pocket. The sleeves were neatly rolled up. His shoes were polished, and he radiated confidence. "You are accused of stealing the payroll from the safe in Cornelia Johnson's office at COC. Your partners have ratted you out."

"I saw those guys in the hall. They are not my friends. It looks like they got paint on them."

"Yeah. Well. It's from the dye pack parked in the safe. It blew a phone alarm when it went off. We caught them milling around in the woods when the fog lifted."

"Captain. There can't be any dye on me. I've not been in Corney's office since before she fired me. But we're sort of friends now. On good terms. Donnacha know? She knows I didn't do anything. Bunny's her cousin and she should be right here.

Bunny was a compact, athletic woman with a nice open face. Her hair was short, and her dark suit unwrinkled.

She and Paul sat in what he thought of as the squad room. "Paul. I practice general law. I do real estate closings, divorce, wills, and such. I have handled a few criminal matters. I can help you for a day or so for a fee of one-hundred-fifty-dollars an hour but not more than one thousand dollars per day even if I work overtime. The clock will start now, and I must be paid in advance.

My retainer will be two thousand dollars. If this goes beyond Friday, I'll find you a criminal lawyer or public defender who may be paid by the court,"

"Is that okay?"

"Yes. Thank you.

"But how can I pay you. I have the money in the First Citizens Bank, but the cops took my papers, including my checkbook."

"Don't worry then. I'll get a blank check before I leave.

"Now tell me your story."

Paul told her his life's story up to and including his relationship with Archie and Jim Bob, and his love affair and impending wedding to Dahlia. I've been saving my money since I was a teenager, and I don't need to steal. If I have more money than some other people, it is because I spend very little.

I have friends in the community. Elizabeth and George Auberson know me very well and so does Corney Johnson. I think there are a lot of COC staff that know me, but they are mostly gone for the season."

Bunny made a list of negatives and positives and declared, "Paul. Given the fact that there is no physical evidence against you and that they, literally, have caught two people red-handed, I may be able to get you out. I believe that we may be able to end this right now. Are you willing to leave your passport with the police and promise not to leave the country?"

"Yes. But I need to go to Germany in the spring to meet my fiancée's parents. I want to leave for Swan Harbor, North Carolina right now." The only reason that I stayed when Dahlia returned to Germany was that the festival was the best place to sell my boat. I don't foresee white water boating in the near future – he paused…Bunny I guess the boat money will go to you."

"Some people call this the Banana Republic of Clancy. The Chief of Police and the County Attorney are the key people I need to talk to. Let's see what the cops want to ask you. Don't tell lies and wait after each question for a nod from me. Just answer their questions. Don't volunteer anything. Understand."

He nodded.

Sergeant Brown and Captain Myers were invited back into the room and allowed to question Paul in the lawyer's supervision.

The officers took turns voicing questions.

"What is your name?"

"Where do you live?"

"Where do you work?"

"Where were you last night between sundown and sunrise?"

"Do you know Archie Phillips?"

"Do you know Jim Bob Bryson?"

"Where is the money?"

"Besides the post office box and the tent, where is your home?"

"Do you have brothers or sisters?"

"Why did you have so much cash on you?"

"If we release you, how will we be able to get in touch with you?"

"Why does Archie say you were there?"

The last question elicited the longest answer from Paul. "I don't know exactly why, but Archie has had it in for me since the day he came to work for COC. He told a some lies about me that led to my getting fired.

"He was the restaurant manager, you know. He may have gotten jealous over my girlfriend, I mean, my fiancée Dahlia. She's home in Germany now but we mean to get married in the spring. I think that Archie knew that I'd be a suspect because I was camping there. I don't think he knew I had permission."

Paul's answers seemed to jibe with things they'd been told by Cornelia Johnson and others.

Since there was no longer the possibility for browbeating and threatening behavior the session went well with Bunny not making a single objection to the questions or procedures. In fact, the police now seemed doubtful that Paul had anything to do with the crime.

He had Archie and Jim Bob's situation correctly in his mind. Archie knew the combination and reached the dye pack only because Paul had reset it to the old number. Stupid choice! He berated himself. I should have used another number. Who knew? It would have been better to pick a brand-new number that nobody would know. He shrugged his mental shoulders and looked at his captors with his open, friendly face, thinking how lucky he was that he had gotten to the safe first and made his quick getaway

MONDAY – October 30, 2000

Mitch left Paul standing by the bridge in the fog. Driving on the foggy road was very difficult but he knew it well and was a very good driver. At first, he kept the passenger side tires off the edge of the road to feel his way along. He managed to drive at three miles per hour in heavy fog and thirty miles per hour in the when it thinned. He crossed the border into North Carolina in medium fog and made his way to Exit 24 on I-40. This was out of his way but it had the elements he needed: a country gas station and diner where he could park without raising suspicions and a nearby public dumpster.

He sat in the dimly lit cab and pulled on Paul's rubber gloves. He methodically stripped the bundles of cash out of each vinyl bank envelope. The stacks of credit card receipts, cash register tapes, documents, and empty plastic envelopes went into a tough twenty-five-gallon plastic bag pre-positioned in the backpack by Paul. The plastic bags were the kind that contractors used for demolition debris.

An impressive weight of cash went into a smaller black garbage bag to be stowed under the passenger's seat.

Mitch pulled out of the parking lot and back toward I-40. Halfway to the interstate he pulled into an untended county trash station and tossed the tightly closed contractor bag into the dumpster. He was back on the highway before the sun was up and opened his store at the usual hour. He planned to slip a few hundred dollars into his store deposits every week to launder the loot. He did not yet know that it would take more than a year to get that job done.

Paul was released in the morning. The county and city police had talked to Bunny, Corney and Elizabeth and realized that they had no evidence other than Paul's self-confessed enemy's accusation. There was no case. There was no physical evidence. Paul's demeanor was the picture of innocence. Compared to

Archie and Jim Bob he seemed like a solid citizen. Corney had moved into his corner too.

The night in jail was actually comfortable for Paul. He was used to sleeping on rocks and pebbles with the thinnest of camping mattresses. In jail the air was warm, the toilet in his cell flushed and he had a mattress and blanket. They had given him a Hardee's chicken sandwich, French fries, and a thick shake for dinner. He was more used to bread and beans.

ON THE ROAD – Tuesday, October 31

Paul was in a good mood when he handed Bunny a check for $750.00.

"Thank you, Bunny. May I call you from time to time to get news about the case against Archie and Jim Bob?'

"You're welcome. Thanks for the check. You're a really lucky guy by the way."

"What do you mean?" questioned Paul."

"Well. It's just this. The police told me that this is the biggest robbery ever. Not only here in Clancy but in the entire region. They've never heard of so much cash in a single location, without security, and they'll move heaven and hell to get to the bottom of it. For a while it looked like they were going to try hard to get you for it, but you look so innocent, and that guy Archie looks so guilty that they don't have the heart to foul you up."

"Wow. Thanks Bunny. You really pulled through for me.

"No problem, Paul. Call me any time. I'll be glad to give you updates. Do you have a ride to COC?"

"Yep. Same way I got here. They're gassing the police cruiser and they'll pick me up right here."

He ventured to give her a shoulder hug and an air kiss. She made it easy, and they parted on good terms. He had her card with his cash in his shirt pocket.

He had to ride in back seat of the police car, and they asked him about his plans.

"I'm heading for Alabama as soon as I can pack," he lied.

Paul's camp was a mess, and his tent was full of leaves. Someone, Corney he supposed, had raised it on its poles and zipped it up. He moved his bus as close as he could get it and made several trips up and down his hill to load it up.

He drove straight for the nearby North Carolina border, away from Alabama, and thought he would not see COC again.

Paul was a deliberate driver. His buggy would not accelerate quickly anyway. Tired of driving in the late afternoon he pulled off the road at Lake Lure, North Carolina and rested. He felt his gear was disorganized. So, at sunset he was hard at work tidying up. He didn't require much space, but he liked a neat bunk.

He splurged on a meal in a barbecue restaurant and talked the waiter into asking the manager for permission to park behind the building for the night.

Things quieted down early, and he slept well dreaming of Dahlia. He began a letter to her in the first light of morning,

> Dear Dahlia,
>
> I miss you so much. I am on the way to Swan Harbor, sleeping in my bus tonight. I'll see Mitch this morning and be in Swan Harbor Thursday, November 2.
>
> Guess what! Somebody broke into the office at Corney's and stole a bunch of money. Archie and Jim Bob Bryson got caught and are in jail. They thought I might be involved too and I had to pay a lawyer $750.00 to get me out! I believe they think I'm innocent now.
>
> I dream about you every night and can't wait to get you back into my world. I'm working on our dreams.
>
> Love ~ Paul

He mailed the letter at the tiny Bat Cave, North Carolina post office and began the drive to Charlotte.

Paul was stunned by the amount of cash they had stolen. $114,000.00! Mitch had decided that his share would be

$50,000.00 and that Paul should have the remaining $64,000.00. Their deal had been for a 50/50 but Mitch wanted Paul to have the bigger share. Paul felt he was settling boyhood accounts with Mitch.

Mitch agreed to hide Paul's share for him until he was ready to launder it so that he could possess it without fear of discovery. He had no idea of how he would accomplish that feat. It seemed like a fun project.

They talked about feelings of guilt and decided that they did not have to worry about their victim. COC would shortly get the credit card receipts automatically and insurance would probably pay most estimated cash and check losses. So, they were somewhat removed from their victim.

Paul explained the move to Swan Harbor to get far away from COC and start a new life as an artist. Mitch agreed to come to the wedding. He would drive their parents if necessary. Paul was on the road again by early afternoon.

He followed route NC24 from Albemarle, North Carolina, and passed through a long succession of small towns. He was road weary when he stopped for the night at an RV park and negotiated a fee of $5.00 since he needed no electric or other hookups.

He'd start out in Swan Harbor first thing in the morning.

PART TWO

Nothing could be finer than to be in Carolina in the morning.

SWAN HARBOR – Thursday, November 2

Swan Harbor was exactly as Elizabeth had described it. It seemed that the fishing village it had been was still there with a layering of newer residents who worked for the Jacksonville based government activities. The population of twelve hundred souls maintained a community that was pleasing to Paul's eye. He felt comfortable.

There were no tourists at this time of year. Restaurants were barely open, and a cool ocean breeze kept people indoors. Paul wandered the historical business district and spotted a ROOM FOR RENT sign on the door of a run-down, self-service coin laundry.

The two-story building's walls were unpainted, its tin roof was a little rusty and the generous corner lot it occupied was littered. It had a porch with dormer windows visible overhead. That's ugly enough, he thought - let's see how cheap it is. The building looked old and tired. It had light Victorian embellishments at the roof peak and in the top corners of the porch.

The small laundry wasn't bad. Paul decided to do a load while he hung out and observed the place. No one came in and no one left so he finally, while his load was drying, almost out of boredom, rang the bell next to the door, which was located right nest to the laundry entrance. He heard noises as someone shuffled slowly to the door.

She was at least eighty years old, dressed in a long bathrobe, and wore a scarf wrapped around her head and neck.

"Yes?"

"I saw the room for rent sign," Paul smiled at her. "Could I look at the room?"

"How long you planning to stay?" she asked suspiciously.

"I don't know ma'am. I'm looking for a place to buy. So, it's up in the air." He tried to give her a reassuring smile since she seemed ill at ease. He thought that it might be his shaggy hair. He gave her his best smile.

"Could I look at the room? How much are you asking?"

She didn't answer. She turned and pointed to the end of the porch. "Use the outside stairway around the corner. The door's unlocked. Take your time and have a good look. Knock again when you're done."

The open stairway began near the farthest end of the porch and reached the second floor with a landing on top. The stairs terminated as a little deck with an L shaped bench. The wood was weathered but seemed sound.

The room felt huge. It was 25 by 40 feet, all open, except for the bathroom. There were three dormer windows on the longest side, two windows and the cube of the bathroom opposite, and two windows on each end. He could see outlines of partitions on the old wooden floor that might once have divided the place into bedrooms, a hallway, and a stair well. It was surprisingly light, slightly musty, and sparsely furnished.

The table with four wooden chairs had seen better days. There was a bed in the far corner and a long kitchen counter with no fridge or stove. The sofa looked okay to him. It would be better than the tent he'd been living in for the past five months. It looked shabby and cheap - just the way he liked it.

He walked down the stairs and knocked at her door.

She came immediately and he said, "Ma'am. My name is Paul Hunter, and I may be interested. But I have a few questions. Like how much is it? Where can I get a little refrigerator and stove? How can I keep it warm?"

"How long do you want it?"

"I really don't know. What would be comfortable for you?"

The woman seemed to like the question. "The thing is I plan to put the place up for sale and I need you to be month-to-month. It's off-season so I would only charge you fifty dollars a week including electric. I can get double that in the summer."

"Month to month is fine. Can I park in the lot next door?"

"Of course. But you'll have to pay a month in advance.

"I have an oil-fired furnace and you'll probably get enough heat from that. But I'll lend you a kerosene heater if you want.

You'll see that will be more than enough. The weather here is cool in the winter but freezing? Not so much."

Paul had noticed that the noon temperature was about seventy degrees on this early November day. That boded well for a mild climate.

He took a moment to consider and said, "What is your name ma'am?"

"Alma Carter"

"Mrs. Carter. Would you accept $125.00 a month and let me do some work every week for the difference? I could start by cleaning the yard and getting rid of the trash. I can paint, do repairs, and even plumbing or electric. If you are selling, my work could make the place sell better."

"Paul. I like a man who bargains, and I like a man who is a worker. The answer is yes. When do you want to move in?"

"Today please and I'll pick up the yard before I move my things upstairs."

She gave him a sweet smile and offered to shake his hand.

"Thank you, ma'am." He gave her another smile and dug into his shirt pocket for the money and counted it out into her palm. "Ma'am. I won't need a receipt. I'll pay you again on the first of every month until you need me to leave."

That made her really grin. "Thank you.

"Would you step into my apartment and have a cup of tea with me before you begin."

Her apartment was cute and chintzy. It was much smaller than the space upstairs because it shared the square footage with the Laundromat. But it was enough for a single person with simple needs. It's way bigger than my tent he thought.

He approved. "This is very cozy Mrs. Carter."

"Small you mean." She laughed. "I've lived here for the last two years. Since Mr. Carter passed. I'm moving upstate with my daughter now. She thinks that keeping this place up is too much for me. And she's right you know."

The teapot whistle interrupted her, and she poured two mugs of tea and placed two muffins on a plate as they sat at her table. She offered him milk and sugar. Paul enjoyed her presence, her wise eyes, and her mastery of her space. She spoke of children, grandchildren, and her sadness at leaving Swan Harbor.

"We came to live here in anticipation of retirement. My husband Ken worked for the Department of Defense and commuted to Jacksonville for three years before he retired. We were happy here. I've always been a housewife. This community is very caring. It's been a great town to live in. What do you do Paul? I mean your profession.

"Well. I'll be twenty-three years old next month and I just discovered that I love to paint. I lost my job at a company in Georgia where I'd worked for two seasons, but I stayed there because I fell in love with a girl from Germany and didn't want to leave her."

"And now?"

"She's back in Germany. My art teacher told us how much she enjoyed Swan Harbor and we decided to try to move here and get married in March."

"I may go to Germany to meet her family."

"Congratulations Paul. Tell me about your art."

"He explained his watcher theme and how he liked to construct a picture with washes, light colors, and dry-brush lines – masking the whites of his characters' eyes to give them a brilliant shine.

"Can you show me?"

"Sure." He stepped out to his bus and brought in a very thin portfolio. Elizabeth had most of the work he'd done over the summer. But he had a few sketches and partially finished pieces.

"Nice," she said. "These look very professional."

"Are you looking to buy a house or a business location?"

"I don't know. I want to look around and see what things cost and then find out if I can get a mortgage."

"Shouldn't be a problem." Alma said. When you visit the bank, you'll find out that they are anxious to make real estate loans."

Paul finished his tea and asked Alma for a rake. "I want to do my rent work as soon as possible. I'll rake the lot and pull some weeds before I park my bus."

He worked up a sweat even though the day was mild. He produced a large pile of raking's and used three of his big contractor plastic bags to contain it all. Next step, he thought, would be to whack weeds all around the property and rake again. He would buy a weed trimmer if she didn't have one in her shed.

He trekked up the stairs four times carrying his bedding, clothing, cook pot and books. He sat at the window in the waning light of day and doodled a budget and a list of needs. He worked on his daily letter entry for Dahlia.

> Yay! I got a place for the winter.
> Tomorrow I explore the town: library, bank, real estate office and city hall. I want to learn everything.
>
> I'll mail this Monday. I love you. XXX

The room was plain and quiet. Alma's Television was barely perceptible. He reckoned the building was well constructed in the old post and beam technique.

Because he now had electric lights for the first time in months, he read parts of Walden Pond and Beachcombers' handbook before closing his eyes.

Paul woke late, ate cereal with the last of the milk from his cooler and set forth to explore the streets of his new town.

He passed block after block of modest homes intermixed with shops that appeared to cater to summertime visitors.

He ventured into the Carolina Bank and opened an account. He drew down the balance from his Clancy bank by writing and depositing a check to himself.

A quick stop at the post office was made to rent a box and arrange for his mail to be forwarded from Clancy. He mailed his letter to Dahlia with some new brochures he'd collected from the Chamber of Commerce porch racks.

The real estate office visit was an eye-opener for Paul. He met the owner Marlyss Midgett. She was nicely dressed while he was a bit shaggy.

He thought that his long beard and tangle of hair gathered into a ponytail must be off-putting for her. She gave him a list of properties in the downtown area that might be converted to an art gallery with living quarters. There were few properties available and none under $200,000.00. He walked about, looking them over, and decided that his dream of a small down payment and modest mortgage wouldn't work here.

On a whim he stopped in the barbershop and got the first haircut he'd had in years. The barber Bill flatly refused to give him a $5.00 cut. He smiled and said, "My young friend. You'll need a double haircut to look human."

"Please sir, could I have a triple?"

"What do you mean?"

"I want to get a buzz cut and have my beard cut to a number one on your electric razor."

"Sure, but if I do all that work, I may need to charge you twenty."

"Okay. Let her rip. Charge me whatever you like and if I come out alive, I may be a regular customer."

The job went quickly, and Paul was surprised by the transformation that took place in the mirror. He looked like a normal citizen again. Over the next few months, he cut his hair ever shorter and finally sported a shaved head and minimal beard. He became Mr. Clean.

Bill charged him $10.00, and Paul added a $10.00 tip in a fit of gratitude. He was sure that Bill would remember his name.

He bought an electric weed whacker and a 50-foot extension cord at the Ace Hardware Store for fifty dollars. This shopping was the most money he'd spent since he'd bought Dahlia's ring.

He was hungry but reluctant to spend money. So, he hiked to the Seven Eleven and bought a hot dog and soda for three dollars and ten cents.

Mrs. Carter seemed pleased when he returned and went to work cutting weeds all around the property and edging the overgrown grass where it grew over the sidewalk.

"You've done enough for now Paul," she called out to him. "C'mon and have a cup of tea with me on the porch. It's nice out of the wind and in the sunshine.

"The yard looks really nice," she said. "Thank you."

"No problem. Just keeping my word on the rent deal. I'll do something every chance I get."

"What have you been doing today? ..."

Dearest,

The old woman who rented me the room is really sweet. Mrs. Carter. She's desperate to sell her place. She's using the property as a coin laundry, and it is in pretty bad shape. It needs paint and general upkeep.

She told me today that she's going to talk to the local real estate office tomorrow and I told her, before I could stop and think, I said that I'd like to buy the place if the price is right.

I suggested that I'd make a $5,000.00 deposit and that if she would hold a $95,000.00 mortgage, I'd pay her $500.00 a month. She said that taxes and insurance don't cost much here. I think we could make a go of it.

Paul

PS I'll add more to this letter tomorrow.
Xxxooo

Paul had switched his unemployment claim to North Carolina with surprisingly little paperwork and no resistance. His unemployment checks now came from his new state and the benefits would last until he got a job. He had to report in once a week. He explained the remoteness of his new town from a town where there would be jobs and his plan to into business. "No problem," said his counselor. "Just report every week until you open your store."

He had fifteen thousand dollars in the bank and five hundred in cash. Joan Taylor, the lawyer whose services Paul and Mrs. Carter shared, said it would take about a week before the title insurance company and the bank were ready to go.

The bank president leaped at the opportunity to make a mortgage loan. The bank, at closing, would pay Mrs. Carter the selling price, add Paul's closing costs to that, and he would sign a mortgage and promissory note along with a goodly number of other documents the bank felt it needed for protection. Paul's main duty was to give Alma a cashier's check for $5,000.00.

The mortgage was an Adjustable-Rate Mortgage. His interest for the first five years would be three- and one-half percent and then go up following the market. His possible rate increases were capped so that there would not be a dramatic increase in his monthly payment in any one year. The first payment would not be due until the first of February. He thought that it was a smashing deal.

People. The barber, the lawyer, the Chamber of Commerce docent, the post office clerk, told him that property values were on the rise and that he'd indeed gotten an impressive deal.

SWAN HARBOR – Friday, December 1, 2000

Mrs. Carter had left for her daughter's home, gifting Paul with her assorted furniture and kitchen items she wouldn't need. Her son-in-law had loaded her and boxes of stuff into a rental trailer and departed the day before. Her part of the closing was done on November thirtieth and Paul signed all his papers in the lawyer's conference room at nine o'clock. He shook hands with Joan and left with a lively step jangling the keys in his pocket.

His plan was to clean the place up, remodel it with his own labor to wind up with an inviting coin-laundry, a gallery where Mrs. Carter had lived, a hot dog stand that would serve food through a window onto the porch or over a counter indoors. He had walls to knock down, woodwork to paint, surfaces to clean and signs to build.

Mitch had told him that the lighted box sign he'd put up on his building had doubled his sales and tripled his income from the furniture store. Paul got it. He too would need signs.

Paul often sat and reviewed the upcoming days of his life. He enjoyed the contemplation of various tasks, imagining the different steps and tools that each job required. He had a large number of different tasks to do that he needed to make lists of things to do and even lists of lists.

The drug store sold him a pad and clipboard. The pad had quarter inch squares to facilitate the drawing of plans and such. He bought a bundle of three lined pads, two clipboards, and a plastic sleeve of mechanical pencils.

His tool kit in the bus consisted of a heavy-duty carpenter's hammer, pliers, a saw and a few screwdrivers. The saw was dull. He knew that he'd have to tool up.

He made his first list with only four items:

Clean and paint everything.

Remodel the first floor to eliminate Alma's old apartment and turn it into an art gallery with room for his paintings, Dahlia's wreaths, and a hot dog stand – all sharing the space with the laundry.

Make and install three electric signs to attract business.

Clean and decorate the second-floor apartment into a perfect love nest for Dahlia.

He pictured and listed five income streams and made another list:

Laundry.
Retail items.
Watercolor paintings.
Wreaths.
Hot dog stand.

Before long he had multiple lists covering every project he wanted to do.

SUNDAY – December 3, 2000

Paul knew that he had no experience as businessman but that did not deter him from dreaming.

So, Dahlia,

The building is ours! But it needs work and TLC. Far better of course than camping in my tent in the woods, but not as good as you deserve and not as good as I plan for you. I wish you were here now to share in the experience of creating a home and business for us. I am enclosing a $1,000.00 Traveler's Check for you to buy a ticket to the U.S. Your destination should be Charlotte again, just like last time. Let me know and I'll be there to give you hugs.

Mitch has agreed to give me a few days a week to work on things like pressure washing the exterior, wall demolition and removal of construction debris with his pickup truck. He'll be here tomorrow and Tuesday. This is the biggest, most exciting project of my life and I'm determined to get it ready for the tourist season beginning in April.

Coincidentally that is when my unemployment benefits end. They are okay with my working on getting the business ready as long as I'm not getting a salary. Remember reading Thoreau together. I am living the life I imagined!

Do some wedding planning. Think of dates and who we'll invite. My list will include Mitch, my parents and a few friends, new and old. If the date is early enough, we can get bargain rates for out-of-towners at the local B and B across the street. If the date is soon, we can get some of the guests to help us get our house and business together. If it is later, we'll be able to set up a dorm situation.

Just fun things to think about. Love you more and more.

Your Paul XXXOOO

He mailed the letter Monday morning on the way to the tool rental shop. He was going to get a ladder, a pressure washer and another hose. He didn't think the hose in the shed was long enough to reach all around the building. Mitch would arrive at ten o'clock and he wanted to put him right to work.

Mitch was overjoyed seeing what Paul had accomplished is a short time. He'd relished his drive to the coast and a quick driving tour of the city. He was playing hooky from work while his girlfriend ran the shop

He found the house with ease. "Wow." was his basic comment when he saw the interior and heard Paul's plan. This is going to be a moneymaker. "Upside potential and very, very low rent. Your mortgage is like a gift from the bank."

"The bank seemed overjoyed when they found out that I wanted to borrow money. They saw my balances and had zero questions about my income and credit history, which, as you know is none," Paul laughed.

"At least there was nothing negative. I've never borrowed money before.

"My lawyer says that just cleaning this place up will be 'sweat equity.'"

"I'm prepared to sweat. How about you bro?"

The plan was to pressure wash the outside of the building from top to bottom in a day and return the rented pressure washer. On Tuesday they would do the demolition on the ground floor to make into one large, multipurpose room. Mitch would quit early enough to load the demolition debris into his truck and get it to the county landfill before closing. He'd drive to Charlotte and be ready to work the next morning. He said that he felt he might be able to come for a couple of days a week until the job was finished.

"Business has been wonderful since I put the sign up. I used a little of the swag to self-finance the sign but, honestly, I don't know what to do with the money. I bank a little every week so that it seems like it comes from the store. But I don't need much to live on.

"Molly's a great girlfriend. She works, saves her money, and worries if I spend too much on her. I love her and, one day soon... I mean very soon; I'm going to pop the question. You in for the best man spot?"

Paul gave him a beatific smile and a warm hug. "I'm happy for you. Dahlia and I are getting hitched as soon as she figures a date to be here. I've been getting a letter from her almost every day not that my mail is caught up."

They devised a system of putting the power washer on the top of the pick-up and they were able to reach the entire building. First the roof was blasted to remove the grime accumulated over the decades since it was new.

The unpainted building had started the day in a natural, darkly discolored, wood way with mold and dark moss growing in the crevasses. It was not a bad look for an older building. It finished the day looking like a new building glowing with a younger complexion. The slightly pink, almost salmon colored, wood looked terrific. They were delighted with the result.

The covered porch that ran down the street sides of the structure looked wonderful. Cleaned up now, it was a great place to sit and rock and not just than just shelter from sun or rain.

The gutters were heavy with compacted leaves and sky debris. They decided just to remove them and let rainwater cascade where it would. If this proved to be a problem Paul would deal with it later.

They celebrated with chicken sandwiches from Arbys and turned in early. Mitch slept on the floor on Alma's mattress. They were up before sunrise and consumed cereal and coffee at the little table.

Mitch said, "I brought you ten thousand in cash in case you want it. If not, I'll continue to keep in in the safe at the shop. The safe is really a joke. It can't be locked but it has a false floor that is ideal. It's fireproof and has a slick latch that only the maker would know – he died over a hundred years ago. I got it from a great-great-grand child, who was older than the hill. I put a big price tag on the ugly thing so that it'll never sell. It would take a crew with a forklift to move it. Your loot is safe."

"Mitch. Keep it for now. I don't believe I'll be reconnected to the theft, but I was wrong before. I'll let you know what to do with it when the time comes."

The demolition was hard work, but they enjoyed it and took pleasure from working together. Mitch brought a selection of pry bars and an electric saber saw. The old wall was down and out in a couple of hours. They kept usable boards, electrical bits, and anything they thought would be of use.

Mitch said his goodbyes at two thirty. He had to get to the landfill. He promised to be back the next week. He kept the $10,000.00 for return to his safe hiding place.

Paul sat in the laundry for a few minutes looking at the expanded space. He imagined a sliding window and counter for hot dogs. He could see white floor to ceiling shelves to retail soap and fabric softener, cans of beans, paper products, aspirin, candy, tins of tuna, jars of mayonnaise, paper plates, plastic knives and forks, and the comforts he himself needed for daily life.

Paul took pleasure in thinking about how it would be to shop at Willy's Cash and Carry one day soon. He had found Willy's Cash and Carry roaming the area near Jacksonville one day. It sold wholesale groceries, large packages of food, household supplies, candies, cigarettes, to stores and vendors.

He checked out the hot dogs at Willy's in-store snack bar. They were delicious. Their skin initiated a pop of flavor when pierced and provided a great texture. They were big dogs and cost less than fifty cents each. He would buy cartons of mustard, relish, and sour kraut in little plastic pouches. He'd need squares of paper to wrap the dogs and cases of coke to wash them down. He felt he could charge a buck for a dog and 50 cents for a drink and his costs would be about a third. He'd adjust the prices as possible.

He would have to get a state sales tax number to shop there. He thought that the dogs, laundry, and gallery would reinforce each other in a symbiotic way. He would give the arms of his businesses great attention and experience would teach him the right emphasis for each.

He walked to the Ace Hardware to buy some paintbrushes and rollers. He was high from the excitement of all the good the changes he was making to his property.

The next day his first destination was Spring's Salvage Company. This was a giant, Home Depot-sized box store and lumber yard that sold architectural salvage, doors, windows, plumbing, electrical wiring, and home decor. His mission was to buy a big bathtub, an exterior grade sliding window in a frame and paint. He wanted to let the day warm up and his building dry after its power-washing.

He bought an ancient claw-foot bathtub, faucets, feed and drain lines and the bits and pieces it would take to make it work. The tub was big enough for two friendly people. He purchased a framed stainless-steel window with a shelf bottom that would allow people to buy his dogs while standing on the porch.

He bought cans of paint: clear weatherproofing for the whole building, red for the fascia around the roof and porch and white semi-gloss for the windows.

He didn't have a North Carolina driver license yet, so he knew in advance that he'd have to pay cash. The bill totaled eleven hundred dollars. He smiled as he reminded himself that he was investing in real estate and not just blowing the money. The tub almost fit into the bus through the side door. It stuck out over a foot but was securely tied. The long window stuck out through the rear hatch, and it too was tied and had a red flag on its end.

The bus was heavy on its springs, and he was glad to get home but couldn't figure out how to get the tub up the stairs. The paints and his giant stainless window unit were less of a problem.

Paul walked back to Ace and asked Jeff the owner for help.

"Sure matey. When I close up, I'll come over with my two sons and a couple of heavy mover's pads. We'll get it up for you."

"Thanks Jeff. I'll be happy to pay you."

"Never ya mind about that. Give the lads twenty and they'll be happy enough."

Paul bought an expensive can of off-white enamel paint from Jeff. He felt bad that he'd bought so much paint from Spring's even though it had saved him money, so he hid most of the cans under a drop cloth in anticipation of Jeff's visit and tour of his shop and home.

The day was fine, and the building was dry. Paul used his Ace brushes to prime and paint the window frames and sills white. The difference was startling. He was creating a thing of beauty. The last thing he did before Jeff's visit was to measure and mark the wall where his new sliding hot dog-window set would go.

It took four of them to get the tub upstairs and in place. Jeff had brought a dolly to roll it across the upstairs floor to its place next to the bathroom at the far end of the room.

"You need a tub or shower pan under this tub. Best thing would be to hire my tile man to build it. You'll be surprised at how little it will cost and it'll save your floors and ceilings when slop and spray go flying. I'll have Ed the tile guy call you."

Jeff and his two grown sons had all given Paul's efforts rave reviews. "You sir are going to have a showcase here. You must join the Chamber of Commerce and we'll have a meeting here when you're ready and show 'em what's up. They will all become customers. Even the restaurant people will come here for a break.

"Listen up. There's a meeting tonight at the Swan Harbor bank. Come as you are, and we'll let you join for one hundred dollars. Join tonight and I'll win another chance in the contest for a prize. Don't worry about paying. We know where you live and can send you a bill for the initiation fee."

Paul was happy with that idea. He had not known anything about how a Chamber of Commerce would work. But the idea made sense.

He did not go as he was, but put on clean slacks, shoes and shirt. His hair and beard were easy to manage now. He thought that he'd never go back to the look he had when he first arrived in town.

To his surprise he had already met many of the attendees. They gave him a round of applause when Jeff told them what he was up to at The Carter Place and that he was joining the Chamber that very night. Suddenly, in a way that had never occurred to him before, he felt proud to be a member of a real community.

SWAN HARBOR – Monday, December 11, 2000

Mitch arrived early on December eleventh. The painting project was already moving along. The weather had been fine for doing the outdoor things and Paul was saving the interior for later when the days would be cold.

Together they marked the window opening and used the Sawzall to make the opening. Fastening the new stainless steel sliding window with its built-in shelf was easy with four hands and a level. Paul caulked and painted while Mitch made braces and frames for both the inside and exterior. The result was another home run. The window would suit its intended purpose perfectly and, as a bonus, it let in lots of light.

"Say Mitch. There are two doors in play here. Maybe I'll buy glass doors at the salvage place and make it into one big door. I wonder what it would be like installing them?"

"Probably heavy and hard to handle. But if you find them at a price, I'm good for the next few weeks to keep helping. By the way, do you need money yet? I brought your ten thou again just in case you changed your mind."

Paul laughed. "Not yet. But thanks."

Now that the ground floor was a single large room, with a restroom taking up a little space on the back wall, Paul thought he needed to warm it up with some color and furniture. He and Mitch brought down a table and some chairs left by Mrs. Carter. Paul hung a few of his paintings. It looked like a small coin laundry with a big bonus room. The bonus room would soon be his studio and gallery. He took Dahlia's largest wreath and hung it in the new sliding window as a Christmas decoration. He pinned a few red ribbons on it.

There had been a few customers every day since Paul had become the official owner. He tried to be the perfect host by learning their names and helping whenever he could by carrying, providing detergent, or just holding the door open. They were a mixed lot. There were young mothers, apartment dwellers, bachelors, and they seemed a little down on their luck. He figured that if he had ten customers every day, they would pay his mortgage, and his electric bill, and put beans on the table.

He cleaned the dryer filters every day and kept the place wiped down. He perceived a certain lack of customer comfort and convenience the way Mrs. Carter had managed. He bought and installed two long Formica counters to use for folding clothes and acquired four used swivel office chairs on wheels. The chairs reclined and he believed that he'd never seen such a comfortable laundry. Just wait though, he promised himself. By spring there would be music, hanging plants, art on the walls and maybe an exotic German chick to liven things up.

SWAN HARBOR – December 14, 2000

Less than two weeks before Christmas Paul had two surprise visitors.

Corney showed up at two o'clock to boldly march up the steps and banged on the door. Paul opened the door and gaped at her. "What are you doing here?" His mouth gaped in surprise.

"Paul. I'm here to make you an offer."

"Huh? I mean, please come in Corney. I didn't expect you. What are you doing in Swan Harbor?

"How did you find me?"

"Paul. I just called the credit bureau and they had your file. You've been busy I see. Buying this place with someone else's money and trying to be a pillar of the community. Her words dripped with sarcasm.

"The Chamber of Commerce here was happy to tell me what a prosperous citizen you've become. They think it's your own money."

She glared at him as she looked around and took it all in. She saw cleanliness and a changed Paul. He was now Mister Clean with a shaved head and white clothing.

He had been working with a piece of plywood that he was fashioning into a worktable for doing his paintings. Corney chose to sit in a swivel chair and gestured for him to sit across from him.

He thought that she was bossy and tough. He was impressed by her demeanor as well as her words.

"I, I...I know how this must look to you Corney, but I don't know anything about your money. I borrowed to buy this place and I can account to you, if I want, for every penny I've made and spent since the day I graduated from high school.

"Likely story," she harrumphed. I don't believe a word of it. Archie and Jim Bob have been in jail since you left and they are going to be tried for breaking and entering and grand larceny. The only problem is that the money has disappeared, and they claim you have it."

"Archie is full of it. Jim Bob doesn't know anything. He's just a little dumb, don't you think."

"Tell me all about it." Corney invited him, sitting back and clearly not going anywhere until she was good and ready.

"Where are you staying?" he asked.

"Across the street at $100.00 a night, where I can keep an eye on you. At the Cygnet Bed and Breakfast.

"Where is it?" she hissed.

"Corney. Listen up," – he told her his financial history, the $5,000.00 down payment, the $10,000.00 he had had in the bank he'd been saving for since high school, his unemployment compensation and about the beginnings of his dream to have a real business. He told her about selling paintings, COC's severance check for $650.00 and the sale of his boat. "Bunny got the boat money," he said, "I had to pay her."

"So, Corney. What do you think now? Oh, by the way, I've got receipts and paper for everything I just told you. Do you want to see 'em?"

Corney looked composed. "Yes please. Not that I don't believe you."

"Well, you're wrong." Come upstairs and I'll show you."

Paul led the way up the stairs. He sat her at his table and brought her his box of papers, envelopes, statements, income tax returns, and mortgage papers. He gave her a lined pad and two sharp yellow pencils.

He made her a cup of tea, turned on the lights and left her to rummage through his life. She walked around the room first, looked in the dresser and bathroom drawers, and admired the claw foot tub with its costly looking hardware and elegant lines. Then she settled down to study young Mr. Hunter.

Paul had obsessed her since he had walked on the charges. She didn't need money, but it rankled her that he would get away with it. So, she had followed him here at considerable cost in time and explanations to Rolf. Rolf was himself away in Nepal now leading an adventure travel group. This was why she was free to follow her inclination to investigate Paul. She had only been on the road for two days, but it felt longer.

She believed Archie was telling the truth and that Paul was a masterful liar. But she had a sinking feeling that she'd never be able to prove it. Paul was probably enjoying his revenge and she probably deserved it for being lax about taking care of COC's affairs and security.

She rummaged through Paul's bank statements and was able to track his cash position and it was consistent with his words. She thought for a long time before trudging back down to find him spray painting washing machines and driers white with a large spray can. His work area was masked by newspaper and blue tape in a professional manner.

"Well Paul. I give up. I hope you have a good life. But before I go, I want to make you this offer. If you come clean with me and make restitution, I'll forgive you and pay for your attorney to make sure you don't go to jail. What do you say?"

"No can do Corney. I won't confess to something I couldn't have done."

"She handed him an envelope with a COC address and walked out of his store.

He saw her get into her old Toyota and drive away. It seemed final and he confirmed it by walking to the B and B to ask the owner if Cornelia Johnson had gotten away okay.

"Yes, she did," said Norma. "She sure was interested in you buddy. Are you friends or family?"

"I guess we're just friends."

His second visitor was also unexpected. Dahlia came walking down the street just before sunset, dragging a suitcase on wheels and carrying a backpack.

She looked exhausted.

"Oh my God. Oh my God!" They cooed to each other as they hugged joyfully. "You didn't call." Paul pouted.

"I could have taken the day off to get you. I need a day off."

"What do you think?" Paul asked as they stood on the street in the fading light.

"Oh Paul. It is beautiful. It is just as you said in your letters. It looks like a German house with the colors and everything."

Paul carried her valise and gave her a complete tour ending on the bed. She was clearly too tired for sex or conversation, so he tucked her in and let her seek a cure for jet lag in dreamland.

He was overwhelmed. It was just too much for one day. His soul was weary from lying to Cornelia and the world, and his whole being was elated to know that his love had crossed an ocean to be with him.

He went downstairs silently to clean the filters on the driers and empty the coin boxes. There wasn't much. But, he thought, these $30.00 in quarters multiplied by 365 days would be a nice piece of change. He vowed to work hard and make it much more.

He remembered the envelope Corney had handed him when she left. He had stuck it into his back pocket and Dahlia's arrival had erased everything else from his mind.

It was a form letter with a place on the bottom to be checked and signed regarding his contributions to COC's 401K plan. He had a balance valued at $840.00. He could opt to take one-fifth on his birthday starting this year and take four more yearly payments. Or, if he checked another box, he could take the entire balance at the end of the third year. His balance would vary as the value of COC's stock varied.

He had contributed the maximum. He had not thought about the 401K plan. It must have bothered Corney to have him own stock and she must be forced by law to treat him fairly since she could not really prove anything against him. There was a stamped return envelope enclosed with the form to help him return it to COC.

Somehow the revenge he'd sought didn't seem so sweet now. So many good things had happened to him, and he hadn't used a penny of the money other than the small amounts of cash he'd taken during his raids on the safe. He didn't dislike Corney or COC. The project had been a side adventure to his real quest, which had been wooing Dahlia. It was a burden that he must carry by himself. He didn't know how to return it or undo his sin.

The next few days were a time of rediscovery and endless planning and chatting about how they might live and prosper.

Dahlia liked Swan Harbor and approved the business plan. She decided, and helped Paul decide, that they needed to take Mondays and Tuesdays off while things were slow and just Mondays when things got busy.

She made a deep impression on everyone she met. The annual Chamber of Commerce Christmas party would be her coming out event and they both bought something to wear.

Paul had taken to wearing white and people were calling him Mr. Clean. He hadn't owned a jacket since high school and had grown heavier in the shoulders and bulkier everywhere else. Dahlia decided that he must have a new blue blazer and that he could wear that over his daily whites.

Dahlia wanted a "liddle" dress and strap shoes. The mall in Jacksonville was their choice. She found the perfect jacket for him and matched it with a very light, almost white, pair of slacks. He realized that he only owned sandals, boots, and athletic shoes so they topped his look off with a belt, black socks, and black loafers. Paul felt like a kid shopping with his mom. She knew best and she insisted on paying. She knew also about the $1,000.00 traveler's check but hadn't received it yet.

Paul was allowed to sit while Dahlia modeled dresses, all of which he admitted liking. She made the final decision and bought the shoes so quickly that he never found out that they cost more than his entire outfit. He wouldn't have cared.

The party would be on the Thursday the 20th of December. It would be a buffet dinner at Chowder's Seafood Restaurant. The dinner meeting happened only twice each year. He paid for their tickets at the Chamber office the next day.

The business plan took a turn too. He had spent the days painting and building their business infrastructure. The apartment became Dahlia's realm, and she made him take a break and start creating art. "Paul we will be very busy when people begin coming into the shop and laundry in the spring. Now is ven ve must produce our inventory; you must make paintings and I vill start making wreaths. I'll call you upstairs ven I need you."

She developed a habit of thumping three times on the floor when wanted his help. Often, he would find her nude and freshly bathed, posing on their bed shortly after the thumps called him. He was always willing to come when she needed him but he never quite knew whether she was feeling horny or in need of a furniture mover. He loved her more and more. She was the ornament of his life.

Dahlia loved Paul right back. His new appearance had surprised her, but she quickly realized that he was the same kind and quiet man without his beard. She loved the fact that he had proceeded to plan and make things happen without her. This seemed to be the mark of a good provider for her and their future babies.

They decided "yes," on children "but not right now." She visited the local gynecologist and got a prescription for birth control and a plan for switching from the morning after regimen she'd been following. The couple agreed on making the decision for her to stop taking pills on some near future date.

Dahlia felt like the Belle of the Ball at the Chamber of Commerce party. There were so many new faces for her. She had a great memory but made many notes on the small pad she carried in her purse.

Like Paul, she had never thought of herself as an entrepreneur. Her hospitality schooling taught her a lot about different kinds of businesses, but she'd always thought that she'd like to work for an airline. What they were doing was hard work, not yet very rewarding yet, but fun for both.

Meeting people predisposed to like her, and the idea of networking was thrilling. They were invited to several other holiday parties including a New Year's Eve party. She chuckled when Paul realized that it would be his birthday party too.

"I'm used to spending my birthday with Mom and Dad and Mitch if he can get to Alabama. By the way we have to figure out when we can go there and meet the folks. Mitch's place is on the way, so we'll see him too when we go. By the end of the evening, they were socially exhausted and were glad to retreat to their nest.

This was their honeymoon even though they had decided on March for the actual marriage ceremony. Calls made to Germany and Alabama and North Carolina helped them set the wedding day for Saturday, March tenth.

The sex was amazing for both. They seemed to have landed in a sweet spot of the earth. Out in the community every day, the rough edges of Dahlia's accent faded. Her melodic voice was enjoyed by all. Nights were trips to paradise for them. They reveled in creating their own comfortable nest.

They needed a telephone and home mail delivery. Paul insisted that they contact a lawyer to make sure that Dahlia would remain legal and begin the process of citizenship.

The lawyer talked them into drafting a simple prenuptial agreement and wills to give her protection even under dire circumstances. The real estate and all their improvements were now owned jointly.

Dahlia began to seek woodsy and brushy areas around the parks, waste areas where Christmas tree dealers threw their branches, woods, and even grasslands. She would return with the back of the bus full. She would carefully sort and stack her sticks, vines, and grasses out of sight at the back end of the porch.

In their shrinking workroom and gallery Paul arranged two workbenches at different heights: one for his painting and one for Dahlia's wreaths.

Watercolors were mounted on foam boards with special Plexiglas corners protecting the work and providing a means to hang the picture. Each painting took a few minutes to frame and could be easily hung.

Dahlia began making wreaths in a variety of sizes and materials. The smallest were made from yellow grasses with just a garnish of green leaves or red berries. They were dollhouse sized, no more than four inches across.

She labeled these "Little Darling" wreaths - $5.00. Her nimble fingers could craft a dozen of these an hour. Paul made her a board with pegs, which would hold dozens of Little Darlings.

Her larger wreaths carried higher price tags and more ornamentation. She used a wire matrix to make the largest of her creations. She aspired to have a large inventory hung ten to a peg on the back wall and she would display a selection in the front. She didn't relish the idea of careless hands pawing through her inventory racks.

"Paul. It might be a goot thing to sell out occasionally. Once I see what people like I'll have some guidance about what to be working on."

Paul's efforts usually yielded a painting a day but sometimes, when he found a particular variation of his theme he liked, he could do five or more a day. Much of the time elapsing from start to finish was drying time that took no effort at all.

Dahlia gave him a day a week to work on other projects. Early on, he built shelves for a retail inventory of non-perishable items. The shelves were simple carpentry and always painted white.

They had a phone installed and bought a cash register from the salvage company. They loved bargains and negotiation. In the end, the $500.00 cash register cost them 79 bucks.

The feeling came over Paul that he was an adult at last. He was creating a life with some deliberation, looking ahead more than one year at a time, forging a marriage with Dahlia, and dealing with his past shortcomings.

Dahlia felt like she had just jumped off a tall building only to learn that she could fly. She was soaring over her new country, her new town, and her new man. The world was hers.

SWAN HARBOR – January 5, 2001

Paul was not quite sure how it happened, but they wound up in pastor's office at the Grace Presbyterian Church. Pastor Maryanne McLaurin told the couple, "Easy Peasy. I'm available, the church is available, the fellowship hall is available, and you can name your own price for the entire package."

She was a beautiful woman of about forty years of age, with blond hair and a complexion to die for. Her youth had not been spent in the sun.

"Tell me. Where did you go to church before you moved here?"

Paul answered first. "My parents were not big on church. We belonged to a Methodist church. When my brother and I became teenagers, we moved to a new house in Huntsville, and we never found a church. I went to Sunday school for years though and we always studied the Bible there."

Dahlia said, my family were Lutheran, but we just went to church on holidays like Easter and Christmas."

"I see," said Maryanne. "We would welcome you at Grace Presbyterian. I think as newcomers to Swan Harbor it would be good for you to have a church where you could find friends and fit into the community.

"No pressure," she added. "I'll get you married and off to a good start. How many guests will there be?

"How about the wedding party? Do you have a Best Man and Maid of Honor?"

"My brother Mitch will be the best man. Dahlia is still shopping for a Maid of Honor."

"Yah. I just got here. I'll ask our neighbor Norma tomorrow. She owns the Cygnet Bed and Breakfast. Our parents, Mitch and about ten chamber members who have been friendly should be there too. We'll ask them. So, we'll have the ceremony in the church at one in the afternoon and we'll plan a reception at the Chowders Restaurant for two o'clock. I think we might be around ten to twenty people. If the restaurant is not available, we'll find another place and let you know. We'd like you Maryanne and your husband to come to the party as well."

"But look – about the price of your services, please give us some guidance," said Paul. We are not rich, but we don't spend much and have savings. Don't cheat yourself. Besides we will need spiritual advice and you must earn a living and pay the expenses of the church."

"Well said," replied Maryanne. How about I just surprise you with my bill after the service and you can negotiate then if you wish?"

"Yes," they chorused. Paul gave a fist pump.

She told them how to get a marriage license. They parted on the friendliness terms after filling out a couple of questionnaires giving Maryanne information.

Working days were fun. They had designed their hot dog stand and shopped for the health department required, refrigeration and sinks. They needed a dedicated hand washing sink and a three-compartment sink large enough to handle their preparation tools. The salvage yard provided these two items with faucets already installed. They bought a used hot dog cooker, a stainless steel, under the counter, refrigerator and some tongs, tools, paper hot dog trays, mustard, relish, sauerkraut, and napkins. Including building material, and visits from the electrician and plumbers they figured that the new arm of their business had cost only one thousand dollars and that even with minimal sales they would recoup their investment quickly.

Laundry was hungry and thirsty work. If a customer could have lunch while getting clothes clean it might create an incentive to come back. They had similar thoughts about the gallery and retail shelves. They would learn what customers wanted.

Norma from the B and B was their first hot dog customer. She had agreed to stand up for Dahlia as her Matron of Honor. Workers from all over Swan Harbor soon found lunch at Mr. and Mrs. Clean's to be easy and cheap. They walked and did not need to maneuver their cars at lunchtime.

Now they needed a sign. Neon that is. Lit anyway, with ART GALLERY, HOT DOGS and LAUNDRY all featured so that it could be seen from Main Street without driving the neighbors crazy. At night they themselves wanted to enjoy a more natural light level.

They solved the lighted sign problem by changing their minds.

Instead, Paul made enough beautiful card racks so that every business in town could place cards and brochures by their cash registers. The idea became very popular.

The racks featured a painting on the front and each of his brochures had reproductions of his paintings. Virtually every business in Swan Harbor made their Gallery/Laundry/Hot Dog brochures available.

When they began placing their brochures around business picked up immediately. Owners and employees alike were able to direct business to them. Visitors, the few that came in the cool months, also found a friendly, comfortable place to get their duds clean.

The inside counter had only two stools, so most customers had to stand or use the porch on fine days. Many stood at the counter. That was a popular spot for the men when Dahlia was taking her turn at the counter.

SATURDAY – January 28, 2006, Ten O'clock

Tired from the week and the day of labor they lay in each other's arms and talked.

"Paul. You seem down tonight. What's wrong honey?"

"Nothing. I'm just tired."

"Paul, you can't fool me. Confess!"

Paul broke into tears and lay sobbing. "Ah Dahlia. I lied to you about something big and I'm afraid that it will change things." He twisted away from her and swung his legs over edge and sat with his head down. He felt ashamed and didn't want her to see his face.

Dahlia was astonished. "Okay Paul. Tell me. Vas it anodder voman vile I vas in Germany?" Her heart sank at the thought of losing her dreams with Paul.

"No. Never. It's much worse. Oh Dahlia. Telling you is the hardest thing I've ever done." His body shook.

She came out from under the sheet and hugged him from behind. "No Paul. You must not vorry so. Tell me and it vill be better. Tell me now and don't hold back." He nodded and tried to get his weeping under control.

"Ah Dahlia. I didn't tell you the truth."

"About what?" She clung to him and tried to turn him to face her. She was frightened. She'd never seen a man break down like this.

"It's about being in jail after the money was stolen at COC. I told you they no longer suspect me. They have Archie and Jim Bob Bryson red handed. Literally. But they haven't gotten the money back.

"Corney came here the day you arrived and accused me again."

"Oh my God! She vas here. In our house?"

"Yes. She had a room at Cygnet Bed and Breakfast. She just showed up and accused me of stealing the money. She said that she'd forgive me if I made restitution and confessed to the crime. She said that if I'd do that, she would even pay for a lawyer to protect me.

"I lied and told her that I didn't do it." There, he realized as he broke out into a sweat. He'd told her.

But Dahlia didn't get it yet. "What do you mean that you lied when you said you didn't do it? Does that mean that you took the money?"

"Yes," he gasped. I took the money," and, through his tears and weeping, he gave her all the details including Mitch's involvement.

"Oh my God. Poor Paul." She hugged him hard and now they were both crying. She finally turned him around and was able to hug him to her breasts while she straddled his legs. She had been afraid that he was going to leave her.

"Paul. Poor Paul. I love you so much. Vat a burden to keep this to yourself. But I understand how you had to until I got here. I forgive you. Now dat you've told me I will help you carry the secret. But promise me not to tell anybody else."

"I wish that I hadn't done it. I like Corney and COC even though they didn't handle things well with me. I don't need the money and I don't know how to make it right without going to jail.

"What do you think I should do?"

"I tink ve should get married and have babies. Fuck Corney and those bastards at COC." She laughed as hard as he ever seen and understood in that moment that she wasn't a saint. She was a tough woman, and she was on his side.

"Mitch has been offering you cash every time he comes. Right?"

"Yeah."

"Vell it's time to start taking it from Mitch and using the laundry business to clean it up. You can be Mister Clean just like the guy on television in Germany selling soap powder.

"Later on, you can give money away and make up for your sins. Now you haf to take care of me! And get rich."

Their lovemaking had progressed since their first wonderful times on the Clancy River. In this moment of fear and forgiveness they seemed to join in an inspired way.

"Dahlia."

"Yes."

"I have another favor to ask you. I mean in addition to forgiving me."

"The answer is yes. Paul. Vat is it?"

I want to go to church tomorrow and spend some time thinking about what's good for me and you and begin to try to get right with God."

"Okay."

SUNDAY – January 29, 2006, Ten a.m.

Joanna McLaurin conducted a beautiful service. She welcomed them at the door and the people seated nearby cordially greeted them. There was beautiful music from a choir and verses from the bible. Hymns that the congregation could sing along with, were fun and everyone was invited to participate in the Holy Communion, taking a sip of wine and a square of bread. The sermon was about forgiveness and salvation.

If Paul understood Joanna's sermon properly, God was prepared to forgive him his sins, but Paul had to do something in return – something more than just attend church. He had to ask for forgiveness and accept Jesus as his Lord and Savior.

These were impossible for him because he did not believe in God in the same way that the church members seem to be saying. He felt that proper behavior meant not hurting others. He felt a little uneasy about the punishment that Archie and Jim Bob were facing but he rationalized the fact that they too had committed a crime.

His own crime, the way he felt about it, it was a sort of a social blunder. He had made people feel bad, but the businesses of COC and the insurance company were not harmed. But he knew that Corney was hurt and pissed off at not being able to get the money back. And she'd tried so hard.

"Dahlia. Here in America many great fortunes were started amid rumors of crime and scandal. Is that true in Germany too?"

"Of course, Paul. Sometimes the great fortunes were got by theft or other illegal means. But a generation goes by, and no one remembers or cares. I understand you. You need to forgive yourself. Go about your business and count your blessings.

"You already have great fortune. You own a house and a business. You have money in the bank, and a vonderful voman. Yah?"

"*Yah.* Thank you for helping me get over it."

Their wedding day was a delightful blur to Dahlia and Paul. He found her parents very agreeable. Papa spoke perfect English with a Brit accent. Mama had a terrific accent but was understandable. They had both been practicing by joining an English club at home. Dahlia got her looks from her mother, and her 'get up and go' from her dad.

Paul's parents adored his bride, so they had a family love fest that went on until the day the parents had to return to their lives.

The dads, Gunter Schmidt and Michael Hunter hit it off immediately. They, the architect, and the builder, took great pleasure in walking about Swan Harbor and discussing the age, construction, and architecture of the various town buildings. Including, of course, Paul and Dahlia's home place.

They collaborated in creating a list of problems and potential improvement possibilities they'd noticed with the house for the young couple. They made a prioritized schedule for the work. Fortunately, most of problems were within the skill sets possessed by Paul and Mitch. Gunter took pictures of everything with his new digital camera. The moms and Dahlia were taken under the maid of honor's wings for shopping excursions. Norma was a dynamo. Monika, Dahlia's mom was the biggest beneficiary of this as she found the U.S. prices very economical and had to buy a new suitcase to hold her purchases.

All the out-of-town guests, including Mitch, and his girlfriend Molly, stayed at the Cygnet Bed and Breakfast.

SWAN HARBOR – March 15, 2001

Mild weather was the rule this year. No more freezes were anticipated. They had ferns hanging on the porch. Windows were cracked and the sun shone brightly on their fully painted building. On this, the first official day workday since their wedding, they sat at ease, opting to avoid chores. They served the occasional hot dog, coke, and coffee, listened to the sound of the washing machines and dryers as their wash customers did their laundry. They were reading the Charlotte Observer.

Paul read a story about a writer's visit to the Carson House in Old Fort, North Carolina. The part of the story that caught his interest was the way the house had been built in stages over many years by a succession of Carson generations.

The Carson House had started as a large post and beam cabin in the 18th century. It was first a plantation home, then, later, a tavern and a stagecoach inn as well. It was framed with chestnut. An identical structure was built next-door just 20 feet away. Years later, the two separate buildings had been joined by a roofed breezeway which eventually became the grand entrance foyer for the building. In its final stage the house was a colonial mansion with stately columns.

Paul had a sudden insight into how they might proceed to improve their property. He felt it was within their capabilities and means.

"My love. I just got an idea..." He broached the idea to Dahlia,

Dahlia looked up from the story she had been reading about the rising prices of homes. Their minds clicked as they began talking.

"So, we are agreed?

"Yes, we vill build an open-air breezeway first. This fall. That vill gif us an outdoor studio next season and the year after we vill build an attached house. Ve attach it to the other side of the breezeway Sort of like they did at the Carson House."

They were both excited and agreed that they'd go to look at the Carson house in person on Monday to see how it looked. "Suddenly Dahlia, I can see a route to wealth. We can use my $64,000.00 COC "inheritance" to finance the construction if we need it. Or we could just use the bank if they'll do it.

The season progressed as they had hoped. Business was good. They sold paintings, wreaths, food, drinks, and launderette services. Their income from their assorted activities paid their obligations and grew their bank balances. But they'd never get rich in the businesses they'd chosen.

Paul grew tired of creating 'Watcher' paintings in early 2001. He began experimenting with and then painting intimate portraits of ponds and streams. His work was inspired by his history with Dahlia. He did not dwell on the man and woman or on the sexual elements of their outings but rather on creating a beautiful and natural environment.

Their secret place featured transparent water. He created luminescent watercolors with a minimum of paint. The technique served as an invitation for the viewer to supply the missing elements. Sometimes he would include suggestions of human forms or even representations of colorful boats. Rocks and flowers were featured in every painting. These were soothing works and his public readily accepted them.

As time passed, he evolved again into doing sky and water inspired by Swan Harbor. Bay water, islands, dunes, and birds took over. These paintings were usually without people because he felt inadequate about his ability with figures and faces.

He liked sketching and painting the old buildings in his neighborhood. He experimented with impressionistic and surrealistic works and eventually began producing a wide range of themes. The possibilities were endless, and he found inspiration in his daily life.

His sketchbooks were also full of human elements. He drew hands arms, ears, torsos, eyes, and eventually whole figures. People gradually began to appear in more of his paintings. He moved on to portraits with Dahlia as his favorite subject.

SWAN HARBOR – June 2001

Paul liked painting on the top landing of his staircase – his deck. Only eight feet by eight feet, it sported an ell shaped bench built into the railings. It was secluded because it was on the rear of the building and screened in the canopy of trees. He took to painting there. At first, he wore shorts but he worked nude on fine days, often smudging wisps of paint on his skin. He liked the feel of the rough wood under his feet and the whisper of air on his skin.

He rigged a system to chime if anyone approached the bottom of the stairs, around the corner. When the bell chimed, rarely, his procedure was to step into the door. Pants, tee shirt and step in sandals took a few seconds and he'd step back on station within fifteen seconds – fully dressed. Dahlia thought it was cute.

She loved to sunbathe and frequently posed there in the corner of the bench. She'd patiently read, snooze or chat, as he wished, lounging on padded cushions. He had the prettiest model he could imagine. His skills advanced with practice.

Dahlia had altered her appearance slightly. Her hair remained short, but she began to emulate her new set of girlfriends by shaving her legs and armpits. Her pubic hair remained dark and nappy but not too bushy he thought.

Dahlia was not shy about having her image in the paintings and often sold them herself to somewhat smitten men. Paul loved the way she looked and thought of her as his perfect woman.

SWAN HARBOR – December 2001

Business softened after September 11th. The world Trade Center and other terrorist attacks kept the usual shoulder-season tourists stay home. Paul and Dahlia decided to execute the big plan immediately, while business was somewhat off, instead of doing it in stages. They would erect a mirror-image building, ala the Carson House, and connect the old and new with a center hall to serve as the main art gallery and entry. They wanted to get it done while they weren't too busy.

The work would be done over the winter, off-season, to minimize the inconvenience to customers. Both dads, Michael, and Gunter, contributed to the plan. They hired Sam Ellison, Swan Harbor's most prominent citizen, a state senator as well as an architect, to draw the final plan, take care of getting the necessary permits and review bids submitted by contractors. Sam would check on progress on a regular basis for a fee of $5,000.00. This seemed like a bargain, but Sam said, "Don't worry. I can see this job from my office, and it will take very little time.

Paul's dad would be the general contractor, using a North Carolina licensed friend to sign off documentation as necessary.

His dad, Mitch, and Paul would do the interior finish and painting as far as practical.

Gunter provided them with proposed floor plans and elevations. Sam had an automated drawing program in his computer and used to produce paper drawings. The final plans showed a handsome building with ample space for parking and gardens.

Paul wanted to do post and beam to really match the original building, but his dad overruled that. "Paul. People today don't know post and beam. They know frame and so that's what to use. In the end you will save money because your people won't be standing around scratching their balls while they're dealing with unfamiliar construction problems.

"The differences between the two wings won't be obvious from the outside. Remember, painted siding will cover everything."

The finished job would result in their having a sixteen hundred square foot residence with a hall connecting the second floor of the new residence to their existing apartment. There were options regarding the use of the space. The connecting upstairs hallway was 14 feet wide and could be used as either an addition to the existing apartment or as part of the new residence with simple partitioning.

They could use the apartment as a rental until their own family needs dictated otherwise. They also talked about renting the new two-story residence and continuing to live in their apartment as an option that could change when their family increased. So, their home could be of substantial size and the business space would double. Dahlia decided the final use of the addition by getting pregnant.

They decided to live in the newly constructed residence themselves. They would enlarge the existing apartment to generate more rental income when it was done. They did this by making the second floor above the new central gallery a part of the rental unit rather than part of the new house. Everyone was pleased by the result.

They needed additional mortgage funding. Their present cash balances were almost fifty thousand dollars and growing even in slow times. Mitch had been slipping them money but they had almost all of the stolen funds still unlaundered and available, hidden in a fire and water proof box and buried on the property.

Dad, Michael, would remain with them while footings were formed and poured. Paul's job was to scour the countryside for bargain building materials. Dad's long bed pickup truck was good for most hauling, but heavier stuff had to be trucked in and staged on the property. Mitch would be on standby until early 2002 when he would start working with Paul a few days a week.

Jeff at the Ace Hardware store volunteered his "lazy, good-for-nothin, giant, sons to work whenever needed. Jeff said they could do general labor, carpentry. Painting, and, in fact, anything Paul asked. With supervision of course. "Be sure to smell their breath," he advised with a wink. Paul knew that the men were excellent, reliable workers - Jeff was just kidding.

Architect Sam gave Paul a letter estimating the cost of the addition at one hundred and fifty thousand dollars including the presumptive value of free owner's labor. Paul thought that the actual cost might be much lower.

Banker Ben King was happy to do a construction loan with the final permanent loan package totaling two hundred and ten thousand dollars. Progress payments were made as architect Sam certified progress to the bank. The architect thought that the post construction value of the property would exceed three hundred thousand dollars. Dahlia and Paul were content with the numbers.

SWAN HARBOR – December 2005

Dahlia's life was blooming. Their two children, Janice, almost four-years old, and Billy two years old, filled her life with energy and joy. Paul was doing well in his art business, but things had changed greatly from the first year.

Paul had originally created an original painting almost every day and would sell them one at a time for $150.00. He shipped a few to Elizabeth in Clancy for her to sell.

Now that they had children, they hired college students on summer break to work in the business. Dahlia said her job description was Queen and Paul was her Consort.

Paul was happy about their situation too. He loved Dahlia and the children, he was comfortable in Swan Harbor, and he took pride in their business progress. They worked hard, to be sure, but they had fun as well.

The VW bus was history now, replaced by a beefy F250, King Cab pickup truck. They had bought it new when the great addition to their house was in progress. It seemed to offer great safety for the family on the road, and it served their business needs, carried their sea kayaks, and was a roomy traveler when they ventured forth once or twice a year.

"Paul!" called Dahlia with some energy in her voice. "Paul. It's Elizabeth on the phone. For you."

After a little small talk Elizabeth announced that she and George would like to come for a visit. "The first week of January would be best for us."

"Yay!" shouted Paul. He looked at the calendar by the phone and said, "Elizabeth. Just say the date and we'll be ready. Stay with us for as long as you like. Use us as a motel on your way to other places. We're all yours."

They agreed on Wednesday, January fourth. The kids had heard the excitement in Daddy's voice and were running around yelling, "Aunt Elizabeth and Uncle George are coming!" over and over again.

Paul and Elizabeth hung up on a happy note. Elizabeth was a hero to Paul. In addition to teaching him about painting watercolors, she had suggested new and better ways to do his art gallery business, sharing things she had learned.

In early 2002 Elizabeth had sent him a letter reporting sales and suggesting that he might take some of her paintings to sell for her in his gallery. A nice reciprocal arrangement he thought. She had also told him that she had just found a printer to make reproductions of her work that allowed her to earn much more from each work of art. Her originals sold for more substantial prices.

She had two classes of reproductions. The first was called a limited edition that she would proof at the printing press. She signed, numbered, and dated each one.

Glycees were reproductions and could be sold for twenty, or more, dollars each. The reproductions tripled her revenue for each day's work. Within a week of getting Elizabeth's letter, Paul was hanging reproductions of his paintings with $50.00 and $100.00 price tag. They sold well and he spent some time with a local printer making good copies.

He found a more specialized printer in Greenville who, for a higher price, would make reproductions with archival inks on elegant art paper. These limited editions brought a higher price and Paul signed and numbered each one. In the world of art, the signature was regarded as a promise not to make more copies – thus they were worth more. He now was creating a large inventory and did not have to work so hard to create new art every day.

The limited-edition reproductions cost him the trouble of going to Greenville at an appointed time and waiting while the printer set up his press in addition to the actual expense of the printing. It was an all-day excursion and he had to leave Dahlia at home to tend to business and the children. But, in a few months, he had an inventory of reproductions and began taking time away from painting; he had enough paintings and reproductions to open a larger store.

They hung and displayed some of Elizabeth's work and it made their little gallery more interesting. Now, five years into their Swan Harbor residency Paul had made arrangements with gallery owners throughout the area to reciprocate with him so the income from his work rose significantly.

SWAN HARBOR – January 2006

One of the many pleasures Dahlia gleaned from living in Swan Harbor was a stroller walk with her children almost every day.

She started downhill. Sometimes Janice would walk next to the stroller and sometimes she would ride in tandem with Billy. Either way they'd make it to Main Street and window shop.

Dahlia's exercise would be accomplished in the end by walking fast and long, up and down the town's gentle slopes. Sometimes the kids on board would be sleeping while she sweated.

She paused in front of the real estate office one fine winter day and looked at pictures of houses for sale in the window. She saw prices in the window on a variety of properties all over the county. Home prices were tending up. Way up. Then she saw a price that galvanized her. Holy Mackerel! There was a house on their street listed for $750,000.00.

It was a very nice house to be sure, but not so much nicer than hers. They had two acres of property, a new residence that could be made into a much larger home or, alternatively, expanded on the business side.

Dahlia was out of breath when she called out to Paul. He was rocking on the porch with a sketchpad in his lap. They could hear the hum and soft thumps of laundry in the background. They thought of it as the sound of money.

"What's up honey?"

"Paul! I was looking in the window at Midgett's Real Estate. The Smith house down the street is listed for sale."

"So what?"

"Paul. They are asking $750,000.00. It makes me wonder. What do you think our place is worth?"

"Wow! That's a lot. I can't believe it! I'll bet we could get more than that for ours."

"Yeah. But why would we want to sell?"

"I don't really want to move but think about what we could do with the money. We'd have hundreds of thousands left afterwards. How much do ve owe the bank?"

"About one-hundred-eighty thousand."

"So ve vould haf over a half-a-million dollars cash if ve sold?"

"Well. I guess so. But what then? Would we buy another place? Move the kids – is that a good idea?"

It turned out that they listed their place for $900.000.00 and waited months for buyers to notice and submit offers.

"Marlyss, should we lower our price?"

"No. Not yet. The problem is not that people are saying it's too much. We just haven't had the right lookers yet. Wait. The market is very strong, and someone will come along.

PART THREE
Prosperity

ASHEVILLE, N.C. – June 2006

Marlyss was right. The offer, when it came, stunned them. They countered and sold their place for $850,000.00. They had from all sources, $857,000.00 in the bank the day they moved out. The place was sold furnished with the complete laundry business and an empty art gallery that the new owners would use for something else. Paul's share of the stolen cash, $64,000, remained in Mitch's custody.

The fact that they were on a large lot had helped them get a good price. It meant off-street parking. Driving and parking in Swan Harbor was always hard due to the narrow streets. The same narrowness that made it feel so cozy and old-timey made the driving difficult.

It felt a bit like winning the game of Monopoly when you have all the money.

Their possessions, including their inventory of paintings and a few wreaths, fit into the U-Haul trailer and the long bed of the F250 with its fancy tonneau cover and fiberglass bed liner. They were off to Asheville North Carolina to try and continue their good fortune. They'd been to Asheville many times and loved the vibe. The city was like a magnet for artists.

Paul brought something else with him besides the possessions in the truck and a beautiful family. He had a malaise, a guilt in his heart, about the theft from COC. He had stolen other things besides. As a lad he and his friends in Alabama had filched candy, comic books, baseball cards, and such from neighborhood merchants and never been caught. He and his big brother had done larger thefts too, when they were a little older, and had paid a heavy price for getting caught.

Now in his inner mind he felt like a lesser man. He had not felt guilty as a kid but now the COC theft was another crime on the list. An adult crime. He wished that he had not done it.

The main thing was that he had nowhere to go with the problem. Dahlia had forgiven him, and he felt that she did not wish to talk about it further. He was afraid to tell others, so he had to process it internally.

Paul did not think about it every minute, but he had dreams about the event at night. He would wake fearful and downcast. The depression would stay with him until he remembered that it was only a dream and deliberately gave himself a little lecture; get over it Paul. No one else thinks about it – neither should you. Then the cloud would lift until next time.

He just didn't know what to do about it, but the sharpest edges of his culpability lessened as the years went by. He'd long ago gotten his 401K money and he had no further contact with Corney.

He'd thought about matters of conscience, morality, and mortality, almost every Sunday in Swan Harbor as he reacted to Marianne's sermons. Sometimes he felt like Robin Hood, even if he was both the thief and poor peasant who got the booty. More often he felt the need to make amends but knew that his innocent family could suffer if he made the wrong moves.

He had called the lawyer, Bunny Johns in Clancy several years ago. She told him that Archie was convicted and serving a five-year felony sentence. Jim Bob had cooperated first and got three years on a lesser charge. Bunny said they'd get time off for good behavior. Paul shuddered to think about what they would give him; the big liar and the guy who got away with the loot. He worried about Mitch getting involved too.

Asheville had a reputation for being an artsy town with a high tolerance for alternative lifestyles. Sort of a tiny San Francisco moved into the mountainous areas of western North Carolina. Lush with municipal flower gardens, decorated with elegant sculpture and finished off with a great diversity of cultures. Old people,

309 alternative-life-style youth, businesspeople, poor, rich, and middle of the road rubbed shoulders on the picturesque streets.

Mitch had lived there for a while once upon a time ago and Paul had enjoyed visiting. The plan was to rent for a year or so to decide if Asheville was for them and to learn the area before being tied to a mortgage. Janice would be in kindergarten in the fall. Billy might start preschool. Their lives were full of promise and excitement.

Paul's motivation for earning money was a somewhat diminished now that they felt well off. He craved an outlet for his need to work. Paul wanted meaningful work

The family lived simply in an old rental near the center of Asheville. There were five bedrooms, one bath and a picturesque fireplace. It was cheap relative to their means. They had a steady stream of income from savings, paintings, and the reproductions that Paul had hanging in a dozen galleries. He had an inventory of paintings, mostly his own work. So, the first task work-wise was to find a way to sell them.

He found two local places to hang his work. One was just a stall in an artists' mall outlet in nearby Black Mountain. He didn't have to man it. The owner would call him once a week and tell him if he needed to provide more paintings.

The other spot was an ancient low-rent shop on a downtown Asheville side street, a few blocks from home. Here he had room to paint and good light from big plate glass windows. It overlooked a quaint street with experienced a decent amount of traffic. He painted in the window so that passersby could watch him. Prints with their reasonable price tags visible from the sidewalk enticed people in to look at his gallery.

He organized the gallery with his original paintings in frames as befitting their much higher price tags. The reproductions, both of his work and that of other artists, rested in canvass slings so that browsers could conveniently view them.

Dahlia's wreaths had a place too. She brought the kids in their stroller around noon most days. Paul took his turn parenting then while she worked in the shop or went off to do errands and food shopping. These were great times for them both. She needed alone time, and he liked being with the kids. His inner child was very active, and he loved to play with them.

Asheville was better than Swan Harbor in many ways. The streets and byways were old and historically interesting. The shops and restaurants were plentiful and the street walking public almost always in a good mood.

There were panhandlers and street performers. Particularly on fine weekends when tourists were likely to be in the mix. Paul had a rule of thumb when it came to giving money on the street. He always said, "Yes."

Dahlia frowned when she first noticed this tendency. "Paul. They should work for their money. You are just encouraging them to be lazy and feeding their alcoholism." They were walking down Biltmore Avenue in Asheville at the time.

"Yeah. I know. But Marianne made a speech once that I always remember. She said her mother was from Spain and there was an awful time during the Spanish Civil War when her mother was young. They had nothing to eat, and her grandmother begged for food and money in the streets of Madrid. She, Marianne, said that whenever she is asked for money on the street, she goes out of her way to give. Sometimes way more than requested.

"If she's asked for a dollar, she'll give ten or twenty. She said it made her feel good and she thinks that Christ would approve."

Dahlia pondered this. "I know it was awful in Germany too after World War II. I'll bet there was a lot of begging and need then. But it is sort of unpopular to give money to a beggar. I think I will be nicer about it now Paul." She gave him a public hug and put the brakes on the stroller so that she could fish small bills from the depths of her purse for the sole purpose of giving them away. "I hope someone asks soon," she said to Paul. "I have just switched sides on this."

She was not disappointed. She gave a shaggy, worn-out guy, sitting with a cup at his feet, a smile and two bills.

"God bless you," he muttered.

She thought he looked a little like an older Paul before the haircut and close-trimmed beard; before her husband became Mister Clean. The gift made her feel good and she resolved to make it a permanent habit.

The street performers were looking for money too, and the couple agreed that the music makers and mimes added to the city's happy ambiance. Paul often stopped and gave them his business card, as well as the money, and invited them to play in front of his store when they needed a spot. He liked their presence and felt they might bring traffic. He let these people use his bathroom facilities and, occasionally, they bought pictures, sometimes even pricey pieces.

Thus, Paul and Dahlia progressed through these years of their marriage. They began to attend Church at Christ Presbyterian two blocks from their home. There was childcare for Billy and Sunday school for Janice while they went to services. Paul chose to participate in the church's efforts to help the poor and homeless who were suffering in Asheville as well as every other city in the world.

Paul accepted that many of the people showing up for shelter and food at the church's downtown shelter facility were mentally ill, addicts, or hopeless alcoholics. Mostly they were shabby, hungry, dirty, cold and hopeless. Paul remembered his improved acceptance in the civilized world when he got his hair cut and his beard trimmed. He felt sure that a little barbering and a fresh wardrobe could help some of the people showing up every week.

He spoke to the pastor about his ideas. "Arthur. The food and shelter we give these people, mostly men, is lifesaving. But do you think we might do a little more. How about making a shower available. I think I can get my barber to volunteer once in a while and. Plus donated clothing might be enough for some of these poor bastards to get some kind of work."

"Sounds like a good idea to me Paul. Go to work on it. Let's see what you can do?" Arthur McAuliff was a good leader for the church and a good delegator. Many ideas were sent his way almost every day. He needed people to help do the work.

"Will do," said Paul. And he did. He was able to get three downtown barbers to come to the mission for two hours each on Wednesday afternoons. The quick print shop made a sign that said,

BARBER SHOP OPEN HERE
WEDNESDAY
NOON – FIVE P.M.
FREE

The three barbers arranged their own schedules with each other and it turned out that business was brisk. After a few weeks they recruited two more hair cutters, including a woman who told them to use her for females if they wished. The program expanded to three afternoons a week. Guys that looked like hermits looked like businessmen when they were shorn, cleaned up, and dressed in fresh clothes. There were fewer females, but they needed help too.

The shower facilities were not hard to arrange. Two plastic shower stalls and a water heater were soon installed, and Paul paid the plumber. Paul rigged curtains for privacy for two bathers and hooks for clothing. Dahlia made up plastic zip kits with a comb, motel soap, shampoo, washcloth, and bars of motel soap.

Paul, who stopped by frequently to sweep up and help out, came to understand that keeping clean was the hardest thing on the street. There was just no way to stop from getting dirty. He thought about the months he'd spent camping at COC. His needs had been simpler because he was in an environment where simple living, as in staff housing, was the norm and he wasn't that far from his peers then in the matter of personal grooming and hygiene. He had had money, transport, and access to laundry facilities as often as he felt the need. He could afford to buy a new tee shirt or sweater. He had time around camp to clean up his boots and privacy to wash himself.

On the street it was different. The smelly, dirty and ragged people had nowhere to turn once they lost their place in society. They were harassed by the police and suspected by merchants even if they had enough cash to make a petty purchase. They had no bank accounts, no bank accounts, no benefits and, likely in most cases, no family to seek out. Their bridges had been burned one way or another. Worst of all for them, were their own bad habits and antisocial behavior.

Paul encountered a down-and-out guy named Marty one day. Wearing a pink fedora hat and matching hi-top pink sneakers, he seemed a pleasant and sunny guy. Dirty, broke and hopeless. He got a shave and a shower, a haircut, and new clothes, from the Samaritans of Asheville Society. The members of the church knew it as SAS. Marty kept his hat and sneakers on after his hygienic makeover.

"Dang. You clean up real nice," called out Paul who was lounging on a bench in the shade watching the barbers work. "Come over here and sit for a minute."

Marty introduced himself and said, "Thanks. My name's Marty Smith. I understand you are the guy who started this clean-em-up program. I feel a thousand percent better."

Paul said, "Well. We're willing." He saw Marty as a handsome man of slight build with stained and damaged teeth. What else can we do for you?"

"I need to do laundry," said Marty. I have a backpack full of dirty clothes and I haven't been able to clean 'em."

"Call me Paul." Paul realized that there were no laundries nearby that could be reached on foot or by public transportation.

"Here Marty. Take this and I'll give you a ride to the laundry and pick you up after your clothes are done." He handed Marty a five-dollar bill. "You're spending the night with us. Right?"

"Thanks. But Paul. What planet have you been living on? You can't do laundry for five bucks." His rather angelic face peered intently at Paul.

Paul smiled. He knew that Marty was wrong, but he didn't care to challenge him, so he dug another bill out of his pocket. "Let's go Marty."

"Nice rig!" Marty said as he climbed into the F250's high and wide bucket seat."

"Thanks."

"You got a family," said Marty. It was not a question. It was a remark on the toys and coloring books having a party in the pack seat.

"Yup. A girl and a boy. Five and two," Paul answered questions not yet asked.

"Ah. You're so lucky. Me? I haven't done so good. I've been drifting forever and now I'm so fucked up, excuse my French, Padre, that I don't see how to make it now. I'm bumping along the bottom."

"Hey Marty, there's always hope. And I'm not a preacher. Listen. You look good now. Like a citizen. Get some help from the Samaritans for your drinking problem and you could get a start."

"Nah. There's one thing you've got to understand about me Paul. I'm not an alcoholic!"

Paul looked at him expectantly.

"I'm just a drunk." He laughed as he carefully exited and took his backpack into the laundry.

"I'll be back in an hour Marty." Paul waved as he pulled out. He headed for the bank to make a deposit. Checks arrived almost every day from the painting outlets he maintained, and he had sold a few paintings yesterday. He was not making a good living, but it didn't matter. Interest rates were high, and his capital was secure.

Paul got back to the laundry a little sooner than he thought but Marty was not there. His backpack was on a chair and Paul spotted his laundry in the bottom of a silent drier.

Paul waited for a few minutes then went looking. There was a pizza joint on the next block, and he strolled over. Sure enough, Marty was eating a slice and had two empty beer bottles on the table.

"The laundry is dry," said Paul.

"Good," smiled Marty. "I got a little hungry and I was just about to go back to wait for you." He took the last bite of his slice and swallowed the last drops of his beer. They ambled back to retrieve the dry wash and climb into the truck for the return to SAS

Paul frankly did not understand the pull of alcohol. He had been brought up watching his dad drink beer while watching sports on TV and his Mom relished a glass of wine with dinner on occasion. He had drunk beer at parties when it was socially necessary, but alcohol made him sleepy and not more social.

Dahlia had insisted on champagne at their wedding and wine for the guests, but it had not affected them much.

"So, Marty. I guess you spent all the money I gave you. And that's okay. But what are you going to do next?"

"I gotta get to Georgia. Not so far from here. I got a friend who's holding a job for me in his restaurant. I should have been there sooner, but I got delayed."

"Oh. That's good," said Paul. I was a little worried about you."

When they got back to SAS the guests were lining up for dinner. Marty sat under a tree by himself and Paul could see him nodding off as he worked in the kitchen window. He was thinking that Marty needed dental care and wondered if he could get a dentist in the program for some basic pro bono treatment.

On a whim he walked over to Marty and roused him by saying, "Hi."

"Hi Paul. Gosh it's nice today. I'm holding back on the chow line because I had the pizza for lunch. I'll be hungry in a little while."

"Yeah Marty. That's good. Look here. I like you very much. I know you have to go to Georgia now but don't hesitate to come back here if you need to or if you'd like to work with us here." Paul had no idea that those words were going to come out of his mouth. He was a little sad to think about Marty on the road again.

Marty marched off the next morning before Paul got there. Paul heard from the manager that he looked good. Had a spring in his step. Said he was whistling and wore his silly hat at a jaunty angle. Paul assumed that he was off to see his friend and forgot about him.

ASHEVILLE – September 1, 2006

Pastor Arthur McAuliff asked Paul to become an Elder of the church. The committee of Elders elected him as a Fellow and gave him the job of overseeing The SAS program.

Paul lived parallel lives. Each was intense and in competition for his time. Dahlia was first. He was in consultation with her about his schedule, his motivation, and his expenditures of their money. He was a husband, a lover, a father, a painter, a businessman and head of an important church program that benefited the whole community. He was a member of the chamber of commerce. These were all compelling activities.

A lot of Paul's time and energy was devoted to staying in touch with the gallery owners that were displaying each other's paintings. The owners he favored were artists as well as shop keepers. They all kept ledgers for each work they shipped out and the rule was to pay each other promptly. He got a fist full of checks each week and this, if fact, was more than half his art revenue. His gallery did well enough and their annuity income from capital invested was more than adequate.

Dahlia was a young American mother now with hardly a trace of an accent, unless she was very excited. Her parents came to visit once a year and she and Paul had gone to Germany once when Janice was a baby. They stayed in good contact with Mitch and Paul's parents. Mitch was married to Molly now and father of two boys. Charlotte was not so far, and they saw him frequently. They had a social circle and friends from their other cities, Clancy and Swan Harbor.

Dahlia's life revolved around her children and her church friends. Paul was a great friend but girls needed girlfriends. Mostly she found moms with children. They often had similar interests and problems. The group began at the park before the kids started school. They evolved into semimonthly gatherings celebrating life, anniversaries, and birthdays. In fine weather they'd be outdoors, in foul they would take turns hosting.

Dahlia worked on arrangements and wreaths a couple of days a week and she spent shifts shop keeping. It was Dahlia who worked out an elaborate accounting system for tracking the paintings; both Paul's and those of cooperating artists. When they became computer literate in the middle of the twenty first century's first decade, they hired a programmer to make a spreadsheet system that was driven by weekly inventories submitted by participating artists. Dahlia was able to get a copyright on the application and sold copies for $199.00 each. This was not a big business, but it helped create and spread Paul's celebrity status in the world of art galleries. She was updating the program to reflect the new realities of the business where printing on demand made large inventories obsolete.

Dahlia loved walking in town. She had a good fitness program that involved very early morning water exercise at the Y and daily walks involving kids and a stroller. Asheville was a great walking town. It boasted wide sidewalks, protected crosswalks, parks and interesting buildings.

Like many cities Asheville had a case of Walmar-itus – meaning that the big box stores and shopping centers had shifted shoppers away from downtown. So empty buildings, once prospering with offices and stores, now stood empty and neglected. She wondered what could be done with such buildings.

She told Paul, "There is an empty building on the corner of Biltmore and Second. It is a sort of tan brick and might have been a car dealership once. There are three stories above the ground floor and I'm wondering if we could think of a way to use it. Maybe we could even try to develop it if we can make a good plan."

"We can talk about it but I don't know if could handle the financial end. How about a gallery downstairs and apartments up. I heard that downtown apartments are a thing now. Is there any parking?"

"I'm not sure. Let's walk over after supper and poke around."

"Okay. That will be fun. Just looking. Right?"

The streets were still busy at seven o'clock, but they took their time. Parking was available on the street. It was just one short block to a new municipal parking garage. The property had space for about twenty cars along one side including space under the cantilevered second floor.

They copied the telephone number and made the call when they returned home. They expected to leave a message but I woman answered, "Sloe Realty. Jolie speaking."

Paul explained their interest. "Hi Paul and Dahlia Hunter, here. You're on speaker phone. Asking about the building on Biltmore and Second."

"Ah. The old Biltmore Cafeteria Building. That's my listing. They are asking a million five and it has been empty, and for sale, for about two and a half years. It may be a teardown. What do you have in mind?"

"Not too sure. Could we get a tour before we talk about what to do with it?"

"Sure. When." She spoke quickly but her tone was warm and friendly.

"Tomorrow before noon or after five o'clock, before it gets dark, would probably be good for us.

"Right Dahlia?"

"Yah. Dat's good."

"Okay. I'm good for nine in the morning."

Jolie turned out to be a slender, redheaded woman in blue jeans and an expensive looking sweater. Paul judged her to be mid-thirties and very prosperous. She parked her Ford Expedition with assurance and had an air of success – almost a swagger. Her manner was direct but engaging. They both liked her.

The outside looked all right but the ground floor was suffering from demolition interruptus. Later they agreed that it needed to be fully gutted, and everything thrown away to fully appreciate its generous size and high ceilings. There was no elevator, but a wide stairwell led to a mezzanine and upper floors that had been used as offices once upon a time ago.

They could not access the roof, but she assured them that it would probably pass an inspection, but she didn't have a key to the door. "The owners couldn't find it and I've shown it so seldom that I haven't been too worried about getting one. If you guys are serious, I'll get a locksmith over later today."

"Well. Don't worry for now. I want to call my dad. He's a general contractor in Charlotte and we'll want his advice. What would it take to have an option to buy this place?"

Jolie said, "The thing to do is figure out if you want it and then make an offer. Usually, an offer is made with a deposit and a period of time for the owner to respond. It's just like a deal on a house but larger in scale and with more civic involvement."

"What do you mean by civic involvement?"

"When you buy a commercial building in the city you must get approval from several departments before you can get building permits. The odd one you may not have thought of is the Parking

Authority. Like most cities we must make sure that we don't add traffic without providing additional parking.

"You will find, however, if you should decide to buy this building, that the building department will work very hard to make your project possible and not just enforce the rules."

"We don't have a lot of experience," confessed Dahlia. "We will need all the guidance we can get."

"Amen," said Paul.

Paul took out his checkbook and gave Jolie a $10,000.00 deposit check to tie the property down while the many preliminary activities were accomplished. She assured him that the conditional contract for purchase would be signed by morning. "Call an architect," suggested Jolie. "He'll give you the real skinny."

Dad, Michael Hunter, came by himself two days later and took the complete tour. "Good news and bad news," he said.

They were standing in the middle of the first floor. "This place could be a gem," said dad. Jolie was standing at a distance to give them privacy. "The roof is probably good for ten or more years. We'll have to check building departments permits to get details and dates on what work has been done on it. There is no way to get an elevator to the top floor – so it'll be a walkup forever. The columns you see now on the ground floor carry loads from the roof to the foundation and they must stay. Otherwise, you can partition this place anyway you want. Have you been informed about either lead paint or asbestos?"

"The asbestos and lead have been mentioned but we're waiting for the architects to tell us more."

Then the questions are: What is it you want to do? And can you afford it?"

"Oh, nothing much Dad," Paul grinned, "Just create the premier art gallery in western North Carolina on the first floor and five or six luxury apartments above. We'll do one furnished model on the second floor and create floor plans for the others. We're talking about long-term, prepaid leases with separate maintenance agreements. I don't know if it has been done here before – its

Dahlia's idea. We need to talk to an architect and a banker about the concepts, but we may make a really lowball offer soon."

"Wow," said dad. "You guys have come a long way in the scale of your thinking. If you get it and decide on a project or need my help let me know.

"Things are slowing way down at home and we're all scrambling for work. Mom and I could move here just for your work. And Paul and Dahlia – for you I work very, very cheap.

"Tell me more about the project."

"Ve are tinking that the top floor vill be a thirty-six hundred square foot residence and the other two floors will yield four eighteen hundred square foot apartments. I am dreaming about vat dey vill look like," Dahlia gushed. She was practically dancing.

"When will you be seeing the banker and the architect?"

"Today, Dad. The architects are due here at noon and I'm going to the bank after. We have been lucky enough to have a real personal banker who is already considering our situation. The architects will give us a brief written report, but they've been engaged just to listen to the idea and give us a verbal, totally non-binding, costs range estimate today so that we can make a decision to begin planning or give it up. We really just need a conversation to tell us what ballpark we're in."

The architects were equally enthusiastic about the prospects, so the Hunters made an offer $850,000.00 with three days allowed for an answer. That, they deemed, was about the value of the lot without the building. They attached a check for five thousand dollars to the offer. Jolie was thrilled.

They were alone in their bedroom with the lights out. Dad was watching television in the living room. Paul whispered, "Dahlia. This is crazy. We've got a project that will last for years, and I can't really see how we can do it even if the bank lends us the money."

"Let it rest for tonight, Paul. We'll work on it tomorrow. Just hold me tight and think good thoughts."

Holding his wife tight was very much on Paul's mind. The magic returned. He pretended they were lying in their secret place on the Clancy River having sex for the first time.

Morning dawned and the kids were parked in front of the TV. The three adults sat around the kitchen table noodling about how to proceed. There wasn't much energy of conviction in their voices. They were all three thinking "No." It's too big a project and we don't want to work so hard.

The phone rang. Paul reached the kitchen wall phone without leaving his chair, "Hello."

Jolie said a cheery good morning.

"Paul. Are you sitting down?"

"Yes I am. Hi to you too."

"Paul. I just got a phone call. There is a national retailer interested in the property. I don't have the name. But the indication I got from the signal is that they knew about the price the property had on it and they were very interested. They have optioned the property next door and will have enough land to use for parking or maybe a parking garage.

"Would you like a suggestion?"

"Yes. Of course. Hold on a second." He whispered the nature of the phone call to Dahlia and Dad.

"Go ahead Jolie."

"I think you might flip the property without actually closing on your purchase and I believe we might even ask a higher price and let them negotiate. I'm so excited I can't sit. I'm heading for my lawyer's office right now to consult about what kinds of agreements he would need to draft for us and I suggest that you get a lawyer right away and we'll make sure that we all profit. I'm out for a bigger commission but you might just hit a home run!"

"You mean like ask for two million?"

"Any number you care to name. Might as well go for a homer."

"Two-million-three-hundred thousand," chimed in Dahlia who had gotten the gist of the conversation."

Paul's dad sat with his mouth hanging open.

"Okay Jolie. Two million five hundred thousand!"

Legal fees, Jolie's commissions, and the architects took a cut. They said, "Ouch," when they realized the tax consequences. Paul's dad was given a check for $50,000.00. He protested but, in the end, accepted his good luck. Paul and Dahlia got rich. After taxes their net worth was $3,000,000.00.

Paul told Dahlia, "Sweetheart. I don't know how any of this happened, but I don't want to jinx things buy spending it all. Let's buy a house that doesn't cost too much and make sure that the money lasts.

When Dahlia began shopping for a house, she discovered that the market was softening. Even commercial property downtown was becoming reasonable as an economic recession settled in. She was in no hurry because, even though their rental home was a little shabby outside, she had decorated the inside and she loved the neighborhood.

Paul bicycled to work and, most days, to the Good Samaritan House. Because of Dahlia's coup he began to pay more attention to for sale signs on buildings. He spotted a three-story building on Montford Avenue across the street from a national, eat-in, hamburger restaurant.

The building included a vacant store downstairs and appeared to be apartments above. There were no glaring signs from nearby businesses. Upstairs, on the second and third floors, long banks of windows looked out on tree shaded parking areas and there were churches on the other two intersections.

The neighborhood included many solid Victorian homes on large, tree-shaded lots so that even though the building was on a traffic-light-controlled intersection, the feeling was peaceful and the traffic not obtrusive. There was a city park a block away. There he spotted benched mothers with young children frolicking in the playground.

They asked Jolie to negotiate. Dad helped inspect the building.

The architect's design combined four apartments into a single two-story, four-bedroom residence with four bathrooms. The master bedroom had a large *ensuite* bathroom with a monster, freestanding, claw-foot tub. Partitions were removed and they were moved in before the snow flew in December 2007. They had profited from real estate transactions royally. They congratulated themselves for riding out economic cycles and buying wisely.

They'd spent less than $400,000.00 and, when they got around to moving the gallery from Lexington Avenue, their business was rent-free. There was a single parking spot next to the building which just fit the truck. Customers would park on the street.

Their financial picture had improved vastly since they had sat on the sidelines as renters while real estate prices across the country plunged. Then they bought back in at the bottom of the market. The situation was just luck as they had no more foresight as the rest of the world.

ASHEVILLE – May 2007

Corney came to town a few weeks after their move. Corney had not forgotten about Paul. She was stuck mentally; unable to figure out why or how he had worked with Archie and Jim Bob, or how they had gotten into the safe. When she relocked it after the theft, it could not be reopened. She had to call a safe repair shop for service.

She had not thought to ask the safe technician, who'd reset the safe's old combination, about the combination on the day he was there, and he later had no recollection of the number. His job had been to get the safe open and reset the combination.

Therefore, she did not know that it had conveniently been set to a combination that Archie knew. Most importantly she could not see how they had made the money disappear so quickly. She had personally examined the woods, the paths, the river's banks and the rocks for a goodly distance around COC many times over the years looking for the swag and clues. She found nothing.

Keeping tabs on Paul and Dahlia was an obsession. Dun and Bradstreet reports showed that they were prospering. She had scanned property records from Swan Harbor and from Asheville with a knowing eye so she knew about all their real estate transactions. She saw where they were living and ventured into the gallery when she saw that Paul was not there. The clerk praised him as a great artist and a good boss. She was surprised to see original works and prints from other artists including Elizabeth Auberson who she had hanging in her own home. Despite her intention to be critical, she actually enjoyed her time shopping and bought a dramatic Watcher Period print for her home. She gave herself a wry smile realizing that the print had probably cost her, COC that is, over $100,000.00.

She made the shady restaurant parking lot her spying headquarters. She had plenty of time as she was on a two-week vacation from her life and duties at COC. Rolf had been furious at first.

"Cornelia dear. This is a waste of your time, and you should not be taking off like this in season. You are setting a bad example for our staff."

She endured his lecture and said, "Rolfie. I have to go. My heart's in a twist and the time when I am young and brave enough to confront him is ending. You know it's not the money. My soul is aching to do this. Please, please give me a little time off. After twenty-nine years I deserve it!"

Paul's whole routine was easy to see. He rode a bicycle in streets that needed his whole attention, so he could not see a little red Toyota lingering behind him as he visited the bank, the Chamber of Commerce, a nearby art gallery and, finally, the Good Samaritan. After observing clients' comings and goings and the signs, she understood that it was a church activity and came to believe that Paul was an authority figure.

Corney followed Dahlia too. Dahlia seemed to walk or run everywhere, often with the kids in a stroller. Their red truck stayed parked except for days when Dahlia made a grocery run to the Fresh Market. Corney understood that they lived in an apartment above the store with an enormous number of windows. She thought that the top floor must have a nice view.

After five days of shadowing them, she resolved to confront them at nine p.m. when Paul would be home, and the store closed. She ate a burger and returned to her hotel for a shower and nap. She wanted to be sharp and strong for the encounter.

The bell rarely rang. Dahlia called out, "I've got it Paul," as she trotted down the stairs. Paul had already settled the kids down for bed in their third-floor bedrooms; Billy to read in bed until eight o'clock and Janice to read in her room until her eight-thirty lights-off.

Dahlia couldn't believe it. She stuttered, "Corney. What are you doing here? Are you okay?"

Corney's face was contorted with emotion as she faced the beautiful young woman. She looked ill but was just at a loss as to how to proceed. She said, "Hello Dahlia.

"I'd like to see you and Paul together," she croaked.

"Yah, sure. Vy don't you come up and I'll get Paul. Just follow me. He may be a few minutes, but I'll tell him you're here."

She led the way up a nicely painted, carpeted, and decorated stairway. The second-floor landing was open to a modest living, dining, and kitchen space. It seemed larger because the rooms were in a great-room format. Windows, unadorned with curtains covered the entire street wall. Privacy was assured by the many trees outside and by careful placement of furniture and potted plants inside.

"Please vait here a moment." She left Corney standing. Dahlia quickly walked through the room and slipped into their bedroom. "Paul," she hissed. "Corney's here. She said she wants to talk to us together. Come now," she whispered urgently.

Paul looked much as he had last time, she'd seen him in Swan Harbor. He sported a shaved head with a little goatee, wearing all white clothing. He actually looked better. He was a fit, mature man with a confident bearing.

He gave Corney a smile and shook her hand. "Please come and sit with us. He led her to the sofa but did not sit down himself.

Dahlia perched on the edge of a chair looking scared. Paul put his hand on her shoulder and said to Corney, "I'm putting on tea. Okay?"

The women nodded.

"Corney. We just moved here. We were able to buy the building at a good price and we have totally rehabbed it. It was ground floor commercial with four apartments in the second and third floors. Could Dahlia give you a tour while I do the tea?"

"Yes please."

Dahlia shyly let Corney around. "This was two apartments in the original building," Dahlia explained. The master bedroom suite was splendid. The large room, perhaps 20 feet to a side, had a huge walk-in closet. A double pocket door led to a bathroom that featured both a two head shower and the biggest freestanding tub Corney had ever seen. It was like a spa room at the Maupai Inn. The two apartments are now our kitchen, dining and living rooms ant the master bedroom."

The third floor had also been divided into two apartments in the beginning. Now it was a large family room, four bedrooms and two Jack and Jill baths. The family room was sweetly cluttered with children's toys. They looked into the guest rooms but not the children's bedrooms. Dahlia said the kids might wake if their doors were opened. There were lots of windows on the long street wall but no window treatments. Corney noticed a large skylight that would shed daylight on the top landing of the stair as well as the family room.

"Very nice," said Corney. She felt slightly jealous. Her house at COC was not this grand. It had been built of natural materials a dozen years before and had both a modern and a country feel. This was one of the nicest apartments she'd ever seen.

"Thanks for the tour."

It was as sweet a nest as Corney could have imagined. She murmured her approval each time Dahlia showed her another feature.

"Paul. It's driving me nuts." Corney was able to speak as he puttered because the space was open. "What happened to my money? Again, I am prepared to make you an offer. Tell me everything and I won't tell anyone anything. Not even Rolf. I just want to know, and I'll pay your lawyer to write up an agreement to protect you and your family. I don't want revenge. I just want to know what happened.

The teapot whistled and Paul brought it to the coffee table on a tray holding cups, sugar, lemon, milk, and tea bags.

"I hear you Corney. Let me think a moment while I pour." They prepared their cups in silence, spoons skirling in cups and clinking when they were set down.

"Corney. I think that you didn't lose anything in that robbery. Tell me, did you file an insurance claim?"

Dahlia was very uncomfortable and said nothing. She just nodded slightly in support of Paul.

"Well, yes. We filed a claim that paid us the many man hours it took to recover lost records and we recovered a calculated seventy-five percent of the cash."

"What about checks and credit card stuff?"

"Well. We think we recovered some of the checks and there was no loss on credit cards. Just a lot of fuss and work in figuring things out."

"Paul. What do you know about this? How do you know any of this? Did you take the money?" These were the questions she'd been aching to ask. She sat erect and looked at him.

"Corney. I'm a businessman now. I have insurance.

"You made a big mistake firing me without notice but you did me a favor too."

"What do you mean?"

"Well, I spent a lot of time working for you each day, commuting, and playing on the river. I loved my job. I sold beverages with every meal and got great tips. Archie probably lied about everything he ever told you about me. I think he was jealous of my relationship with Dahlia.

"You forced me into a different life path, and I have prospered. But I didn't know that that would happen when you shit-canned me.

"I can see you're wondering how we acquired the things you see. You are wondering if it's your money at work. Well, it isn't. Here's what happened. The folks at the bank in Swan Harbor loaned me enough money to buy that place. I was unemployed. Go figure?" he shrugged.

"I had fifteen thousand in cash and that was enough to get us started. I told you all that when you snuck up on me in Swan Harbor that day. I let you look at my bank accounts and mortgage statements. I thought I had you convinced.

Corney said, "I was confused then Paul. I believed you when you showed all of that to me but afterwards, I thought you were lying and I've been stewing about it ever since."

"Well, Corney. This time I'm just going to tell you a funny story and not show you anything." He hitched forward and looked at Dahlia.

"Honey. May I tell Corney how we got the money for this place?"

"Paul," Dahlia said. "This is shocking to me but if you tink it vill help Corney, tell her the story." She got a little closer to him and tried to be composed and to show solidarity with.

"Corney. I've been so lucky that you probably won't be convinced this time either. We made a lot of money selling the place in Swan Harbor. A lot – we had $900,000.00 in banks when we arrived in Asheville. We started with about fifteen from my savings and fifteen from Dahlia's. You remember I showed you the records. We sold at the absolute top of the market and waited out the downturn by renting.

"We remodeled that house we were living in on the cheap – sweat equity, don' t cha know. It was a big job almost tripling the square footage.

"Corney, have you ever been to the Carson House in North Carolina? Look it up on the web. That was our inspiration.

"We never got into expensive habits, and we lived simply here, renting a little house, and covering our expenses with art sales and interest. And then a crazy thing happened. Right Dahlia?"

"Yah Corney." Her eyes were gleaming, and she said, "Tell her what ve did Paul."

Corney was sitting back now but her posture betrayed great interest in these statements layered with suspicion and skepticism.

"Corney, we made a low offer on a nice commercial building. We got it for eight hundred and fifty thousand and sold it for two point five million before we took possession or even closed on the deal. We became millionaires! Bought this place, at a bargain price, for cash, and fixed it up as you can see. Do you have any questions?"

"Paul. Did you steal the money?"

"Corney, you were wrong to fire me. But I didn't take the money.

"I like COC and I like you. I'm sorry that this troubles you so much. Is there anything else you'd like to talk about?"

"How old are your children?" Corney asked. The conversation was a little stiff, but they asked about people they knew at COC. Corney seemed resigned to not solving her mystery. She left and things settled down to their regular tempo.

ASHEVILLE – July 2011

Some things are relative. Dahlia and Paul felt rich in many ways. The kids were both in elementary School. Janice, ten, was an ideal student; Billy two years younger, was a little more rowdy because, they suspected, he was a boy. Girls were the gentler sex.

They lived and worked in a wonderful space and their finances were spectacular. They decided not to be real estate speculators but sometimes discussed properties. Dahlia made and sold wreaths and dry flower arrangements in their store. Paul sold his paintings there too but sold even more in other galleries and on the internet. He painted in one window when he tended shop. Dahlia, in her free time, used a workstation in the window in the other side of the entrance. The apartment's foyer could be reached from the street or from the inside of the store. They had one employee to give them time away from keeping shop.

Foot traffic was good but not spectacular. The churches, the restaurant and a coffee shop recently relocated to the building next door, provided a lot of the foot traffic. They put a bright yellow awning with a painted sign on it to attract drivers' eyes. It had a good effect.

Church activities took a good deal of time. Especially for Paul in the work he did at the Samaritan House. Paul was instrumental in providing additional services from time to time. His mission was trying to help Asheville's homeless and hungry. The church now owned a 40-room motel across the street, to help individuals and families get off the street for more than one night at a time. They had job counselors and cash assistance programs were designed to boost people back into self-sustaining lifestyles. Paul doubted that they changed many lives because demon rum, drugs, and the lack of social abilities were rampant. Many of their clients were mentally or emotionally disturbed. He felt that they were fighting a losing battle but one that demanded to be waged anyway.

Pastor Arthur McAuliff was very grateful to Paul for his continual gifts to the church and his work and leadership at the Samaritan House. Paul accepted Christian gospel on Sundays and membership in the men's Christian Fellowship Group. Yet, even with his good works he felt a kernel of guilt twisting within. He spoke to Dahlia about his troubles. She gave him love and acceptance, friendship, a great home life and everything but he seemed not to be capable of self-forgiveness. He knew he had to get it on his own.

The crime was now over ten years in the past. He often had troubling dreams about being in the woods and creeping about the COC property, planning his attack on the safe. The hurt he'd experienced when they fired him seemed trivial in the face of the success he'd enjoyed with Dahlia and with his career.

Paul and Dahlia sat in their truck eating hamburgers beside the road in Bryson City, North Carolina. They had two kayaks and a tent in the bed of the truck. They were heading home from a camping weekend on the Little Tennessee River and Fontana Lake.

The two of them had spent the day paddling the rapids where the river flowed into the lake. The lake had hundreds of miles of shoreline and coves to explore.

Paul's parents were baby sitting in Asheville. Movies, pizza and kid stuff were on their agenda.

"Dahlia. I'm suffering."

"What my love? What can I do?"

"I don't know how to say this. My life is so perfect, but I feel like my soul in going to hell. I have bad dreams almost every night and I don't feel deserving."

Dahlia paused and gazed into his eyes. "Paul. Shut up! You're driving me crazy with your stupid guilt. Look. Ve haf the money. Vould it help to just give it back and go to jail for a while?

"Ve have plenty of money. Money ve don't even need. Give everything away, feel better and ve can get jobs like everyone else? Vould dot help? I will always love you and take care of you. Just like you do for me."

They were both crying now.

"Dahlia. I need to talk to Arthur about this and maybe Corney. I think that I need their forgiveness too. I can't find it in myself."

"Ven do you vant to do dis? Now?"

"Arthur. This is Paul." He was choked up. He could hardly breathe.

"Paul. What's wrong? Where are you?"

"I'm in Asheville. At the church. I have a big guilt problem that is hurting my life. I'm unhappy and I want to unburden myself to you and ask for advice. Dahlia's here with me and she knows about my problems, but I want to talk to you alone."

"Okay. I'll meet you there in ten minutes."

Arthur pulled in and spoke briefly to Dahlia. "Is there anything I can do for you Dahlia? Are you okay?"

"Yah. Tank you Arthur. Just talk to lunkhead here and fix him for me, vill you please." She gave Paul a hug and a kiss and dealt Arthur a peck before she drove off for home, leaving Paul to make his own way home. "See you soon," she said through the window with a smile for Arthur and a blown kiss for Paul.

They sat in the guest chairs in Arthur's office. They were close, sitting eye-to-eye, knees almost touching.

"Come on Paul. Tell me what I can do for you."

Paul began the story of how he worked for COC and met Dahlia. He spoke slowly at first then with more urgency, leaving nothing out.

Spent at last he paused and looked Arthur in the face. "What should I do?"

"What do you want?"

"I want to be forgiven."

"By whom?"

"Now you got me Corny, I guess… You. God. Me."

Arthur had heard many confessions in his twenty-year career in the church. Paul looked anguished. It was surprising really. He had thought of Paul as a rock. He was strong, able, rich, talented, well-married, and familied up. He seemed a very good man indeed and yet he needed something that Arthur probably couldn't give.

"Paul. That was a very good story. Thank you for telling me. Let me share a few things with you before we talk about what you could do. I too have much guilt in my life, and I feel it every day, morning and night. I have committed every sin including theft, taking the Lord's name in vain, fornication, and manslaughter. I have even deliberately hurt others in petty ways. I've hurt people who were not able to defend themselves. So, when I tell you, my friend, that I forgive you, and I do, I must also ask you to forgive me."

Paul nodded, "Thank you Arthur. I forgive you not knowing what you've done. But I still hurt. I've got to do something."

Arthur looked at him and asked, "Paul. Will you pray with me?"

"Yes." Paul could hardly speak. Tears streamed down his cheeks. He bowed his head and clasped his hands together as Arthur intoned,

"Our Father who art in heaven,
Hallowed be thy name,
Thy Kingdom come, thy will be done,
On earth as it is in heaven.
Give us this day our daily bread.
Forgive our trespasses as we forgive
those who trespasses against us,
Bring us not into temptation but deliver us from evil,
Maketh us to lie down in green pastures,
lead us beside still waters.
Thy rod and thy staff comfort us.
Annointest my head with oil. My cup runneth over.
Surely goodness and mercy will follow me all the days of my life,
and I will dwell in the house of the Lord forever."

They said, "Amen," together and sat in silence for a few moments.

Arthur cleared his throat, "For me Paul, this prayer is very much at the center of my life. I say it every day and try to think about the meanings of the words and the wonderful intelligence and love behind those words.

"Just image 'here on earth as it is in Heaven.' We all need forgiveness. I like to think that if God forgives me, why can't I forgive myself too?"

"I see what you mean, and I feel better. I think just sharing my sorrow has lightened the burden. I need to work at being better to myself. I mean feeling better about the things I've done and the things I'd like to do."

"Does Dahlia know about your burglary?"

"Yes. I told her before we got married. We were always close emotionally but when I unburdened myself to her, I felt closer than ever. She told me not to tell anyone then but when I told her how it was eroding me, the way I felt about my life and my peace of mind, she agreed that I should tell you and see what you thought. I did some bad things as a teen that I haven't told her. "

"She's a smart woman."

"Amen and Hallelujah."

They laughed at Paul's joke.

"Paul. You need a lawyer. If you are thinking about talking to that Corney woman, I would not tell you whether or not it's a good idea, but you definitely need to know how bad it could be.

"Regards restitution, you have given the church a great deal of money, time and effort and perhaps if restitution to COC's insurance company is too dangerous to you and your family, you might consider making a conscience-salving gift to a charity. I don't mean our church. Advising to give it to this church might not be good for my conscience.

"Too self-serving don'tcha know."

Paul seemed glum again. "Arthur. I know that I have given money to the church and Samaritan program. But somehow it doesn't relieve my internal, infernal, bad feelings about my biggest sin. My gifts were just celebrating success in a couple of real estate deals. I wasn't trying to ease my conscience."

"God forgives you. Jesus forgives you and you should forgive yourself and try to build your relationship with Jesus.

"I want to be your friend Paul. I think you are on the right path, and I just don't want you to hurt yourself by winding up in prison if there is another way."

"You know, I feel much better Arthur. I am grateful for a loving church that doesn't want to punish me for my sins. Forgiveness seems so much better since we all do or think wrong things."

They parted on good terms. Paul walking home across his beautiful city and Arthur back to his church calendar.

Paul felt that there were three people helping to carry his burden now: himself, Dahlia and now Arthur. Maybe he should tell everyone and lots of hands would carry it with him. He'd better talk to his brother, Mitch, about things too.

The kids were asleep and the house quiet. Dahlia hugged under the covers. Now they were free to talk.

"So, Paul, what did Arthur say?"

"I really like Arthur. It was a comfort to tell him what's really on my mind and I respect his view.

"He said Jesus and God forgive me and he does too. We prayed together and I look at the Lord's Prayer more literally now. But, even so, I have to talk to Mitch and to Corney. I don't think I'll be prosecuted but I want to make the journey on my own darling." He paused and Dahlia jumped in.

"You vould like me to stay home while you go on a dangerous quest." She was making a statement, not asking a question.

"Aw, Dahlia, I love you so much. But you did not commit the crime and I won't take a chance on you being involved.

"But how do you feel about my coughing up $114,000.00?"

"My God Paul. Dat's a lot of money but ve have it. In cash, yah?"

"Well, not exactly cash but close enough. I can write a check and the bank will pay it out of our money market funds. It won't affect our lifestyle. Hell, money is the least of problems. We have been very lucky.

"I want to go by myself and have your blessing to play it by ear. If I have a conversation with Corney that I don't like I may just lose my guilty feelings."

"Yah," she sighed. I can understand why you feel like you must go alone but I tink that I want to go with you anyway. We can leave the kids with Mitch.

"You know what? I want to take our kayaks and go for a paddle on the Clancy. Just like old times, yah. You can confess to crimes and ve vill make love in our special cove if it's still there."

They lapsed into lust as thoughts of the old times by the river wriggled into their heads.

Afterwards Dahlia said, "Thank you for being you, Paul. I'm sorry about your guilt but I want to be with you at every minute and help you get up if you stumble."

"Thank you, sweetheart."

They slipped into dreamland and Paul dreamed about Corney. He was alone with her in the woods at night. He could hardly see her, but she was talking. He couldn't make out her words...

GEORGIA – July 2011

The Maupai Mountain Lodge came into existence after the Civil War. It provided wealthy Atlantans with relief from the exhausting heat of summer. It started as a country lodge with 12 rooms. Guests would tarry there for weeks at a time, always clamoring for more accommodations and longer stays.

Now just over an hour by auto from Atlanta, a short jump over state lines to the Mountains of North Carolina and Tennessee. The mountains still offered cool relief from the heat and the hot springs were considered to be healthful as well and enjoyable.

The resort grew in good times and bad. It now provided convention capabilities, a world-class spa experience, golf, restaurants, lodging, and even a shopping galleria.

Paul and Dahlia stopped there for a weekender while on the way to confront Corney. It was their first luxury resort experience, quite contrary to their usual low-cost camping and paddling vacations. And they liked it.

Paul saw that there was no art gallery and that the new shopping facilities were under construction. He inquired about renting retail space for an art gallery and, to his very great surprise he was greeted enthusiastically by Fred Huttaug, the onsite real estate agent. "Mr. Hunter, would you be able to stage a grand opening by October 31st?"

Dahlia and Paul looked at each other and nodded. "Dahlia, would you consider coming back here for a couple of weeks in October if we could get accommodations at a good price?" His wink was masked because he had turned his head away from Huttaug.

"Paul. You know the kids will be starting school then and that is our busiest season in Asheville." Then she said to Huttaug, "Dat is a hard time for us. And the expense would come at a bad time."

The negotiation had begun. When it was over, they had gotten the resort to pay remodeling construction costs and give them six months free rent. Paul gave Fred a check for $25,000.00 as a deposit. They got a floor plan and store elevation and promised to get drawings to the realtor by the first day of August. They were also comped for their weekend stay, including meals, and also would be comped for their late October grand-opening stay.

Fred showed them a list of new tenants scheduled to open before the end of the year. Caverns Outdoor Center leaped off the page. "Fred, do you know the Johnsons from COC?"

"Yes. Corney was here a few days ago. She signed for the corporation and will be ready on time for the Grand Opening party."

Later, in the comfort of their room they lounged in bed.

"Paul. I can't believe it. That is really prime space and everyone walking by or stepping in the door will be in financial brackets vere dey can buy original paintings - I think ve just struck it rich! Again. You better be careful tomorrow and not spoil my opening party," she giggled.

""Dahlia, it's all you. You have a great eye for value. You carry me in all our great adventures."

"Dat's nonsense. I didn't know how to live until I met you. Even though ve have a lot of money ve really don't spend anything. Just like Thoreau told us ven ve vere in the tent. Ve are living high this weekend, it's der big exception, but ve give away much more money dan we spend on ourselves." She crossed the bed with a wiggle and a leap and hugged him hard. "Paul, I love you so much.

You are a very good man and I'm very proud of you, but you better do the right ting tomorrow."

She had asked him what he was going to do but he refused to give her details. "I'm going to play it by ear. Maybe God will put the right words in my month and help Corney and us all to see the best way.

They set out for COC early in the morning. Paul was silent and Dahlia, responding to his mood, held her peace feeling that he would find the right words.

PART FOUR
Gotcha

COC – August 2011

Corney walked to her office before eight a.m. and was surprised to be greeted by her old nemesis and his cute wife sitting like school children on the bench outside her office, just as they would wait for the principal of their high school. They squirmed as if they were in trouble.

"Good morning," she greeted them. "To what do I owe the pleasure of your company?"

"Corney, I need some time." Could we get coffee in the restaurant?" It was just across the road and Corney did not mind at all.

"C'mon," she said. "I'll buy this time." As usual she was puzzled about Paul and Dahlia.

Comfortably seated, looking out over the river Paul began a rambling talk, "Corney, Dahlia doesn't know exactly why we're here or what I'm going to say. But this is serious business for me.

"I've sinned against God, COC, you, and Dahlia. My conscience is driving me crazy. I've lied about everything. I took over one hundred thousand that night and I did it on my own. Archie and Jim Bob were acting independently. We didn't know anything about each other's activities. But they were out to steal and got caught by the dye pack and my stupidity."

"What do you mean?" asked an astonished Corney.

"I mean that you were right. I'm a crook and I got away with it. There is no excuse."

Corney sat silently, stone faced. Dahlia put her hand on his arm looking very troubled.

"Corney. It was an act of revenge at first. I mean while I was thinking about it. Then as I settled down and fell in love with Dahlia it became a stupid adventure; like it was the most outrageous thing I'd ever dreamed of.

"Ironically, I never needed or used the money. I gave it all away over the years. Anonymously, mostly through my church. I've also given them a lot of money and time to help the homeless and hungry in Asheville. Now I'm wondering, Corney, is there a statute of limitations in your heart? Will you forgive me? Please." Paul put his hand, palm up, in the center of the table and looked at Corney.

"Paul," she said. "I don't know how I feel. I'm angry with all your lies. I feel a little better, I guess, to know, after all these years, that I was right about, you little sneak." She was not smiling. She ignored his hand, and he slowly withdrew it.

"What do you want from me she said?"

"There are several things. The first thing is the hardest; it is an apology for your firing me, even though it worked out so well for me. The second thing is your forgiveness for my trespass. I have decided that God will forgive me, I have forgiven myself, Dahlia and my pastor have forgiven me, but I don't sleep at night because I need your understanding and forgiveness too,

"The next thing is about money. I know that you and Rolf are loaded. You sold the COC to the employees' co-op for millions and you were well off before that. I need money now, real money. More than I have, to fund an idea to help the worst-off people among us.

"In Asheville there are plenty of folks without shelter or food or any of the comforts most of us take for granted. Each night we go out and round them up to place in the shelter or give them blankets and food. In cold weather it is an emergency just to keep 'em from freezing.

"I want to try to improve the lot of these people with a pilot program to guarantee them a decent place to stay, a job, life counseling, drug and alcohol addiction treatment, dental and health care and try to get some of them back as self-sustaining members of society."

"Paul. You are talking about millions of dollars." Corney's face and posture radiated disapproval.

"I know."

"What makes you so interested in these people Paul?"

Paul was silent for a few minutes, pondering an answer. I know I told you that the reason I stayed on the hill that summer you fired me was that I wanted to be close to Dahlia." He looked at Dahlia and took her hand tenderly. "Dahlia. It's true.

"But there was something else going on. I could have gone home in a few days after I got my bus fixed. I discovered painting and the theft was just an idle daydream that segued into an adventure. The other thing going on was that I felt rejected, humiliated, homeless and, sort of delusional. I felt disconnected from my family. I was homeless in my mind.

"Dahlia's love saved me.

"When I got arrested, I saw how I could easily lose control of my life. I guess now that I deserved it. It was a close call Corney… especially because of your suspicions. You were so right about me."

He paused, "So what about it?"

Corney answered, "About what? Forgiveness or a million more dollars for the homeless in your hometown?"

"Both Corney." He clung to Dahlia's hand, his shoulders rounded, his face clouded over, nearing tears. His eyes darted from one to the other. "But, on your say so, I'll move to your hometown, Atlanta, and we can do good work there. Corney, there's a huge need. They say there are thousands of such people in Asheville. I'm sure that there are even more in Atlanta. Whatever the number they all need help."

"No. Hell no! I won't give you a million dollars. And I'm mad as hell about all that you put us through all this mess. I feel like an old fool." She pushed her chair back angrily.

"Dahlia. I like you both and won't do anything to hurt you and your family at this late date. But your boyfriend is nuts." She rose and stalked out of the restaurant.

Paul looked at Dahlia and shrugged. "Well, it was worth a try. I'm going to write her a letter and restate my case, but I don't think we can talk to her just now."

"Paul. She's right. You are nuts." Dahlia rose and left him sitting there as the waitress brought him a check. He signed it 'Corney' and left a $5.00 tip.

Dear Corney,

Talking to you this week was definitely one of the hardest moments of my life and, again, I say I'm very sorry about everything. You and Rolf have had blessed lives and I see how much of your joy you have been able to share with the world. I love COC and I love you.

Funny thing is that, even though people do wrong things, like unfairly firing workers, getting divorces, and stealing, the consequences of these actions are not always bad. Sometimes the world seems to right itself like a seaworthy boat knocked down in a storm.

The purpose of this letter is to again tell you that I am willing to invest one million dollars in a joint project with you in an effort to do some good in this world, and to give back to society. And I want to share with you, some of the blessings I've received. It's hard to explain to you why working with me will benefit you but it has to do with forgiveness.

I've been a member of the Asheville Samaritan Society for over five years. We own a 40-room downtown motel where we provide housing for individuals and families who, otherwise, would be sleeping outside. On an adjacent property we provide emergency shelter for up to 80 people a night We feed as many as 300 people every day and provide showers, clothing, barbering, dental, medical, counseling, and transportation services. Most of our providers are volunteers.

The problems our clients present are overwhelming. City and county services to this population are very limited. The clients need to escape from drugs, alcohol, and boredom into the adventure of living and working productively. They need work, self-esteem, and coaching.

I think the problems in other cities must be even worse – I'm thinking about your native city Atlanta now. My check will go to Reverend Arthur McAuliff in Asheville unless I hear from you by October 31st.

The money will be used to hire professionals to render services not presently available. Our million dollars will support the program for two years. Your money, if we go in it together, will not only make it better and make it last longer, but it will also give it the critical mass to serve as a pilot program - so that any success we may enjoy will be repeatable in other communities.

As you know by now, I am opening a gallery at Maupai Mountain Lodge and will attend the Grand Opening Gala. (Fred Huttaug told me he gave you the complete guest list and pointed us out when he spoke with you.)

Telephone me if you want. Help me make a better plan. We can start by making notes on the back of a napkin. I'll do most anything you suggest to make our society a better place. I want to work with you and really earn your forgiveness.

You can talk with the reverend Arthur McAuliff at the Samaritan society in Asheville to get his views. I've confessed my sins to him, and you can tell him anything. He has years of experience and many good ideas.

Love Paul

    Corney and Rolf wore their city clothes to the party. In his case chinos, a blue button-down shirt and blue blazer with clean hiking boots. Corney wore a white dress with a long, fringed vest and white sandals. Her revolver was holstered under the vest as usual.

Paul wore his church clothes and Dahlia wore a new cocktail dress. They stood in the entrance to their gallery and gazed across toe wide passage toward COC's entrance. Corny and Rolf stood looking at them. Eight eyes locked in a crowd of partygoers whose eyes were looking elsewhere. Corney stepped forward and advanced on the Hunters at a measured pace. She stopped a few yards away and raised her arm.

Paul froze as he focused on the big gun in her hand. He could not breathe. The gun was pointed at his chest. It was a creepy pink color.

Corney pulled the trigger and there was a loud pop. A silk flag came out of the barrel and danced at the end of a stick. Corney turned her body so he could read the word "Gotcha!" on the flag.

Corney took two steps forward and said, 'Paul. Dahlia. Let's go to the fireplace lounge and have a drink... I have an idea for the employment of your homeless friends."

Speechless, they followed her to the bar.

# # # #

POSTSCRIPT

ASHEVILLE, January 2012

Marty had a new red hat but the rest of him was a mess. His black eye and pungent clothing made him a standout even among the homeless guys in the chow line with him. Paul walked up to him with Corney in his wake.

"Hi Marty. Remember me? Paul.'

Marty did remember. From the time they did laundry a few years ago and from other encounters at the Good Samaritan.

"Sure. Paul. My old laundry buddy."

I'd like you to meet my friend Corney. Cornelia Johnson."

Corney smiled warmly, "Hi. Good to meet you, Marty. Call me Corney. We don't want to take you out of showers line, but could we sit with you afterwards, for a while, as you eat your dinner?"

"Sure," grinned Marty. His teeth were white and looked to be in good order. He was a regular client of the Good Samaritan Center. He was a pleasant, not bad looking fellow when cleaned up. He'd been at loose ends for most of his fifty years; without family and friends to keep him straight he'd get wasted on alcohol and drop out of sight.

Whenever Marty had received counseling, lodging and sustenance. He'd improve for a while but soon drift away to a bar and they'd see no more of him for months at a time.

Paul had an idea that a man like Marty Smith just got bored and had nowhere to light other than a bar. He and Corney had discussed many cases, but Corney liked the story where he'd said, "I don't need help. I'm not an alcoholic Paul. I'm just a drunk."

"Paul," she'd put his hand on his arm. What if he had an evening job that he loved, that paid well and that was terribly important to the community? Would he still drift off and get drunk?"

"What if, on his day off, he had an activity that wouldn't let him drink?"

"Tell on," said Paul.

"Let's say he had the job of managing an activities center that welcomed our clients. That he was given the task of operating a game room that would give people a place to be after dinner until eleven at night. I'm thinking checkers, card games, monopoly, scrabble and such. How about a media room? Ping-pong, WI, exercise and other healthy activities. He'd get coaching and his responsibilities would keep him busy. Give him a day off every week and we'll help him learn white-water boating, COC style. He'd need transportation. We could recruit others to experience rafting and outdoors activities. He'd be too busy, too engaged and way too tired to mooch off to a bar."

"I dunno Corney. It feels good. Let's talk to Archie and to Dahlia and see what kind of support they'll give us."

They had spoken to the Samaritan's program managers and then decided to try it.

Marty heard their proposal and burst into tears. "Sorry gang," he choked, "there is one thing that you need to know about me. I'm not a bum. I'm just a weak jerk who has almost ruined my life on earth. Your deal sounds like heaven. I am so happy. I have never felt so good about life as I do today. Thank you." He beamed energetically.

Corney womaned up and forgave the trespasser.

Paul and Dahlia lived happily forever after until...

# # # #

HUNTER III

BOOK THREE – BEYOND THE YEAR 2055

Continues Paul's tale in 2055 when he Reaches 75-years-of-age.

PROLOGUE – December 31, 2388

Paul Hunter lay dreaming about the day he found his secret place on the banks of the boisterous Clancy River. His arms and body twitched slightly with muscle-skeletal memories of the canoe maneuvers he was making.

He was paddling alone but was not yet an expert whitewater paddler. He made frequent turns into minor eddies trying to be totally technical with his strokes and balance. Just practicing skills needed for the exciting sport.

He nosed his canoe into the bank behind a boat-sized rock, only to find no bank; just a screen of bushes that masked a side stream entering the Clancy.

It was a flat area. The slow-moving water was crystal clear. The shallow brook had stones and pebbles strewn across the bottom. Grasses and bushes screened it from sight in every direction. Thick moss covered the rocks on the riverbank.

He liked the place so well that, afterwards, he always paddled there when he was alone. That was where he and Dahlia had first made love. It was a spot where he liked to exit his boat to sit and dream on the bank. Sometimes he fell asleep...

Happy Birthday to you,
Happy Birthday to you,
Happy Birthday Dear Paul,
Happy birthday to you!

The song made him smile. Light applause brought him fully awake.

Paul opened his eyes in surprise. He couldn't see the singers because his eyes were watering with tears. He hadn't expected any celebration and was having a hard time getting his bearings. Oh! And it couldn't be his birthday yet.

Strong, caring hands helped him sit upright in his bed. He pressed his knuckles into his eyes to clear them, but it didn't work very well. He was so tired. His eyes drooped and the commotion went away. He thought that he had just imagined it anyway. He sensed that both his mind and body were failing in the last few months. He felt like a spectator to his own story.

He remembered…

PART ONE

April 2055

Paul was tired. He trudged past the entrance post to the campground and didn't pause. At the age of 76 he did not walk fast; however, he'd covered over 25 kilometers since morning.

His youthful dog, Spotty, followed attentively.

This was the first day of his hike. He considered it a series of long walks with a rest every hour. He saw a white blaze on a tree, indicating that it was an official part of the Mountains to the Sea Trail. He had seen a hundred of these marked trees, but this was the first that spoke to him.

The soft voice inside his head said, "Hi Paul. Welcome to MTS Dunes Campground. If you are staying for the night just go to Camp Three. It is one hundred meters ahead. Your account will be charged for each night you stay. Call 704 555-1515 if you have questions or problems. The Ranger will stop by to say hi at around six p.m. Have a good stay."

Paul's belt buckle had received the message, forwarded the voice via his implant, and paid the bill with a debit to his general account. The implant helped him manage routine parts of his life including financial transactions, health care and communications.

He had his first implant procedure in 2020 when he was just over 40-years old. A renewal device was put in his brain every few years since then. The current 'gizmo,' as he called it, his eighth, was quite advanced over the original. It was recharged, of course, through an induction process from any source in his immediate vicinity.

Now, in mid-century, just about everyone in the world was implanted. His personal information was not so private, and his identity was generally available to anyone within range. But, the benefits outweighed the downside. The only private element was his personal password. An implanted person could go off the grid with the proper gadget and the password.

Usually, a citizen must get permission from his government to go off-line. The one exception was death – no 'by your leave' was required.

Most often the devices' recharges came from his hat's solar collector while he was hiking. The heels and soles of his ankle high boots were a better source of PEE, personal electric energy, on dark and rainy days. Selective induction made this all possible. At home, in the city of Asheville, North Carolina, there were multiple recharge points everywhere he went.

He was a vigorous human being despite his age. He just moved slower and tired quicker. And he held his thoughts better than he did as a young man. He was hiking to sort out his life. He needed to get away on his own to make some important decisions. He had plenty of time to think about fewer things, as a famous newscaster once said at his retirement dinner.

A natural multi-tasker, Paul was also writing a book. His memoirs. It would be a picture book featuring his watercolor paintings as well as photos and sketches. His voice monitor made it very easy to do the written part of the work. He just talked about things as he walked. In the evening hours he could lounge in his tent area and see the spoken words as text on the holographic monitor implanted in his corneas. He could edit his words with his mini-board that was a part of the E-package he always carried with him, or he could do it with voice alone.

His productivity as a painter was low now, compared to his younger years. To some degree, his hike was an attempt at reconnecting with his muse.

As a wealthy man he had the best MacroNanno E-kit available. It weighed less than 50 grams. Other capabilities included a telephone with both video and audio, e-messing, Facebook, Twitter, Jawbreakers, holographic keyboard, and a Finger-Rat. He rarely used the keyboard. All these bits interacted with his belt buckle and implants to perform many tasks.

The amazing capabilities and productivity of his light E-array were possible because it was just a portal to links with his other computers at home, in his office, his vehicles and so-called cloudland. Nanocomputing made everything very fast.

He thought that he was a bit long-in-the-tooth to be out for a major trek, but the need to occupy his mind was urgent. He was mad at himself. He felt guilty because he blamed himself for his wife's death and he was discontented with his life in general.

The day before began with a conversation.

"Buffy."

"Hi Boss. We going somewhere?" His car's female voice was youthful, and enthusiastic.

"Yes. We're going to Jockey Ridge State Park in North Carolina. Power up. Pick up our purchases at Mast General Store and at Fresh Market. They have your code, and the orders will be ready when you get there.

"Spotty and I will be ready to leave when you get back. Call me when you get to the corner. Don't go into the garage. We'll be at the front door, ready to get in and go."

"That all Boss?"

"Yep." Paul replied, and rang off with a practiced but very slight, blinky squint of his right eye. It still amazed him that he was able to interface with his car and gadgets by simple gestures. Voice commands came long ago but the gee-whizzers soon enough figured out that human communications were gesture driven as well as voiced events. His repertoire consisted of thousands of facial nuances, hand movements and body and posture signals.

His equipment was all attuned to him and it all rebooted from time to time as his habits evolved. A reboot was very complicated but with nanotechnology the speed was astronomically fast. He never noticed a reboot. Redundancies abounded in case of a failure somewhere along the line. If it all shut off he would still be a healthy human. Maybe a little frustrated.

He spoke on the phone but without visible equipment. He still used a slight hand gesture, pinky out and thumb up, when in public, to let others know that he was not babbling to himself. It was automatic.

Paul was dressed to travel and hike. He figured that the errands would take his ride half an hour at most. So, he bade Spotty sit near him while he enjoyed his second cup of coffee and mused about his day.

The ride to the coast in his Buffalo would take seven hours. Traveling I-26 at a steady 150 kph would be easy. The eastern trailhead for the Mountains to the Sea Trail was about 500 kilometers away. The last 200 klicks would be on slower roads. He would be in full-out napping mode for most of the trip. They would stop only for toilet breaks. When the hike actually began he would be walking westward, away from the sea and towards the mountains.

He had already packed the vehicle with his tent, consumables, personal toiletries, and clothing the night before. The last-minute shopping was to have the freshest veggies possible for his journey and to get another potable water jug to keep him on the trail as long as he wanted.

Night One would be spent at a B and B in Nags Head, North Carolina. In the morning he'd drive to the trailhead in the nearby park and Buffy would self-stash at the local police department parking lot.

ASHEVILLE – November 2054

"Paul. Get the hell avay from me!" she yelled, as he advanced on her with a sudden release of Viagra IV for motivation. Dahlia, Paul's wife of over 50 years, was full of life and very playful. She glared at him in mock anger.

He needed some help in that department lately. Just out of his morning spa, airflow dried and powdered, he felt frisky. He caught her leaving the apartment on the way to meet friends for an outing to the Grove Park Inn Spa just down the road. She was dressed in a frothy afternoon ensemble, on task, and in no mood for sex.

Dahlia was a very upbeat person. Kind, lively, funny and energetic, she liked taking care of people. Her husband Paul and their children were the main beneficiaries of her loving ways.

She grabbed the towel from his waist and backed up snapping it. Whack! She got a lucky hit near his crotch, and he fell back giving her a lead that he could not overcome without going out on the street naked.

Dahlia fled down the stairs, leaving the towel halfway down and called back to him, "Honey. Remember dat thought and tell me again later. I'll be back at two." Her light German accent still returned in times of stress and excitement.

Leaving the drive with a burst of acceleration, she went through the light at the corner of their street. She had over-ridden the Autodrive and slid on a patch of ice.

Dahlia had time to observe the rapidly approaching rock wall with a look of surprise on her face. It was a freak accident at a relatively slow rate of speed, but it had managed to ram a boulder from the retaining wall through the window and break her skull.

Paul, preoccupied with giving up the chase, and seeking out clothing for his day, ignored the sound of the accident. He found out about it when the ER physician from Mission Memorial Hospital reached him several hours later, looking for a Mr. Hunter.

He was with his old friend Marty Smith when the call came. His face fell and his shoulders slumped. He collapsed onto the sidewalk bench outside the church office. They had just finished meeting with the Senior Center Advisory Board.

"Paul. What's wrong?" Marty's face was furrowed in concern as Paul sagged, hugged his knees, and began shaking.

Marty, sitting on the bench opposite, jumped up and reached Paul as he fell to the ground. "Paul. What's wrong buddy?" He helped Paul get back on the bench.

"Marty. That was an ER doc at the hospital. Dahlia's been hurt. I gotta go now."

"Okay. But let me take you. Let's go."

It seemed that everyone dear in his life went away when Dahlia died. Their children, Billy and Janice, came to her funeral, of course. Billy, a veterinarian, and Janice, a surgical nurse, lived in Indiana and Wyoming.

Dahlia's funeral was huge. She got a good send off.

"Mom sure had a lot of friends," Billy said to Janice. Dahlia and Paul's children had come from their faraway homes for their mother's service. Their five grown children and an assortment of friends, cousins, nieces, and nephews constituted the crowd that filled the apartment. They were a somber bunch, mostly dressed in fashionable jumpsuits of the day.

Billy and Janice had grown from babies to adults in this apartment. They retreated to Janice's old bedroom on the third floor to find quiet for a talk.

"What's Daddy going to do without Mom? What are we going to do without Mom?" Janice slumped into her old armchair as she choked out these words.

Billy stood next to her. "I can't believe this happened. Why was she even steering that God-damned car. Autodrives are so much better than people. Never should have happened."

"Daddy said they'd been playing, and she snapped him with a towel and ran out of the apartment. She must have been feeling excited and happy. You know how much I miss driving these days."

"The freaking car should have saved her. Nobody dies in car accidents anymore."

He was right. Cars and trucks drove themselves and handled navigation, parking, tolls, and traffic better than people ever could. They were never inattentive, overtired or intoxicated. There were only a few thousand vehicular deaths per year now in the entire world of ten billion souls. Before Autodrive technology there were many more deaths than that each week and tens of thousands of injuries every month in just the United States.

"We need to talk to Dad, "Janice said. "He must never override his autodriver. He's in great shape but it's 2054 and Mom should never have been driving."

SPRING 2055

Life without Dahlia seemed drab. Paul had a few remaining friends and as much work as he cared to do. His interior life was rich, but he missed their days of plentiful friendships and meaningful activities.

He spent a lot of time alone, sallying forth to church on Sundays and church-related meetings on other days. He did not work much otherwise. His three art galleries located at Asheville's Grove Park Inn, the Maupai Mountain Lodge in Georgia, and on the first floor of his apartment building, ran without him. University art students kept the places open six and seven days a week. The business did well but he didn't need the income and intended to keep them in operation to preserve memories of his old life with Dahlia. He could have done well by renting the stores but chose to let them go on.

One of the activities he liked was shopping at the old Mast General Store that was within easy walking distance of his home in Asheville. It sold camping gear as well as outdoor clothing. The new-fangled tents, backpacks, cooking gadgets, and trail food attracted him every time he browsed the store. Knowledgeable and friendly staffers made this a fun outing. He picked up a book about the Mountains to the Sea Trail there and that spawned his idea about hiking. The MST.

He was lonely for Dahlia and sometimes a little blue. He bought a dog – adopted it really. He named the puppy Spotty, and they soon became close friends. Paul spent a not-so-small fortune for his new best friend's implant. Daily walks were good for beast and master.

Paul's soul was not happy. Dahlia had passed too early, and their children were busy with their own lives thousands of kilometers away. He was lonely. He had found many friends in life but at his advanced age they were scattered and old. *Or maybe mostly dead,* he thought, *like me in a few years. What do I have to show for it all?* He shrugged his mental shoulders and muttered, "more than some I suppose."

Deciding to walk parts of North Carolina's Mountains to the Sea Trail with Spotty, engaged his mind with coordinating details and planning.

Paul believed that he had a charmed life despite misadventures, misdemeanors, and crimes and resolved to share his story with his descendants and family by writing a memoir he named *Paul's Falls*. The walk would be good for him. Help him to sort things out and maybe even find a direction to follow for the remainder of his life.

He eventually completed much of his book while hiking along hundreds of klicks of spectacular and challenging wilderness trails. Both the hiking and the writing projects took years.

He needed to prompt his recorder to begin each session as he walked on through the countryside. So, he began each bit of manuscript copy by saying, "Dear Diary." He soon shortened the phrase to, "DD."

Spotty was a slightly mixed-breed, but mostly Bernese-Mountain type dog. His face had a big black spot in the middle of his forehead, floating on a pond of pure white fur. Overall, it was hard to decide if he was more brown, white, or black. Regardless of his genes, he was the cutest dude on record and passersby could not help stopping for a pet and a friendly sniff.

Both pet and master enjoyed the vigorous brushing after each walk. The brushing was needed to keep the mutt's hair out of the apartment. Dahlia would not have approved of dog mess. But, Paul thought, she would approve of his new friend as *she* didn't have to alert the dust mop when Spotty strolled through the apartment.

Septuagenarian Paul was fit because he never smoked; because he had advanced medical care; and because he possessed great longevity genes. Oh yeah – and that implant thingy too.

His head was shaved, and his whiskers trimmed to number zero on his shaver. He looked like an aging Mister Clean.

APRIL 2055

"DD..." His feedback tick told him he was recording properly. "I am walking comfortably on a sandy path. Rover tent is following me at a precise distance of five meters. Its four big wheels are good on almost any terrain. The power unit takes care of itself in a variety of ways – sunlight, downhill braking, induction stations and even a hand-crank. So far, first day of my great walk, I've had to use the towrope twice.

"The Rover carries my sleeping bag, a mattress, food, water and my general supplies. Everything is very lightweight. It sure is different from my camping out back at the turn of the millennium. In 1999, or was it 2000?

"Spotty's walking order is between me and the tent. He sometimes bounds off, full of young canine energy, but his implant is tuned to my wavelength so I can check him when he wanders or keep him at heel if there are traffic or pedestrian concerns"

Paul had plenty of time to muse about his life and the changes he'd seen over the decades. He had seen inflation brought under better control in 2034 when the world's great currencies merged into the Universal Dollar – Udol as it was called. The universal digital tagging of all manufactured goods and commodities had helped make that step possible. Improved worldwide transportation, storage, distribution, and communications had made the old cycles of punishing inflation and ruinous recessions and booms disappear and they now seemed ridiculous.

"DD. It's hard for the average person to remember how the Udol related to the value of currencies of yore. For one thing its value has been set to the value of human work in the modern era and that changes, by edict, every year as people became more efficient. It is managed to achieve the greatest good for all. No one carries cash or manages a checkbook.

"I've lived through times of great change. There are now currency accounts for every human being on earth and it doesn't matter too much if an individual overspends in a single year or even a decade. Accounts are eventually settled at death. Just as the average man no longer worried about tigers and bears so much in 2000, the citizens of 2050 don't worry about money. That beast was under control.

"The wars, riots, and upheavals of the early 21st century largely resulted from the unemployment and poverty. Religious zealots and political true believers fanned the pains of poverty into flames of change – but the changes followed no one's plans. Big change started with cellphone and internet technology enabling people, everywhere on earth, to see beyond the range of their eyes. They saw prosperity and peace on a large scale and obtained it simply by demanding it for themselves.

"When the 'Bright Lights' at Harvard University declared that it was no longer desirable to have class divisions based on wages, since there were not enough jobs to go around, they figured out the Universal Reverse Tax to spread the wealth equitably. Crime all but disappeared; poverty and hunger became obsolete. International cooperation became the norm and outlaw nations could not withstand. Central government planning was mostly abandoned as a bad idea. Free Market economies were the norm."

He switched off to give it a rest but thought about the remarkable way things had improved for people. *The average Joe in the year 1000, vs. the average person in 2000, vs. the average man now, only half a hundred years past the millennium…*

"DD. The thing with crime was that the incentive to steal was just about gone. Cash was no longer of any use and many possessions, in the face of worldwide plenty, were no longer so desirable.

"As I said earlier, I was sneaky as a youngster – a thief and a liar and my actions were damaging to myself and others. I've made apologies and restitution as well as I could, and I try to do good in the world now.

"I was out of a job and homeless – but that's another part of my story.

"There were many reasons that there were not enough jobs to keep everyone employed in the 20th century model. Individual productivity had blossomed with the marvels of computers, fast communications, modern transportation, and robotic factory workers.

"Automobiles, kitchen appliances, tools and all manufactured goods had advanced in durability and quality. They did not need replacement as often.

"There was a green movement throughout the world that preached smaller houses, environmental concern, and less waste. The world needed energy to prosper but used so much less to achieve the results of decades past. Fewer workers produced and distributed more goods at lower costs.

"There was a time in the second decade of the century that global warming trends were in the news and linked to severe weather. No matter if the winters were too severe or the summers too cold; man messing up the planet's climate was the popular culprit. News outlets always turned to stirring weather problems if the other news was slow. Governments, eventually, did cooperate to reduce the output of greenhouse gases.

"But by the early 2020's, scientists postulating, and politicians posturing were outshouted by volcanic activity.

Activity which, with a little "more than the usual geothermic belching, tossed chemical vapors into the high-altitude atmosphere that shaded the earth just enough to start a cooling trend. It turned out that global cooling trends were neither better nor worse than warming. Heh hee. I always knew that it wasn't my fault!

"Irregardless of governmental actions, efficiencies in lighting, heating, manufacturing, transport and all areas of human enterprise suddenly reduced the manmade emissions to levels that were deemed as acceptable." *(Paul's spell and grammar checker made a fuss about that word, chiming in with "irrespective and regardless" – He didn't care and let the irregardless stand. That was a word his dad always used, and he liked it.)* "The ice caps and glaciers are still coming back along with polar bears. Siberians are not happy campers.

"DD. Speaking of the news, I always subscribed to a newspaper and, when I finally got a TV of my own, I watched the news on the television. Later on, I dropped the real paper, and eventually the televised news. Now I get it all from worldwide web agencies. The new news.

"Farming is no longer a hit or miss proposition. Yields went off chart with modern hydro. Inefficient and cruel meat production was eliminated by manufactured products. Wasteful suburban living was being replaced with marvelous cities that preserved old treasures while providing a healthful environment. Oddly, many, otherwise unemployed people, reverted to small farming in an updated version of earlier eras. 'Make the earth happy' was a popular slogan."

Paul himself was rich enough and benefited from a much higher than average income. He enjoyed income from both social security and a jumbo variable annuity. In addition, a trusted agency took care of distributing and marketing the art that he had created over the years. The art generated plenty of income. He did not need to jobshare and paid no attention to the job lotteries that apportioned available work to people participating in the pools.

He was no longer in love with creating art. He realized that most of the paintings he had produced were not masterpieces either in his portfolio of work or in the world at large. He felt he'd produced a few worthwhile paintings and had been lucky that they were valued enough to make his name known in the contemporary art market in a minor way. His signature on a work made it salable. He became well known partly because he had made so many paintings. The technology of reproducing good copies had made him a lot of money. Now with advanced 3-D printing, it took an expert examination to tell a copy from a genuine original painting.

Despite his success as an artist and as a businessman, his riches were the result of a few lucky real estate deals. He eased through the first half century of the millennium untroubled by the unemployment or poverty. Now, as an old man, no one cared if he worked. He didn't have to pretend to be busy with a career in art.

Perversely, as worker productivity soared, and the economy produced bountiful goods and services, unemployment rose dramatically. Greater efficiency produced enough for America and her trading partners without needing the number of workers once required.

Paul put those thoughts into the record and continued. "DD. At the same time that productivity soared, the quality and durability of the things we used improved dramatically. If one looks at the life of a typical Chevrolet or Ford over the decades from 1950 through 2050, the odometer at retirement rose from 300,000 kilometers in the year 2,000 to 3,000,000 plus at mid-century mark. My big Ford Buffalo had 2,000,000 K on it when I bought it. It looks and performs like new."

Paul tried to be selective in his preaching. He wanted his readers to understand that his life was good before the digital revolution. It was good when he had no money and few needs. At the age of 18 he spent years living in tents without plumbing or electricity.

"DD. Other factors in the always, ever increasing, unemployment were the aging of the human race and reduced birth rates. With the reduction of the stigma of unemployment, no one cared. There was plenty of money and material goods for everyone. Lots of people worked at some point and unemployed people usually wanted jobs. Work was thought of as prestigious, fun, and interesting, as well as a way to have more money to spend. Others thought that just taking care of their families was enough. Stay-at-home mommying and daddying was popular."

He laughed out loud. "Me? I always liked my jobs. Even when I was my own boss. Just the way I'm wired. I like to work but goofing off is better…" He was interrupted in midsentence.

Lucy Lu's voice came to his ear. She had a very musical voice but she spoke softly. "Hi Paulie. You awake?"

"Yep. It's seven a.m. here. Where are you?"

"Paris. Having lunch on the *Champs Élysées*. My favorite café – *Les Deux Magots*. Just a *croissant* and *café*. Got to watch my figure, ya know."

He turned on his eyeshare to let her see what he saw, and she reciprocated.

"Wow Paulie. Where are you sitting – in a tent? Is that Spotty?"

"Yep. Paris looks beautiful through your eyes. Wish I was there."

He laughed softly, "You better watch your figure. I'm working on mine." He was lying on his sleeping bag and mattress in his Coleman Supertent enjoying the closeness of Spotty's head resting on his outstretched leg. Growing light and the morning breeze flowed through the open flap. He sipped hot coffee.

She gave an audible pause, "…Um… Paul Honey," she breathed as if next to his ear. "When are you coming to see me?"

The phone connection was so intimate. When he had taken the raft guide course at COC, the Caverns Outdoor Center, in mountainous Clancy, Georgia back in '97 - or was it '98? - they had not been close. The classmates had sorted themselves into age groups and she was a few years his senior. He had recently graduated from high school and had no career goals. She was a young M.D. of Chinese heritage and a genius to boot.

Lucy graduated first in her medical school class at age 25. She was a slightly burned-out ER physician at Emory University Hospital when they met. She had an idea that she could work fewer shifts in the Atlanta emergency room and then spend restorative time on the rivers as a whitewater rafting guide.

Paul saw her hand reaching for a croissant and then the street scene with pedestrians wearing smart outfits and quiet busses passing by. She saw speckled sunlight and his hand absently patting the dog.

As personal communications improved in the second decade of the century, Paul had reconnected with virtually everyone who had been important in his life. Lucy was barely on that list. The only thing they had in common was the one-week Whitewater Guide Rafting class at the now famous COC. They had only shared a passion for whitewater kayaking. They were not really friends and had not seen each other in over 50 years. She was a tab on his list of friends. When he had sent out the announcement of Dahlia's death, he had renewed friendships with people from his past as expressions of sympathy came in.

Paul and Lucy learned things about each other over a 6-month series of calls. He knew she was divorced and working part-time as a physician in a French clinic. She said she did not need to work but she had skills that were better when used.

She claimed to be as healthy as a horse. She told him once, "Paul. I think that age 80 may be the new 40 nowadays." She had extended the invitation weeks ago and he had accepted without formatting exact dates.

"HONEY?" She had never called him Honey before. Wonder what that meant, he mused.

"Uh… Lucy. Soon. Right now, I'm on a camping trip. Just me and my pooch Spotty, on the Mountains to the Sea Trail in North Carolina. I'm not sure how long I'm going to keep at it. Right now, I'm thinking I'll be ready for a break soon. I could fly over, say about May 15th and we could do *Paris* together. *Oui mon cherie?*"

"That's a date then. I'll pick you up at the airgate stop. I suggest you come 'Comfort Class' and terminal at Notre Dame.

"And Paul, I …er, have a roommate, so, for your first visit I suggest that you get a hotel room. She is a retired Catholic Bishop, and I don't want to offend her if… if there should be any hint of improprieties… *comprendez vous?* Can I pick the hotel for you?"

"Yeah. Sure. I don't need anything special. Quaint and cheap would be all right but if it turns out quaint and Ritzy, I can handle it. Money's not much of an issue, ya know.

"So okay!" He waxed more enthusiastic, "I'll make the airline arrangements and let you know ETA and gate. You make any other arrangements you like. Sky's the limit," he blurted out. He began to imagine Paris in the springtime.

His vision returned to normal as they rang off.

The gate would be in the middle of the city of Paris. The detachable coach pod from the jet would make its way, without a driver of course, to one of several in-town terminals, picking-up and dropping passengers just like a bus. Jumbo jets were the norm now and airport facilities could not keep up with the traffic. The Boeing PodJet left the drawing boards in 2030 and was now the standard of the world for moving people more easily in the air and at both ends of a flight.

He would carry no baggage. Not even a toothbrush. He could get resupplied with saniwear, wardrobe items and toiletries as he went. His essentials: power shoes platform, belt, hat and glasses would go everywhere he went.

Aside from her time as a Caverns Outdoor Center raft guide Lucy and Paul's life paths did not cross. Something else had sparked their interest in meeting. Curiosity about how they had turned out as mature adults he thought. Perhaps over-ripe adults he chuckled to himself as he thought about it.

He opened his tent flap more fully after they rang off to let the outdoor air engulf him. He'd slept in his walking togs and felt gritty. He walked a few meters away from the tent carrying his toiletry kit and camping spade. Spotty watched with interest but did not stir from his nest next to Paul's sleeping bag.

First Paul peed into a bush. Then he dug a smallish hole in the forest mulch close to a tree, stripped, and leaned against the tree trunk to relieve himself. He wiped with his disposable saniwear and put it on top of his pile before covering the hole with a handful of leaves.

Paul fished a large moist folding towel from the bag. He scrubbed his face, underarms, feet and privates with the towel before poking it under some leaves. Out of its pouch it would become brown, disintegrated mulch in 24 hours. The saniwear would disintegrate too but on a slightly delayed schedule. He felt refreshed and sanitary. He would brush and floss his teeth after breakfast. He had rinseless shampoo and soaps but he chose not to use them this morning.

The personal sanitation outfit he used was first developed for military and the old NASA organizations. Boaters and campers loved them.

He actually had a foldaway portable toilet with him but it just wasn't needed under the day's conditions.

He had hot oatmeal with ButterX, brown sugar and raisins for breakfast. He set the package to deliver 1,000 calories. He'd need a good deal more energy before the day was over. He folded his airbag camp sleeping bag, evicting Spotty who made his own morning toilet nearby. Everything packed easily into his Supertent. His camp chores included washing a pair of wool socks and draping them over a line positioned for that purpose on the front of the superlight tent rig.

Before moving out for the day he popped the Bubble easy chair out of its pocket and let it self-inflate. It was a lightweight but brilliant addition to his camping outfit. It was very comfortable, supporting his back and lifting him off the ground. It was covered in a strong plastic material that he would have difficulty puncturing, even with a knife. Its terrycloth seat and back cover prevented him from getting damp when he sat in it. It was the most comfortable piece of furniture he'd ever owned.

While Spotty ate his breakfast and roamed, Paul sat comfortably and made arrangements. He secured a reservation on the ten p.m. Paris flight from Atlanta on the 14th of May. He'd arrive on the morning of the 15th, fresh from a night's sleep in his airbed.

He arranged for his friend Marty to take care of Spotty while he was gone. He spoke to Billy and Janice. Calling his children with a 'Welfare and Whereabouts' report was a daily routine.

Paul had a hard time explaining Paris to Janice. "Sweetheart. I'm just taking a vacation from my life.

"I'm at loose ends right now and need to fill the time while I look for a direction. Lucy Lu is an old friend from my days at COC."

"Daddy. What the hell! I just googled her. She's a sex therapist!

"What's going on with you?"

Paul was stumped. "I...I... I didn't know that," he stammered.

He thought about it a nano-second and said firmly, "Janice. I might have sex with someone sometime. Not Mom." Oops had he said that aloud?

"I mean. Things have changed. She has a Catholic Bishop for a roommate, and I am not going to have sex with Lucy. I have never seen Paris, and this is an opportunity to have a Parisian show me the place."

Janice laughed so hard she peed her pants. "...Just a little Daddy. I am over 50 years old, and you don't have to explain yourself. I was just shocked for a moment.

"I'm sorry. I've got to ring off now and change my sani." She disconnected, still laughing.

"DD. We goin' to *Paris*!"

APRIL 18, 2055 - Day Four

Walking was a pleasure now that his legs had quit aching. Day three was the worst and then the pains had mysteriously gone away. He felt strong. The tent followed brilliantly. He was glad he had fitted the wheels with short horizontal treads to help it negotiate the softer sandy areas.

Standing on a grassy dune in the Cape Hatteras National Seashore Recreation Area, he did a slow 360 to look at his horizons. Nearby he saw his tent where he had stopped it for a rest. Spotty lay next to it on the beach. Waves crashed endlessly on the shore and the relentless wind stroked the craggy dunes and grasses.

The horizon was sharp. Seaward and off to the west there was only water. Looking west he saw the Pamlico Sound stretched to the horizon. It was at least 50 kilometers wide, he thought. He wished he could get out on the water. "Maybe I'll get me a boat someday," he murmured.

Walking on the sand was not as hard as he had feared. Keeping to the littoral areas, between the low and high tide marks, it was almost as easy as walking a road. The sand was hard enough to support the tent's wheels and the thin layers of shells littering the surface helped a lot.

The cold sea chilled the morning breeze. It was spiced with a salt tang. He breathed deeply and squinted at the brilliant azure-blue sky.

Paul needed to resupply water on day six. He needed dog food, Paul food, sanis and towels. He wanted a restaurant meal as well as supplies. He studied the map of the area on the hi-def images supplied by his implants.

Walking the trail was not too complicated. Joining the organization called *Friends of the Mountain to the Sea Trail* had been a good move. This gave him a circle of people he called his 'MTS pals.' Their website provided detailed information about each section of the trail.

Man and dog traversed dunes, beaches, trails, country roads, parks, highways, villages, and towns. Sea breezes and clean air were a part of the daily diet. Mostly Paul and Spotty were by themselves. About once a day an MTS pal would call him to say hello and offer assistance and information. He declined company when it was offered, and no one intruded on his solitary jaunt. At his age he felt lucky to have help near at hand.

He tapped into the members list and reached out to the 'manager' of each trail section before he traversed it. They told him where to camp legally and, if camping was not allowed, they'd tell him where he could crash with a nearby 'friend,' or, even better, told him where he could safely camp without permission, usually less than ten meters from the track he was on. Law enforcement in the area, and on the problem of illegal camping, was very light. No one bothered him, yet he spoke with people every day. The few folks he encountered were very interested in his rig and in his story. "Why are you doing this?" "How long have you been on the trail?" "Where are you going?"

Although there were houses and condos lining the beaches and clustered into tiny settlements, he felt removed from civilization. Too early in the season for swimming, the beaches he traversed were virtually empty. He was near the beach for the first five days. Even where he crossed bridges to cross the inlets, the sound was a pristine water world with very few boats, vehicles, or other signs of human habitation.

He had ample supplies packed into his Ford Buffalo SUV. Bags of water, crates of freeze-dried food, sanis, fresh utilities, and more. He rang up the vehicle and arranged a rendezvous at noon near the ferry dock in Davis, North Carolina. It was currently parked at Jockey Ridge State Park near the trailhead. He used his Google and Apple maps to scout the area. The Buffalo would come to him, be on time, and keep him informed if there were problems.

Davis was a tiny village with a ferry terminal. He loved North Carolina's free ferry service. It tied the Outer Banks to the outside world. He got a hot dog at the lunch counter near to the ferry parking area.

He was doing the trail backwards. For him it was the 'Sea to the Mountains Trail.' He figured that he could build up his legs and wind better on the flatter coastal regions. He knew that he didn't want to do the entire trail in a single trek but in increments lasting a week to a month. This first outing was a learning experience for him.

His most expensive purchase from Mast General Store was the Coleman self-propelled tent. It had a reputation of being able to recharge its batteries even on overcast days. It used its hub-mounted brakes and a wind powered turbine for energy as well. With over-sized bicycle tires it would proceed about its business even if it flipped. The tires had removable sand vanes to give it better traction on soft surfaces.

It was set to follow Paul's belt buckle at a distance of five meters. Paul had a miniature remote control button on his belt buckle to shut it down when he needed it to wait for him. It could roll faster than he cared to walk.

"DD. Before 2020 pneumatic tires were the only kind available. They were noisy. Even out in the wilderness, 30 kilometers from the nearest highway, you could hear motor traffic. Sometimes it was engine noises, but it was tire noise too – inflated tires making a ruckus, sucking up energy and wearing out.

"Someone, I can't remember who, solved the noise problem, the inefficient use of energy, and the problem of wearing out tires all in one *swell foop*. A woman I believe. She figured out wheel geometry and substituted a slightly flexible wheel and rim covered by a solid neoplastic tire – very energy efficient, extremely long lasting, and whisper-quiet. She designed sound insulation into fenders, and car tires became as quiet and efficient as their engines. She put millions of workers out on the streets. Tire manufacturing, tire repair, tire service, and tire noise were all gone in less than five years.

"That has been the trend my entire adult life it seems - fewer workers producing more than enough goods with technological unemployment exceeding the need for workers in the new industries and product lines. Old industries and services are getting more efficient and reaching more of our world's population. Sigh…! It wasn't easy at first…"

Paul arrived at the rendezvous early and napped under a stunted tree while he waited. He was fitter now that his body was readapting itself for daily walking. His legs were certainly stronger, and he walked faster than on the first day.

Spotty flopped down in the shade nearby. Paul lay dreaming again about the day he had found his secret place on the banks on the Clancy River. This recurrent vision had been coming to him for more than half a century. His arms and body always twitched slightly with muscle memories of the canoe maneuvers he'd been making. Sometimes Dahlia was in his dreams lying naked in the sunlight after the lovemaking. Sometimes he was alone, happy as always in the dream, but thinking about others in his life. Sometimes his brother Mitch would appear, and they would reminisce about their boyhood escapades.

Today he was giggling over something Mitch had said as a joke when the Buffalo beeped. It had arrived so silently that he had not heard a thing.

He opened his eyes and stretched with the luxury of having time to enjoy the vibe of being. How lucky I am to see clearly and feel so good. The air he breathed was warm and well moistened by the onshore breezes of the day. Life was good.

Spotty sat alert as Paul loaded fresh supplies into the tent.

The tent was plugged into the Buffalo, super charging its batteries while Paul placed a small amount of accumulated trash in the dustbin compartment of the vehicle.

They had about ten-days of supplies now.

Buffy was dispatched to the city of Havelock to park in the municipal parking lot. He called the town police department for permission. The female voice asked him for its color and ident signal. She promised, "We'll look after it for you sir. Let us know when you decide to move it."

MAY 15, 2055

The flight was comfortable - Paul slept the whole way. When the wheels touched down with the slightest bump, he was rested and excited to be in the City of Light. His pod separated itself from the airship and trundled away from the airport towards the city center toward the Notre Dame stop.

Passport formalities were largely a thing of the past. His implant identified him for authorities. His passport was not a paper document as it had been in younger days. He well recalled that intercity air travel used to require that he be at the airport two hours prior to departure to accomplish security and other details. He recalled long lines for customs and immigration at both ends of international flight. Those kinds of delays were no longer necessary. It was a safer world in the mid-21st century.

Paul's seat neighbor was a University of Florida history professor going to France on holiday. He casually pointed out some of the sights for Paul as they passed. Paul had the window seat and took in Paris with appreciation. He had read much but never visited France. He and Dahlia had made many trips to Europe over the years to Germany, Italy, and Spain. As an avid reader, Paul had been here in his imagination.

They skirted the Montmartre, and he glimpsed up the sloping street where his seatmate told him the Moulin Rouge was situated. They circled the Opera house and The *Gare du Nord* Train Station. At last, the River Seine appeared and the pod stopped in full view of Notre Dame. Paul was excited and took the scene in with pleasure.

The Seine flowed just below the old *quai* where he stood. He saw vendors and strollers everywhere along both sides of the river. He could see the massive towers of Notre Dame Cathedral looming above sparsely leafed trees and a short bridge. He had studied maps of the city and knew that many of the famous places he wanted to visit were mostly within 1,000 meters.

A crowd of 30 or so people milled around the pod terminal. A porter opened the baggage hatch, and she was passing out shiny suitcases and plastic-wrapped packages to the passengers. A few people were giving the girl new luggage and boarding. Paul scanned faces looking for Lucy.

No luck. He was looking for an older woman. There were two women chatting by a bench. The younger, smaller one was eyeing Paul. She was only slightly oriental. The stouter, older of the two sat in a wheelchair. These two were the only possibilities.

Wait. Could she be Lucy or her daughter? She didn't seem old enough. She vibed European as well as oriental. Paul moved toward them. The woman jumped up and called out, "Paul!"

She embraced him and, as she reached up, he focused on her face. This was not a girl but a woman of forty. She looked young due to her slender frame and smooth skin. But she was actually several years his senior if not already eighty years old. He realized that this was indeed his old friend.

"Why Lucy. You look terrific! How do you stay so young?"

She laughed. "That's a long story. I'll tell ya later. Here. Let me introduce you to Polly."

Polly looked up from her chair. "Hi Paul. Welcome to Paris. Sorry I can't get up just now. I had knee surgery yesterday and they want me to rest the leg for 48 hours. Then, they say, I can go back to playing tennis."

He shook Polly's hand and saw a black woman of his own age with a prominent cross on a chain around her neck. She was dressed in an ordinary jumper. "Pleased to meet you. I'm glad the chair is temporary."

Lucy said, "Polly is my flat mate. I told you about her. She's a retired Catholic Bishop from Ohio. She's in Europe and North Africa for a yearlong sabbatical studying comparative religions. She's writing a book and knows everything you can think of about religions except how to convert me to Christianity." They all laughed at that remark. Paul looked at Lucy in a questioning manner, "Okay my friends. Lead on. I am without knowledge of a place to stay."

"Not to worry Paulie. We took care of that. We got you the Royal Suite at the Hotel Plaza Saint Michael. We plan to move in with you for a couple of weeks and let you pay the bills. Three bedrooms, decadent dining, en suite spa, and all. And the hotel is easy walking distance to everything. Polly will be rolling for now of course.

"As you suggested we booked for two weeks and, Paul, this is very important." She took his arm and peered into his eyes, "You must give them your credit number as soon as we get there. If you don't do it, I'm going to have to look for a hovel in the burbs. I won't be able to pay my rent.

"Paulie. I hope you are as rich as I think."

Paul grinned at his friends. "I'm comfortable with the arrangement for now. My banker might notice in a year or two, but the main thing Lucy is that I'm delighted to be here." He reached for her and gave her another hug. She was very short and very slender.

He patted Polly on the shoulder and asked, "Polly. Can I push for a while, and you can tell me where to go?"

Polly looked up and challenged him to a race. "I can get over the bridge before you, my son."

The chair didn't need pushing. Its systems included a strong propulsion unit. All that Paul needed to do was stroll along as the women told him details about the things he was seeing for the first time.

He was impressed by their knowledge and was falling in love with the city. It was so damn old! So much had happened here. Not all of it good.

Paul was amazed by the amount the hotel charged his account - it was just over UD100,000. He figured it as over three years of earnings for a worker at minimum wage. He didn't share his shock with his companions. Their quarters were splendid. The hotel manager accompanied them on a tour of the suite. It included a generously equipped workout room and spa containing a steam room and hot tub. There were six bedchambers, seven bathrooms, and a modern kitchen. The large living areas had glass doors leading to an impressive balcony. The furnishings were modern with many nods to the history of France and Paris. They had a butler and maids at their beck and call. There was a concierge on duty outside their door 24 hours a day. They were introduced to the staff as a part of the tour.

"*Monsieur et madams. S'il vous plait.* Please do call on us. We want to be of service. A comprehensive list of services is on the tablets in each room. You will like our bicycles and access to our free auto rental fleet. You, of course, will have a driver at your disposal. The vehicle is automatic, but he will serve you in many ways to make your visit pleasant and productive.

"By the way. There will be no extra fees for those services or meals unless something major like a private aircraft is desired."

Paul thanked *Monsieur* Vale with a handshake. Then he quietly thanked God that there would be some freebies thrown in. The bill didn't scare him, but it got his attention.

The hotel was only 30 years old. It was built of modern materials, but it had many touches of the grand turn-of-the-century style that typified his American stereotype of France.

The three friends sat in their grand saloon and formatted a plan for the remains of the day and the next few days as well. Frank the butler brought them tea and cookies and retired to the kitchen to await their pleasure. He would be on duty until six p.m. A single maid would stay until after the dinner hour to give them turn down service and freshen the bathrooms.

"Tell me what to do Lucy. I'm in your hands. And yours too Polly."

Lucy took charge. Her plan was simple enough. "Paul. Polly and I have discussed this at some length. We have two weeks to fill, and we have decided that, because of our ages, and because of Polly's knee, we don't want to be full time tourists. So maybe we could plan for just one event each day and dinner together, and some free time for us all. Except for today and tomorrow.

"We've got that all mapped out: tonight, Notre Dame. We'll follow that up with dinner at the hotel. Tomorrow afternoon we'll go to the Musée d'Orsay.

"The D'Orsay will be your favorite. They are having an American art round-up. Twenty-first century artists. We'll venture out for breakfast at the crack of noon, or whenever we get up. We'll stroll along the quay on the way to the museum and wander *les arrondissements* afterwards. That means the neighborhoods.

"Notre Dame is only 200 meters away and we'll go there tonight. Polly has arranged a VIP visit. The hotel dining room is on the roof. Sunset is after eight. So, we have time to rest, walk and visit Notre Dame today. I'd like a nap and I know Lucy wants one too. Let's leave for the cathedral at five o'clock. *Oui?*"

"*Tres bien.* Sounds good to me. I'd like to freshen up and have a snooze too."

Paul turned to Polly. "Polly. How do I address you? Mother. Your majesty? Your Reverence?"

"Good questions Paul. I am one of the first generation of female Catholic priests. Early on we decided that Mother was confusing as the title Mother Superior was already in use. Sister might have been good but that was also taken. We finally decided that Pastor was appropriate. When I was promoted to bishop, and I was not the first, it was decided that Holy Pastor would suffice. Most Reverend is okay for written letters. As a friend just call me Polly. If you introduce me to someone in a formal way you can say Bishop Polly or Most Reverend. It's confusing. Yes?"

"Yes. How did you become a priest?"

"Well. I did not start life in that direction. But I was a serious student at Loyola and my bishop was an old renegade who was seriously interested in bringing women into the church. He felt it was a necessary but not recognized way for the church to survive in this century.

"Despite the resistance of centuries, the church was desperate for priests by the year two thousand. I studied comparative religion, and my seriousness of intent was recognized by the first generation of female pastors.

"My ordination was just before my 28th birthday. It turned out that I was a better administrator than a teacher. I served a series of churches in Baltimore, Washington, and Indianapolis before my elevation to Bishop. It was a great career. And yes. I did miss the company of men and having children, but I saw the opportunity for the church to progress as something good for mankind. I sacrificed. Now I'm a retired warhorse."

Polly looked ready for a rest, so Paul excused himself and retired to his royal bedroom.

Paul thought that the tour was terrific. Because of Polly's exalted rank, they received special attention at the church. There were met at a side door by two young priests named Sean and Nancy. One was Irish and the other American. There would no language impediment to Paul's understanding of what they were told. The American escorted Polly to a wheelchair ramp for an informal meeting with Monsignor Gotti, Rector of the Cathedral, and other visiting dignitaries.

The climb to the tower was interesting in several ways. First, it was a 400-step climb and he and Lucy handled it easily. Sean, in the lead, looked back at them frequently, saying each time, "Please help me set the pace," with his charming Irish accent.

"Step it up Sean," Lucy replied each time. "I'll let you know if the old-timer back there gets winded." She looked back at Paul each time to make sure he was keeping up. He was.

Paul brought up the rear as their party climbed. Lucy's jumpsuit, following the fashion of the day, was blousy on top, snug in the hips and had bell-bottom cuffs. It was a pretty blue color with very sparse ornamentation. There was, however, a pair of colorful peacock patches made to look like the back pockets used 40 years ago. The birds danced as Polly lifted her leg for each step. They hopped and jiggled, and he saw that the birds' movement involved Lucy's very active butt underneath. There must be some horsepower there, he mused.

Sean said. "Well. Here we are in the footsteps of the Quasimodo and Esmeralda. You are seeing a modern version of what he and Victor Hugo might have seen in the 1820's. Hugo's Paris was much different than ours, however. And the construction on this beautiful church was started in the 12th century, 700 years before these fictional icons haunted the shadows here."

Paul shivered thinking that 700 years after his visit, which would not be commemorated, his bones would be gone but this building would live on with the help of constant maintenance. He was interested too in thinking that the Catholic Church had been building places of worship for over 2,000 years.

How long, he mused, could I last with good maintenance? I might be gone at this time next month.

He was interested in the idea of flying buttresses. The external supports had not been a part of the original plan. When the walls began cracking under the stress of the weight of the roof, the ancients had devised a support system that now looked like a part of the original plans to the uninformed person. Thanks to Sean he now knew better.

Sean droned on about the architecture of the structure, the history of Paris and his reason for being assigned to France. "As ye most likely know, the priesthood is in trouble. Our numbers are declining despite the ordination of women and the reluctant move of the holy mother church into the 21st century. I had a gift for language as a lad and I'm here to improve me French.

"So, I works like a dog eight days a week mostly climbing these friggen steps. Oops. Excuse my French." Sean laughed heartily at his own jokes.

"Nah. Truth be told I love me job and I have strong feelings of purpose around this cathedral. My French is improving by leaps and bounds. My duties require only 40 hours or so each week. So I spend time in cafés and mingling with people. I'm taking classes at the Sorbonne too. I'm only 32 years old and I have the best legs in the archdiocese. I'm moving to Africa in the fall and will likely finish my career there. Teaching as well as pastoral duties."

He questioned them about their lives and was delighted when Paul reported himself as an artist.

"Artist now. What do you paint?"

"Yes. Watercolors. I've done a lot of landscapes and impressionistic work. I'm retired now. Mostly I just sell prints of my work. I maintain shops in Asheville, North Carolina and Atlanta, Georgia. And Amazon, of course."

They ended their climbing lecture at half past six o'clock. Paul noted that Lucy looked fresh while their guide leaned against the wall resting. As they eagerly examined the exhibits, the bell mechanism and the view, he stayed at her side. "Should we think brief," he said, "so we can get back to Polly before she gets too tired?

"Besides. I'm hungry and I can't wait for dinner. Eight o'clock reservation. Yes?"

The three friends arrived at the tenth-floor entrance to the hotel's Restaurant Europa at eight o'clock. Dressed in a tux with tails, Maître d', *Monsieur* Viktor Hakl greeted them with a flourish, "*Madames et Monsieur*. Welcome to our establishment." He had a charming accent.

He led them through the spacious dining rooms and galleries to a table nestled into a bow window overlooking the twinkling city lights in the deepening twilight. Paris' treasured Eiffel Tower was lit in alternating hues of red, white, and green. Inside the restaurant, only a few tables were occupied.

Monsieur Hakl gave them menus and then presented his staff. The waiter and his assistant were introduced in person. The Maître d' invited them to visit the rest of the staff on their menu screens.

Under Viktor's tutelage they met the chefs, the dishwashers and other back staff in the kitchen. Each of these persons was working but alerted by a tone, they each looked up from their tasks, in turn, and said "Hello," or saluted their guests in French.

The waiters were dressed in Tuxedos, but the kitchen workers were in traditional kitchen attire. The chefs' tall toques gave them an august presence.

They studied the electronic tablets and saw not only a written description and explanation of each menu item but, if they wished, they could look at recipes and videos of the preparation.

"Ladies." said Paul, "This is not MacDonalds."

Paul looked at Viktor and his companions and announced, "I worked as a cook and waiter in my youth. I loved the work and, *Mansour* Viktor, if you permit, I would like a tour of the kitchen one day soon."

"Of course, monsieur. Do not call or make an appointment. Just come at your convenience. Perhaps it would be most interesting in the evening when we are busiest. If I'm not here, Henri will escort you."

"*Merci.*"

They chose *crudites* for the *hors d'œuvre* course, *medallions de boeuf* for the *plat principal*. They opted for the *fromage de maison* and fruit to top off their meal. Paul asked for regular and the women for petite portions.

They all knew, of course, that the meat was textured vegetable protein and that the veggies had not been grown in the bountiful soil of France. The French had opted for the efficiencies and other benefits of modern hydroponic farming. They always, however, maintained their long tradition of fine, inventive cuisine. The food was delicious.

Paul was starting to feel mildly jet lagged. He said, "Thank you my friends for a delicious day." They all agreed on escape to their apartment for a nightcap and a good night's rest.

The threesome sat in lounge chairs on their balcony a short while later and watched the city from above. The Eiffel Tower was bathed in blinking lights that changed hues every few heartbeats. It was sharp and distinct as its colored lights sparkled and pulsed against the dark sky. After a while, Polly said goodnight and rolled away.

"Tell me about your work Lucy. My daughter Janice googled you and told me you are a sex therapist. Is that true?" He tried to keep a straight face.

"Well. Yes and no. I do physicals for a clinic that specializes in sex therapy. Mostly we work with older men. We do not supply surrogates, but we are very, very effective. I know all of the methods," Lucy peered into his eyes. Her large, unblinking dark eyes were riveting. Then she grinned impishly.

"Paul. How are you getting along without a woman?"

"How do you know that I haven't found a woman?" His tone was teasing.

"Face it Paulie, if you had a woman she would be here. You wouldn't have come without her, and she would not have let you come alone. Also, you said "yes" as soon as I asked you – no consultation. And of course, you haven't mentioned anyone."

"Wow. You don't need a detective, Lucy. You are very smart."

"Paul. Now that we're alone, I want to tell you more about my work. For me it's not only an interest in sex. I am interested in modern medical science's ability to prolong life.

"Paul. How old do I look to you?" Lucy stood and pirouetted several times. She stretched her arms as she twirled to display her body through the thin fabric of her garment. She stopped and rolled up her loose sleeve to display a thin arm with well-defined muscles clearly defined under unwrinkled skin. She rolled her forearm to show the muscles and sinews there. A few blue veins showed too – making the arm look strong.

She moved close to him and put a foot up on his chair. "Here. Feel my leg." Surprised, he complied while looking up at her mischievous face. She took his hand and raised it higher along her thigh under the loose pant leg. She kept her hand on his and pressed it firmly. He felt smooth female skin with firm muscles underneath. She lowered her foot and seized his hand, spread the fingers and pressed it into her belly, leaning her slight body weight against the strength of his arm.

"Well. Paul. How old do I look?"

"Damn it. I don't know. Maybe forty. But you really look good. How do you do it?"

After midnight. Paul enjoyed the unctuous, sensual feel of the heavy ointments being rubbed on his skin. Lying face down was good. He rolled over reluctantly when ordered to do so, because he was self-conscious about his fledgling erection.

As soon as the back of his head hit the pillow, Lucy slapped his belly button with the flat of her hand. Hard. It made a pop and he rose up only to have her push him back with her hands on his shoulders. He farted.

"Scuse me," he said lamely.

"Paul honey. Relax. That was just a popper to help you calm down." She draped a small towel over his groin. His hard-on declined and he mumbled. "Thanks. I needed that." It was an hour after midnight, and he was pleasantly fatigued.

She laughed because his eyes were as wide as saucers. "Here sweetie. Slip this under your tongue and let it dissolve. We're not going to have sex. This is just part of your first anti-aging treatment."

Paul recognized the familiar taste and mouth feel of Viagra IV. He swallowed and immediately felt a flush on his face and shoulders. He closed his eyes.

"Just breathe. Relax. Shhh. We've got all night. Tomorrow won't begin until you've had your beauty sleep Hon."

Lucy had started telling him about her anti-aging program on the balcony after Polly wheeled herself off to bed. Then she surprised him by saying, "Paul. Would you like to experience anti-aging?"

"Well, I guess so!" he said emphatically. But what are the side effects? Does it hurt?"

"No darling it won't hurt. You'll enjoy it and the benefits will come quickly. The main effect is that you will live longer, feel younger and require less medical support. You'll probably want to work more and try to hook up with chicks."

"When can we start then? How is it done?"

"We start tonight. It'll take a few hours of our time, but you can rest while I'm working. And the major side effect is death – but not until you enjoy a longer and better life. Some system in your body, perhaps your brain function or liver, will fail, eventually, and bring the rest of you down. Those ugly events will have nothing to do with your treatment. It is just still our inevitable fate. We humans do not last forever.

"Still game?"

"Lucy. I remember you as the smartest person I've ever met. I know that you were a brilliant student and the youngest ever Fellow of the American Academy of Emergency Room Physicians. I trust you with my life." He stood and drew her onto her feet and embraced her.

She hugged him back and said, "Paul. You will remember this night for the rest of your sorry life." They both laughed.

"First let me give you a physical." She took a mini scanner from her belt and made him bend so she could reach his head. She passed the thumb-sized instrument over his implant. "Good. Got it. Sit down a moment Honey."

She sat and leaned toward him, looking intensely right into his eyes.

"There's another thing Paul. You must agree to keep our program secret. Not even your family and closest friends can know about it. This will involve a big undertaking from you in a few years as your loved ones age and pass on. Your life arrangements must be thought out to deal with your longer life. You must also journey to Paris once a year for a thorough, very invasive, physical, and additional treatments. It will take a few days each time.

"Think it over for a bit and let me know if you can do it. You will be a member of a small club who know the score, and I will undertake to guide you as long as you need me or for as long as I am able."

Paul leaned back and thought about his children and friends, his circle at church and his self-imposed charitable obligations. At his age he guessed he was a short timer.

"Lucy. Now that my dear wife Dahlia has passed on, I need to reshape my life. That's what I've been doing with my hiking on the MTS Trail and why I'm here visiting you in Paris. I need change to reinvigorate myself and regain my *joie de vivre*.

"So. Yes. I'll keep the secret and I understand the big changes in my life that it will entail.

"Lucy. Can I ask what led you to choose me for this honor?"

"I was rather taken with you when we met all those years ago. You were so different from me. I found you very alluring, but I was too shy to do anything about it.

"I was jealous of your ability to seek your way through life without a big plan. I was so opposite. I had my entire career mapped out by the time I was twelve. Then I was chomping at the bit to escape from the life I was crafting for myself. I wanted to be you and live in a tent eating beans and rice and PBJ sandwiches.

"And I'm still envious. I wish I was an artist without a care in the world."

She gave him a big grin. "Paul. Go take a bath and meet me in the spa room at midnight." She was studying his implant health data output on her device as he left the room to do her bidding.

When they met in the spa room in the quiet of the midnight hour, he was dressed in a hotel robe and his sanis. Lucy was well covered by a hotel robe. She made him discard his 'rags' and lie face down on the massage table. "Don't be shy Paul. I'm just your doctor tonight and you have nothing to hide from me."

He lay face down and bare-assed with just a towel between him and the table.

"Paul. Tell me about your diet and exercise regimen. Whatever it is, you look good for an old dude"

He explained that he mostly ate in restaurants and leaned toward lots of greens and vegetables. That he had a daily routine involving a 40-year-old Total Gym system, the stairs in his apartment, and walking all over Asheville. "I run up and down the stairs between sets on my Total Gym. Up one flight to the top floor and then back down one flight to the ground floor. It's totally private and I figure that it is a perfect aerobic exercise between sets of arm, core, and leg strength work. I stretch before and after I start the workouts."

Lucy began rubbing an ointment into his skin.

He told her more about his therapeutic walk on the Mountains to the Sea Trail. She murmured approval. "I'd love to do part of the walk with you one day. Is that possible for you?"

Paul nodded assent. "Sure Lucy. I just have to ask Spotty." They laughed.

That's a very good regimen Paul. This is about your skin now. We have learned that the skin, your body's largest organ, does a lot. It is a sensory organ that helps us understand the world outside our bodies. It does more than keep bad stuff out, grow hair, regulate your temperature, and secrete yummy odors to attract females.

"Its most important role is to secrete chemicals supporting the vigor of the major organs of the system including your blood and connective tissue. It is also a great portal for the chemicals we are using tonight. This is better than injections and high colonics, eh?"

He thought that over for a moment. "Yeah. In fact this is great, even if it is good for me."

"As your skin begins to fail on the outside, getting wrinkled and dry, becoming thinner - the rest of your body suffers from the loss of a host chemical compounds, once produced by the skin. The body loses abilities - like superman in the presence of kryptonite.

"You lose your ability to live without the total chemical support of your skin. Your vision, hearing, muscular vigor, sexual prowess, ability to resist microorganisms, mental acuity, etc. all suffer. The effects you experience from aging will be a growing frailty and eventual death – probably before your 100th birthday.

"DNA damage, stem cell replacement decline, slowing rate of cell replacement, frailty, accelerated aging and death. Failure of our cellular metabolism and reduction of growth factors gradually get us all.

"My chronological age is 79 years. I test as a fit 40-year-old woman. I can have babies and jump fences. I feel wonderful. Sadly, it won't last forever. Not only is it expensive, but also there could be side effects of the treatment. We don't know enough to live forever and eventually something will fail and suddenly cause us to die. It seems that the treatment may be more effective if started while we're young. So, the primary side effect is death. Also, there are psychological considerations. You will outlive your family and friends.

"So, Paul. Can we continue with the treatment? Would you like to add some good years to your life span?"

He nodded and emitted a muffled, "Yes," as she did her work. The bottoms of his feet were ticklish, and he definitely noticed when she inserted a finger into his rectum to supplement his physical exam.

"Damn Paul. Your prostate feels good. I can tell you are a lucky guy."

Lucy continued to work the ointment into his skin - every square inch. She droned on, "Science has been working on the 'Ponce de Leon' effect for centuries. In the last part of the nineteen hundreds, they began to understand hormones like testosterone and estrogen. You've heard of them – but many other chemical factors have recently been discovered that control the reproduction of cells, growth, and metabolism. These factors change as we progress through infancy, childhood, puberty, adulthood and old age. Old age can be divided into early, middle and end stage, as frailty takes over and robust energy dwindles."

Paul had not been aware while he was on his stomach with his mouth and nose pressed into the breathing-mask hole, but Lucy had slipped out of her robe and was naked. It had happened quietly while his face was pressed into its depression on the table. He saw her when she made him roll over. She was a small woman with dark pubic hair and pointy breasts. Only her face looked oriental.

Her glistening body would have placed her as a beauty anywhere in the world. She was very feminine in her hips and rear end, as he had noticed while climbing the stairs of Notre Dame behind her. She seemed muscular and fit. Her smooth thighs were well rounded with muscles. He tried not to stare, but pretty much failed, straining to see her golden skin out of the corners of his eyes while she moved up and down the table.

"In this program to rejuvenate your body, fixing your skin is the first and most important step. As I said, it's the largest organ in our bodies and far more integral to the aging process than we imagined years ago.

"I want to take a little time tonight, as I work, to explain that a lighter diet, rich in raw foods, heavier exercise, and use of sun blocker creams on your face, hands and every part of your body exposed to the sun, will be good things. By the time you wake up tomorrow, and over the next few days, you will be feeling better and better.

"I don't know what your effective age will be when we are done here, but I suspect it will be about a fit forty-five.

"Congratulations on keeping yourself as fit as you have." She worked the gunk, as he thought of it, into his front from the top of his head to his feet. She pumped a blob into his palms and said, "Paul. It is probably better if you do your own genitalia, I'll do it for you if you like, but I think, in the end, it's better if you do yourself. Work around your anus too."

While he complied with her request, Lucy asked him, "Do you drink?"

"No. Not much. Maybe a beer now and then. Is that a problem?"

"Not at all. The thing I'm getting around to will sound counterintuitive. Your mental attitude is very, very important to your continued health and rejuvenation. I recommend that you learn to relax with a drink or two in the evenings. Establish a sunset ritual which is relaxing to you and which will put you in the mood to be with others. *Capiche?*"

"Yes. *Si.* Of course. I'll work on that."

When he was done, she gave him a one-liter bottle of pills and a booklet. "Read this tomorrow. You'll dissolve the pills in water and spray your entire body with the solution a few times a week and air dry. Begin the day after tomorrow and keep it up forever. This bottle of pills will last for two years, and I'll ship you a real supply after you go home. Maybe I'll deliver them in person.

"And take this now. It'll help you sleep." She placed a tablet on his tongue and offered him a sip of water.

She shrugged on her robe, letting him watch her sleek body on purpose. He thought her action was a kind of challenge. She took her time and enjoyed watching his eyes wander over her body.

"Wrap yourself in sheets tonight so you don't mess up your nice bed too much. Don't wash tonight. God only knows what the maids will think."

They parted with a peck and a hug. He was exhausted.

May 16

Paul woke from a wet dream clutching his happy, throbbing penis as it squirted its fluids into his hands and onto the sheets wrapped around his nude body. Lucy, in his dream, had been giving him a hand-job, her dark eyes gazing into his with great intensity to be sure that he came hard.

He lay gasping and pressing the last drops from his organ as he tried to squeeze sense out of the dream. She had been lecturing him.

"No sex tonight, Paulie. You have got to keep these ointments on your skin as long as possible."

In the dream, he had been nodding in agreement as her hand suddenly gripped him and began masturbating him. He wasn't surprised – only pleased that she had read his need so well.

Oh. Wait a minute! He realized that he hadn't had such an intense sleep event for many years. He might have been 20-years old last time. What had happened?

He gradually began thinking about the practical aspects of rescuing himself from the tangle of sticky sheets – moist with sweat and the oils from Lucy's ministrations. His bedside clock told him it was almost noon.

There! And that was another thing – he always woke early. Lucy had dismissed him at about two a.m. He had followed her instructions not to bathe until morning, but he had expected to sleep in until maybe eight o'clock. He had overslept four hours by his reckoning.

The shower was refreshing beyond belief. He even shampooed and rinsed his bald head, even though it was virtually hairless. It all felt good.

He put on the fresh street clothes the hotel had placed in his closet and wandered into the saloon to find Lucy and Polly lingering over coffee and the remains of fruit and croissants. He asked the maid for *café Americaine,* croissants and fruit.

Lucy stood up when he approached and said, "Paul. You're looking mighty chipper. How do you feel?" She appraised him with her eyes and placed a hand on the back of his neck, stroking him as if he were a cat.

"Well. Great! Never better in fact. I believe I just slept as well as I possibly could." He looked at Lucy and glanced at Polly to ask if the bishop was in on their secret.

"Paul. Polly knows everything. She has been in juvination therapy for over a year. She looked at her roommate and said, "Polly. How do you feel?"

"Well young man. Lucy has given me back my youth. I'm ninety-two years old and, except for my knee, I feel like I'm 60 again. And I was a hellova 60-year-old too. I was very spry and youthful then and I feel that way now."

Paul noticed that her wheelchair was not in sight. "Are you done with the rolling chair now Polly?"

"I'm going to use a cane today, but I'll have the chair follow to make sure I don't overdo it – especially late in the day.

"Do you feel any different today?" Polly asked him. "It was an intense experience. Wasn't it?"

Paul looked down at his hands. He was used to seeing a patina of wrinkles, spots, and veins. They were still his old hands, but the skin looked smoother and brighter.

His jumpsuit felt snug in the arms and chest. "Holy shit! Excuse my French. But I do feel younger. I expected to feel jet-lagged, but I just feel good."

Paul jumped out of his seat and said, "Ready when you are girls. Lead on."

They took a bathroom break and then set off on foot in the direction of the *Musée d'Orsay* followed by Polly's wheelchair. Polly walked lightly using her cane for balance when they encountered steps and curbs.

The left bank teemed with strollers from every nation. Stalls of art, books, flowers, and souvenirs were lined up so closely that the River Seine could only be seen sporadically. The press of people was most on view when they came to the bridges. They paused at each span to have a look at the city up and down river.

They passed through throngs of street entertainers juggling, posing, making music, and miming for UDs. It was a fun atmosphere and Paul soaked it up. It was like Asheville on a Saturday afternoon when the street folk came out but on a scale that boggled his mind. He could see that both sides of the river were busy and that side streets were also alive with humanity out for a good day in good times.

There was a massive line at the front of the Musée. Lucy made a telephone call and said, "We're here at the front. See you in a minute." She led them to the side of the building where they were met by a tall, mustachioed man who seemed somewhere south of 60-years of age.

"Percy my dear." Cried Lucy as they embraced and shared a triple face kiss and a bit of grinding around on Lucy's part. She seemed overjoyed to see him.

"Percy LeGran. Meet my friends Paul Hunter and Bishop Polly Pinter."

"An honor to meet you sir," said Percy as he wrung Paul's hand. The greeting was a little over the top and it put Paul on guard. He didn't know what he was nervous about.

Polly was greeted likewise. "Your Grace. Thank you for coming. We are so excited." Polly chose to sit in her wheelchair at this point and Percy LeGran ushered them into the main saloon of the museum. The building was a train station when it was erected at the beginning of the 20th century. The grand space was bright with sun filtering through walls of glass. It was big enough to require a day's stroll to see all of its individual galleries.

The French penchant to view the nude human form as the ultimate work of art was evident everywhere. Wonderful alabaster sculptures of full-bodied, youthful women were abundant. Godlike warriors with oak-like arms and legs menaced them from every side.

The central gallery was magnificent. Vignettes of sculpture and vistas of paintings were on display. The painters' names registered with Paul, but he did not know much about them. He saw Monet, Goya, Picasso, Renoir, Van Gogh, Lautrec, Gauguin, Manet, and others.

They wandered slowly toward their goal of viewing *American Painters of the 21st Century*. The *Gallerie Américaine* was marked by a large banner and, as they stood in the center of the room Paul saw that there were several rooms connected by sizable archways. His eyes flitted from painting to painting and suddenly fixed on a work two rooms away. Brilliantly lit, and hung in a place of honor, was his own painting! Paul's jaw dropped.

He saw a large work, 750 by 1,200 millimeters, hanging by itself. It was an early version of his *The Watcher* paintings. "Lucy. Polly. Percy. What the hell is that thing doing here?"

He turned to their host. "How did you get it? Percy. Did Lucy and Polly have anything to do with this?"

As they drew closer, he could see that it was a dark palette – an image of a vague form high in the dark branches of a tree, with stark masculine eyes staring down at a form at the base of the tree. A female figure crouched in the foreground, vaguely suggested by serpentine white lines terminated in a pair of feminine eyes looking back at the watcher.

The work had been inspired partly by an incident from his teenage years when he had peeked through a window at a girl from school. The images were also born of his feelings at the time he made the work. He felt himself to be an outsider looking into the community campfire but kept out by banishment. He was lusting for the woman in the painting.

"Paul. We were very lucky to get that painting. We paid UD200,000. Does it not look magnificent?"

Percy was grinning from ear to ear with pride at his acquisition and pleasure at viewing the work with the artist. This was, in fact, a first for him. Surprising an artist with his own work.

Paul was astonished at the price paid for the work. It did look magnificent sitting in the perfect light. As they drew closer, he recalled everything about the picture and its history.

He did not make many paintings that size when he first started painting because the young artist could not afford the large paper. Many of his original paintings had been sold over the years. At first, he was happy with 50 or 100 dollars. Then he had discovered a limit. At about $150.00 people would no longer buy his work. He didn't care because he made a nice living selling limited editions and lycées of his paintings.

He started working as a painter at the age of twenty-two. Over time, five decades, he produced well over 10,000 works. This particular piece was special for him. It had been an emotional time for him. He remembered putting the paint to the paper and his teacher's comment.

Elizabeth Auberson had said, "Paul. This does not look like a watercolor. Don't get me wrong Paul. I Actually like it. But this technique of making the work so dark is not what I like to do myself."

"Percy. Thank you so much for showing this. But I have something awkward to tell you."

Percy, Lucy, and Polly stood by Paul and heard him say, "As much as I appreciate it being here, it is a copy, and not the original."

"Paul! How can you say that? It's too awful. He paid a lot of money for it," cried Lucy. "There's no way you can tell. Is there?" she challenged.

Paul looked sad. "Percy. This is like shooting myself in the foot."

"But Paul. We had it authenticated. The paint and paper samples passed our standard battery of tests. The seller is a reputable firm."

"Yet, I did not make this picture. I know because of the size and the paper. It must have been made from a print of the original. I sold hundreds of them over the years at an average of $50.00 each."

"What do you mean Paul?" said Percy, somewhat in shock.

"I painted a picture just like this, same size and color but I painted it on hand-made paper given to me as a gift by Elizabeth Auberson. She made the paper and was disappointed that I made such a dark mess of it."

"I know of Elizabeth Auberson. We have one of her paintings being framed. I want to show it to you." Percy was wringing his hands with worry. He led them through a staff-only door, and they made their way to a workshop deep in the recesses of the museum.

The Musée's 'Auberson' was clearly a work on handmade paper, the same size as Paul's *Watcher*. The material was thick and coarse with bits of fiber dotting its surface. The edges were uneven. The subject of Elizabeth's painting was a fierce eagle with outspread wings and intense eyes.

"I know this picture," said Paul. We painted together on certain Tuesdays – those were my class days with her. We painted together. The bird lived in Texas and that's where she made the drawings that she based the painting on.

"She'd take days making paper out of discarded bits of paper, cloth, dried grasses and such. She had a secret recipe that she didn't share with me.

"I once suggested that she could harvest fibers from the driers at the town's main laundry. She made a face at me and said, "I don't like that idea, Paul. Too much hair I think."

"My 'Watcher' painting was made on this same kind of paper. Handmade by Elizabeth." Paul got close to the painting and, without touching it, inspected the margins. "Yep. Just like my painting."

Percy thought it over as they stood around the Auberson. "Paul. That was a long time ago. How can you be so clear that the work we have on display is not the real thing?"

"Well. In addition to the size and paper, I have the original at home in my art vault. I'll be home in two weeks, and I'll be glad to ship it to you for inspection and then inclusion in your display. I'll throw in a few others that you might like. The only condition I want to make is that you return them to me when the *Americaine* exhibition is over. Unless..." Paul engaged in a pregnant pause and big grin... "You could buy them Percy. That would make my collection of original paintings worth a fortune." He grinned thinking about how many paintings he had stashed away and doing the outlandish arithmetic in his head. *Billions!*

Paul knew the number of paintings he had retained, thanks to Dahlia's accounting system, devised when they were young, and she began to take an interest in the escalating numbers. He still had over 9,000 paintings in his vault. If they could fetch UD10,000 each, he calculated that they'd have a total value of UD90,000,000. But Percy had paid UD200,000 for just one painting! The value of his collection might be much – very much, greater than he had ever imagined.

Paul had a small gallery in the ground floor shop underneath his apartment in Asheville. It was an interesting, but not an elegant space. Its high tin ceilings harked back to the beginning of the 20th century. It represented the architectural style of the times. The shop's 88 square meters was open except for a washroom in the back. The front facade was glass with an inset, centered door to shelter people as they entered. The doorway separated and defined two plate glass front display areas. Sometimes he painted while sitting in the larger window.

He owned a much larger gallery near Atlanta at the Maupai Inn. Here he sold original works for bigger bucks. Up to UD5,000 for the works he liked best - the larger ones.

At the Asheville business, his friend Marty Smith worked as the manager. Marty's main duty was to hire and supervise students from UNCA who tended the shop and rang up sales. He also swept the floor, cleaned the plate glass, and made the occasional trip to the bank.

Many paintings, mostly reproductions, hung on the walls. Other artists were represented as well because of reciprocal arrangements with other artists that Dahlia had helped to devise. It made the shops more interesting.

Paul accumulated thousands of his own original paintings because they did not sell at the prices he wanted. He long recognized a need to protect them from theft and other mishaps. He sold limited edition prints and glycees, but the originals languished.

Going back over 35 years - his brother Mitch acquired a big safe – an antique that couldn't be locked. The steel lump was part of the decor of his antique shop. It weighed over 500 kilograms and had a big storage volume. It was highly rated for fireproofing standards. Mitch had gifted him the safe and delivered it to the shop in 2020 when Paul offered to buy it.

Mitch and Paul wheeled the safe into the rear of the shop on a Friday night. They loaded it with almost all of the unsold originals. Paul reckoned that he could start selling them in earnest if the need ever arose, but his busy, and otherwise, very successful life, allowed him to procrastinate.

The shop was six meters wide. Take away 1.5 meters for the washroom and he was left with a 4.5-meter-wide rear wall. That same night Paul decided that better protection would be achieved if he completely walled the safe off from the rest of the shop. So, with Dahlia's permission and help he partitioned the safe room overnight. He now called it his vault. He had good carpentry skills and was able to build a room, with no doors, for the safe. One would need to breech the wall to enter.

He did the work when there was no one around. A stack of studs, six pieces of sheet rock, a bucket of drywall compound, and a can of latex paint were used. The room, with his originals inside, was now fully hidden. The space was virtually invisible to the naked eye. He hung some framed works, left some in canvas sling racks, but most of his original paintings were in the fireproof vault. There was no door or other entryway to the space. Its wall was now the store's rear wall with paintings hung for display on the shop side.

Inside the room, a single forever-light bulb warmed the room slightly to keep it dry. He broke in periodically over the years, using a utility knife and sheetrock saw to create a small opening, to add paintings to the stash, or to remove some for sale. Each time he would reseal and repaint the wall to keep it from being discovered. The entry and exiting would take about an hour, including repairs and painting.

Now with Dahlia gone, only Paul knew about the hidden safe and its suddenly precious contents. It was mentioned in a sealed codicil to their will, so he knew that it would be discovered when he died.

Percy agreed to buy the original 'Watcher' painting and Paul was overjoyed. The sale would pay for his trip. The penny-pinching part of his soul was satisfied.

"By the way Paul. Your comments about Auberson were very interesting. About how she made the paper, where the bird was painted and how she viewed your work. I would appreciate it very much if you could write a short article with those personal details. We could include it in our monthly postings and as a placard by her painting."

Paul agreed. "Sure Percy. I miss Elizabeth. She was a good friend as well as my teacher. I am in touch with her children."

Percy agreed to meet Paul and his friends for dinner at the hotel at eight o'clock.

Paul asked him for advice over cocktails. Paul was drinking a virgin Bloody Mary. At Lucy's suggestion he was abstaining from alcohol for 30 days to obtain maximum benefit from his treatment.

That dinner for Paul consisted of fancy raw veggies served with a delectable raw hummus made from a secret recipe. To his surprise he actually got enough to eat. He had a honey-sweetened, meringue-coated fruit for dessert. The rest of the party had duck *orange* for a main course. No actual *canards*, of course, were sacrificed for the meal.

"Don't worry Paul. You can have regular food tomorrow maybe. I'll give you a physical in the morning and see how your numbers stack up.

Paul could not tell if Percy was a member of the anti-aging club, and the subject was not discussed. The dinner conversation revolved around what Paul should do to convert his art collection to cash.

"Paul. I advise you to get a well-connected art agent and collaborate with an auction house. One with an international, high-end reputation. Establish a long timeline for your business plan. Think big!

"Give yourself a few years and don't cash in all at once.

"By the way. Are you still painting?"

Paul had to shake his head. "Before my wife died, I dabbled – perhaps one or two paintings a month. Now? It has been over six months and I haven't even looked at my brushes."

His audience was sympathetic. Lucy put a hand on his arm. "We can only imagine how it is for you. I hope you are getting over your grief – frankly, I think you are doing amazingly well. Your spirit seems good."

"Thank you for understanding. Not needing income, my painting motivation was low.

"But, since being here, just for the last two days, my eyes are brighter, and I see paintings everywhere. And remember, I've been hiking with my dog Spotty. The images from being outdoors so much have been inspirational. I want to start painting again."

Percy provided Paul with the names of several New Yorkers who could steer him in the right direction.

PART TWO

JUNE 2055 – New York

Paris, France, the French countryside, and his sojourn with his friends sped by. Paul decided to spring for an upgrade to ultra-first class for his trip home. He sat back, feeling wonderful as the giant aircraft leapt into the sky. Destination New York.

Paul leaned back in his wide luxury seat with a Clamato juice Bloody Mary at hand and nodded off as the clouds became the only view through his screen in the nose of the airplane. He was happily remembering his last few nights with Lucy. She loosened up on her rule of no sex and became the first woman, not his wife, to do the deeds with him since the year 2000. Over five decades.

Lucy had been more a teacher than a lover. Every move he made, she'd say, "Go for it Paulie. That's the way. Deeper. Harder. Hold on. Don't come. Do it with your tongue. Don't stop there."

Her hands would grasp something - his head, his hands, his penis, or his butt and push him where she wanted him to go. Lucy was very oral, and Paul had a hell of a time.

She made him wash and lie on his back after the air dry. Light aromatic oils would be warmed between her palms and massaged into his skin. He now thought of his pelt as his favorite organ.

When he began to beg for genital contact, she would distract him. She gave him chocolates to melt in his mouth. Spankings to warm his bottom. She would mount his head and press her vagina into his mouth, holding his hands to her breasts and making him squeeze her nipples hard.

The sex games would go on for hours until she gave him sweet release as he lapsed into sleep land from the un-named drugs she made him swallow.

"Don't worry about it sweetie. Momma won't give you anything bad." He believed her whole-heartedly. He felt well cared for.

The plane flew and Paul slept. He dreamed about what to do with his years, his new youth, and his hundreds of millions of UDs as he drifted off.

Paul gazed out as New York City appeared as a beautiful miniature growing larger as they neared the New Jersey coast.

He recalled that New York City had been in a decline in the years of his young adulthood. It was then choked in traffic and exhaust fumes, and besieged by homeless, jobless, helpless people. The city struggled with aging infrastructure and financial turmoil. Its politicians were deadlocked over solutions. Its reputation heavily tarnished.

Mayor Willie Rodham Jackson was a cousin of two Presidents. He was a brilliant Harvard PhD Political Scientist and economist. He came up with the idea to quit hammering the downtrodden unemployed and find special ways to challenge New York's fabulously wealthy to take care of the underclass. The elite stockbrokers, bankers, law enforcement, medical and teachers and employed citizens of every stripe were led to contribute time, expertise, and cash to ease the underclass into a healthier state of existence. Willie liked to tell a fifty-word allegory about the workers and the arrow. He called it the *Mini Saga of the Happy Village*.

> *The Happy Village. Ten women provided plant food and clothing for the tribe. Their men used slings to get animal food. Everyone was*
> *happy.*
>   *A wanderer gifted them with bow and arrows. Suddenly one man could provide meat.*
> *As a result, nine men were suddenly unemployed - no longer needed to hunt.*

Jackson then leaned toward his audience, looked them in the eye and asked his famous question, "Was the tribe better off?"

In Jackson's *new* New York, the able poor were given a chance to work, if they were able. Necessary jobs cleaning streets, parks and restrooms, painting curbs and such. Necessary work that could be done by almost anyone but contributed to the general wellbeing. Dental care, haircuts, childcare, clothing, apartments, food, utilities, and primary education became universal New Yorker rights. The cost was astronomical, running to the hundreds of millions but the benefits were well worth the cost. The creation of good jobs was one of the outcomes.

During Jackson's first six-year term as mayor the crime rate plummeted, emergency rooms were no longer delivering inadequate primary medical care, and unemployment was better understood in a town with only four million jobs available for ten million people needing income to provide for their families. The teeming souls who called the city home were justifiably proud of their accomplishments.

The biggest change was the idea that unemployment was the fault of the unemployed. In a land where there were ever fewer jobs due to skyrocketing efficiencies in the manufacturing and distribution of food and services, unemployment was inevitable. The three-day workweek became standard, and the idea was soon copied on a national scale. Europe and the rest the world was already ahead of the United States on some fronts.

Worldwide, post-elementary education shifted into the computer–internet realm. Cyber schools improved teaching techniques and lowered the cost of education. No more expensive schoolrooms were required for advanced degrees. E-books cost pennies. The best teachers were available to thousands of students. The best lectures could be repeated many times.

University education was totally different in these modern times. The time and expense of higher education had plummeted by the year 2025. Brilliant teachers in Uzbekistan were teaching eager students in the Philippines. Chinese teachers lectured Mexicans and Frenchmen. The world had shrunk so the best of the best could share their insights and methods with tens of thousands of students attending each lecture. Each student progressed at his or her own pace, garnering gold stars - the old reward-driven method pioneered in the first decades of the last century.

The biggest cost of an advanced degree was often testing and certification of graduates. Typically, an unskilled worker's pay could easily cover the finances of advanced education.

In the old university system, the students had to devote years to attending classes and often had to work at unskilled jobs to achieve their degrees and/or borrow obscene sums through student loan schemes that could not be repaid until years after graduation. People learned at their own pace now and the process was not metered in semesters and years. It was gauged by knowledge and abilities attained.

The planet has always been hungry for engineers, chemists, mathematicians, physicists, and technically trained people in every field. Now these skills were widely available and large corporations routinely designed the curriculum needed for their operations, even for locals in remote areas where facilities were located to be near raw materials. The world was getting smarter every year.

Charismatic business leaders in New York became elementary school teachers for a few days each month. Religious leaders manned daycare centers for a few days out of thirty. Each working person was privileged to serve in needful ways on an ongoing basis. The New York Community and character improved so dramatically that the rest of the nation, and the world, took note and followed suit. Taking care of each other was clearly a better way than blaming the unemployed in an ever-shrinking job market.

Paul arrived in Manhattan without setting foot in the airport. He had no luggage and walked from the air coach corner stop to the New Joy Hotel. His room was splendid, but the cost did not compare to his digs in Paris. It seemed relatively cheap.

He had chosen the hotel because his attorney, Andria Morgan, was in the hotel tower's business suites. Morgan had been highly recommended by Percy. While Paul had spoken to her many times in the past few weeks, they had not met in the flesh. He saw her image on his holos while they were talking and knew that she was an attractive woman. Of course, he supposed, all females these days seemed to be younger and more attractive.

He had an appointment with an internationally recognized art agent. Terry Perleman had told him on the phone, "Paul. With your backstory I have blocked out the entire day for you. I expect your collection to be the capstone of my career." His voice was raspy.

Terry, in person, was an ordinary looking guy of middle age dressed in a sports jacket and open-collar shirt. The style might have dated to the first decade of the century. He stood out not only for his old-fashioned manner of dress but also for his long hair. His ponytail hung to his shoulders.

He wrung Paul's hand. "So privileged to meet you sir."

"Please. Just call me Paul and don't worry about anything but making us a lot of money. I need your guidance to map out a plan that will be safe as well as profitable." They were seated in the opulent lobby of the New Joy. A waiter appeared to take a drink order. Paul wanted flat water and Terry ordered sparkling. Paul was glad his companion seemed sober minded.

"Okay Paul. Let's start with my fee – I can either charge you a thousand UD an hour plus expenses, or 5% of sales, but I cover my own expenses. I way prefer the latter even though it may take me years to make some money. I'll have an incentive to work hard for you either way. If you opt for the hourly fee, I'll need 100,000 up front. With the percentage contract, I'll give you monthly statements. No money from you until we have some sales."

Paul had already discussed fees with his advisor Percy, in Paris, and quickly declared, "I trust you, Terry. I want to go the percentage route."

Terry turned away and made a call. He spoke quietly and, in less than a minute, turned to Paul to say, "My associates will produce the contract for your review and have it available for your signature right here in the lobby in a few minutes. Give me the name of your attorney so that he can review it before we sign it."

Paul called the attorney, who was on stand-by, and arranged a review.

"Terry. Send it to Andria Morgan at this number. "She'll produce the actual document and get it here to us while we sip our bevs. Her offices are in this building. I think we'll agree on everything and can get started." He showed Terry the contact number and waited for him to relay instructions to his office.

Their drinks arrived with a tray of carrot sticks and dipping sauce. They settled back to talk while their teams scurried.

"Terry. In a matter like this, how much attention should I pay to the physical security of the work? Can you help me formulate an action plan that will involve getting started in my hometown vault in Asheville, North Carolina tomorrow? What about insurance? What other considerations should I involve myself in?"

Terry told Paul that he should be prepared to receive a catalogue staff from the Mathews Auction House at his earliest convenience. "As soon as the paintings can be photographed and labeled, the catalogue staff will arrange proper shipping containers and secure transport to the nearest suitable airport. The airport may not be Asheville.

"You can't ensure the paintings for their proper value until the curators have a look at them. By the time that happens, here in New York, your work should be as secure as possible."

Andria arrived with a folder in hand. Introductions were made and they moved to a lobby table to conduct their business. In high heels she was as tall as Paul, and he felt a great connection to her. Her blue eyes were clear, her posture confident and she looked like a person who liked to get her way. Her jumper fit her like a fine glove. Paul was falling in love as she shook his hand.

"We meet at last. Hi Paul. I'm here to help make this happen for you."

She turned her gaze to Terry. "Hey. You too Terry, my old friend."

Paul saw that they knew each other and gave them a quizzical look.

"We have worked on deals before," said Andria. "We keep each other in line. In this deal, I belong to you Paul. Nobody else. I'm watching like a eagle."

They all chuckled at her joking tone. But Paul felt confident that he was in good hands.

Contracts and letters of understanding were discussed and inked. Dates were arranged for the auction house to view the paintings in Asheville.

"My God Paul," said Andria. "Nine thousand paintings. Why aren't they in a bank vault?"

Paul shrugged. Embarrassed. "You know I don't have a good answer for that. It just happened over a lot of years. I wasn't ambitious enough and I think that it's just a freak thing that they suddenly have such a value. They are very safe. No one knows where they are, and they are well secured and protected. Not even Terry knows where they are. The auctioneer's cataloging team will meet me at my main gallery in Asheville Monday and we'll go to them from there."

The afternoon was growing late, and Paul invited them to dine with him and his daughter Janice. They declined, citing prior commitments, and the three parted with warm handshakes, each clutching a folder of signed documents.

Paul now felt that his return to the States was somewhat a triumphant event. He had already contacted his children, Janice and Billy, to see if they and their spouses were able to meet him in New York – his treat for airfare and hotel. Janice was the only one available for the event. He was very anxious to talk to them about his newfound success in the art world.

Janice knocked on the door of his suite at seven. His daughter was a slender woman of fifty with stylish gray hair, a form-fitting green coverall, and high heels. She carried a large purse that contained the essentials for a two-day visit to New York.

After a big hug she stepped back and said, "Daddy. What the hell have you been up to? You look terrific." She hugged him again and then held him at arms' length while examining the details of his face.

"Daddy. You've lost weight. Have you been working out? You seem so much better than the last time I saw you."

"Yes. I have a new regimen that seems to agree with me. Doctor Lucy Lu showed me what to do. She's older than me but is in amazing shape."

"Keep it up please. You look more like Billy than your old self. Gosh I wish the gang could be here."

Billy, two years younger than Janice, was unable to meet them because he was in Toronto speaking at a convention of veterinarians. Both sets of grandchildren were in the final weeks of school and uber-involved with term-end exams, proms and other school activities. Two of them were graduating from high school.

School had evolved since Paul's youth. Once reading, writing, arithmetic and behavior were dealt out in the first four grades, most kids were home schooled, using computers and the brilliant internet courses that entertained as they taught advanced subjects. Many kids, especially those with working parents, were involved in professionally managed neighborhood study groups. Physical education, sports, social events, and field trips were a regular part of each student's life. The costs of primary and secondary educations were reduced and there were fewer but better paid administrators, teachers, and non-professional workers in the process. Even small countries were able to bear the costs.

Paul and Janice settled down on the comfortable sofa in his suite and chatted while they connected with Billy in Toronto. Billy's smiling face bloomed from the wall holo. "Hi Dad. You look great. Hi Jan. You too. How was your trip from Laramie?"

They engaged in small talk for a few minutes missing the presence of Dahlia. They had always been in more contact with their mother since Paul, although he was a loving father, tended to step back and let Dahlia take the lead with the children and grandchildren.

"So, Dad," said Billy. "Tell us what's up? Why did you need to talk as soon as you got here and not wait till next week?"

Paul suddenly felt shy. "Look kids. Something interesting came up in Paris and it will affect both of you. I wanted to tell you in person, but events are moving so fast with this that I had to tell you now."

"Daddy. Are you getting married? To that Lucy?"

Paul hesitated. Shrugged his shoulders and said, "Well no. Lucy and I are great friends now and I can't wait to tell you all about her and Paris. But it's something else.

"It's about my collection of paintings. You know that I have a lot of original paintings. Mostly I made a living from selling reproductions. Yes?"

Janice and Billy nodded and looked at each other, puzzled by the direction the conversation was taking.

Paul explained about the exhibition at the *Musée* d'Orsay, the fake painting, and the subsequent sale of the original for UD200,000.

Janice blurted out, "Holy shit Dad!"

Billy couldn't talk. He was laughing. They saw that he'd gotten up from his chair and was doing a celebratory dance around his Toronto hotel room.

"Kids I don't think my paintings will all be worth that kind of money but, the part that you don't know is that I have thousands of unsold originals and a marketing plan that should bring in mucho dinero. I think the inventory of my paintings will come in at over nine thousand." He paused again for his children to do some math. They both looked serious.

"Dad," said Billy in a hushed voice. "That's a lotta money. It's hard to fathom."

Janice was looking at him with a loving but puzzled expression. "Daddy. You're going to be very famous!"

When they settled down Paul told them that he intended to give them an inheritance - a gift - as soon as he could. "I'm shooting for UD3,000,000 for each of you." He had determined that amount based on his current finances. The gift would deplete his ready cash assets, but he was confident that his plans would start a great windfall.

The expressions on their faces ranged from surprise and delight and then to concern for Paul's health. "Daddy are you all right? You're not getting ready to die, are you?"

Billy nodded agreement in the halo.

"No to death just now. I have never felt better. Really good!

"I intend to use the bulk of my wealth, present and future, to advance the cause of elementary education in Africa, North Korea, Bangladesh, and a few other relatively unenlightened areas of the earth. They might have needs I could help fill."

He leaned toward Janice and gazed at Billy's image. "I based my decision to give on the good effects my work in Asheville, accomplished when I was a young man and you two were kids. It was good for me and Mom too. So, I decided to do this in Paris as soon as I figured out the implications of the value of my inventory of work

"I know you both have sound personal finances, but I want you to have an inheritance now because the future is uncertain for me. I mean to travel to funky parts of the world. This gift of money is from both Mom and me. There's no telling when an old guy like me might kick off…"

"Daddy…" Janice protested. "Don't say that. You just said…"

Paul interrupted her. "Kids. You both know that I love you very much. I may live forever but I want the huge pleasure of seeing to it that you get this money now while you are young enough to enjoy it. I sure don't need it. I have a hard time spending the retirement from the government and my monthly interest and dividends."

He gave them the details of the arrangements he had made earlier in the day with his new agent and the attorney.

"Billy, I can't tell you on this open line where the paintings are stashed. It's a secret until they are secured by the auction house. But, in case something should happen to me, you, my heirs, can get the secret location from the *Upon My Death* letter I left with attorney Andria Morgan here in New York. She's right here in this building." He added, "I'll tell you, Janice, about their location when we hang up with your brother. Billy, I'll make sure you hear all about it in a few days."

"Dad. How much are you going for? What do you think the work will bring? And when?" Billy was keen for details.

"Kids. First let me ask a big question – is it okay with you two if I use my new fortune this way? Give it away I mean.

"I believe that there might be many million UD involved here. Hundreds of millions.

"Also, I am going to start painting again. I have big ideas about painting scenes from my hike on the Mountains to the Sea Trail and my visit to France as inspiration. I haven't been sketching like I used to do, but I have thousands of EPICS in my Boss Cloud.

"We spent several good days in Brittany and Normandy, taking in the sights. Lucy and Bishop Polly were just there for fun (and games he thought) but I was working on my image collecting too."

Paul quit talking and just sat back to hear what his children to say.

"Billy," sighed Janice. "This is a lot to take in. What do you think?"

"I don't need money. I'm happy with my profession, my family, including you two, and I have no money problems. The three million, if it happens, would be like extra icing on my cake. Great if it happens, okay if it doesn't." He looked directly at Paul. "Pop. You look great. If this plan keeps you busy and happy, and does some good in the world, I'll be very happy for you."

The three of them began crying as Billy finished. "What about you Janice?"

"Me too. Daddy. I don't need money. I just want to keep you happy and healthy." She shifted on the couch and gave her father a big hug. "Daddy. These are tears of happiness. We were worried about you."

After they rang, off Paul and Janice decided to stroll the streets of New York and wound up at the bar in the original Carmine's Restaurant in the theatre district, on 44th Street to wait for a table. Paul made a reservation while enroute from Paris and planning his time in New York. Janice asked for a California Martini - she admitted to adoring the taste of the fresh peaches - and Paul had a large, fresh-squeezed grapefruit juice, without ice. They toasted, "To Mom."

"See you soon," Paul added, with a sigh.

Paul leaned close to his daughter and whispered, "Kiddo. These old paintings of mine seem to be worth a lot. Mega millions. So that is why I'm telling you about their location in person, here, and not on the wire. Don't tell anybody but the prince and only in person. Not on the phone." Prince was Paul's private name for Janice's husband, Huey.

He described his cache and the secret room built into the back room of his gallery in Asheville."

"OMG Daddy. What a clever fellow you are. If anything had ever happened to you, we would never have thought of that. Or even that there was such a treasure trove."

"Would you like to be there Monday for the grand opening? Billy told me he can't, but I'll have my friend Marty to watch and help and it would be wonderful if you could come."

"Darn Daddy. I love my job and my kids need me. I must go home tomorrow.

"I'll move heaven and earth if you say you really need me." She was clearly upset at the thought of letting her hospital, her work group, and her family down.

"No babe. I just want you for the pleasure of your company. I'll have all the help I need."

They carried their drinks to their table when it was ready and enjoyed an Italian feast, splitting several dishes. The sausage was from plants and factories, but it tasted as good as any they had ever eaten in the old days.

They strolled the bustling streets after dinner for more father-daughter time before bed. They would fly out in the morning, each going different directions.

"I remember my first visit to NYC in about 2015. Say some 40 years ago," said Paul.

Janice listened attentively as they walked past old buildings and historic parks. She liked hearing about the old days and stories her mom and dad told.

"Mom and I left you kids with grandpa and came to what was then called the Big Apple; what we now call Supertown. We brought some sample paintings with the idea that we could get into a gallery somewhere. The city was disgusting. Overcrowded congested streets and accumulation garbage spoiled the ambiance. And we utterly failed to make the connections we'd hoped for. But we had a great time anyway." He had already told her that they'd just eaten in the same restaurant he and Dahlia had enjoyed together.

"The town is so nice now Daddy. I guess we don't make as much garbage as we used to."

"Yep. It all began happening when you were a teenager. Better wrapping and packaging, less waste, more recycling and social improvements have changed the world and the cities.

"New York had a reputation back then as a dangerous place. Travelers were warned to be watchful. Nowadays it is just as safe as Caracas or Mexico City. Humankind may be mellowing out."

Central Park was about a kilometer distant from the restaurant. As it came into sight Janice cried out, "Oh look Daddy!" She pointed toward the horses and carriages tethered along the street. Let's go for a ride in the park." She was dancing on her toes with excitement.

Paul willingly assented. He had never felt so close to Janice. Just the two of them on the town was exhilarating. He mulled his future over and was chilled by the thought that there would not be many more times like this. She was aging and he seemed to be younger every day. He deliberately slowed his pace and relaxed his posture to seem older.

"Mom and I did this four decades ago. It wasn't half as nice as this," he said. They rode quietly for a while listening to the cabbie whistling a movie tune from long ago. There was virtually no traffic noise in the city since electric cars were the new norm and their tires made little noise. There were no horns – just the restful sound of the horse's hooves on the pavement.

"I think the city has mellowed. The new vibe is much happier and less inpatient."

He called out to the whistling driver," Hey Bertie. Cheer up."

Laughter was her merry response...

JUNE 12, 2055

The weather was delightful in Asheville. Paul took a brisk walk through the Montford section of town before meeting with Marty at his favorite café. The city seemed festooned in flowers. Pots of bloomers were at every street corner in the downtown area. Individual property owners put their own colors on the side streets

Just a year older than Paul, Marty looked tired. He wore his usual jaunty red fedora fat and red tennies. Marty had been a homeless drifter when Paul met him at the church shelter decades earlier. Marty had fought his alcoholism and self-image problems with the help of Paul, and others, to the effect that Marty had become a productive, happy and prosperous member of the community.

"Thanks for taking care of things on the home front Marty. Paris was very good for me. Spotty was glad to see me. Thanks for taking care of him too." Paul reached over the table and put his hand on his friend's forearm to make sure he had full attention. The arm felt thin.

"Marty. I'm doing something special today – at the gallery. I'd like to share it with you."

He told his friend about his secret stash of paintings and about the sale of the *Watcher* painting to Musée d'Orsay.

Marty was stunned when he figured out the scope of the fortune that was just sitting hidden away in back of the store.

When Marty settled down Paul told him, "Here's the plan.

"I've hired off duty city police officers to help with the security. The cataloging team from the auction house and a representative from the Travelers Insurance Company will show up at noon. We'll open the wall and clean up the mess. They are bringing tables, crating and other packaging materials, photographers and art experts to record and preserve the paintings. A special transport will arrive at six o'clock and we should be done by seven.

"I want you to help me soap the windows for privacy, move the merchandising and shelving materials out of the way, help me clean up and…" he paused for effect, "enjoy the show as my best friend. If anything is ever questioned later, you can be a witness to the proceedings. "Okay?"

"Sure buddy. I'll be happy to help. I just wish that Dahlia and the kids could be here for you too."

They reached across the breakfast table and shook hands warmly.

"Thanks Marty. You being here means a lot to me."

They walked to the gallery together and found an executive from the Mathews Auction Company waiting with a young woman in tow.

Introductions made, Harry asked, "We'd like to commemorate this event from start to finish Paul. Do you mind if Julie here, indicating the video-photographer, records everything we do?"

Paul was surprised but assented to the request. So Julie shot everything as Marty sprayed white foam on the windows.

There was a *closed* sign on the door and Paul replaced it with a *closed for remodeling* sign. The clerk had been given the day off.

Paul greeted each person that arrived and asked them to park across the street in the shady Fudruckers' Restaurant parking lot.

By the time the cataloging crew assembled there were police officers, carpenters, camera operators and stenographers to help create a record. Harry narrated events on camera as the day wore on. It was a busy affair.

Paul and Marty cleared space for three large tables in accord with instructions. Paul used a utility knife and a hand-held sheetrock saw to enter his secret room with its giant safe. The carpenters quickly made a larger opening in the wall.

"Holy shit Paul, how did you ever hide this space from me? I thought I knew the whole setup."

"Sorry buddy. Even my kids didn't know until yesterday. Dahlia and I decided to keep it to ourselves. There is a sealed codicil attached to our wills. I never believed it would be such a big deal."

Marty used the feather-duster vacuum to clean up the dust and the carpenters hauled the demo material to their truck. Their main job was to encase the paintings in between plywood and load sizable blue shipping crates with the paintings as they were catalogued. The shipping cases had built in dolly wheels.

The two craftsmen agreed to put the space to rights afterwards. Paul had prepositioned sheetrock and supplies to do the job. He also supplied paint and supervision. At the end they left part of the partitioning in place and built some shelves into the corner for later use for store supplies.

The giant green safe was pushed against the rear wall with its door well ajar. Paul imagined Daisy, the UNCA student, store manager, being surprised Monday morning - by clean windows and a space that seemed larger. She'd be happy with new storage shelves in back and curious about the strange safe where once was just a blank wall.

The cataloging team took over to do their work. The final count was 9,125 paintings. Each work was photographed, measured electronically, described in a few words and, if Paul had named or dated a work, the name information was included.

When the last hand had been shaken, and Paul was assured that he had appropriate copies of everything, the trucks departed.

One truck held his life's work in special cases and the other the carpenters' tools and debris.

Marty was exhausted. Paul convinced him to sleep over in the apartment upstairs. Marty took a nap while Paul walked Spotty. After the walk they heated recon pizzas in his flash oven.

The friends settled in Paul's entertainment cell to watch a movie – something with naked women, flowery smells, frightful volcanoes, and a saber tooth tiger. They donned the sen-jackets and gloves and lay back for the rush. When the pizza was history and the screaming was over, Marty asked, "What now Paul. What are you going to do?"

"Good question my friend. I have decided that I can't live here any longer. Too many memories. I think I'll sell this joint and move to the country somewhere."

"God Paul. I wish I could go with you." Marty sighed. "I'm getting too old to travel though. I'm wearing out."

Paul commiserated and, at the end of the evening, hugged him. "Marty, I love you, but I've got to go alone. I think I have one more adventure left in me."

"Good night, buddy."

The next big step for Paul's team was a grand gallery exhibition.

Terry's people conceived a gala party for the elite and well-connected poohbahs of the art world.

They decided that Asheville was too small for the kind of success they sought. New York was too competitive and preoccupied. Philadelphia had the potential, but Atlanta was closer to Paul's home. And he had connections there. His first gallery was at the old Maupai Inn in the foothills of the mountains he'd known so well as a lad. But even the Maupai was too small for what they had in mind.

The new Hemisphere Convention Complex near the old State Capitol Building was chosen for its elegance and the size of its facilities.

Invitations were sent to museum directors all over the world. The sought-after invitees had prepaid, first-class airline tickets attached. Major gallery owners and notable artists and collectors were summoned in the same manner - all would stay at the *Le Grand* Hotel. The event was billed as a house party and RSVPs poured in.

Percy helped design the showing to meet the tastes and needs of the big players. Five hundred works, representing less than one twentieth of his collection were hung, but the video catalogues were accessible for his entire inventory They were not disappointed in the results – over a thousand paintings were sold for record sums. Never in history had so much money been spent on art in such a short time. Percy bought two more paintings representing different periods in the artist's life.

Paul's inner circle stayed with him in rooms just under the tower's revolving top. They were all on the same floor. Lucy, Polly, Percy, Marty, Billy, Janice, five grandchildren and Spotty. Only Lucy, Polly and Percy shared in the longevity secrets.

Spotty was certified as a service dog and, with his implants, was emotionally and intellectually up for the challenges of coping with hundreds of humans who would be sure to pet him. Spotty spent more time at the beauty parlor than Paul did.

Paul wore his trademark white clothes for the entire event. Each of his white jackets, the old-fashioned linen kinds, had a bright splash of paint on the shoulders. He was building a trademark and logo. The splashes of paint were to imply that he had just been working on a painting.

Paul felt very strongly that many, perhaps most, of his paintings were not very good. He liked certain ones and those were the ones that decorated the walls. No prices were displayed. If price was important to a ticket holder, and this was almost always the case, reproductions were available. Signed, limited editions were popular with many buyers.

2070 - Daytona Beach, Florida

His airy apartments were on the top floors of the 15-story condo building. He purchased two units, one atop the other, and combined them into a single thousand-square-meter apartment. The two levels were connected by a stairway in addition to the buildings keyed elevator. He lived in the top floor unit with rooms for painting, and for his gym and spa. The lower floor was used for business.

His team included a lawyer, an accountant and a personal assistant who did a wide variety of tasks. Harry, his personal trainer came four days a week to supervise his training regimen and measure his fitness level. His goal was to stay ahead of Lucy who teased him about his conditioning when they were together – they visited just about every month for friendship and frolic.

Lucy finally got to hike with Paul in the mountains in mid-April. Years after she first expressed the desire to go with him. Something had always seemed more important when they talked about it - so the adventure was delayed. He was on his final assault on walking the entire Mountains to the Sea trail. They met in Asheville, and she finally saw first-hand where he had lived with Dahlia before their first meeting in Paris. They shopped at the Mast General Store with Spottytoo tagging along. Lucy geared up for the woods.

Spottytoo was a clone of Paul's first dog and behaved in the same cheerful canine manner.

The couple was able to make a nostalgic visit to Caverns Outdoor Center where they had first met.

"Gee Paulie. It all seems smaller now. Everything was so much bigger in my mind's eye." They were rafting on the Clancy with a rented raft, remembering the days when they had trained as guides. He showed her his secret spot but they did not make love or tarry overly long. Being there with Lucy made him nervous and ill at ease.

"Let's go Lucy. You be the guide and tell me what to do. You up to it?"

She answered by splashing him with her paddle and he responded in kind, getting himself soaked in the process. Cold water felt good on a sunny day as long as they were protected by wet suits.

Buffy took them to Clingman's Dome Mountain on the Tennessee, North Carolina border where the Blue Ridge Parkway, the Appalachian Trail and the MTS Trail came together. It was one of a handful of peaks higher than 2,100 meters in the Eastern United States. Paul had walked the oceanic and the piedmont sections of the trail in a series of month-long treks spread over several years. He found the mountainous sections very challenging when he finally got around to them.

They left Buffy, took in the views, and commenced walking to a shelter ten klicks downhill. Lucy found that going down was hard on her knees and back. Going up was even harder.

The Coleman self-propelled had to carry a lighter load in the mountains. Paul, Lucy and Spottytoo each carried a pack calibrated to their body weight. The tent rolled itself much of the time but it was exhausting work getting it up hills and over obstacles because it needed a lot of pushing and pulling.

They planned to be on the trail for a week. The late spring weather was often balmy but, just as often, rainy, wet and cold. They saw snow twice but their biggest problem, sucking energy and slowing them down, was the slippery ground on the steep parts. They had numerous streams to cross. They wore tough Teva sandals to wade frigid water that was too often above their ankles.

"Paulie. I'm having a wonderful time. Really. I like shitting in the woods and walking all day with this load on my sweaty back. But 4frankly, I'd rather be doing something else.

"So. When we reach a good enough road, I want Buffy to come and save us.

"Lu. I get it. This place is beautiful, but our bodies aren't able to cope with all of this. I'm 100% with you."

So, their long-anticipated sleep-out was over after the third night and they headed for a luxurious hotel in Cherokee, North Carolina. The casino there was in full bloom and the Cherokee Tribe was busy getting its financial retribution on the society that had hurt it so badly in the 19th century,

The booming volume of sales for both original paintings and reproductions created an income stream that had to be examined by an independent auditor to keep the core team on the straight and narrow.

He had never had any thievery affect his business but, when he was a young man in Asheville, fresh from being a thief himself, he worried about someone crippling his business from the inside. Just after the turn of the century a friend in the architectural salvage business had been ruined by a bookkeeper who wrote checks to herself and wrote his creditors' names on the check stubs. The friend's ruin had been total – the business and his own reputation were spooged. His faith in humanity diminished.

Paul no longer used checking accounts, checks or bookkeepers but the lesson was not lost on him. He had a lot of UDOLs swirling around him and he intended to use them for good, as well as his own substantial upkeep.

"Get a friend in town," advised Lucy. "Start a hobby." "Get laid at least." He was already sorry he'd been whiney about having lost contact with his family. Lucy was referring to other people. When she was around Paul they were as intimate as any married couple. Her world involved other men and women and she made her home in Paris where she had work, access to cutting edge longevity research. and her pal Bishop Polly.

"Paulie. You are alone too much. Your trainer and your employees don't count. Find an activity." She was right of course. His children were mostly out of his life now and his oldest friend Marty was gone.

They had been on a romantic Caribbean sailing cruise aboard a borrowed yacht when they had that conversation. There was a paid captain and his wife, who was the mate and cook, to do the work and manage the little sailing ship. Paul and Lucy were able to participate as much as they liked in every department. They became friendly with the couple and Paul briefly considered taking up sailing as a hobby.

"The trouble with boating," Paul ventured to the group gathered for a pre-prandial sunset cocktail, "is that I always feel apprehensive and sick when the boat heels and rocks. I think it's just minor seasickness. But I love the idea of moving with the wind and the beautiful outdoors."

He had always been drawn to the kayaking rivers in the mountains. He had also loved the waterfront when he lived in Swan

Harbor, North Carolina. He liked hanging out in marinas and looking at boats. But the high seas on a small boat were off-putting.

2071

Lucy sighed in his ear.

"I know it's sad Paul. But you had to do it. We are probably going to outlast all of our friends and we can't yet explain it to them. I don't know if it's worth it."

He had just told her that he wasn't going to visit his kids any longer. It was too emotional for him. He had a hard time watching them age so fast while he seemed younger than ever. He did not look his age. He was strong as ever due to ongoing longevity treatments, good genes, and a vigorous healthy lifestyle. He was bald, clean-shaven really, and he no longer knew his hair color.

There was a strong element of guilt in Paul's psyche. Not so much over deeds committed but over lost opportunities to bond with and know his grandchildren and their kids. He was a multiple great grandfather now. At this point there were dozens he would never meet. The number of unknown descendants increased every year.

Lucy was in Paris and Paul at his hideaway condo in Daytona Beach, Florida. He relaxed on a chaise lounge dressed in shorts and flip-flops. He had an icy V12 juice at hand and was awaiting the lunch call from his butler Larry. He had views of the Atlantic Ocean and the splendid Halifax River from his full floor residence.

"Ooh. You look great Paulie. You getting any?" She was able to see him because he had enabled his patio monitor. He was not able to see her.

"Naw. Not so much. I'm shy about making friends because, you know, I don't know how I'll fit in. I feel like I'm masquerading under false pretenses."

"I know what you mean. There are more than 60 of us old farts now; people who have had anti-aging treatment. We're like an experimental group. The general population is enjoying increased life spans, but we're staying very far ahead. Some of our members are older than 100 but they act and feel decades younger.

"Most of us are well off – a few not so much. But I'm thinking that we should meet up together and form a kind of a club or secret society. It would be good to have friends in the same situation. Oui?"

"*Mais oui*! How about here in Florida? It's a popular destination. I can arrange a mini conference meeting. Say in early January. We'll have good weather and folks will be glad to escape winter.

"I'll look around and figure out a place if you can send out a 'Save The Date' notice to the old folks."

"Okay Paulie. Do it. Make the arrangements and we'll let them know the details later. I'll get the boss's approval. You and I can be roomies if you like. Polly will be there, but she knows me better now and the shock factor is long gone since she knows now that we've already been having sex for all these years."

"Ooh. You told her."

"No. She's very intuitive. She told me. As soon as she found out. Before you left Paris two decades ago. Wanted to know when we are getting married and if she can officiate."

They laughed at Bishop Polly's astuteness and rang off on a happy note. Lucy promised him a head count and he promised her a happy site for the old timer's party.

2O72 - Mar Paz, Florida

Paul finally got to meet most of his peers. They were mostly Europeans, professional, well off, and convivial. Some were couples, both gay and straight; many had met before. Paul knew that Bishop Polly and Musée d'Orsay Director Percy LeGran would be coming, and he had bumped into other group members while in Paris. But getting together was a seminal event.

Members didn't talk about longevity much. The 62 people he had booked into the Daytona Halifax Resort Hotel and Spa were busy, interesting, seemingly middle-aged, go-getters. They met for breakfast and supper, sitting at tables set for eight with no reserved seats. That was Lucy's strategy for letting the people get to know one another. She felt that, if left to their own devices at a huge, long table they would take the same chairs every time. Like assigned places in school. She even had the tables moved and changed in other ways. Sometimes they would seat four- or six-persons time at each table.

Members who wanted to talk to each other in more depth could get together at other times besides scheduled meals.

Golf, sailing, wildlife excursions, raceway tickets, fine dining at area restaurants, every other night, and simple hanging out at the beautiful, tropical hotel pool completed the program.

Cocktail hour began each evening at 6:30. Attendance was never mandated but it was rare for a member to miss the event. The only crowding they encountered was at the Spa's gym and workout rooms in the mornings. They were all exercise freaks.

While Paul was the official host, Lucy was the social maven. The Big Kahuna was Dr. Ricardo Filippio, of mixed Euro heritage, whose headquarters was in Paris.

Paul had been going for his physical on an annual basis forever. HQ ran like an exclusive medical practice. Paul paid substantial retainers every year without inquiry or complaint. His payments, along with the fees he assumed the group paid, supported Dr. Filippio, Lucy and. the staff of medical researchers keeping him alive and kicking. Given the excellent state of his health, he never questioned the amounts. "Wellness," he opined to Lucy, "is priceless."

One big payoff for Paul was that he now knew the names and contact information of five-dozen people he could relate to without awkwardness over the fact that he would be outliving them. Over the coming years he would enjoy new friends' visits regularly. It was a success as far as he was concerned.

There was only one real meeting during the ten-day event. It took less than 60 seconds before supper on the first night. Dr Filippio stood and gestured a military style salute to Lucy and Paul, "Thank you two for hosting this event." He then said, "May you all enjoy being friends with each other. Please feel free to capture me whenever or wherever you wish if you have questions or concerns." He gave them a big happy face and sat down.

Paul learned that a tall, silver-haired woman named Shirley Baker, at 198, was the oldest member.

"Well, well, well. Paul Hunter. I heard about you but never thought I'd meet you in the flesh." She reached out with her wine glass to clink with Paul. He gestured for them to sit on the sofa where he had been standing, hoping to talk to Polly again. He wanted to pump her about her new job as Vatican Ambassador to Thailand.

"Hi Shirley. Pleasure to meet you too. What do you do? Who are you?" Such questions were common in the group. They had a brief window to meet and needed to be efficient in their social reach-outs.

"I'm the third wife of Ricardo Filippio. And his first 'subject.' I mean, after himself. He was the real pioneer."

"Wow." So' you've been at this a lot longer than me."

"Yep. And I've got the scars to prove it."

"Scars. What do you mean?"

"Oh. Maybe I shouldn't tell you. I don't mean real scars, but figurative scars. I've had to die twice. Just like Ricardo. When you get over 150 years old the authorities and the families start to ask too many questions. Questions that Ricardo isn't ready to answer. For example, what would happen if the treatment was available to everyone?"

"Oh. That's a big one. A question that has been fomenting in my head for a long time too.

"I guess the population shift would change in a big hurry. I know that as countries get more prosperous the birth rates drop and if the rate gets too low, things will change in other ways. Cultures might disappear. Prosperity could reverse itself too. If human consumption outpaces production, we would all be poorer."

"Exactly!" said Paul. "Fortunately for all of us, production is soaring. We make stuff faster than anybody would have believed at the beginning of the millennium. And our transport and distribution systems are far better than at any time in history of man.

"Things are good in the world, but privacy is pretty much a thing of the past. One can only hope that governments will remain benign for the remainder of our lives. Living for several times the usual human life span will change everything. Eh."

Paul had several conversations with each of the attendees. They talked about their lives, their accomplishments, about the state of the world, and the future. Optimism prevailed. But his talks with Shirley Baker and Ricardo himself were the most meaningful.

Ricardo told him even more about how he had to disappear several times. It seemed that the French authorities, above other governments, was interested in tracking its citizens. All governments had similar abilities but the officious government in Paris felt that it had to regulate things better than the Germans or Ukrainians. Go figure! Paul believed that the United States was not far behind the French.

Paul had lived abroad for several decades in a kaleidoscope of exotic places including India, Sri Lanka, Slovenia, and Morocco. He had visited every continent and many countries for business and pleasure. He appreciated his homeland even more because of his travels.

Invitations to visit and be visited were exchanged with many members. It gave Paul something else to look forward to besides old age. It was uplifting to have others in the same boat and to learn how they dealt with their problems.

JANUARY 2116

It came as a text message and cost him big UDs and sleepless nights. He needed help and felt that a blood relative would fit the bill. He needed someone to take possession of his massive and exceedingly valuable art collection and manage it for him. He had other duties in mind too. A trusted person who would know his secrets and have the education and savvy to act in his stead and free him from being his own manager. So the report lying in his lap was very important.

SPECIAL REPORT FOR PAUL HUNTER

JASMINE HUNTER KENNEDY, AKA JAZZ KENNEDY, IS A 22-YEAR-OLD LAWYER. SHE'S BEEN PRACTICING FOR 3 YEARS HAVING TAKEN A YEAR OFF TO TRAVEL THE WORLD AFTER

TAKING HER UBAR EXAMS AFTER HER 18TH BIRTHDAY. HER DEGREE ENABLES HER TO PRACTICE IN THE US, MEXICO, PANAMA, CANADA AND BELIZE.

SHE IS BILLY HUNTER'S, GREAT-GREAT-GRAND DAUGHTER. SHE LIVES IN WASHINGTON, DC WHERE SHE HAS ACCEPTED EMPLOYMENT AS A JUNIOR ASSOCIATE IN THE LARGE INTERNATIONAL FIRM OF HARVESTER AND REAPER. SHE WILL BEGIN HER JOB THERE ON THE 15 OF FEBRUARY THIS YEAR.

THE SUBJECT IS ON VACATION, WHEREABOUTS UNKNOWN. WE WILL SUPPLY YOU WITH HER RESIDENCE ADDRESS, TELEPHONE AND OTHER METRICS IN THE ADDENDUM TO THIS REPORT.

JANUARY 2116, Isla Margarita, Venezuela

"Jasmine is not a slut!"
"I am not a slut."
"She only lies when necessary."
"Damn it. Morgan." Jasmine scowled. She looked fierce with her lip curled and her white teeth glinting. "I want you to tell me what to do – not un-assassinate my character. Besides. It was just a white lie. We did not do it in bed."

Tears ran down Jazz's face and she sniffled as her nose tickled with an annoying drip. She ripped off a couple of sleeve bands to use as face towels. Her left sleeve was now shorter than the right but she still looked chic in her bright blue skins.

They sat at the bar overlooking Casino Iguana's gaming floor. Translucent clouds rose above the gamblers. Blue smoke from the cannabis laced e-cigs and red haze from the e-ciggynonos of the people toying with nicotine.

Neither Jazz nor her best friend Morgan smoked the silly things. Smoking was a European thing. The government of the U.S. had campaigned against smoking for so many generations that tobacco addiction was virtually unknown at home. Here in the small Venezuelan casino, risky behavior was more the norm.

"He was so cute. I just wanted to screw him a little – you know, just enough to hook him on me. I'm not looking for love right now. I've got you for that."

The girls sat knee-to-knee, holding hands, and trying to shut the world out. Jazz wore a short blond shag wig and Morgan's bald scalp gleamed with perspiration.

"Jazz. I promise you it's all right. You didn't hurt my feelings. I might have done the same thing if he'd spilled his drink on me. You just did him that one time. Right. In his room with no one around while I was out running on the beach?"

Morgan's head was permanently hairless to accommodate her implants. Like most women, she had wigs, hairpieces, and scarves to dress her head up on occasion. Time with Jazz did not rise to the formal level that would cause her to cover her baldness.

Besides, she thought. Hairlessness is hotness nowadays.

Jazz nodded. "I just wanted to towel off. His room was closer to the elevator."

"Was he a fun lover?"

"Not as good as you sweetie." They laughed and hugged and sipped their beverages as they strolled the casino floor again – soon perhaps to get ready to retire. Jazz had forgiven herself.

Paul watched the young women stroll through the crowds with their arms linked.

He caught up and tapped Jasmine on the shoulder. "Excuse me ladies. Jasmine. Could I have a word with you?"

They stopped and looked at the tall, middle-aged man who had used Jazz's name.

"Yes sir. How can I help you?" she replied.

Paul was mesmerized by how much she looked like his long-lost Dahlia.

"I know it's late, but I would like to talk to you for a minute." He looked into her eyes.

"It's pretty late," Morgan spoke up. "Could this wait for another time, sir?"

"I just want a minute – Jasmine. I think we're related. I found out that you were here through your facebook postings and thought you might take pity on me and forgive the surprise."

"What do you mean related? Who are you?" Jazz looked at him closely and saw that he looked like her great-great grandpa Billy when he was younger. She had seen the family photos. In fact, she had the photos in her computer.

"I knew your great-great-grandfather. I've been doing some family research and thought we might enjoy a meeting."

Paul saw distrust in the girls' eyes.

"I'm staying here at the hotel in suite 55. Perhaps you would allow me to buy you two brunch. Say the time and we can meet in the hotel café. He kept a respectful distance and, successfully, tried to look harmless.

"Is it okay with you Morgan? We could see him at noon?"

Morgan nodded.

"Excellent ladies. You know my room number if you need to contact me. See you in the dining room at noon."

Paul gave them a two-finger salute in the current fashion. "*Vale. Hasta mañana.*" He walked away and went straight to his room. His heart was pounding. He wanted to get this right. To reconnect with his family. Learn more about them and plead his case. He needed help.

The government was becoming interested in Paul. He had too much money and had been filing Excess Income Tax Returns for far too long.

Lucy had warned him that he should disappear - stage his own death and reappear as a newly minted human being. The population growth factors, including a reduced death toll from disease and accident, longevity of general population, and declining birth rates were interesting but not highest on the world list of issues to solve.

If the authorities decided to investigate his longevity, it might compromise their program.

But, at the age of 137, Paul was the oldest living human being on the books of the United States Government. He had received letters of inquiry regarding his continuance in the records. Someone, or more likely, some machine, wanted to know more, too much, about him. He was in an emergency mode now. He wanted a descendant to take charge of his affairs and the thousands of new and original paintings he had created over the last nine decades of his life.

Lucy was waiting in room 55. "My love. How did it go?"

"Good, I think. We have a date for noon, and we can begin to execute our plans for her."

"Very, very good." Lucy patted the edge of the bed where she was lounging in wait. "Give me the scoop."

Paul sat and said, "They're a little standoffish, naturally, but we can split them up in the dining room so I can tell Jasmine what I need. You keep her friend Morgan occupied at the other table and I'll signal you when we can sit together."

They knew a bit about the relationship between the girls, but they needed Jasmine's assurance that she would cooperate and preserve his confidences before they had a general conversation. Better that Morgan does not know everything.

Paul and Lucy passed the morning anxiously waiting for the appointed hour. They arrived in the dining room at 11:30 and sat in wait. The plan was to give Paul a chance to sit with Jazz for a few minutes.

"So, Jazz. Here's the thing. We're related through your great-great-grandfather Billy Hunter. I see a great family resemblance."

"How? I mean how are we related?"

"Jazz. I've got to make this short and sweet. I have a family secret to tell you, but I must ask you to promise to keep it to yourself for the time being. Especially not to blab to your friend Morgan." Paul's voice did not betray his emotions, but he was afraid of a quick rejection.

"How can I make promises like that? I don't know you. You must tell me more or just leave me alone." She sounded slightly offended.

"Here's the thing. I want to make you a business proposition and I have a cashier's check for you to buy your promise. I just wanted to meet you for now, but I want to see you in Washington, before you start work. I want to make an appointment now. You pick the time and place. A good restaurant would be fine." He laughed, "Or a bad one. Wherever you'd feel comfortable.

"Here. Put this in your pocket." He handed her an old-fashioned cashier's check for UD10,000.

She looked at it with wide eyes. Jazz looked like she was deciding not to take the money. Her face was reflecting her uneasiness at the strangeness of the situation.

"You don't have to do anything. Just put this in your account and agree to meet me.

"For now, I want to introduce myself as your Great Uncle Paul Hunter. You can call me Uncle Paul. Please." He put on his best face. He saw that Lucy and Morgan were returning. "Please say okay. Just meet me in a couple of weeks and I'll explain everything. I promise you an interesting tale and, for now, just call me Paul or Uncle Paul." He offered his hand on the deal.

"Uncle Paul. I kinda like that. But it's an awful lot of money for me. Are you sure? You didn't need to pay."

"Remember. I'm just paying for your promise to keep an important family secret. We must just leave it at Uncle Paul for now and have a nice meal with your friend now. On me. Okay?"

"Yes. Okay Uncle Paul."

"Welcome back girls." Paul rose as Lucy and Morgan approached the table. "Did Lucy explain?"

Morgan smiled and reached out her hand for a knuckle bump. "Uncle Paul. Yes. It's very nice to meet you. What a surprise. Lucy told me that you went to a lot of bother tracking us down and that you are on a secret mission, and I must not tell anybody about you."

"Yes dear. Sorry about the mystery but I'll explain it all to Jasmine when we get back to Washington. I'm starved.

"Lucy. Can we eat now?"

Paul waited patiently in the bar at Old Ebbitt Grill. He was early and expected Jazz to be on time. He wasn't sure of exactly how to proceed.

Lucy had made him an amazing offer. "Paulie. I liked the girl very much. We are looking for youthful volunteers right now. What do you think of adding her to the program?"

"I dunno. How long do you think we have before governmental regulation catches up with us?"

"Not long now. But so what?" Lucy challenged him. "Once a person gets the original treatment the whole body resets in a good way. There is no downside for Jazz insofar as her health is concerned. I don't see how you can say no to the idea of propositioning her. Look at how wonderful you turned out and you were 75 when we started on you. I was only sixty. She will have a long full life and it should be her choice anyway since the offer is on the table."

"Lucy. You're so right. I need to tell her how it is with me and give her the choice."

Jazz strode up to Paul and offered him her hand to shake. "Hi Uncle Paul." The hand was smooth, young, and firm. He took her hand but held it while he shifted off the stool and ventured an air kiss over her left shoulder. She reciprocated.

"Hiya yourself Jazz. Ready for lunch and a story?"

"Sure. I'm starved."

They sat and enjoyed a leisurely meal. Jazz had not yet started her new job at the law firm, and she had told Paul that there was no rush.

Finally finished with small talk, Paul began, "Jazz. I'm not your uncle. I'm your great-grandfather Billy's father."

She looked skeptical. Puzzled. "Naw. You're too young." She laughed as she leaned in for a closer look at him across the table. "You are kidding? Right?"

"Afraid not Jazz," he continued, "I was born in 1978 and led an ordinary life until 2055 at the age of seventy-six. I *am* your great-great-grandfather..."

Jazz tried to reserve judgment while Paul talked about the details of his life and told her things about the family and finally explained about Dr. Lucy Lu and the anti-aging treatments. It sounded true and he looked very sincere.

"What if I believe you Paul?" She had already dropped the uncle. "What do you want with me? Why now?" She looked and felt beyond skeptical. She was flabbergasted.

He made her an offer she couldn't refuse.

She thought about the check he'd given her and finally decided that he was seriously getting her attention.

JANUARY 2, 2120

Kelly Elres was a 35-year, veteran government employee - a lawyer of the Department of National Welfare. She had worked in virtually every section. Despite her law degree, she loved applied mathematics and assiduously studied the many statistical reports generated by the department. Her final position, before mandatory retirement when she reached age 75, was in Fraud and Enforcement. There were about four calendar years left before that great date.

She arrived at her tiny office at 7:30 a.m. this first working day of the year. At age 70 she was strong, slender and active in sports that might have been beyond her age group some years ago. She played volleyball in her church league and golfed with her husband. She skied and sailed her own sloop in the Potamic River Yacht Club. She was also busy with grandchildren. She enjoyed a blessed life and had no desire to hurt anyone. Government's place in the world was to help people was her motto.

Elres had worked in support positions as second or third banana and was firmly in the middle of the executive corps pay scale. She had done research into obscure matters and served as a consultant to other departments in need of legal opinions.

The average statistical age of Income Recipients was forty-nine. They arrived at this figure by eliminating children under 1-year-old and the aged population over a century old. The youngest recipients were newborns with the payments going to parents or guardians and the oldest were old-timers over 100-years of age. The attainment of a century birthday was becoming more common but, even so, those over 100 were less than 1% of the total population.

Although Elres was not an actuary, she enjoyed playing with numbers and trying to discern the meaning of statistics. She knew that many fallacious arguments were backed up by irrelevant statistics and she tried to avoid contributing to that sort of thing. But she was curious.

It was thus, in her position as third in command, that the question of, 'who is the oldest payee?' arose in her mind. Hunter was a common name, but one Paul Hunter had outlasted the many thousands on that 'Oldest' list by several decades. He seemed to stand alone.

There was something familiar about the name, so she googled him, and artist Paul Hunter popped up first on the list. Aha! She knew his name because he was the guy who gave so much money away a zillion years ago.

She recollected that she used to have a Hunter print, but she gave it away when she downsized after the kids left home. It was kinda nice – a signed, limited edition, showing beach sand and grass with breaking waves to the horizon. The colors were soft and went with her big sofa.

Paul's case was not chosen for investigation, but he and several other old people stayed on Elres's to-do list for the time being. She thought they might make for a good human-interest project for her to get a story into the department's monthly magazine *Fare Thee Well*. She was taken with the idea that someone so rich might be a cheat. This could be just the kind of case that would serve as a deterrent to others who might want to scam the system. She tried to reach him by ordinary email.

Elres didn't have a demanding job. She was expected to work 1,000 hours per year and had a flexibility regarding time off. If she had an interesting project, she could work as many hours in a week as she chose and would arrange time off later.

The grown children and grandchildren in other states gave her lots of incentives to take time off and travel. She was not in a job-share situation so no one would work on her files to cause her confusion.

Most cheats involved people who were collecting multiple stipends under assumed names. Some were widows or parents who 'forgot' to file a death notice for loved ones and continued to collect unearned funds. Penalties were administrative unless there were massive amounts involved of more than UD100,000. Very few people went to jail. The United States Federal and states prison populations had fallen from over 2,000,000 in the year 2000 to under 100,000 by the beginning of the current century. No one wanted to kick-start that industry again. Fewer laws meant fewer crimes.

These questions interested her - 'How many cheats are still on our rolls?' 'Who are they?' 'What are the penalties?' 'How can we catch them?'

Paul got the email and forwarded it to Jazz.

Months passed before Elres got back to her musings about the oldest man in the system. She began to research Hunter and found that he had a rap sheet in (Holy Cow!) the year 2000. He was arrested as a suspect in a big grand theft case in Clancy, Georgia but no charges were filed. Insufficient evidence. Two other men were charged and convicted of the crime.

"So, this guy has been collecting since 2030 when the program started. He claimed to be 51 then and that makes him..." Elres paused while her boss took a call.

Arthur Nuttley rang off and returned his attention to Elres. He was not very impressed by Elres. The old girl had been around forever, and held her position by virtue of a long-ago law degree and very occasional promotions for party loyalty.

"So. That makes him..."

"One-hundred-forty-two years old. Born 1978 and still going strong. It's a hoax. Gotta be...

"I think he's a different guy posing as Paul Hunter. What should we do?"

"Give me a few days on this Kelly. My plate's full and I'm off for my annual leave next week. I'll get back to you when I return."

They chatted about vacation plans and reviewed three other cases that were going into enforcement.

Elres shelved her slim file on Paul Hunter. There was no paper file and no actual shelf of course. Her tickler system brought him to the surface once a week, but he was deferred repeatedly because of more urgent business and unresolved complaints.

It was July before she had a few minutes to clear her to-do list. She was getting ready for annual leave and only had about 200 hours left in her work contract before her yearly professional performance reviews. Hunter was ignoring or not getting her occasional emails.

She called a friend in enforcement and asked this question, "Benny. I have an artist's fingerprint in my file. Would your print scanner work on a painting hung in the National Gallery of Art? I mean like a camera. Can you shoot for prints from a short distance? Like a tourist?

"I don't have any paper, so I mean as a favor. Just between the two of us on our lunch break."

"Sure sweetie. I'm at loose ends here. The crime business sucks. Just tell me where and when to meet. You have a warrant?"

"Oh Benny. You're a love. No warrant. Just you and me on our lunch hours. Okay?

"How about 11:30 this morning? Short notice, I know."

"*No* problemo. Which entrance?"

"East. *I'm* sending you his prints now. Can you load them in your machine before we meet?"

"Yep. As we speak."

Benny was a short, portly man in an age of tall thin dudes. Elres spotted him a block away as he strolled from his office toward her vantage point in the lobby window of the Modern East Building. She led him to the American Art display, and they soon stood before several Hunter paintings from different times in his career.

They started with the oldest work, a water scene that included an old-style kayak tied to a dock with some trees and shacks sketched in. It was labelled 'Still River ~ 2000.' They looked at several others; 'Nude ~ 2002,' 'Asheville ~ 2019,' 'Mountain Trail, ~ 2055,' 'Florida Sky ~ 2070,' 'Pelicans ~ 2119.'

Benny raised his camera thingy each time and slowly took pictures. Elres watched anxiously. He muttered to himself and bobbed his head, but she could read no real language from his mouth or gesturing.

"Benny. Whatcha got?"

"Wait a minute... He was busily running his hands over the screen and continuing to bob his head in rhythm with his hands.

"Okay. Look Kelly. There are several different prints on all of these. But they're clean. Especially the newer paintings. Few prints – like they were handled carefully. But your guy Hunter is on all of them.

"Do you want me to send you a print-out of the results? It'll show the names and Idents of most of the people who handled the pictures."

"Yes please. What are your thoughts here? It would seem that the oldest painting is about 120-years old. Fingerprints last that long?

"Sure. In some instances. The oil on our fingers might go away, but the underlying surface can be slightly etched - enough for my baby to read, anyway." He looked proud.

"Benny. Thank you. I don't know what this means but I need to look at the data in my records again and see if I can noodle this out."

They were old friends and she stepped in for a hug and kiss on the cheek as they parted. Lawyer Elres was deciding, as she walked, that there was something going on, but she wasn't sure what it might be, and it must be illegal. *If things don't add up,* she mused, *I just have to study harder.*

A mild spell meant windows open and the hum of air conditioning blessedly absent.

Paul and Lucy lay dozing in Jazz's king bed as the morning breeze moved the diaphanous curtains gently in and out of the tall windows. The room overlooked the pool patio, and they heard the water lapping and the chirps and cries of birds. A hawk cried in the distance.

The baby suddenly began crying in the next room. The red LEDs on the ceiling monitor told them that it was eight o'clock.

"Let me see what's up Hon. Stay here." She ordered. Lucy's bare feet were silent as she crossed the cool bedroom floor tiles. Her silvery blue robe swirled as she walked.

She moved quietly down the hall to the next bedroom door of the luxurious home. As she neared the door she began to coo and whisper, "I'm coming sweetie. Don't cry. Lucy's here." The baby wailed louder.

She pushed the door open and froze. There was a strange man holding the baby under his arm, ass backwards, and he was waving a stunner at her.

He hissed, "Shut up bitch or I'll put you down." He turned slightly and hitched the baby up in an awkward stance. He was a heavy-shouldered, dark-skinned man with the look of a drug addict or insanity radiating from his squinting eyes and alarmed posture. His front teeth were missing.

"Be quiet you... or the kid dies too."

The baby cried louder, and she heard Paul call out though the monitor, "Lucy. What's up in there? Do you need me?"

"It's okay Dolldoll. Go back to your breakfast now." Lucy called back

"Please sir. Tell me what you want," She whispered. Lucy collapsed to her hands and knees, looking up at the intruder. Her diaphanous robe had fallen open to reveal her form. The man stared at her.

Babysitting was not Paul's favorite thing. It seemed an enormous responsibility with many opportunities for grief and limited rewards. But Lucy loved it. So, when Jazz called to ask for help while she honeymooned with her new lover, Paul assented.

"Only condition Jazz, is that Lucy be with me. She loves the little ones, so she'll be mad if I don't include her. *Capiche?*"

"Sure Dads. I love Lucy too and I know that my Andy will be safe with you two."

Paul mulled over what Lucy said and a dread feeling came over him. Dolldoll? Breakfast? He heard the mutter of a strange voice and the cry of the baby. He was naked but, without hesitation, he reached into Jazz's top drawer and pulled the stunner from its case. His feet were quiet as he approached the baby's door and, to keep low, he dropped to the floor and peeked through the partly open door.

He saw that Lucy was on her knees. A big man whose back was to him, stood while Andy was squealing under his arm and reaching for Lucy. The man saw Lucy's eyes fix on something behind him and started to turn. Paul pulled the trigger.

Lucy lunged to break the baby's fall as the intruder, immobilized, began to sag. Paul and Lucy stood over him.

"Oh my God. It's Peter – the baby's father," said Lucy.

"She told me he had a breakdown and was in protective custody. Peter was a semi-pro hockey player with too many concussions. His dementia is probably permanent unless they can implant a dispenser, but he seemed to be allergic to the idea and they won't do him by force."

Later, they gave Jazz a full report on the holo. "He was a maniac. The police were looking for him. Somehow, he had skipped his meds and slipped away from the asylum. We were very lucky."

"Oh my God," keened Jazz. "I'm so lucky you were there. I don't know what would have happened if I'd been alone. I have such terrible judgement in choosing men.

"You are a couple of tough old birds."

Lucy grinned at her. "We physicians see such people in hospital settings all the time and I've had a few experiences. It was Grandpa's quick action that saved the day. Naked as a jaybird too."

"I have such bad taste in men," groaned Jazz. "I hate that butthole. Just wait. They'll throw away the key now. No more street privileges for him."

"Makes me think how fragile our lives are, even with Lucy's anti-aging interventions." Paul was feeling some aftershock. "Any of us could be gone in a second. Just like my Dahlia went. Never saw it coming."

"I'll be home tonight. Thank you. Thank you. Thank you." She was sobbing now. Andy was her first child, and she was not used to trauma of any sort. In a few years she would toughen up a little, but this was a big event. It would be a long time before she would again leave her baby behind.

Working for Paul was a great boon for her. She was at his beck and call, but she had no other clients, no office outside her home, and no fixed hours. She had fallen in love with Lucy too.

They cared for Jazz as well. When she was through childbearing, she would join the longevity program. She hoped that anti-aging would eventually extend to her children, but she accepted that no promises could be made.

One of Jazz's most important functions was to be the front person for Paul's treasured paintings. He could not do it himself because he was supposed to be dead. She, as a family member, was able to claim that she had inherited a treasure trove of art and she disposed of the works in several ways.

Some were sold for big bucks. Some were anonymously bestowed on her many cousins, Paul and Dahlia's other grandchildren. Some were warehoused at Paul's favorite museums.

The museums chosen were allowed to exhibit the works, but ownership rested with Jazz. The benefit for the paintings' owner was that the museums knew how to care for precious works of art. It was a good deal for everyone. When she chose to market a painting from a museum, she would substitute another work so the museum's collections would remain viable and interesting.

There would always be more than enough money even though Paul had stopped his annual federal stipend. He had never needed it. Income from his art supported elaborate lifestyles for Jazz, Paul and Lucy and a few others lucky enough to be in his employ. Lucy was not only part of Paul's family, but she was the very core around which Paul and Jazz revolved.

Jazz saw the email from the Feds and decided to ignore it and wait to see what else they would do. Paul had broken no law, that she could determine, but he was very particular about not being outed for his advanced age. He was protecting Lucy and the others as well.

Jazz realized that her own ability to cheat death and old age was on the line. All hell could break loose if the longevity program was publicly revealed.

December 31, 2120

A crisis loomed for Paul. It led to his asking Polly and Lucy, "Say. What would you all think about helping me alter my identity so that I don't get any more of these scary letters?" They were celebrating his birthday party. Just four people including Jazz.

He sat with Polly and Lucy and handed them a printout of the latest missive while Jazz was out of the room.

CERTIFIED DELIVERY SUMMONS

Office of the Secretary of National Welfare
1 Maple Street
Atlanta, Georgia 303021
October 2120

Paul J. Hunter
1 Halifax Towers East
Daytona Beach, FL 32118
Dear Mr. Hunter:

We have tried to contact you numerous times to help us understand your age record vs. the annual income subsidy established for you by 56, U.S. Code, 1.

Despite numerous attempts to contact you, we have not resolved the issue of illegal or excessive collection of your pension.

As a final attempt to satisfy our concerns, you are ordered to appear on the 1st of October 2128 at 9:00 am, at Room 1821, 1 Maple Street, Atlanta Georgia 30302.

Fail not to heed this summons.

Kelly Elres (SIGNATURE)
Enforcement Division
for
William Huntly, SNW, Regional Director

"Well. Yeah Paul. Do you mean to tell us, sitting there in front of your biggest fans that you and Jazz can't handle a routine matter like this?" Lucy was on her third cocktail and feeling feisty.

"No. Yeah. I mean, would you two come with me to hold my hand while I pretend to off myself in Africa in a couple of weeks?

"I've already shipped two balloons and a box full of gear and I have tickets for you two. I'll need some corroborative witnesses according to Jazz. She's the ringleader but she felt that I needed to get you'uns to agree to come on my own. Without her."

Lucy and Polly sat with round eyes and gaping mouths.

Paul had also had one cocktail too many and was slurring his words slightly. He was scared and his life was about the change.

The women took pity on him. Polly stood and patted his back while Lucy plopped into his lap, butt first, and gave him a big hug.

"Paulie. We knew all about this. We were just kidding you. Of course, we'll go and hold your slippery little hand."

Jazz joined them, having overheard the conversation. "Okay gang. Good on you Paul. There's no hurry. I know the summons seemed urgent, but I can put them off indefinitely.

"Paul. I'm going to claim ill health, dementia, and foreign residency *and* threaten to sue them if they don't leave you in peace. I'll play those cards one at a time and I think I can get them to slow down. This can take years. Both Elres and her boss Huntly at the Enforcement Division will probably be gone or out of office by the time we really have to appear.

"Remember. These government guys may use the best computers, but they get a lot of time off and they have heavy caseloads. It all plays in your favor. Especially if you just die like you're supposed to." They all howled with laughter.

2124

Paul did not lead an entirely solitary life. He had daily morning contact with his fitness coaches. They kept him active and strong when he was in residence. He was 145-years old. He looked and felt much as he did in his fifties. His in-house administrative staff included accountants and a lawyer.

His studio and office were below the level of his living quarters. The studio was on the North side of the building, and he spent time there each day creating new paintings and doing business with his agent, his lawyers, and his galleries. His plans to become a billionaire and gifting the world's poorest places had worked out very well.

He learned early that it was better to act through existing agencies rather than always being involved at the giving end. He had visited North Korea, Bangladesh, Somalia and many other poor regions, and felt emotionally enriched by the efforts. He once figured that if he added up all his foreign travel to date, he had spent over ten years in other countries. He had many adventures and some misadventures.

Most of the 500 million udols he had given to the world, so far, went toward hardware that poor folks could use to explore the world, to get an education or even for business purposes. He used other peoples' well-established charitable trusts to help with the actual work.

The digital pads he gave were very far advanced over those he'd had as a young man in 2010 when he'd joined to the trend. Now they were more durable, more feature packed and enormously energy efficient. Quantum computing was leaps and bounds beyond his wildest imaginings as a turn-of-the-century man. If electric power wasn't available for recharging, an hour in sunlight or even a few hours of light on a cloudy day would do the trick. The devices used power sparingly and mainly functioned as portals to the knowledge of the world and as a device to keep people in touch.

The planet's E-versities reached the remotest corners of earth through satellite links. Cell towers were relics of the past and were recycled metal in this age. Students needed a pad to go to the best training on earth. Classes were virtually free and once a student successfully finished a module of study he could be certified through testing procedures.

The money he gave was a pittance compared to the resources of even humble governments, but his gifts were inspiring, and had triggered a multiplier effect.

He got a ton of media attention when he began to successfully sell his paintings – worldwide. It seemed that the more he gave away the more he got. It did not require much skill or attention on his part. Jazz did the heavy lifting - she was a Godsend. She had taken over and seemed to know his wishes and desires before he could voice them. She was wickedly smart and very funny and decorative.

Within ten years of his first and biggest charitable efforts it was determined that every person on earth had an e-pad and was connected by Facebook, Google, and Ratfink. His UD500,000,000 helped, to be sure, but it was the catalytic effect on the 'powers that be,' and thoughtful individuals, that constituted the bulk of the effort. Implanting was almost complete too, and he had contributed both his celebrity and his fortune to that effort.

Paul was taking an East coast motor tour trip without Buffy. His recently purchased flying car, 'Bumpy,' was a lot of fun. It was a four-seat Ford Flitter. Because all flight systems were automatic, flying car owners did not need pilot licenses - they needed bankrolls. His old hometowns of Swan Harbor and Asheville were on his itinerary.

Vertical takeoff and landing obviated the need of runways. They could be driven on the ground if the driver cared to steer, but accident prevention kicked in at the slightest misstep. In the air they were automatic and controlled by drone pilots if a situation developed.

Paul traveled light – just the tablet pouch he carried on his belt. Hotels would provide fresh outerwear and toiletries. He chose the colors, sizes and styles when he made reservations. He liked the Grove Park Inn in Asheville because it housed one of his art galleries and because it was near his old Montford section neighborhood.

Paul enjoyed visiting the gallery anonymously. It was the oldest establishment in the shopping promenade. It had the status of a museum, and the hotel would probably have given him the space free or paid him to stay. School art classes made field trips there to see it and stayed for lunch afterwards.

Paul belted in and told his GPS, "Asheville to New Smyrna Beach."

"Yes Sir, Chief. We'll have to stop in Jacksonville for the night. Do you want a hotel or motel?"

"The New Omni Marriott please. Call them with our ETA for me please. I want to leave Jacksonville for New Smyrna Beach to arrive at 4:40 in the morning. What time will we need to leave Jax?"

"Are we going to the Air Show?

"If yes, we'll have to park at the satellite parking and take a bus. Departure time no later than 3:30 a.m. Okay?"

"Yes. Ten-four all that. Take me away. I'm napping. Gotta get up early."

"Yes boss. Enjoy the ride."

Paul settled back as Bumpy quickly rose high over the city and then headed south, gradually rising to a cruising altitude of 2000 meters. The views were splendid but the air over the mountains was bumpy, as usual. The ride would be smoother once they circled Greenville's restricted air traffic zone and the landscape flattened.

The winter had been harsh in the mountains of Asheville, and he was seeking warmer weather and fun when he saw an ad on his holo for the "Biggest Party Ever."

The New Smyrna Beach Balloon and Sky Fest was the first Hot Air Balloon Rally he ever attended.

He arrived in New Smyrna Beach at five a.m., more than two hours before sunrise, intending to wander through a huge field filled with inflating balloons where scores of brightly colored balloons were being inflated to the roar of flaming gas. The brilliant lights of the mighty fires were filtered and reflected by the brilliantly varicolored bags. It was an exciting-otherworldly scene as the forest of giant, glowing balloons rose around him.

Paul made a friend on the bus. Kenny was a youthful Brit with a pronounced accent.

"Yew been here before?"

"No." Paul admitted as they bumped off the road onto a grassy field. "How about you."

"Oh yah. Oy been goin' for years. Oy used to 'av a loycence at 'ome. But it was so expensive, oy couldn't afford to keep it up. Oh. And there was a divorce and some choinge in me emploiyment. Oy emigrated 'ere to America. Virginia oy mean. And oim taking a week off to see the balloons."

Paul enjoyed the sound of accents. They evoked far-away places for him and different, maybe better, ways of doing things. After a few minutes he began to tune Kenny's accent out and was happy when his seatmate said, "Tag along with me if you like and maybe I can exploine a few things for you."

"I'd be 'appy for the company." Paul answered.

They smiled. Shook hands and agreed to hang out for the morning

Paul didn't know anything about the sport, but they saw teams of men and women scurrying around the vehicles working with rigging, rattan baskets and the horizontal ducts that led the super-heated air into the bags to create lift.

"Watch the guy in the white tee shirt," advised Kenny. "'Ee's the pilot. I can tell because he's so clean. Look at the mud and junk on the crew's jeans and shoes.

"Effing pilots are the rich ones paying all the bills. Course we wouldn't have a meet without them. Dang. I'm jealous."

Food and souvenir vendors had a big area staked out between the balloon launch area, a temporary airport operations center, where the old airplanes were on display close to the carnival rides. Nearby, huge tents sheltered entertainment venues. Public parking was some distance away and electric buses silently shuttled festival visitors back and forth. At this early hour there were few passengers returning to their cars - it was a one-way highway of excited attendees.

Bleachers were set up for the air show that commenced at ten a.m. Paul wound up there, led by Kenny. "Up 'ere. All the way to the top for the best overview."

They stood as high as they could get as the sun peeped over the horizon. The balloons were all upright now and tugging at their mooring lines. Colors blazing each time the burners fired.

"The only time the balloons can fly is when the breeze is down. Like it usually is at sunup and late in the afternoon. Today it's ideal. The air is hardly moving. These guys will probably fly until the wind kicks in and then look for a field. Parks and schools are typical landing areas."

Kenny's accent totally faded for Paul as he became accustomed to the man's different way of speaking.

"Gee whiz," said Paul, "I'd like to be going up with them today. I tried to get a ride, but the baskets are booked up with family and friends."

The beautiful aircraft shed the surly bonds of earth and rose directly overhead with the strong morning light illuminating every detail. They drifted south, away from the airfield, and soon were specks above the horizon. Off on their adventures. Chase vehicles left the immediate area to stay in touch with their flying crews and help retrieve them for the next flight - maybe in the late afternoon.

"Where do all these balloons come from?"

"You'd be surprised. Literally, all over the world. There's even two from down under. One from New Zeeland and the other is an Aussie."

"I had no idea. Tell me more about ballooning."

Paul knew a lot more at the end of the day. He decided that he would find a way to participate.

Kenny stuck with Paul through lunch. They had fair-food on the carnival midway.

They'd seen the air show and a model airplane demonstration. Some of the models were jets and helicopters. All were controlled by serious men and women with their little joysticks. The models' pilots had screens showing the view from their tiny cockpits.

Smoke streamed from stunt and formation air show planes. A few vintage planes flew, including representative craft from every American war since WWI.

One highlight was a two-ship flyover by massive lighter-than-air cargo ships. The ships were longer that football fields and easily rivaled oceangoing ships and trains for efficiency. Their biggest advantage was that they could deliver cargo anywhere without tracks, ports, or other expensive infrastructure. Their powerful engines rumbled, and they eclipsed the sun to throw the fields into momentary darkness.

The crowd loved the auto dealership flyovers. Fords, Chevies, Tatas and Teslas whizzed overhead in elegant formations.

"Look there Kenny. That's my new ride. The Ford Flitter. The red one on the left."

Kenny was suitably impressed. "All right mate. Good on you!"

Paul was tired but stuck in out until well after noon. He was there for nine hours. Alone, on the way to the bus he came to a tent erected for Embry Riddle Aeronautical University. He picked up a copy of the course offerings and admission requirements for later study.

Paul enrolled in the Embry Riddle Aeronautical University's flight school the very next semester. His intention was to learn to be a balloon pilot.

He wanted to have fun and to take advantage of the huge opportunity to further travel the world attending balloon rallies.

Most students in this era were online, but flight training was very much a hands-on, group effort in a real brick and mortar school.

He had the time and resources for the activity. The training curriculum was much the same as for a fixed wing pilot. He accumulated the flight training hours and passed the FAA tests with ease. Considerable sums of money were spent on buying two mid-lift balloons and all the gear that went with them. He warehoused them and his chase-vehicles near the school in Daytona.

The process took over a year. He had to learn to be a competent ground and chase-crew member. Launching and retrieving the beautiful, colorful balloons was fun but very important to the safety and comfort of the pilots and passengers. The flights were followed by chase-vehicles. The pilot and the drivers had good communications and detailed, up-to-the-minute meteorological data.

The classes covered airport operations, emergency procedures, FAA rules and maneuvering. He accumulated an e-library of books on weather, flight planning, post-flight procedures and communications.

It was an exhilarating time for him. He often thought about his early experiences and training in whitewater guiding and kayaking. The skills were not the same, but the intensity of the experiences matched. Some fear and some triumph.

Actual flights were wonderful. He became close to his paid ground crew and relied on them for his recovery after each flight. Winds in the area were calm in the early morning hours and he would launch from fields near the beach or inland depending on the forecasts.

There was much ado in getting ready. The flight systems including the envelope, the gondola, burners, fans, and fuel tanks took a lot of work. This was not a solo sport.

"Lucy. Do you realize that with a few more credit hours I could qualify to pilot a cargo lifter?" The connection between their implants was clear.

Everyone knew that giant, lighter-than-air ships were rapidly replacing trains, bulk carriers, and airfreight. They could lift hundreds of tons and move cargo at 300 KPH. They did vertical take offs and landings, and were not too challenged by winter weather, ice, road congestion or other obstacles. The big airships were very economical. Helium, once purchased, and purposed for airship use, would last indefinitely.

"Yeah. But, Paulie, you don't want a job. Leave that work for someone else and paint me some more pictures. Eh."

He laughed. "Okay. I was just saying..."

Paul often mulled over how his life would really end. And what indeed would happen in the afterlife? Would he go to heaven or hell? And indeed, was there a purpose to his life.

When asked, long ago, by Bishop Polly, he squirmed and had to confess that he was not a believer in an afterlife. "I guess my mind will go to sleep and just never wake." She guffawed when he added, "I'll skip the resurrection too."

In his travels and years living abroad he had a lot of helpful exposure to different ideologies, especially those to which most of the world's population professed. He had met many Christians,

Muslims, Hindus, and Buddhists. He was very interested in how these groups had fought, sought forgiveness, and finally came to peace with each other. He often wondered how religion could hinder or help his causes.

Some of the Long-Life Club members were devout non-Christians. They were often willing to share their opinions and beliefs.

Paul learned that the four largest groups comprised about 80 percent of the world population. Fifteen percent of the people in the modern era were not religious and only five percent were members of the less populated spiritual persuasions.

He had been comforted by membership in the Presbyterian Church in Asheville when he was being tormented by guilt for youthful crimes against property. He'd seen some of the grief and other consequences of his acts and was trying to atone.

At this point in his life Paul was a respectful non-believer. He did like many of the ideals and behaviors promoted by the different religious people he had befriended.

Early on, lounging in the Royal Suite of the Hotel Plaza Saint Michael in Paris, Catholic Bishop Polly lectured him on love. They had just met and were lounging over tea on the terrace of the most beautiful hotel suite in Paris.

"Paulie – I like calling you that. Christ said that love was the thing. Love of God, and love for each other. Forgiveness, helping each other and respect are a part of love. I think that's what is making the world a better place.

"And not just Christian love either. I have many Muslim, Buddhist, Jewish and Hindu friends who agree that Love for God and love for others is saving the world from chaos.

"I think that, on balance, Islamic people suffered very much at the hands of Christians. Yet Islam, historically speaking, is more tolerant of other faiths than Christianity. Consider the history of Spain, for example. The Muslims ruled for 800 years, and the Catholic peoples were not unduly harmed. When the Christians took over Spain, they kicked out the Muslims first and then the Jews. Total ethnic cleansing. A horror to think about such things now, but there you are.

"Christians will try to convert you by word or by using the rack and, if those measures don't succeed, they'll kill you off or drive you out." She was very animated while they spoke of those things. Mostly she lectured and he listened.

"What do the Muslims believe Polly?"

"I'm not an expert yet," she said. "But I'm working on it in a serious way. *Mon proffeseur*, at the Sorbonne, said that the main thing is belief in Allah and belief that Mohammad was his messenger.

"The so-called pillars of the faith, the obligations of every Muslim on earth, are straightforward. The majority of Muslims are peaceful people trying to make the earth a better place. They are charitable, hospitable, and happy people.

"Belief, like I just said is the first step. It must be declared at least once. To say it to yourself is enough.

"Worship. They have obligations to pray five times a day. They can do it privately, publicly or in mosques. This is a very important obligation and is not excused for any reason.

"Charity or *Zagat* is an obligation. Generally, two-and-a-half percent of a person's income or profit is required. Anyone in poverty may be excused from *Zagat*. As a rule the money goes through governments to help the poor. Muslims are expected to be charitable.

"Fasting during the month of Ramadan is required. Ramadan is a month in the Islamic calendar. It changes every year vis-a-vis the regular world calendar – by about 11 days."

Lucy had been listening to Polly's lectures too. "Polly," she said, "When are you going to get to the good stuff? The eastern religions."

Polly laughed. "Not today dear. Maybe next semester if I'm still in the program."

"Back to fasting. This means abstinence from food and water, sex, and pleasures like smoking, chewing gum, etc. from dawn to sunset. This has several purposes. They believe the practices bring them closer to God and make them more aware of the plight of the poor and so on. Travelers, sick people and others can be excused.

"A pilgrimage to Mecca is a big deal too. Every Muslim is required to go at least once if he can make the journey. The poor and the frail can be excused."

"So that's it. Pillars one through five. I like Muslims. They are so sincere and friendly. Not Ku Klux at all. Except for the nuts. And the nuts are very much in decline."

Paul loved the teachings of Christ but did not consider himself to be a conventional believer - neither in Christianity nor Islam. He thought that his being would just dissolve into the universe like a drop of water into the sea. Eternal rest then. Free of guilt or blame.

After years of bumping heads with Polly and Lucy over the religious aspects of long life, he learned the health benefits of Buddhist meditation.

Daily meditation, several times each day seemed to improve his outlook and mood.

Lucy told him, "Paul. I love what meditation does for you." On many occasions she passed her scanner over his implant before and after he finished a session. Impressed with the numbers, she too began to make meditation a part of her routine.

Paul ran into many problems after a few years in the limelight. People accused him of being addicted to plastic surgery to remain youthful. His children rapidly caught up in age. His friends were all dead except for Lucy, Polly and the few other people he knew to be on the treatment. He felt that he needed to become invisible and more reclusive to keep his special circumstances hidden. Janice and Billy had passed.

The move to Florida had been done quietly. He was removing himself from his society. He kept a residence in Asheville, in a gated up-scale community, but virtually never went there. It was a ruse. The only time he visited was for occasional business trips to visit his galleries.

Paul sometimes went into an elaborate charade when he had to go out in public as himself – without a disguise. He assumed an elderly posture, used white wig, grayed his beard, used a walker, and moved slowly pretending to be much older than he felt.

When not pretending to be old, he looked younger than his grandchildren who were in their sixties. He thought he might outlive them all. His defense was to remain aloof, and he had just devised a strategy.

He arranged his affairs to fold all assets and income into a trust to benefit the foundation that had already given away half a billion udols so publicly. And he arranged his own death.

The big hurdle was his implant. It kept track of his comings and goings and allowed a medical team to monitor him – he had to unplug himself from his life. And get away alive.

He did the surgery in Uganda with help from Bishop Polly and Doctor Lucy.

His new implant password code identified him as a 60-year-old South African millionaire. His new persona was a confirmed bachelor with outstanding health named Pablo Alonso.

The staged death of the celebrated artist Paul Hunter was the result of a freak balloon accident over Lake Victoria. Balloonists had gathered from a score of countries. He and his Ugandan guide had been on a practice flight when a sudden storm swept them offshore. Their bodies were never recovered but pieces of the balloon and rig were eventually found 30 kilometers off the Ssese Islands where he had been staying. The accident put a damper on the rally. They held ceremonies in his honor,

"My new name is Pablo girls. If you call me Paul, I must learn not to respond. Call me "Pee" for a short while as I get used to my new identity."

The conspirators sat on Adirondack chairs on the verandah of the lake house. They were recounting the adventure in the evening twilight.

"Pau...I mean Pee. It went brilliantly today. You are lucky to be able to afford such a spectacular exit from your old life. What will you do now?" Barefooted, Polly wore old-fashioned shorts and a tee shirt. She did not look like a bishop of the Catholic Church. In fact, she had driven the rescuing chase boat.

Lucy interjected, "He's going to spend some time with me and come up with a plan for pursuing happiness." She turned to Paul and said, "Pablo, you are due for your annual. Let's test your new passport and go to the clinic in Paris. We can take a motor trip from there to anywhere in Europe. Whadda ya say?

"But I'm calling you Paulie from now on. *Valé?*"

Pee shrugged. "I suppose you can call me Paul too. I don't believe the feds are watching. Jazz will see to that."

He would always be Paul to himself and his friends.

Publicity had been very useful to Paul's fortunes and gifting activities. In addition to the obvious marketing benefit for high end 'Paul Hunter' paintings, it focused a lot of attention on his mission of educating children in out-of-the-way places in modern methods. He wanted to share his bounty with them and at the same time let the greater society learn resilience and innovation from subsistence level peoples. His leadership in building the basic skills of pad, cloud and internet did make a difference and the renown helped him sell more paintings for more money. A lot of UD flowed his way.

But it was not good to be so well known and recognized if you were trying to disappear. So, Paul grew a beard. Because it was more pepper than salt, he tinted it red in the fashion of the day. It was like a fancy frame for the lower portion of his head. Hair on top was harder to grow so he stayed bald. Altogether he was very fashionable.

One of the neat features of modern computers was the rat and RatFink. This feature enabled folks at any level of society to put a searchlight on wrongdoing, or waste and inefficiency of government.

Should a politician accept a bribe, an ordinary citizen with knowledge could blow the whistle with impunity, or, for example, should a village elder have inappropriate sexual relations with a child, the whole village would soon know. The deeply worn path of kleptocracy, governing for the purpose of personal enrichment, became more difficult and righteous behavior more common.

People were flawed as always, but bad behavior was harder to hide. Better communications and better education made the world a better place. Its resources were abundant and more available to all.

Privacy was no longer as prized in a world where it had been largely sacrificed for the benefits of widespread wellness and security from poverty. But Paul got away with his crime and continued to enjoy life.

Paul had to avoid rat finks.

2140

He kept a reverse genealogy of his and Dahlia's descendants. The current generations were on top of his charts. He kept his notes spread out on the large, unfolded table in the main salon.

One of Jazz's responsibilities was to keep track of things like contracts, agreements, inventory, sales, authorized reproductions, and such. She was very good at it. She was Paul's chief legal adviser and replaced a platoon of lawyers scattered among several cities. This made Paul's life much easier. He sought simplification.

Perhaps her most important duty was to keep a flow of valuable paintings heading towards Paul's numerous grandchildren. The recipients would only know that they had received a bequest from a long forgotten, departed relative. These loving gestures gave Paul a feeling of reconnection with his children in an obscure but meaningful way. He supposed it was bizarre, but he persisted anyway.

He spoke to Jazz several times a day.

Jazz would start her own anti-aging treatments after her 50th birthday. They had long been promised her, but she waited until her childbearing and rearing days were done.

Sometimes Paul called just to pass the time of day. It was more pointed when he said, "Jazz. I'm having recurrent bouts of mild depression. Sometimes I feel that there's no point to my life. Maybe I can get a hand on feeling that I'm doing some good in the world through my offspring. I feel terrible that I haven't been in touch with them – on purpose – and for so long. I couldn't break the pact with Lucy. Until you, of course."

"Grandpa. I understand." She was sitting at her kitchen table in his hologram breastfeeding her newest child; it was to be her fourth and last. The baby's wisps of flaming red hair paid tribute to his red-headed father as well as to the mother's German genes.

"I understand the point of your life. It's me and my thousands of cousins." She exaggerated.

"We wouldn't be here without you. And, furthermore," she lectured, "your ongoing gifts have helped educate us and they link us to your life as we imagined it was. They all think you are dead. I get it that that it is sometimes a problem for you. But just fegitaboudit. It's okay with me. I forgive you on behalf of the entire tribe. You just did what you had to do to get through.

"C'mon. Give us a smile." She popped Andy's grip on her nipple and switched breasts. "Sorry about that," apologizing to the baby for the interruption.

"I'll keep updating the spread sheets and we will continue to cram it with as much formation as you need. We'll work on it together when we get there."

PART THREE

2180 – Swan Harbor

Paul was happy to be back in the tiny village of Swan Harbor in North Carolina. He and Dahlia were married in the church down the way. His watercolor paintings had been produced, at a lightning quick pace of one or more a day, when the 21st century was new.

The town had not changed much in the 175 years since he first arrived there to begin his married life with Dahlia. They had many friends and acquaintances here then, but those friends were all long gone now. Some of the names on the village shops were the same indicating, perhaps, that children and grandchildren had taken over.

Paul rented a furnished house on the water for a year. He bought a boat. The runabout enabled him to gunkhole the saltwater sounds and bays of the area. Bogue Sound, Pamlico Sound and, further afield, Albemarle Sound were all shallow, saltwater expanses sheltered from the open Atlantic by a great stretch of barrier islands.

Jazz was closing his other residences and disposing of properties in Florida, North Carolina, and New York. Apartments, galleries, warehouses full of stuff would all be merged into his estate trusts for eventual distribution to his many heirs and charities.

He wanted to paint and write, to make a few friends, and spend some time being a waterman. While he wasn't a great fan of fishing, he wasn't totally averse to going through the motions of being a self-supporting outdoorsman. His painting had evolved in a natural way and his writing interest was far beyond the memoire stage.

Paul's Falls had long-since been completed and made public on Kindle, but actual sales were mostly to family and business associates. He finished the book with the story about his first jumbo sale to the museum in Paris and how he had used the wealth that ensued to provide educational tablets to lagging pockets of poverty in the world.

His new writing interest was in documenting the changes he saw as society developed at an ever-increasing pace. He called it *Paul – After the Fall*. Its contents were a deep secret as his arrangement with Lucy and the society were never to be revealed.

After the Fall was a series of digital journals. They covered so many years, places, and adventures, that they could never be published. It was over 500,000 words. His were paintings well represented. A companion piece explained his paintings. It too was illustrated and lengthy.

Physically Paul felt good and healthy. Not exactly young but free from pain. Perhaps, he thought he felt better and younger than before the anti-aging treatment began. He felt terrific most days but wanted to vacation from himself.

The house was not an expensive or expansive abode. He intended to live alone for a spell, in a new community, and to cultivate new interests. He was trying to downsize the support teams too.

Lucy was visiting for the first time. They stood in the living room and took in the 2020's Carolina-comfort furnishings. It was all somewhat dated, but he loved the feel.

"I'm not getting stale. Am I Lucy?"

"Not you honey. You're too full of piss and vinegar. This will give you a chance to stay out of sight and ponder the meaning of life and all. It's nice. Comfortable like my place in Paris." She gave him a hug. "Can I come and visit you whenever I'm able to get away from the institute?"

She was kidding him again. Her being here with him was like a housewarming present – some sex and romance to christen his new way of life. She was not totally in agreement with him just hiding out too. Officially she was Lucinda Lewis, a British subject, living abroad in Paris. She no longer worked for the sex clinic. She was a researcher at the sub rosa institute that produced the discoveries that kept her, Paul, and a few old associates alive. She answered to Lucy. She had paper-faked death twice to avoid the prying eyes of the official world that might be too curious about her long life.

They embraced and slowly toured the house, gradually disrobing as they prepared to make love like an old, caring, married couple. No rush. No pressure.

Although the house was a hundred years old, the floors were radiant heated, the windows an efficient design and the furnishings neat and clean. Paul shucked his pants in the kitchen. Lucy was naked before they got to the bedroom. Her wig was hooked over the bedpost when they finally got down to serious foreplay. Lucy was in charge and spared nothing to get Paul fully aroused and dedicated only in pleasuring her before he climaxed.

When they finished it would take a fifteen-minute effort to get the mattress back on the bedframe and the contents of the drawers back in place. There wasn't always breakage but, on this occasion, Lucy apologized, "Paul. I'm sorry about your saniwear. And the lamps. I'll help you shop for replacements tomorrow."

Paul slumped on the floor with his head in the dark corner and the lower half of his body sprawled over the mattress and a couple of pillows. He was somewhere between losing consciousness and dropping off to sleep. "S'okay Luce," he slurred, "Splain that again later." They were both joking.

"Oh Paulie. That was great. You are my favorite stud although I feel a little like your mother. I taught you everything. Didn't I?" She rested her head on his belly. Her hands wandered over his nether parts wondering how soon he'd be ready again. Not soon, she thought. Both were sated at the moment. It was fully dark outside. The sun went down just after five o'clock.

"What's next sir?"

"Let's nap, shower and try for food at the diner. I'm too tired to cook. Okay?"

"Okay."

They didn't make it to the restaurant. They slept the night, woke late, and made love the following morning. It was almost noon before they arrived, famished, at the marina restaurant.

"I like this better than the diner," Paul said as they strolled the few blocks to the pricy eatery that looked down at a fleet of docked boats.

The elevated dining porch admitted a lot of sun but the clear windscreens kept the temperature comfortable. Paul sensed heat rising from the floor. Wind sigh, halyard clanking and wave splashing music came faintly to his ears.

"Lucy. I have never felt better. Ain't this grand?" he grinned at her.

The waiter delivered coffee and took their lunch order.

Lucy leaned toward Paul. "I like being with you Paulie." She was smiling too and reached out her hand to him. They held hands and looked at each other and the nautical ambience of the marina. Pelicans and gulls wheeled through their lines of vision. The water sparkled like diamonds in the sunlight.

There were all kinds of pleasure and workboats. Sport fishing was a tourist draw in season, but the commercial fishing boats of yore were gone. Fish factories now supplied the world's needs. They dined on fried seafood – lobster, crab, bluefish and ample coleslaw and crisp sweet potato fries. Nothing they ate actually came from the sea or farms.

"Me too Lucy. Thanks for saving my life."

He paused to consider his words. He gazed at her a moment and reached for her hand across the table. "I mean for everything that's happened to me since Paris. For not letting me grow old and die as I was meant to do.

"I have made some good use of these years. I regret losing my family and friends, but my hope is that it's for the greater good – to help you guys figure out optimum human aging management to keep everyone healthy longer."

She squeezed his hand. "Paulie. I've been in love with you forever. I did it for selfish reasons, but you have made wonderful use of your life force." They leaned forward over the narrow table and kissed tenderly.

His interludes with Lucy were always too short. Soon he would be alone again and would look forward to seeing her in Paris or back in Swan Harbor.

2181 Swan Harbor

On his own for a few months – loose on the town, Paul bar crawled in the evenings. There were only three choices in Swan Harbor, so he took a different route every night and usually sat at a bar and kibitzed with the bartenders while watching sports events on the holos.

There were few alcohol drinkers these days, but pot and buzzers were popular. The bars stocked displays with brightly apothecary jars of inhalers, sniffers, and tabs. The new substances were not to Paul's sober taste, however. He was able to nurse a beer for hours.

Paul made friends with a couple at Ralph's Waterfront Rat Trap, the closest neighborhood bar. Sitting next to him at the long bar, they were a salty couple in their sixties, clad in ragged shorts, dirty white sneakers, faded tees and sporting a pleasantly weathered look.

"Hi. Millie and David." she indicated their names. "What's a boy like you doing in a nice place like this?" The woman started the conversation with a white, toothy laugh and the offer of a handshake.

Paul took her hand. He had to reach across David to do so and then he shook David's hand when released by Millie.

"Soaking up the local color and this box of beer." He had a standard one-liter container of lite. Paul did not watch calories. He preferred the slightly sharper taste of the low-calorie brew and appreciated the lower alcohol content.

His new acquaintances were sniffing towelettes of MetaA. They looked slightly looped to Paul, but their attitude towards him was very warm and friendly. They were discussing politics and included Paul in their circle.

"So, Paul. Do you think that having a job is a right or a privilege? The U.S. Supreme Court just declared that it is a right if a person insists on having a job, municipalities must make room -

for anyone who wants a job. Private companies can decide on their own."

"Well. I believe in work, ya know, but people can stay very busy just tending to the needs of their families and their communities. If a person doesn't want a job and has enough income from the Sharing, he shouldn't be *required* to have a job. For me that's the main thing."

They agreed on that point and moved on to other topics at a table, away from the bar. They all decided on broiled salmon and real coleslaw salad. Garlic bread was included with all meals. They ordered supper by tapping their orders into menu gadgets built into the bar.

After the dinner, which was, in their mellow opinions, "…the best ever." Millie and David invited Paul to have a nightcap aboard their boat that was docked at the restaurant.

"C'mon Paul. Spend a few minutes and see our floating love nest." He accepted and was wowed by the vessel. It was a boxy kind of a houseboat. Everything was white and clean with a few nautical touches like porthole windows and wall murals.

The main salon was the width of the boat, about three meters wide and five meters long. There was plenty of ceiling height. David gave him the tour while Millie prepared three glasses of ice water in the tidy corner galley. There was an ample dining table and built-in seating along the walls and around the table

The boat seemed solid and did not move much as they walked about.

"Forward we have the stateroom and full head." They descended two steps into a small bedroom and ensuite bathroom. Another door led to a small closet. "Look here. We had the drawers built into the bulkheads and under the oversize berth." David seemed very proud of the small but well-organized space.

"What about HVAC?" asked Paul?

"Mostly *Dami* relies rely on Mother Nature. Windows are screened and we have the fans."

"Pardon me?" said Paul. "*Dami*?"

"Yep. That's her name." He laughed. "You'll never guess how we came up with it."

Paul smiled.

He noticed small barrel fans in the corner of each room. He was not a big lover of air conditioning. It wasn't needed in his former apartment home base in Asheville. He too relied on fans in Swan Harbor. It must be even cooler right on the water he thought, wondering what it must be like to sleep on a boat like this.

David showed Paul a small foredeck accessed by walking a narrow side deck at the edge of the boat.

"There are hatches under the deck for the anchors, lines and fenders and such. We don't spend much time in front here – too much sun and wind."

"C'mon." He led aft to show Paul a cabin with bunk beds and a full bathroom. The after deck was spacious with an awning-covered deck holding four chairs and a picnic table. Railings protected guests from falling in the water and built-in stairs made for easy reboarding when swimming.

"*Dami* is three meters in width so it can be transported by truck without special permits when we decide to change locations. That increases our range of options at where we can cruise. Our main base of operations is on the Cumberland River in Kentucky. We decided to explore the Inland Waterway this year. So, we hired a truck to bring it here."

Paul knew that the maximum legal width of a normal highway load had increased some years ago when the United States went metric. He had needed a commercial class driving license when he trained for a balloon pilot's permit in 2080 and had to learn the requirements for a commercial driver's license in Florida. The rules would be about the same in every state.

"How long is Dami?"

"She's twelve-by-three-meters. The boat was built in about 2030 using fiberglass. The power plant is an old Cummings diesel and backup power is our gen-set."

"What's a genset?"

They were on the broad afterdeck now where they had boarded the boat. Millie brought a tray with sweating glasses of ice water and told the men to sit. The afterdeck was furnished with deeply padded folding chairs grouped for conversation. There was a table for drinks.

"I mean our generator has its own diesel engine and it can be rigged to turn the prop in an emergency. We call that the gen-set. This old gal has a lot of modern add-ons, but her old bones are locked in 21st century technology."

"David. I'm familiar with the water around Swan Harbor. I just kayak here or putter around in my runabout. But the water is not very deep. Bogue Sound and Pamlico Sound are very shallow. How much water do you need to operate?"

"Good question Paul. She draws just under a meter. I can run her at ten knots in calm conditions. Maybe 12 if we're in a hurry to get out of the weather."

Paul put on a puzzled face and held his hand palm up to spring the question. "Uh. David. I'm not quite up on nautical nomenclature. What's a knot again?"

"Ah. Sorry. It's about 1.86 kliks. So, we can travel about 18 klicks in an hour. I never go offshore so that speed will let us find shelter quickly if there's a blow.

"She's strong but not very handy. She would not like going out into the ocean or big waves anywhere." Paul was listening intently, the beginnings of a plan forming in his mind.

"The main thing is to keep a close watch on the wind and weather. I don't mind wind and rain, but I want to be securely tied up or anchored if there is a storm.

"Hurricanes. Forget about it. Tie her up and save yourself. Ya knows. You can always get another boat, but your skin is not so easily replaceable."

They spent a comfortable half hour talking about living aboard boats and such. Paul said his good nights.

As he stepped on the gangplank Millie said, "Paul. We're going for a spin tomorrow. Would you like to join us?"

Paul accepted in a heartbeat. He yearned to experience more house boating. "What can I bring?"

"Just yourself buddy. Or, if you're shy, bring a swimsuit." She laughed and he walked to his house feeling blessed to have made friends with such interesting people.

He spent a happy hour Googling houseboats. There were many available for sale throughout the world and many types. He visited the websites of builders and saw a variety of prices ranging from expensive to obscenely expensive.

He saw canal boats in Europe and even a type called Shanty boats – so called because they were shacks on barges with no motor. Most of the boats he saw were too big, too small, too used or too dull. He loved pouring over the galleries of photos posted and the blogs from the shanty boat owners around the world. In Europe they spoke of river and canal boats.

One that caught his eye was a plain 5-meter raft with an old style, wheeled, pop-top camper strapped on the deck. It was tied up to a johnboat that had a light outboard for propulsion. Sort of a private, miniature tug, it appealed to the Tom Sawyer in his personality.

He thought about living in a tent as a youth. It had been hardscrabble in many ways, but there was an unfettered freedom element too. He sometimes felt a yearning to live a more detached life. Hmmm…

It was eight a.m. in Rome when he was finally ready for sleep. He called Lucy to say hi and talk about the events of the day.

She sounded bright and crisply ready for the challenges in her day. "Keep me posted Paulie. Be good. Wait – not too good."

The picnic date on the *Dami* went well.

They cast off at 11 o'clock. Paul had brought a bathing suit wrapped in a towel and a gift consisting of a tube of fine Merlot wine and four stemmed wine glasses. "Thanks Paul," gushed Millie, giving him a friendly hug. "We'll have this with our lunch. We thought you'd enjoy a swim before lunch. Then we can kick back and enjoy the breeze. David was positioned at the wheel resting his butt against a fixed bench that was wide enough to easily seat four people.

David spent a few minutes setting switches in the wheelhouse and then reached below the deck to fuss with some valves.

There was a cough, a bang, and then a puff of black smoke. The diesel engine rumbled to life.

Paul actually liked the smell of the diesel engine. It reminded him of old-time buses and of a diesel-powered pick-up truck he'd used once upon a time ago. He well understood that the fossil fuel was not a plus for the environment. The engine steadied to a low throbbing grumble as it warmed up. David stayed busy with getting the boat ready.

The day was mild and sunny with a light east wind. Wispy clouds and lots of blue sky prevailed. The sun was bright and warm, the air clear of haze. Paul stood by the bow line, as instructed, ready to cast off and step aboard when David signaled. Millie stood on the dock at the other end. The engine started at the touch of a button and rumbled quietly while David stood on the cabin top to have a look around for traffic or other problems.

The engine warmed for a couple of minutes and David called, "Cast off astern," to Millie and "Cast off the bow line," to Paul. The stern eased into the channel and the boat backed into position. Paul stowed the bow dock line as he'd been instructed.

David pushed the controller to forward, and the boat moved into position, through the canal and out into the maze of islands on the edge of Bogue Sound. When clear of the port he throttled up to cruising speed and the resulting breeze kept them comfortably cool. The boat produced a substantial wake even at slow speeds.

They motored North in the Intercoastal Waterway for an hour. There were a few boats in the distance and oceanfront hotels and apartments appeared in the far distance. The nearer shores were low and entirely natural with no sign of mankind's activity. There was an abundance of birds.

David reduced power and pointed the bow toward a sandy islet covered with tall grasses and low sand dunes. He steered carefully to its northern shore. The grassy bottom seemed just 100 millimeters deep.

"How deep is the water here?" asked Paul.

David glanced at an instrument and answered, "About one-and-a-half meters. Looks less to the eye though. Doesn't it?"

"It looks like I could stand up," said Millie, "but it's over my head."

David cut the engine and walked forward on the folding side deck to pull the anchor out of its built-in cubby on the foredeck. It splashed into the water followed by an attached length of chain and the synthetic anchor rope.

The boat continued to move forward until the anchor caught the bottom. The boat moved softly in the breeze and the bow soon came around to face upwind. The air temperature was a pleasing 30 degrees centigrade.

"Woo!" Millie screamed as she flew through the air.

Paul looked up and caught a glimpse of her bare body as she hit the water. The boat rocked again, and Paul looked up to see David leaping into the drink. Naked.

Oh, what the hell, Paul thought. He stripped and joined them. It was a chaste swim despite the nudity. The water felt good. His new friends were in high spirits and Paul felt that he had made a great decision. What a way to spend the day. Inspired, Paul wanted his own fun platform.

Paul launched a research project into acquiring a real boat. He went to the internet 'boats for sale' sites, prowled the local marinas and began thinking up a list of his requirements and desires.

Paul's list was not short. He wanted a platform from which he could paint landscapes and water scenes. A safe and comfortable space for sleeping, eating, hosting a very limited number of friends. Shallow of draft, economical to run, plus ease of operation and the ability to single-hand were key. It must be warm in the winter and cool in the summer, towable by truck, strong of structure.

The vision was to give up his rental house in Swan Harbor and live aboard. Communications and navigation would be handled through his e-array, but he'd need a depth-sounder, battery-based energy storage, signal devices, lights, personal floatation devices, a tender, storage space, weather-proofed environment and more. He could tow his existing runabout for a tender, if needed.

Paul happened on an article in an online magazine, called *Small Boat Journal,* discussing the construction of such boats. He poured over the pictures and plans and his vision sharpened. He would build his own boat! It would be a project to enrich his life.

He had good carpentry and general building skills learned as a youth under the tutelage of his contractor father. He sketched well and fancied himself master of the knowledge of which design elements would make him happy. He began to draw, and to research materials, supplies and equipment.

Paul needed room to build his dream. He did calculations and shopped for available warehouses suitable for his project.

After getting the general concept on paper he scanned the images and notes with his E-array and dabbled with his CAD. In the quiet nights he entertained himself by making a cardboard model, painted to look like an old-fashioned harbor tug.

He decided he wanted a hull three meters wide by ten meters in length. The hull would be propelled by a pair of hydro pumps. It would be energized by induction using solar, wind and wave motion generators to keep batteries charged.

The major panels of the barge-like hull would be constructed of material much like the carbon fibre reinforced plastic used for aircraft – it was called Carfirep.

Carfirep was available in sheets of varying sizes. It came in several thicknesses. It was much lighter and stronger than the wood products he used as a youthful carpenter when plywood might have been the material of choice for such a project. A standard one-by-three-meter panel weighed only 11 kilos.

The hydro pumps would be mounted fore and aft and require only ten cm below the hull. The flow from each pump could be rotated independently through 360°. Thus, the boat could move sideways as well as fore and aft through simple, intuitive controls. It could be made to spin in place.

Paul's weight estimates indicated a fully loaded weight or displacement of over 2,000 kilograms resulting of a draft of less than 30 cm, including the allowance for the propulsion units.

Swan Harbor was home to Francine McDermott, Marine Architect. She was retired but kept an office to get out of her house on a regular basis. Paul approached her door, in a waterfront building, with a pad of sketches, lists of materials and model in a box. Franny shook his hand, bade him sit and let him talk. She was an intelligent woman with a content and peaceful expression.

Her office was decorated with photos and drawings of ships and boats of every description. Most of her work consisted of converting old fishing boats to pleasure craft. As in so many fields, work was hard to get.

She was a tall woman in her middle years. Her attire was the usual casual work jumpsuit, but it revealed a sturdy figure. They sat at a library table with ample space for spreading drawings and plans.

"Paul. Thanks for coming. Call me Franny. Tell me how I can help you. What are your plans – your dreams? Tell me your hopes and aspirations. "She smiled to show the humor in her statement.

Her warmth and helpful attitude allowed him to proceed with confidence. She was, in fact, delighted to have the prospect of a paying customer.

He described his dreamboat and his decision to build it himself. "I'd like to design around a comfortable bed for two and a great couch for hanging out with the holo."

"I want a good deck for plein air painting."

Franny looked puzzled. "What the heck is that?"

"Painting outdoors. Sorry about the fancy terminology."

He recited his list of requirements and later forwarded the details to her computer.

Paul estimated that he'd need about 800 carfirep panels of varying sizes that would weigh about 500 kilograms. The weight of the propulsion, tankage, batteries, and other equipment would greatly increase the total displacement.

Franny asked Paul about a budget, somewhat doubtfully. He had come dressed casually and she knew that he was renting a modest house in town. "How much money are you prepared to spend on this project?"

"This is a rather delicate subject Franny. But the truth is I don't care how much it costs. I'm ready to pay you your regular fee for guiding me and designing but I want to do the work myself. It's sort of a retirement project – both the build and the use of the craft. I have spotted an empty warehouse on the water that will lease for about UD700 per month and I think I can do it in less than a year. Then move to a dock nearby. The yard will supply a moving crane for a price."

This was very good news to Franny. She was getting few commissions due to lack of demand for boats in general and the decline of the fishing industry.

"Paul. I need the work. Perhaps I could help you with the design, purchasing and even the build for a flat fee of UD25,000. I own the welding set-up and that'll save you some time, effort and money.

"It would be a great retirement project for me too. I think I could give you 20 hours a week through completion and advise you when we'll need help with lifting and turning."

Paul was uncomfortable at the thought of her working for 20 hours a week for an unknown number of weeks. He sensed her neediness for employment.

"Franny. Let's work on this basis. I'll pay you UD20,000 in advance, upon completion of a preliminary design and then shipyard rates for your labor."

They made the deal, and she invited him to leave his materials with her for the day and meet in the morning for a more comprehensive consultation and to pay a deposit for her fee.

"Done!" Paul enthused. "What time tomorrow?"

They agreed on ten o'clock and parted with smiles and a handshake.

Paul was amazed by her presentation the next morning. She had set her display on the library table.

His model and sketches had been transformed by Franny's CAD into a holograph of the completed boat, resting in shimmering water. The colors were true to his drawings. There was glass in the portholes and doors. A johnboat was moored alongside. And, wonder of wonders, she removed the topsides, and he was able to gaze into the interior spaces fitted out with furniture, kitchen galley counters, beds and even curtains and pictures on the walls. It was a large display and he had to walk around the table to take it in.

"Wow! Wow! Wow! Franny. This is smashing!"

"Yep," she said proudly. "But really it is your good work and the CAD magic. You'll have to change your sanis when you see how it prices out."

"What do you mean? Is it a lot of money?"

"Yes and no. The cost including materials, tools, construction space, my fee, moving, and testing and all should be about UD200,000.

"Your labor is a big bonus. *If* you are a good worker, you will save about UD75,000. And the boat will be worth more than the cost when you are ready to sell. Your concept is truly different. You have asked for lots of headroom and elbow room and low speed as well as high efficiency propulsion."

"So, I'll need about UD125,000 plus free labor?"

"Yes." She looked at him expectantly.

"When can we start?"

Paul was bemused by the cost projection. "Lucy," he announced. "Do you realize that the price of a single painting is sometimes more than the cost of this big boat?" They had a perfect clear connection despite being separated by an ocean.

"What a gas. You are amazing. You are a regular industry of good ideas. Why do you want to do the work yourself?"

"I dunno exactly. It's been on my bucket list forever. I want to spend a lot of time on the boat. You too of course. It'll be different from anything we've done before."

"Paul. What will you name the boat?"

"Ah. I'm not sure..."

"Well, I have a suggestion. Call her *Dahlia*. That will be a nice tribute name for your beautiful dream."

"You know Luce. I thought I might name her *Lucy*. Maybe *Luz*. What do you think?"

"I think that you should name her *Dahlia*. Okay?"

"Okay then. Good choice good buddy!" he kidded her. The suggestion was more than welcome to Paul.

"Then hurry up and get it on. I'll be there in a few weeks to supervise and keep you off that Frannie person. I want you to myself."

This was not the first time she'd hinted at exclusivity. Paul felt a tug at his heartstrings. "Me too Lucy. Absence makes the heart grow fonder and you've been gone for too long."

SEPTEMBER 2181

The warehouse in the marina was freshly swept. Paul cleaned the windows, repaired the ancient natural gas heating system, and oiled the hinges on the doors. He updated some lights and fabricated workbenches for himself and Franny. Her welding rig was in place and a variety of building materials accumulated.

Lucy was expected at noon. She wanted to participate in Paul's bucket list project (and check Franny out in person). Buffy went to get her at the New Bern Regional Air Station.

The silvery, grey Carfirep panels were stacked on edge to conserve floor space. Some of the panels were one meter wide for the hull sides and interior bulkheads. Ten-liter buckets of Carfirep glue were on strong shelves that Paul had placed to keep the premises orderly.

The boat's glass windows were created and sorted by size. The main salon would have huge picture windows. The glass would be stronger and heavier than the hull panels. The two large sheets that would form part of the outside walls of the main salon would not open - for strength and safety. The smaller ports and windows and glass doors would open for ventilation.

The 25 by 50-meter warehouse had a ten-meter-high ceiling and a roll-up commercial door that would accommodate a sizable flatbed truck. Franny and Paul sat on stools at the workbench to chart out their procedures and create a workflow.

Franny provided meter-long sheets of plans to help them cut panels that needed curved edges. Paul bought a Craftsman Carfirep saw.

"Paul. I know you originally wanted a totally flat bottom, but we have agreed on a mild rocker to make beaching, turning and accidental grounding easier to manage. We are going to build the base hull right-side-up for ease of making the bulkheads strong and leak-proof. We will flip the hull again to install skegs and external stringers and to paint the bottom with superplast. Then we'll reflip onto large, wheeled dollies to build the topsides and outfit the interior spaces."

"The bottom will be heavy. It will weigh over 400 kilograms by itself. What will it take to flip it?"

"You and me buddy – along with a crew of tough guys and some lines. You'll need to find some friends and have a flip party. I'll get the yard to send 'em. Maybe a mobile lift too."

They began by butting panels together on the floor. The forward and after planks were angled upwards, slightly, by resting them on studs and letting gravity establish a slight curve. The Carefree adhesive was applied to the edges and the laser-wielding device did its magic. The wielded edges would be as strong as the base material itself and last forever. If the hull were ever to rupture it would not be at the edges.

Franny looked at the joyful reunion of friends and lovers and regretted her solo status. Lucy greeted her warmly and said, "Paulie sent me the holo plan. It looked wonderful. Thank you."

Buffytoo had delivered Lucy at noon. Her flight had been Paris, New York, and Charlotte. She brought a restaurant take-out lunch with her, and they sat at the workbench by the opened overhead door. Sunshine and a soft breeze soothed them as they feasted on fried chicken, baked beans, and soft, sweet rolls.

As previously agreed, the three worked together placing and cutting panels with an eye on the clock for an early quitting time in honor of Lucy's arrival.

It did not yet look like a boat. It looked like the beginnings of a big sleigh. The panels were not hard to cut but marking the cut lines took time. Measurements were taken and retaken to be sure. The bottom assembly took the three workers a week to puzzle together and then more days to paint.

Paul noticed that the two women were able to outwork him. He was good for about eight hours of physical effort and then began to flag. They still looked strong when he was ready to quit. Still the work went quickly. On the other hand, he thought, besides five fingers, I do more of the heavy work.

The layout of the shanty boat was revealed as the vertical panels were placed. From front to back it showed the anchor locker, head, forward berthing area, the main salon, after berth, and rear decks. The pilothouse would be over the head and forward berth. The berths seemed huge, but they would eventually allow storage drawers underneath king mattresses. The variety of spaces and areas of the vessel, including the ample fore deck, covered after deck, uncovered after deck, and the deck on top of the cabin, made the boat seem spacious beyond her actual measurements.

Paul recruited his landlord, the owner of the warehouse, and two guys from the neighboring marina to flip the boat using a portable lifting device.

They installed the pump thrust impellers and painted the bottom with a special paint to inhibit marine growth like barnacles and seaweed. The same crew later turned the hull over again so that the interior, motors, batteries, built-ins, and topsides could be fully fabricated.

Paul had agonized over his power and battery choices. They used the same power systems used in commercial busses. "So, Franny. Tell me again how long these motors will run on a charge."

"Paul. I can't give you an exact answer." The three workers/friends were taking their lunch break. "This hulk we're building will be very much affected by wind and wave action.

"If the wind and currents are behind her, she could run 24 hours at low speed. Into the wind or current you will just get four or fice hours of full throttle at full charge. But there's a kicker. We're installing two heavy-duty wind turbines. So, the wind will produce lots of charging power for the batts.

"Your electrical management array will tell the story after a few weeks of sea trials. Your boat will be robust and efficient. I think you'll be happy with the results since you're not looking for speed. The Dahlia will be pokey. Handy around the harbor. You can go sideways or backwards as easily as frontwards. I'm guessing that you can pretty much run all day – just like buses. But you will then need time to recharge. Plan ahead and you can do anything but go offshore."

"Yeah. That's my plan. Sheltered waters only."

The exterior paint job made *Dahlia* look something like a harbor tug. The smokestack was placed to disguise an outdoor shower. It took just three more weeks to put most of the panels together. Deliveries of new gadgets and devices made every day seem like Christmas for Paul.

Paul was pleased with the interior finish of the boat. The windows and ports let in a lot of light. The magic glass could be adjusted at will to let in the warmth of the sun or insulate against heat loss in winter. He was able to salvage mahogany panels to create a retro yacht interior with lots of varnished wood. There were painted surfaces too but, of course, no actual paint and no varnish were used. Modern materials were much better than the surface coatings he had used in his youth. The work seemed to go on forever.

Lucy managed invoices and "paperwork." The boat's CPU was temporarily mounted on a desk, and she organized the files with links to manufacturers and Paul's cloudland storage space. She was at ease with computers – better than Paul.

Auxiliary equipment and systems took another month to hook up and test so it was November before the vessel could be put into the water where she would sit while the myriad finishing touches were worked out.

The techniques they used to do the work had been perfected over the centuries. The hull assembly methods were a riff on the old 'Stitch and Glue' of days gone by.

Electrical requirements for lighting and electronics were minimal. Luminescent paints were replacing electrical lighting in the world at large so *Dahlia's* carbon footprint was close to zero.

North Carolina registration and Coast Guard certification requirements were made easy by having a marine architect involved. The vessel was certified only for non-commercial use in protected waters for a maximum of 25 passengers. A large deck locker held the requisite PFDs and an automatic inflatable raft multi-purposed as a table base.

Dahlia was ready for her maiden voyage on the first day of April 2176. Paul hosted a party for his dockyard worker pals and his few local friends and suppliers. Franny, Lucy, and Jazz were conspicuous having devised an orange tee shirt uniform.

There were more than a dozen people on the after deck, sipping champagne punch, and enjoying *hors d'oeuvres* when Franny rang a bell she had tucked into her pocket for the purpose. Conversation paused and all eyes were on her as she rang the high-pitched instrument.

"Ladies and gentlemen. Please take a moment to appreciate this occasion. *Dahlia* was named for Paul's wife who died at a young age.

"We all wish Paul long life, a clear heart, and a happy nature. Salute Paul."

Paul's eyes moistened at the sentimental words. He had always cried on sad and happy occasions.

Paul announced, "Folks. Would you all do me the honor of taking a short harbor cruise to celebrate?"

There was total agreement on this point.

"Millie. Stand by the bow line."

"David," he bawled at her husband, "Stand by the stern line.

"Cast off!"

The gentle breeze that pushed *Dahlia* against the dock was no match for the impellers push. They eased away, sideways, with the water between them and the shore gradually widening. Captain Paul used his hand-held controller with gentle finger strokes for moving forward and steering as necessary. There was a top speed of about eight-KPH, but that speed was reserved for open water and the usual cruising speed was about half.

The motion was smooth and quiet. He caught Franny's eye and they gazed happily at each other. *Dahlia* floated on her lines and was doing well. Their baby lived!

2182 Summertime

Paul and Lucy spent the summer wandering the Outer Banks' bays, rivers and sounds, Bogue Sound, Core Sound, Neuse River, Rattan Bay, Pamlico Sound, Albemarle Sound and as far as the Pasquotank River by August. They took baby steps at first, to learn the Intercostal Waterway and other riverine marker systems. They became familiar with what their vessel could and could not do. The *Dahlia* seemed to take care of them.

Their first voyage was a two hour romp up the Bogue Bay with the wind pushing them from behind and the engines used for steering more than for forward propulsion.

They anxiously anchored in the lee of a no-name sand spit islet that left them in full view of ritzy vacation homes that lined the near shore. He let out 20 meters of chain and line to insure adequate rode. They sat on top deck, the anchor holding them bow to the wind.

They heard gulls calling in the distance and observed a flight of pelicans skimming the bay near the shoreline. The water was still in the windless afternoon.

"Cheers!" Paul lifted his stemmed wine glass to clink with Lucy. The brilliant red sunset lit Lucy's face with a glow that seemed to come from within. "Lucy. This is the most beautiful moment in my life." His eyes glistened. "Here's to my Dahlias."

"Amen and hallelujah she replied."

"I love you, Lucy. I wish we could always be together. What a precious time this has been. Fitting out the boat and finally getting afloat on our own"

"Me too, Paulie. But I must go back to work in the winter. Will you be okay with that?"

"I guess so. We can explore the waterways to the north this summer. We'll maybe get up to Virginia by the end of August. Wherever. Just gotta see how it all works, how comfortable and happy we'll be. I don't have a schedule."

By the fourth day they found themselves navigating the sheltered waterways leading to the Neuse River basin and the waters of Pamlico Sound. Their previous shore-bound existence was fading, and the many boat-keeping tasks became routine.

They kept a close eye on weather forecasts and on the wheelhouse's bank of dials indicating battery power. Solar panels and wind turbines were the main sources of energy for the engines, lighting and other systems making life fun and pleasant. They also had dials to view a water turbine output contributing to their power supply.

The pilothouse became Paul's usual and favorite station while underway. Glass windows on every side allowed him to monitor the boat's surroundings. It was a comfortable space with cushioned benches all around and a walkout to the front deck.

The port side of the pilothouse was positioned over the head. The floor was higher than the rest of the space to give headroom below. It presented as a one by two meter raised bench with a comfy mattress to serve as daybed seating or extra sleeping for guests. Paul would often spend the nights there.

He could hear and feel the effects of wind and water on the hull from anywhere in the boat – the gentle vibrations of the turbines and the quiet hum of the impellers pushing them along. The boat seemed to speak, telling him, "All is well..."

The flat panel mounted on the dashboard gave information on all systems and served as the chart while underway and there were similar displays in his berth, the main salon, the after deck and even the head. The displays were bright during the day and automatically dimmed to night-time settings depending on ambient light.

Night vision was important in the darkness and the combination of Paul's enhanced eyes, and the display panels amazed him. He had so much more information available to him than mariners of previous eras. He could see better than nocturnal animals now.

In the beginning of their maiden voyage, there was trepidation about how and where to "park" *Dahlia*. The prevailing breezes were often very strong. Anchoring was just theoretical until he had to rely on his own ground tackle for safety while passing a dark night on a strange shore.

Although he had a few paper charts and waterway guides, his electronics guided him. The paper items were just antiques and ornaments from another century. Anything Paul needed to know was instantly available electronically. The E-info was always there and always accurate and reliable.

His implants gave him the ability to see in the dark when he needed and to see things at a distance when he grimaced and squinted just so. He used his visual powers sparingly because vision could be confusing if he switched ranges too often.

They make it to Virginia by the time Lucy had to return to Paris to resume her duties. The days and nights were idyllic, interspaced with moments of panic and trepidation - especially in the early days.

Because of *Dahlia's* relaxed cruising speed, they learned to factor winds, tides, and currents to give themselves a lee shore for evening anchorages. If a spot appealed to them, they would tarry for days, lounging on deck and swimming in limpid waters. They often went ashore for walks or more elaborate excursions.

Perishable supplies and potable water were factors in their movements. Buffy could rendezvous with them as necessary. The reliable vehicle would stop at the big Walmarts and other chains that participated in E-shopping for everything

Paul was alone, but not lonely when Lucy was away. He kept busy with navigating from sheltered shore to sheltered shore working his way south before the cruel winter kicked in.

Beautiful nautical and seascape paintings began to accumulate. He thought that they were his best work ever. He shipped them to Jazz on a regular basis. She was the first link in his marketing organization.

Early on he had experimented with living off the 'land.' Really just the water, although he sometimes found useable clumps of berries or grapes. Mostly he gathered greens to supplement salads.

He liked to harvest clams in the shallows in warm weather. He just sat on the bottom with water up to his waist and dug his hands and feet into the sand and mud looking for stones – except that the stones were clams. He tossed them into a bucket kept nearby by a length of string.

After washing the mud and other junk off them, they would go into a net and hang over the side for a while before cooking. The clams flushed sand out of their systems while hanging in clear water.

His steamer would hold salted water and wine. A cup of sauteed onions and garlic then went into the boiling water followed by the clams. The clams would be open and not be overcooked at the end of seven minutes. He would dip the clams out and then run the broth through a strainer into a large cup.

His clam boil feasts would follow the pattern he'd learned from his parents. He would hold each clam by its 'neck,' rinse it in the mug of hot broth, dip it into clarified butter, and pop it into his mouth. The flavor was astounding. At the end of the meal, he would sip the broth, being careful to not eat sand that might collect in the bottom of the cup.

He also caught several kinds of fish from the deck. His top pick was flounder because they were delicious and relatively easy to catch. Fried flounder and seasoned vegetables were very enjoyable for him. He liked root produce because it did not require refrigeration and kept well for long periods. In fact, he had no refrigeration. The only sacrifice entailed was that he had to drink warm beer.

Cleaning the fish was a messy business and the boat smelled afterwards, no matter how hard he tried to clean it up. He found it wasteful too, discarding most of the animals including guts, scales, skins, bones, and shells.

Living off the bounty of the environment proved to be more work than it was worth to him, and he gave it up after the first season.

He preferred to let everything around him live with as little interference from him and his boat as possible. He hung his rod and tackle in the main salon as decorations. He could resurrect them if he ever needed to go into the survival mode - then look out fish!

Watching the pelicans and gulls, the dolphins and fish was enough. They were often subjects in his paintings. He tried to suggest motion and capture the beautiful colors he saw swirling around them. He and his art evolved slowly. When he was a young man, and artist, he felt like an outsider. His paintings were sometimes dark. Now he felt more connected to the world and tried to show his place in it in unique and worthwhile ways. The older artist experimented with line and color constantly.

He would never dare do any killing when Lucy was with him. She told him, "I know fish eat fish, birds eat fish, animals eat animals and they, like us, are designed to do so. But, cruelty should be a part of mankind's past and not his future.

"So, Paulie, if you want to be a hunter, butcher, and eater of animal corpses, do it when I am not around.

"Please pass me that tube of beef protein..."

Paul went to Paris for his personal health overhauls. His original treatment with the age reversing ointments could not be used again. But his annual physical revealed the effective age of his various organ systems, and he took support supplements, custom adjusted each year. He used maintenance skin lotions and spray applications religiously. He felt wonderful most of the time. His body had served him well.

Animal studies had enabled scientists to quadruple the lifespan of small mammals but there was no precedent for really old humans like his peer group. It was difficult to do controlled experiments on long-living animals.

Paul sat cross-legged on a cushion. His face was toward the faint morning breeze and the sun was on the job keeping his face warm. He closed his eyes slightly, breathed comfortably, trying to clear his mind of negative emotions, and thoughts.

He breathed through his nose trying for awareness of the caress of the breeze and the pleasant heat of the sun. He felt calm. Content. He tried not to think about what Jazz might be doing on his behalf. He erased the daily concerns about whether or not to shift Dahlia or when he'd need to make port. Lucy went to his mental back burner.

Today he felt the peace right away. If calm was elusive, or his mood not so responsive, he would try chanting "Boodoo" over and over. This would go on for many minutes and, ultimately, he would shift into the meditative state that he sought.

Meditation was a daily event – twice a day whether he was alone or had guests aboard. Even the cocktail hour did not replace the evening session when he had company. His most frequent guest was Lucy.

The next step for Paul was exercise. His body craved motion and challenge. He would go to the main salon to unfold his Total

Gym System from its niche in the wall and went through his multipart daily routine.

Sit-ups for core strength and push-ups for his shoulders and back. Squats, rowing, curls, and pull-ups worked different muscle groups. He did three sets of each with a brief recovery for each segment. Between each part of the routine, he would use the boat's two steps to the afterdeck for stair stepping. He maintained his maximum heart rate for about 40 minutes and then showered.

The smokestack shower stall was clever. Standing, he was tall enough to see over the edge and enjoy the view while he cleaned up. The products he used were environmentally friendly. The final drain was just above the waterline. Once in a while, if the waves were just right, dollops of water splashed up through the drain onto his feet. This was a fun event and not something to avoid. He rationed fresh water by bathing in warmish salt water and rinsing with hot fresh water.

Breakfast was a tube of oatmeal and raisins with almond milk in the same tube. It was filling but he hungered for bacon and eggs with crisp toast and grits or potatoes. Grits versus potatoes was a hard choice so he alternated between them in reality when such fare was available but only in his mind while he went through his morning mush.

Jazz's up-dated charts arrived every few days. They were impressive. He and Dahlia had really started something. There were over 100 descendants, and he relished the information he had on each of them. He kept paper files on each of them, backed up on his personal networks plus, more solidly he thought, in the quantum cloud.

But he liked the paper. He had some news clippings, nonprint of course, and some photos. There was never any intent to contact any of his grandchildren.

He was so pleased to see that Astronaut P. J. Hunter-Douglas had a Hunter original painting in his apartment near the space coast in Florida. He was considered a hero so his taste in furniture made an article in On-line Architect Digest. Hunter-Douglas was on his way to Mars and would be gone for more than ten years. NASA kept and safeguarded his apartment and personal effects as a part of his remuneration for giving such a large chunk of his life to the Mars Mission.

The colony on the second planet was permanent, but select specialists were shuttled in and out to enable people who would not, or could not, emigrate to the planet's hardship way of life. The moons of the gas giant planets would soon support small colonies as well. Man was spreading his wings.

Paul's charts showed *Hunter* people at different stages of diverse careers. Some just starting, others long retired. There were very few in trouble with legal or medical issues. Sometimes he could steer help their way, anonymously, and sometimes he had to sigh and let matters work out.

Like a chess player, Paul had to think his navigation several moves ahead. Paul's daily runs at five knots per hour allowed him to travel about 50 klicks a day, so he had only two weeks to get to the rendezvous with Polly, Lucy, and Jazz with two of her kids. They were all arriving on the 19th in Norfolk, Virginia. He would have Buffy pick them up and deliver them to the dock at the James River Marina just below the US 17 Bridge.

He would work on resupply there, while waiting for them. Then he would begin his annual Southern migration. Two weeks of navigation down the Intercoastal Waterway with them on board would help him reconnect with the world of living with other people.

He loved his solitary life, but he periodically relished company too. His daily phone chats with Lucy did not totally satisfy his need to be with people.

Buffy delivered his friends and a heavy load of supplies. He tanked up potable water at dockside. *Dahlia* settled a few millimeters deeper with the load but remained perfectly level and stable because the weight was distributed low in the hull.

Polly assumed the role of chef, taking delight in crafting delicious feasts for every meal. In her active work life, she dined in company with her religious co-workers and employees or ate in restaurants.

"Somehow," she told Paul, "I feel like a girl again when I'm cooking. My mom let me work in the kitchen with her. When I was older, she encouraged me to cook the family meals. She worked outside the house as an accountant."

Paul kibitzed while she took care of the evening's culinary offering. They were having barbecued steaks, coleslaw salad and roasted potatoes. Paul used a handy zapper hung overboard to cook the meat. No dead animals were involved in creating the food.

"Mine too," confessed Paul. "Well, sort of an investment counselor. She certainly taught me not to spend money. Other than the fact that the world freaked out and made me filthy rich, I still don't spend much. I mean I have to live somewhere, and the boat is cheap now that the original cost has been spread over so many years.

"If I sold her, or." he paused, thinking about what he was saying, "gave her away, I'd be paying rent somewhere."

Lucy butted in, "Yeah Paulie. Like I'd charge you rent."

They all laughed.

"Yeah. Come and live with me. Dump this money pit. You're getting too old to be bacheloring it like this. All alone without supervision. Live with me Paulie. I'll keep you fit."

Every day was a blessing and every thought a benediction. Paul was happiest when he had family crowded around.

2248

Dahlia was getting old and needed a hauling out and something overhauled or replaced every year. Improvements were constant so that she was more efficient than ever. Paul was aging too, but not necessarily more efficient he thought.

Dahlia was over 60-years old, and many substantial improvements were made over those years. On casual glimpses she looked about the same – sort of harbor-tugish. Unseen, mostly underwater, there was now a bulb at the bow that gave her a longer waterline and greater efficiency. The improvement was so apparent that an after-bulb was added at the next haul-out. Efficiency and speed improved incrementally.

HVAC was good from the start with dorade vents positioned to force fresh air into one end of the vessel and out the other. An impossibly efficient furnace was added. The device was mostly air chambers connected to the main cabin by a duct and low speed fan. Sunlight made a huge difference, even on cold days. This same kind of device was almost universal ashore now in cold climates.

Cooling was augmented by a washboard-like water tower he charged manually on hot days. He'd lift buckets of water for storage near the topside shower. The water would trickle over vanes that cooled air that was then introduced into the bunk areas. It was almost prehistoric in concept, but it took good advantage of evaporative cooling and the fact that the bay water was cooler than the air in summer.

Paul was in love with each part of his boat. The luminescent paint and dorade-fed heating and cooling were nowhere more appreciated than in the bunk areas.

No window screens were needed because mosquitos had been relegated to a non-problem by a paint additive on all above water surfaces of the boat. It functioned just like their clothing to keep pests away when they were not aboard. Lions, ticks, no-see-ums, and mosquitos were in the 'things not to worry about' category."

Paul lay back and listened to Polly snoring in the after king-berth.

The kids and Jazz were right overhead in the spacious pilothouse. They had stopped stirring hours ago. The midnight air was quiet for a change – he could detect no wind. He was warm despite his bare skin. Lucy was a polar bear – comfortable no matter what the outside temperature. The open port let in quiet night sounds of rustling leaves and lightly lapping wavelets.

"Why not us?" Lucy argued in a hoarse whisper. "People on their own can survive for over a hundred years. I'm going for four hundred. What about you Paulie?" she demanded as she attacked him again in their bed.

"Yes dear. But I don't think I can go again."

He almost groaned in pleasure as she began her ministrations. She started with her lips on his ear lobes and then, with her fingers holding a chocolate mint, she began to involve his olfactory nerves with delicious scents. He wondered where she had hidden the mint.

Lucy brought her breasts to his face as she reached over him for the Pandora Radio switch. She liked slow-moving classical woodwinds with light, insistent timpani. He wondered if the others could hear the music. Lucy's body scent, Passion d'Nuit, penetrated over the chocolate aroma. He did not move.

Polly continued to snore in the after berth four meters away, and he sensed no movement overhead.

Lucy touched other switches and the bed began to rock softly. Luminous vistas of blue water, meadows and pink clouds moved across the ceiling the ceiling.

"Don't think Paulie. Just lie there. Be a good boy," she sighed into his ear. He breathed through his nose and tried to clear his mind. He closed his eyes. It didn't work. Whap! She banged her flat palm down on his belly button. He rose up with his shoulders and legs. She pushed him down murmuring, "Down boy. Just relax for a minute. But don't go to sleep. And don't fart."

"Okay." His eyes were wide open, and he reached for an embrace to celebrate her joke...

Just as he was about to ejaculate, she pushed the chocolate mint into his mouth. He erupted with all his senses in high gear. Another triumph for Lucy Lu. Physician. Mistress of the night.

Lucy was splendid. She took perfect care of herself and benefited from proximity to the expert team devoted to keeping each other young and healthy. The old ones, including Paul, had special implants to monitor even more than the standard marvels everyone wore.

Sharing his space with his family and Lucy was the quintessential essence of harmony thought Paul. He relished every moment. Polly bustling about. The kids wrestling and always on the move. The adults double-teaming the kids to give Jazz a break from her motherly duties. It was all good.

December 31, 2328

Paul dreamed, twitching in his sleep, as he executed the maneuvers. He was alone but not lonely. He loved the thump his paddle made when it drummed against the canoe's gunwales.

He made frequent turns into minor eddies trying to be totally technical with his strokes and balance to practice skills. He nosed into the bank behind a boat-sized rock and was surprised that it was just a screen of bushes that masked a side stream entering the Clancy.

The slow-moving water was crystal clear. Just ankle-deep, its river stones and pebbles were strewn across the bottom. Grasses and bushes screened it from sight in every direction. Moss covered the rocks on the riverbank.

He always paddled to this spot when he was by himself. That was where he and Dahlia had first made love. He liked to exit his boat to sit and dream on the bank. Sometimes he fell asleep...

He beamed. Remembering Lucy's visit one spring. They were both getting to be old codgers. Somewhat frail and faltering, they shared many secrets – life had been good to them.

2350

"Paul," Lucy said, "You've got to get off this damn old boat.

"It's getting too hard for you to manage, and I miss my noisy little apartment. Won't you please consider coming back to Barcelona with me? I have a premonition that the end is getting near. I'd like to spend a few more years with you in ease and comfort."

Lucy had fled Paris in 2245 in response to the French government's inquiries into the affairs of AAAFA. The officials had lost interest when she and the other key figures in the operations became difficult to reach.

As a United States citizen Lucy was able to quit France with no notice or bother. She made the journey by zip train with her most valuable possessions in a crate – the *Hunter* paintings that Paul had made for her over the years. She preferred the train because she could roll the flat-wheeled crate to her private double compartment by herself. The train trip took only five hours with stops in Lyon, Toulouse, and Zaragoza.

The wind outside was howling, and Paul had to venture outside every hour or so to check the lines. He had two lines tied off to trees forward and to two anchors aft holding them off the beach. The GPS alarm would sound if they moved off station and the engines would automatically maintain their position. But the ropes would fray if not adjusted periodically.

Rain was falling in sheets; driven hard by the wind it drummed into the boat and would have incapacitated Paul if he didn't wear an insulated dry suit and a visored hoodie when he went outside into the night to tend his lines. He squinted through windows on all sides of the boat, looking for hazards before donning his suit. Lightning and thunder made their presence felt.

This kind of night would have scared him in the beginning of his life with *Dahlia*. Now it was just a part of being on the water and immersed in the elements. He loved being there and raised his face to shout into the wind.

Back inside Paul was thinking about Lucy's proposition. "Lucy," he said, "would it be possible for me to get a folding camp chair and set up an art studio near the Rambla?" The wind was hammering now.

Gusts rocked Dahlia and made things rattle in the lockers and cabinets. Barcelona's mild climate and warm sun was on his mind.

Paul was snug and warm in his bunk. It was as big as an old-fashioned king-size and the sleep cushion was way more comfortable than the mattresses, he had known in his first lifetimes. The storm raged.

"Shoot Paul. Too easy. Let's get an apartment in *Plaça Real* and live in luxury with the *Rambla* and *Porto Vell* at our doorstep. *Vale!*"

"We'll be near your favorite neighborhoods and restaurants. You like Barcelona and the Spanish people, that Pollo Rico place behind the market and the museums in in *Barri Gotic* and *El Raval* are always exciting."

"Ya thinks? That sounds perfect. You know city people get way more walking exercise than other populations. I have to work hard to get my exercise on the boat, but it will be easy to hoof the klicks in town. Let's do it!"

La Rambla was his favorite spot in Barcelona. He had promenaded its tree-lined kilometer with Lucy and Polly on numerous occasions. He delighted in the artists and performers that created their works on the street with throngs of local and visiting passers-by looking over their shoulders. His Spanish now was way better than the Spanglish he'd learned in Miami's hot streets when the 21st century was new.

On A Spring Day

They walked hand in hand into *Plaça Real* and found café seats by the fountain at the sunny end of the hundred-meter long, cobblestoned landmark. The day was cool but sitting in the sun, out of the wind, was a treat. She placed her soft hand on his big mitt.

Paul frowned and paused to look at Lucy.

"Not now Paulie. I mean someday when we get up in years. This is the place." They laughed at their old inside joke.

Vehicle traffic was limited both on the street and nearby neighborhoods to preserve their historic ambience. It would be thronged with happy strollers whenever the weather permitted – which he knew was almost every day of the year. "Who was it that said? 'It's the only street in the world which I wish would never end,'" asked Paul as they strolled its length.

"Don't know. Maybe Garcia somebody. I love it too and it is most of the reason I want to die here."

"Maybe I could learn proper Spanish. I suppose I'd have to get a permit to set up there. Or run when *la policia* patrol comes around."

Lucy laughed at the thought of a world-famous artist having such a humble position in the world – painting while sitting on an upturned bucket on the street. "Paulie. You have the bucks to set up a real shop and wow the world with your cool pix. And your Spanish is great."

"Damn it, Lu. They are not pix. They are paintings!"

He was getting weary of boating. His body was slowing down and he often found himself wishing for the comfortable land life again. The *Dahlia* was now an antique. *Like me* he thought. Its systems and structure had been upgraded many times but the size, which had been just right for many years, was becoming a factor. It was easier when he was feeling like a 50-year-old hunk. Now he felt like an 80-year-old hulk.

I'm a very good 80-year-old though, he thought, not yet frail or tottering. His muscles were strong, his mind was clear – *but he heard the bells tolling.*

"Jazz" he croaked.

"Grandpa. What's wrong?" She heard the pain in his voice, but his monitor was turned off and she could not see his face."

"Nuttin Honey. Just something I need you to do for me." He paused as he turned his monitor on so that they could see each other.

"I'm hauling Dahlia tomorrow for her annual checkup. I want you to get something together for me. I want to give her to somebody, but I don't know who. She's worth about UD100,000. So, pick someone deserving and get her off my hands.

"I'll have my personal stuff off tomorrow.

"I'm moving to Barcelona and getting hitched to Lucy. Well, sorta hitched, heh hee..."

"Oh Grandpa! I love your style. What an announcement."

Year 2350

Aaaaaaaaaaahhhhhhhhhhhh

The painting he toiled at was a depiction of an astronaut flying through a starry black night with wispy visions of a blue-green planet behind his right ear and a suggested reddish Martian desert behind his left. It was a difficult but very rewarding watercolor for Paul. He was happy when passers-by paused to look over his shoulder and comment. He'd always pause and give them a business card with the addresses of his galleries in New York, North Carolina, Georgia, and Spain.

He was emotionally wrestling with himself over the meaning of his life. It was so different than he'd ever expected. Several lifetimes stitched together over a span of centuries rather than decades.

So many years had passed.

What was it about? Paul wondered as he leaned back on the bench and waited. The sun felt good on his face and shoulders. He was tired and he slouched to an even more comfortable position. Lucy was in their apartment in the *Plaça Real* waiting for a delivery.

The sea-kissed breeze felt cool on his face and the bare skin of his neck and hands. He was swaddled in the fashionable long wrap of the day. Its iridescent sheen was a consequence of electrical activity as it adjusted to keep Paul's skin temperature constant.

La Rambla was busy with the murmurs and conversations of passers-by, both creating and soaking up the ambience. Humanity had come together for a celebratory day of promenade, art, food, and street entertainment.

Paul contentedly nodded as he waited for Polly and Jazz to meet him for lunch. He was a fitting part of the scene.

He had grown tired of his painting project before noon. It was too windy, and he had to clip his work to the table while dry brushing and scraping the paper to get sharp and light effects. His tidy bucket of art materials and the folding chair and table sat at his feet. Leaning against the slats of the bench, he heard birds call above the stir of the people.

He thought about the *Restauranté Pollo Rico* while he sat. It was just about his favorite place in the city. It was a going concern long before his parents were born. It had stayed open during the Spanish Civil War and, being on an obscure side street off La Rambla, it had managed to avoid attention from the combatants. The bombs had missed, and they'd roasted real chickens there for over a hundred years. Flocks and flocks of birds. Just a hundred meters away. They would sit on plain wood chairs at a tiny square table. *Mesa*.

The small birds roasting on the rotisserie now were real chicken, but not from living, breathing chickens. Paul could not fault the meat in texture or flavor. The *papas frittas* were real and divinely crisp and greasy. Just the way he liked them. He was a little hungry. *Tengo hambe.* "I wish the girls would hurry," he muttered as he began to nod.

Hell of a ride, he thought, as his lips curled higher. *This is the best part,* he sighed as his comfort level rose. He slept...

#

A NOTE FROM THE AUTHOR
~ December 31, 2443 ~

This third book is loosely based on Artist Paul Hunter's recently discovered *Journals* and his book *Paul's Falls*. Please refer to *Hunter I* and *Hunter II* for details about his early life. BS

Made in the USA
Columbia, SC
06 July 2023

a1575f4b-5cf7-43cf-b289-909e864a01d0R01